MIDIAN
UNMADE

MIDIAN UNMADE

TALES OF CLIVE BARKER'S NIGHTBREED

Edited by

Joseph Nassise

and

Del Howison

TOR®

A Tom Doherty Associates Book

New York

MIDIAN UNMADE: TALES OF CLIVE BARKER'S NIGHTBREED

Copyright © 2015 by Joseph Nassise and Del Howison

A Tor Book
Published by Tom Doherty Associates, LLC
175 Fifth Avenue
New York, NY 10010

www.tor-forge.com

Tor® is a registered trademark of Tom Doherty Associates, LLC.

The Library of Congress Cataloging-in-Publication Data is available upon request.

ISBN 978-0-7653-3542-5 (hardcover)
ISBN 978-1-4668-2362-4 (e-book)

Tor books may be purchased for educational, business, or promotional use. For information on bulk purchases, please contact the Macmillan Corporate and Premium Sales Department at 1-800-221-7945, extension 5442, or write to specialmarkets@macmillan.com.

First Edition: July 2015

Printed in the United States of America

0 9 8 7 6 5 4 3 2 1

COPYRIGHT ACKNOWLEDGMENTS

For all those who have felt that sense of unbelonging
*so characteristic of the Nightbreed—never forget
that you are not alone.*

Joseph Nassise

*For Clive Barker—your kindness, talent, and influence
will last with me for the rest of my life . . .
and maybe beyond.*

Del Howison

CONTENTS

PREFACE

In late 1992 I picked up the Pocket Books paperback edition of a new novel by a writer I'd never read before, Clive Barker. The book in question was called *Cabal*, and I remember the cover quite clearly, for it featured a dark, looming face superimposed on the night sky with the tagline "At last, the night has a hero" situated beneath the bright red letters of the main title.

Within the pages of that slim volume I was introduced to both an amazing world and an amazing writer. The tale of Boone and Midian and the creatures known as the Nightbreed instantly captivated me, drawing me into their dark embrace and never letting go. *Cabal* engaged my love of the dark fantastic in a way that few books before it ever had, turning me into a lifelong fan of Clive and his work.

Just a few months after I had picked up that book, in the spring of 1993, I had the pleasure of attending the first public solo showing of Clive's art at the Bess Cutler Gallery in New York City. Paintings and drawings with names like *Cenobite* and *Books of Blood* and *Frank* hung on the walls, places and characters and worlds that are familiar to any fan of Clive's work but about which, at the time, I was just learning. I bought a print of one of the pieces (*Books of Blood: Volume 1*) and was pleased to have a few moments to speak with Clive as he signed it for me. It was a short but memorable conversation because we discussed the life of a writer and what it meant to be able to bring one's visions to life on the page for others to experience.

Fast-forward eighteen years to the fall of 2012. My own writing career had taken off at this point, with more than a dozen novels to my credit, and I was casting about for a new project to begin when I came upon a battered copy of that original print edition of *Cabal* in a used bookstore. *Wouldn't it be fun to play in that world?* I thought to myself. I imagined picking up where Clive had left off, with the tribes of the moon scattered to the four corners of the globe, waiting for their savior, Cabal, to restore their sanctuary and call them all home again. What would their lives be like? What beauty and wonder and misery and madness would they have found, tossed out into the world like so much flotsam and jetsam, at the mercy of the monsters known as mankind? In that moment *Midian Unmade: Tales of Clive Barker's Nightbreed* was born.

It took another three years and the help of many people—my coeditor Del Howison (owner of the world's best horror bookstore, Dark Delicacies), editors Jim Frenkel and Melissa Singer at Tor Books, the twenty-three writers who penned the stories that appear herein, and, of course, Clive Barker himself—to turn that dream into a reality.

You hold in your hands the fruits of that effort, the physical embodiment of fantasy made flesh and blood, and within its pages you will find the Nightbreed in all their glory as they dance and sing and feast and yearn and hope and dream under the light of the moon.

I hope you find them as intriguing as I have.

JOSEPH NASSISE

INTRODUCTION

(Reprinted from *The Nightbreed Chronicles*, 1990)

Our lives are scattered throughout with periods of *un*belonging; in childhood, of course, and adolescence; but in adulthood too, when sudden loss (or gain) forces us to reassess things we believe immutable.

At such times we all become like changeling children, at odds with our friends and peers, looking to distant horizons for fresh comprehension of ourselves.

The fiction of the fantastic brims with metaphors for this condition: tales of people whose cells are protean and souls migrant, people called by mysterious forces to a place they've visited in other lives or states; a place never understood—at least until the moment of crisis—as their real home.

There, perhaps, they may enjoy the company of their own tribe.

Welcome, then, to the people I feel particularly at home with: the *Nightbreed*. They are a colony rather than a family. A collection of survivors of what were once small nomadic nations: werewolves, vampires, demons, shape-shifters . . .

In conventional Western mythology these are the villains; creatures who possess little more than an appetite for destruction and evil. But in cultures less brutalized by dualism these dream nations are as much celebrated as feared; they are the spirits of our darker natures which healthier theologies don't seek to repress.

CLIVE BARKER
Pinewood Studios, England
September 1989

MIDIAN
UNMADE

RETURN TO MIDIAN

Midian—the name means a place of refuge, a legendary city where all sins are forgiven.

—*Clive Barker's The Nightbreed Chronicles*

Twenty-five years ago, Clive Barker was the tour guide for our journey into Midian, a place he described as a "labyrinthine necropolis" occupied by "an ancient race of mythological creatures." During this sojourn, he challenged our perceptions and prejudices when he declared that "evil hides behind a human mask and even monsters have souls."

Barker's "grotesques and freaks, noble beasts and exquisite transformers" were both apart from and a part of the world. Whether the sense of isolation sprang from an uncommon visage or, like Narcisse, a knowing from deep within, Midian called out to each of them.

More than a literary locale, the "hidden city" represented a liminal space familiar to anyone who felt that he or she did not belong; simultaneously a safe haven and a precarious dwelling where self-destruction, annihilation, or even transcendence was possible.

While no two Nightbreed looked alike, their sins were in essence singular; they were the Other. As such, they were feared and hated, for as Julia Kristeva posited in *Powers of Horror*: "The abject has only one quality of the object—that of being opposed to I."

Even though sympathetic creatures populated other works, they often appeared as loners forced to the dark edges of society. If more than one type of monster inhabited the same landscape, they were enemies. Battle lines drawn, man's oft-repeated history of "us versus them" was allowed to play out, neither questioned nor challenged.

Cabal was a tale written for the readers of its day but also in anticipation of the future. Like Rachel and Babette, the Other was and is a shapeshifter, transforming at the behest of a time, a people, or a nation. The constant? A seemingly insatiable need by humans for this space to be, at all times, occupied.

Although Barker engineered Midian's destruction, he also left among the ruins pieces of hope. For the Nightbreed came together as one, not because they were the same, but because they were different.

LISA MAJEWSKI

THE MOON INSIDE

Seanan McGuire

Once, Midian. Once, the caves carved from the living rock, the warrens and rabbit-runs like veins through the flesh of the earth. Once, a world lived in constant descent, down, down, ever down, until it seemed that one day in their expansion they would strike the hot molten core of the world, where magma flowed like the blood of Baphomet. Once, safety. Once, home.

Now, Seattle. Now, the cold, cruel cities of the Naturals, which rise towering above their foundations like they would deny the very stone that birthed them. They bloom like grotesque flowers, these misshapen cities of the sun, spreading their petals to greedily block the sky from those they have left behind them on the ground. There is no safety here.

Babette curls in her room—a corner of attic in a warehouse whose ownership has become tangled over the years, bills of sale disappearing and deeds being mysteriously lost—and watches the rain patter on her small and fiercely guarded window. Some of the others consider her strange for coveting this slice of the outside; she's too fragile to risk the sun the way she does, she should be more careful, she should move deeper into the communal room, forsaking privacy for safety. But her visions are their only connection to Lori (who came to them in skin and left in leather, wings against the moon, oh Lori, *see how she flies*), and hence, to Cabal. If she demands the window, and the sweet-faced moon beyond, she'll be indulged.

Seattle is a good city, as Natural cities go. The sun shines more often than the tourist brochures they once stole from a travel agent's office promised them it would, but it vanishes often enough that the braver and stronger of them can go abroad in the daylight, hoods pulled over heads, parasols shielding skins from an unexpected break in the clouds. They mingle with the Naturals that way, making their faces known among the community. They won't be caught unprepared if another Decker rises, another human monster with a vendetta to pursue. Even Babette has seen the streets by daylight, thanks to heavy cloud cover and well-placed awnings. She could be happy here, if this were home . . .

But this is not home. This will never be home. Cabal is moving through the world, and his woman moves through the world with him, and together they will find a new Midian, a strong, secure place driven deep into the rock, and the tribes of the moon will come together once more, living and dead alike, in the place where the monsters go.

The sun is setting and the sky outside the window is the bruised color of week-dead man flesh. Babette stills, listening to the sounds around her. Breed move through the shared spaces, whisper in corners, copulate in the rafters . . . but none of them are paying any attention to her, not even Rachel, who is her mother in all but flesh. Satisfied, Babette reaches out with clever fingers and undoes the latch, sliding the window open.

It is a teenage girl who braces the glass with a piece of masonry, keeping it from closing before she comes home, and a teenage girl who drops the bag of clothing to the street below. It is a creature like no other ever seen on this earth that slides through the open frame, dexterous paws finding the soft places between bricks and gripping tight, so tight that no force in this world could pry it loose. Its coat is the gray of a misty sky, stippled with darker spots, like eyes. It blends into the city, blends into the twilight, and it slips away without a sound.

The difficulty of being a teenage monster in a human city is the absolute lack of things to do on a Friday night. She could go to the movies, watch some Natural fever dream of terror or romance play out upon the screen, but she did that last week, and the amusement value wears thin after a while.

She could buy a cup of coffee with the money she's bartered from the more daylight-safe members of the tribe, sip it slow and bitter while she sits at an outside table and watches the world go by—but what difference is that from her window, really? She still has no connection to the people who pass her. They're just closer, the blood in their veins like sugar candy and communion wine.

It's rude to eat the people in your neighborhood. Worse, it attracts attention, and attention is a thing to be avoided. It was attention that drove their splinter tribe of Breed from Columbus, where the corn grew high as heaven in the fields, and from Anaheim, where the sun was unforgiving but the nights were bitter cold and oh, so long. They can't afford another move, not right now, not with two of the women and one of the men of the tribe gravid with Nightbreed yet to be. Pregnancy is hard enough on the dead without adding the strain of another flight to the process.

In the end, Babette settles for breathing her beast back into her belly, where it curls like a predatory fawn, dangerous and waiting for an opportunity to pounce. She collects the bag of clothing from the shadow where it fell and pulls each piece on with a rebel's reverence: the denim trousers, the loose linen shirt, the heavy down jacket that blurs her body's lines almost as effectively as a change of shape. She has come to see clothing as a form of shape-shifting; it lets people hide their true selves behind masks, distorting and remaking their own images. So tonight she will be a child of this city, this obscene flower of a city, and not of Midian; she will walk among them unseen, and she will see.

I see this for you, Lori, she thinks, and receives the barest trace of beating wings and a frozen, distant sky for her troubles, skating across her mind's eye like the shadow of a dream. They are still out there, still searching, still running. Babette aches to run with them but no, no, that is not her lot in death; hers is to wait and watch, to hide and hear the things some would rather have unheard. She did not choose this, but she carries it with her as she slouches out of the alley and into the world of man.

They are everywhere, the Naturals, stinking and prolific, swarming the streets like rats despite the growing darkness, despite the falling rain. There was a time (*before her time, so many years before her eyes were opened*) when none of them would have dared the dark like this. They would have been too afraid of the tribes of the moon, who walked freely under the stars and took what meat they needed from those too unwise to bar their doors at night. Babette remembers that with every shoulder that brushes hers and every body that shoves her aside, a tiny bit of almost-human flotsam bobbing through their hectic sea. Once, they would have feared her. Once, they would have run at the merest flash of her small white teeth.

And once, they would have followed her home with fire and with bellies full of terror, which is like coal: press it down hard enough and it hardens into a form of courage, diamond-hard and impossible to break. It's better not to be feared. She knows that, but oh, she wishes they would not touch her.

The tidal pull of humanity carries her down one street and onto the next, where she turns and swims against their current, heading for the one place that requires no human money and asks few human questions of a teenage girl who appears homeless to adult eyes. (And she *is* homeless, she *is*, because once was Midian and now is Seattle, and Lori and Cabal and the reunion of the tribes are so far away.)

The doors of the Seattle Public Library are unlocked, and quiet as a whisper, Babette slips inside.

———————

The existence of human libraries was a discovery Babette first made in Columbus, on a hot summer night when there was nothing else to do besides sit in the hayloft of their borrowed barn and watch the corn growing in the fields. Within these walls is everything the tribes of man have learned, and everything they have stolen from the tribes of the moon.

"Know thy enemy" is a saying known to Natural and Nightbreed alike, and Babette is hungry for knowledge. She already knew how to read, thanks to the gravestones in Midian. She learned her letters from the names of dead men, prizing their secrets from the granite and marble one syllable at a time. The difference between an epigraph and an encyclopedia is merely one of scale. Both preserve the accomplishments of the lost.

The librarians barely glance up as she ghosts past them, a familiar figure in her mismatched clothes and her oversized jacket. She doesn't shout or throw things or disturb the other patrons; like most of the city's itinerant youth, she is utterly polite while she is inside the library walls, and so she is allowed to come and go unhindered. It is a small and sacred contract, and one that has served all involved well in the months since the Breed have come to Seattle. The librarians do not know there is a monster in their midst, and the monster, unthreatened, sees no cause to reveal herself.

Luck is with her; there is an open space in the bank of computers at the back of the New Media room. Babette slips into a seat and presses the button to log herself on, marveling only a little as the machine swiftly responds to her command. Most of the Nightbreed have never touched a computer. The world is changing—the world is always changing—and this change is among the most dangerous of all, because she knows one day it will reveal them. Too many people are seeing too many things, and posting them to the Internet, where they wait like snares for someone to stumble into them and start seeing the patterns.

She brings up a search engine, drags the mouse to the box at the top of the screen, and types a single word:

MIDIAN

Rachel would call it dangerous foolishness, but Rachel does not go out in the world as much as Babette does; she is older, and wiser, and has learned to mistrust too much freedom. Babette is learning different lessons. Thanks to the oh-so-public slaughter at the necropolis, Midian is urban legend and modern myth now, indelibly etched into the stories of the Naturals. They take her for another human teenager made curious by tales of monsters—and maybe a little bit wistful. What was it Peloquin said once, in Lori's hearing (and hence Babette's, for they have shared so many things since those dark days of fire and fear)? "Oz is over the rainbow and Midian is where the monsters go."

She has learned about Oz since then—more pretty lies for the Natural children—but more, she has found that many among the tribes of man yearn for Midian and its darkness as much as she does. Anyone who sees her screen will take her for one of those yearning children, and look no further.

The results of her search are a tangled complication of narratives. Here is someone claiming to have been at Midian when it fell; here is someone else saying that monsters are real and planning to remake the world in their own image. Here is truth and here are lies, all of them tangled together until it becomes impossible to distinguish them without knowing the true story, absolute and clean and down to your bones. They are still safe. They are still undiscovered.

"Midian again, huh?"

The voice is male, cocky, human. Babette tenses and blanks her screen before she turns to find a Natural boy behind her, his clothes as oversized and mismatched as her own, his hair a shock of bleached-out blond that reminds her of the cornfields in Ohio. "Were you spying on me?"

"No," he says, and then, "Maybe," and then, "Yes," with a grin that clearly aims to make all accusations dissolve into mist and forgiveness. "You come here once a week and do the same searches every time. A guy gets curious, you know? Wants to know what the mysterious girl with the curly hair is trying to find. You looking for monsters, Blondie?"

Babette almost touches her own hair in reflexive response. Her curls are the color of moonlight on dead grass, a gold that is true and cold at the same time, unforgiving and fair. Instead, she says, "I don't think I'd know what to do if I met a monster."

"Scream and run away, if you know what's good for you," says the boy, offering her his hand. There is dirt beneath his nails. She doubts it came from digging graves. "Matt."

"Blondie," she says. Her name is a treasure she will not give to any Natural. She slips her hand into his—refusal will only draw more questions—and watches his puzzled blink at the coolness of her skin. "It's rude to look at other people's screens."

"But this is the library's screen, and that makes it as much mine as yours," he says, giving her hand a perfunctory shake before letting go. "Besides, if you're looking for Midian, I can take you there."

Babette is too startled to hide her confusion. "You?" she asks, before caution tells her to be silent.

It's too late: the word is out, and the boy with the bleached corn hair is smirking, amusement in his eyes. "Me," he says. "You think you're the only one who ever wished she knew where the monsters were? Come on, Blondie. I won't hurt you. But I might lead you to your heart's desire."

The computer's secrets have been spilled out on the floor like pearls, or teeth. There is nothing left to learn here, and the night is young. Babette rises like a wisp of smoke, too graceful for the gawky thing she seems to be, and inclines her head toward the boy who dared to speak to her. "Yes," she says. "Take me to Midian."

Once, Midian. Once, safety and security and home in the deep warrens and the living earth. Babette knows she is not walking backward through time—knows it better than any other member of the tribe. She has *seen* Cabal since the destruction of their sanctuary, *seen* him scouring the edges of the world looking for safe haven. She knows to the bones of her that whatever she walks toward, it can't be home. But Babette, for all her cold-blooded strangeness, is a teenage girl, and teenage girls are vulnerable to dreaming.

She follows Matt through the alleys behind the library like a rat following a piper, her girl-skin drawn tight around her bones, hiding her second face from view. Matt moves almost as quickly as one of the Nightbreed, skipping from one side of the alley to the other, his strong boy's bones moving in his lanky boy's limbs. The smell of him is everywhere, blood and flesh and sweetness. She isn't the hungriest member of the tribe—can be sated on cat flesh and rat flesh more often than not—but she still wishes he would move a little more like a predator, and a little less like prey.

After they have walked too far for her liking and not far enough for her to feel safely distant from her kin, Matt stops. "Here we are," he says, waving a hand to indicate a rusty door set into the hard brick of a nearby wall. "Midian."

Babette frowns, searching his face for the joke she knows must be hidden there. No joke reveals itself. She looks to the rusted door, and passes judgment: "This is not Midian."

"It is if you want it to be. Midian isn't a place, Blondie; it's a state of mind. Places can be destroyed, but ideas are harder to kill." He moves to the door and knocks twice, calling, "It's me! Let me in; I brought new blood."

"What's the password?" demands a voice from beyond the door.

"Midian lives," says Matt. He's trying to sound old and wise and eerie. He sounds like a child playing at things he doesn't understand.

I should go, thinks Babette. Go now, while this farce is still unplayed, while she still has a chance to slip away unnoticed—but curiosity is a strong thing, and she wants to know what lies behind that door. So she stays where she is, stays as she is, as it swings open to reveal a teenage girl in too much makeup and a black lace dress two sizes too small for her.

"Welcome to Midian," says the girl. "Do you fear monsters?"

Here is a question Babette can answer honestly. "Only the human ones," she says.

The girl looks disapproving. "This is not a place for pretenders or people looking for a scare. Do you come to Midian freely and with an open mind?"

"I have always been coming to Midian," says Babette. "Midian is where the monsters go."

"See, Danni? She's one of us," says Matt. "Let us in."

The girl he calls Danni rolls her eyes and steps to the side, holding the door open as she does. "Welcome to Midian," she says. "Enter freely and be unafraid."

There are so many things Babette wants to tell her: wants to tell her that when one enters Midian, one should always be a little bit afraid, even if Midian is home and haven altogether. Living amongst monsters does not come without its share of dangers. But the first part was correct. One must always enter freely, for otherwise, why enter at all? So she slips like a shadow through the door and into the room beyond, where she stops, bewildered by the scene before her.

It is not a large room. It was a coffee shop once, before its windows were covered with soap and cobwebs and these children, these pretenders to Midian, found a way to pry open the back door and slip into their secret sanctuary. There are eight of them, Matt and Danni included. Some are dressed in black with too much makeup; the rest are in patches and rags, layers that don't quite match but echo Babette's own. The unseeables of the city, gathered with the would-be children of the night that never falls.

They are not her kind. She should never have come here.

But the door clangs shut and she is trapped, Matt coming up behind her on one side, Danni on the other. "Welcome to Midian," he says, waving a hand to indicate the tired, dirty space, lit by candles, with faded Halloween decorations and newspaper clippings plastering the walls. He looks to her, waiting for her reaction. When it's not forthcoming he prompts, "Well?"

"It's not what I expected," she manages, after a moment's strangled silence. She wants to laugh. She wants to cry. Is this what they are now, the tribes of the moon? From reality to legend to children telling themselves stories in dark and dusty rooms? The other kids are watching her, taking her measure in a way that makes her yearn to breathe out her beast, to run wild and biting through their ranks until they end their credulous lives on the tiled floor. She struggles to contain herself (*Lori, give me your strength*) and adds, "How did you find this place?"

"Danni's dad used to be the general manager," says Matt, looking proudly to the girl in the black lace dress. "She realized we could use this space. That we could all be monsters here."

"But you haven't proven you're a monster," says Danni, shoving her way back into the conversation like a crowbar. "Why should we trust you?"

Answers pile up on Babette's tongue, each one truer and sourer than the last. She swallows most of them, spitting out the most innocuous: "Because I have no one to tell about you. How can I be a danger if I have no threats to make?"

"She's no monster," says Danni dismissively. "She's a pet at best, and prey at worst. If you want to keep her, you'll need to feed and water her, and make sure no one else eats her."

"Promise," says Matt, with a small and secret smile that Babette can't help feeling is intended only for her. "I won't let her pee in the corners or anything."

Danni snorts—the most monstrous thing Babette has heard from her yet—and turns her back on them. "It's your funeral," she says, and walks away, showing how little she thinks of them. Babette doesn't mind.

It's better to be disregarded.

———

Now, not-Midian. Now, human children playing dress-up in a dark room that isn't theirs (which may be the most Breed aspect of this strange and deepening evening; they're all squatters in their own ways, clinging to the sides of human society like ticks on a fawn), wearing their artfully tattered clothing, hissing at each other in a mockery of monstrosity. Babette finds herself a place in one of the corners and watches them, all wide eyes and silence. She knows there's something to be learned here, if she can just sneak up on it and make it show its face to her.

There have always been Naturals who aspired to become Nightbreed. She was too young in the days of Midian to have had much congress with them, but she remembers their faces, pale with pain and weeping like the moon, and their eyes. You could always tell the monsters-in-waiting by their eyes. Some of them came to Midian full of sin and secrets, and those ones might make it past the doors, down into the dark to be judged by Baphomet. Others came innocent and empty, and they were turned away, if they were lucky. (But Boone came empty of anything but darkness and dreams, and he became Cabal, their savior; Lori came empty of anything but love, and she became *his* savior, and Babette's, and in the end, that made her everyone's. Maybe they chose the wrong supplicants, opened their doors to the wrong design.) Babette searches the faces around her for signs of Midian, for the slivers of moonlight that invite the monsters in.

She does not find them. She finds damage, yes; more damage than she could ever dream would lurk in the eyes of children. This world has used them harder than any monster, and for a moment she entertains the thought of taking them all home with her, handing them over to the members of the tribe who hunger, night after night, for the flesh they cannot have. Babette could feed her people and save the children in the same gesture: every bite would drive the balm deeper into the blood, until those who *truly* dreamed of Midian began to change, to breathe their true faces into the world. . . .

But no. That is not the way, not now, not in this open, exposed place. Cabal will come for them and they will make themselves a new home, far from the prying eyes of mankind. Then, and only then, will they be able to think of saving anyone but themselves.

"Having fun?" asks Matt. He thinks himself stealthy, moving through the shadows to appear suddenly beside her. She does not disabuse him, although he has taken no step without her knowing since they arrived.

She looks to him, trusting the darkness to hide the way her pupils have expanded, the way her nostrils flare and scent the air. He smells of sunlight. "I should go," she says. "It's late."

"You just got here."

"No." She pushes away from the wall. "It's too late."

So she walks through the children of this unhallowed place, looking neither left nor right, until she reaches the door. Danni is already there, a sneer on her face.

"Didn't care for the monsters after all, did you, Blondie?"

It takes Babette a moment to remember that she gave her hair color as a name to these people. When she does, she inclines her head as politely as she can and says, "Not these monsters." Then Danni is opening the door with a joyful crow's-cry of "Don't come back!" and Babette is stepping out into the damp nighttime air, and Matt is running after her, asking what he did wrong, asking why she didn't like their secret little kingdom.

Babette keeps walking. It's all she can think to do. Better not to run; running shows weakness, shows you should be pursued. So she walks, chin up and hands down, and Matt pursues away from the door (which closes behind them with a click, final as a coffin lid), away from the alley, into the warren of the midnight streets.

There are men, and there are monsters, and then there are the monsters who are men; a different thing than honest Nightbreed, who know what they are and do not conceal it. Babette is distracted, trying on different ways to evade her pursuer without giving herself away, and does not hear the footsteps until they come too close.

"What do we have here?" asks a voice, older and harder and colder than any of the children who played at being monsters.

Matt cringes.

Babette sighs. "My brother and I lost our way," she says, turning, trusting the illusionary relationship granted to them by hair color to carry her story to willing ears. "Can you tell us how to get back to Pine?"

The men behind him—worse luck, for there to be three of them, all large with muscle and smiling in a way she recognizes too well—laugh. "Not until you pay the toll," says the one who spoke before. He thrusts out his hand. "Empty your pockets."

"My pockets are already empty," says Babette, looking at his hand curiously, as if she expects it to fill with treasures. "What's in yours?"

"Don't mess with me, kid," says the man, and grabs her shoulder.

Babette twists her head enough to keep looking at his hand, and sighs. "I wish you hadn't done that," she says.

The screaming begins shortly after.

———

Babette is not the most deceitful of her kind: the face she presents most often is that of a sweet-faced girl with a liar's halo of golden curls, and down deep, that girl is real, is not a lie. But that girl is not the only thing she is. The stranger's hand weighs heavy on her shoulder as she breathes out the fog that rests in the swampy depths of her lungs, breathes out flesh and fierceness and fury. *This is a terrible idea*, she thinks, and *He laid hands upon me*, she thinks, and through it all, the beast is unfolding across her person, until she has claws, until she has fangs, until she can make her displeasure known.

The process takes several seconds. The men do not move. Terror that comes too quickly can do that to a man; can freeze his feet in place while his mind denies the reality of what he sees before him.

When her teeth find the throat of the first man, he remembers movement, but he remembers it too late. Babette is not the most deceitful of her kind. Like all of the Nightbreed, she is exactly deceitful enough.

Once, Midian; once hiding through isolation, humans intruding rarely, for they knew the wisdom of staying far from the houses of the dead. Now, Seattle, where isolation is not the only way, for they lurk in the stronghold of the enemy. When they must kill, it is to be done quickly and well and leave no witnesses, for witnesses might remember the things they have seen, the impossible miracles of flesh and claw.

The first man falls, still twitching, as the flash of motion that is Babette finds the second. Cool wetness on his stomach, and he thinks she has missed, thinks he can run, but as he takes his first step his offal splatters to the ground, and the shell of his body follows, landing hard, so much discarded trash. Matt screams. It is the first sound since Babette breathed her secrets into the night, and he is still screaming when the third man falls, and Babette closes the distance between them, her hand over his mouth, his thin shoulders pressed against the nearest wall.

"You said you would take me to Midian," she says, and her voice is broken glass and rusty nails filtered through a mouthful of teeth like knives. "You lied."

He says nothing, only whimpers as she pins him there, and the alley smells of blood, and his flesh smells of fear.

"Forget monsters; forget Midian," she says. "Run into the light, and do not look back. If you do—if you whisper a word of what you saw here—I will know, and I will come for you, and I will show you Midian. Now run, little liar, and forget, for your own sake."

She releases him, and he runs, a fleeing fawn in this obscene, exposed forest of a city. Babette looks at the carnage and sighs before tilting back her head and howling to the hidden face of the moon, blocked out by clouds but no less present. She howls like she could bring back Midian through the sheer power of her grieving, and stops only when an answering howl from the rooftops tells her that her message is received.

Alone in the rain, Babette breathes her beast back into her body, and waits for the Nightbreed to come.

Messes are inevitable; when one world presses up against another, they cannot be avoided. Some messes serve a purpose. There are mouths to feed, after all, and three more of them on the way. Children are always born hungry. The Breed who answer Babette's call are happy enough to remove the bodies, carrying them in pieces back across the city to the warehouse. Rachel resolves out of the mist, her eyes wet with sorrow, and Babette flings herself into her almost-mother's arms, clinging there like a much younger child.

"Are you all right, my dear?" asks Rachel.

Babette does not respond. She is thinking of children who play at being monsters and monsters who play at being children, of men who cross lines they should have stayed far away from, and of the line between truth and legend, between legend and fairy tale. The rain will wash the blood away. The Nightbreed will remove the rest, and this night will enter the uncomfortable country between truth and lies. She has spent too many of her days there. She no longer knows where the boundary lies.

Babette is too large now, to be held with ease; too old now, to be carried. But she closes her eyes and lets Rachel carry her, and all her thoughts are far away, of Lori, and of Midian, where such boundaries will no longer be needed—where it will be only monsters, safe at last, forever.

THE NIGHT
RAY BRADBURY DIED

A Tale of Lost Midian

Kevin J. Wetmore

Nobody walks in Los Angeles, but he walked as he always had. It almost never rains here, but tonight, during the "June Gloom," drops fell from the dark skies. And so he walked, alone. Always alone.

He walked the thousands of miles to the city of lost angels and now he walked everywhere, mostly at night. With a face like his you cannot simply walk into the DMV and apply for a license. Didn't matter. He couldn't pass the driver's test anyway. He had never had much use for words. Not with a face like his. But at night, hidden under hats and clothing and hoods and darkness, he could walk unmolested.

He had been born with a wolf's snout where a Natural's nose and mouth would be. He couldn't speak. He tried to communicate through gestures and through tapping out messages. His birth parents hated and feared him. He couldn't even remember the name he was born with. When they finally left him at a highway rest area, he wandered, walking, until he found Midian. Midian gave him a home, and a name and a function. He spoke through rhythms and percussion, so they called him "Drummer" and let him drum. It was his gift to Baphomet and Baphomet's gift to him. The drums spoke for him and gave him a role in Midian. His voice, through the sticks in his fists, summoned the Breed, warned of danger and marked the rituals in honor of Baphomet. He had a name, a place, a purpose.

Then Midian fell. And once again the Breed now known as Drummer walked. He walked by night to the one other city he knew of where he might survive. Unlike some Breed, he had a silhouette that could pass for a Natural's, but his face, specifically his muzzle and teeth, gave away that he was something else. But Los Angeles was a superficial city. The people looked but did not see. One might blend in, if one didn't draw attention. Because once those superficial people saw, they hated anything not beautiful. And then they would try to hurt him, try to kill him. Yet again.

There were a lot of Breed in LA. Some knew they were, some were unawakened, but you could see their yearning. It was in their hair, colored in shades not found in nature. It was in metal, pushed through lips, and noses, and nipples, eyebrows, cheeks, chins, and other areas less visible. Ink covered arms, legs, backs, and even faces—images dark and beautiful, their meaning sometimes only known to the one whose skin they covered and sometimes not even to them. A lost tribe of addicts, runaways, dreamers, the lost, the broken, and the damned, seeking to fill a hole in them with something, sometimes anything.

He had a new name, too. To live in a real city you needed more than one name. So Drummer became his last name. Now he called himself Iblis, after stories an old man told him when he first got to the city. The man was blind, but had memorized the Koran. Under a bridge, during Drummer's first winter in the city, he heard the story:

> We have established you on earth, and We have provided for you the means of support therein. Rarely are you appreciative. We created you, then We shaped you, then We said to the angels, "Bow down before Adam." The angels all bowed, except Iblis; he was not with those who bowed. Allah said, "What prevented you from prostrating when I ordered you?" Iblis said, "I am better than man; You created me from fire, and created him from mud."

Drummer decided he had been reborn as Iblis, as he had been created in the fires of Midian that night, and while he would try to blend with man, he would never bow down to him.

He lived in a small basement apartment next to the laundry room on the bottom of Coldheart Canyon where it emptied out of the Hollywood Hills onto Sunset, just a few blocks north of Hollywood Forever Cemetery. When he was lonely or homesick, he would spend hours quietly beating rhythms on the tombstones in Hollywood Forever, drumming on the faces laser-etched on granite or marble, next to names written with letters he did not recognize and could not read. He meant no disrespect to those buried there. While he drummed, he sometimes thought of those buried there and offered his drumming up to them. He walked among the graves and felt at peace.

It also allowed for the cosmic joke of his life. He drummed one February night on a tombstone and heard a voice nearby. Ordinarily he remained vigilant and ran at the first sign of anyone—the police were unkind to those in the graveyard after dark and everyone was unkind to Breed. But he thought of the fires of Midian and all he had lost and his arms moved with wild abandon, marking a beat that sang of both a broken heart and a vengeful fury. He was a catastrophe of a creature, and his music that night spoke eloquently of his pain while assuaging it at the same time. He just needed a second or two more to finish the song.

"Shit, man, you're good!"

Too late he saw the two young men. They stumbled toward him. Sticks in his hands, he began to move away from them.

"Hang on, dude! We need to talk to you!"

Too late to run. They approached, but their speed was not aggressive. He knew what that looked like. His hood was drawn low and he had a scarf over the lower half of his face. He tried to look indifferent, but his heart was pounding louder and more rapidly than his drumming had been.

"Dude, that was fuckin' metal!"

"Naw, dude, that was like fuckin' Lars Ulrich combined with Neil Peart combined with, I don't know—a whole fuckin' African tribe or something."

They were excited. Glassy-eyed and looking at him like he was some sort of god. Dressed alike in black leather jackets, covered with writing, torn jeans and boots. Ink on all visible skin. They weren't Breed, but they were a breed unto themselves.

The one with long, greasy hair said, "Me and Ian here, we heard you and were like, 'That guy's the shit we gotta go meet him.'"

Iblis just looked at him.

"What dude here is trying to say is, are you in a band or anything?"

Iblis shook his head, no.

Ian gave him a look, took a long pull on his beer. "You fuckin' mute or something?"

Iblis returned the look, trying hard not to seem scared. He couldn't believe it when he nodded.

The other one spat. "Shit, man, that's fucked up. Still, who needs to talk when you can play like that."

Ian was still looking. "What's your name, man?"

Iblis held out a piece of paper that said, "Name Iblis Drummer. I am poor and hungry." He had had a junkie write it out for him. Sometimes you can panhandle and get money and not worry about being hated and hunted, because all the beautiful people avoid looking at poor people asking for money. It was how he paid the rent most days.

"'Drummer,' huh? No shit? Whatever. Everyone in this town is bullshit."

Ian was still looking at him. "Okay, look—we've got this band, and we need a drummer. You're the fuckin' best thing I've heard in a long time."

Iblis nodded, as if he agreed.

"So anyway, you think you might be interested? Here's the thing. We're kinda like a speed metal band and we wear costumes and masks when we play, like Gwar, you know?"

Iblis nodded, as if he did know.

Ian took another pull, draining it, then threw the bottle into the darkness, where it hit something and may or may not have broken.

"So anyway, if you're interested, we'll get you a mask and a costume and you can jam with us. The money's not great, but it's cash under the table and we can usually get free beer."

"Plus pussy. Man, metal groupies love us!" said greasy hair.

"This is Damon, he blows bass. I'm Ian, lead vocals and rhythm guitar. You'll meet Zack. He's lead guitar. He's like you—doesn't talk for shit."

Damon belched. "Yeah, but he plays that guitar like he's fucking a porn star."

And that is how Iblis, without ever speaking or showing his face onstage, became a drummer for a speed metal band. He would perform, drumming in front of people, for those brief hours passing as something else: a Breed pretending to be a Natural pretending to be a Breed. He even wore the mask and costume to rehearsals. At first the others in the band made fun of him for it, but as he played they came to see and treat him like some kind of percussion saint, and they left him alone to do his thing, take his cash, and never go out with them afterward.

But tonight, as small drops fell, he began walking. Something in the world had changed, and he felt it in his soul. His fingers nervously beat a tattoo as he walked. He kept his head down, but could not stop his fingers and hands from pulsing over objects—mailboxes and phone poles, parked cars and parking meters. He was sending some code he didn't even speak out into the universe, not knowing why, just knowing it had to be sent.

He walked farther than he ever had, passing the clubs on Santa Monica in West Hollywood. The pounding dance music, rhythmic and ritualistic, drew him, but he might not enter. The men in these clubs were beautiful, their bodies hard and their faces sharp, carved by hours in the gym. Beauty and desire. Rejected elsewhere, in small towns and suburbs, they came here to their own kingdom, where they were the beautiful ones, where they were the Naturals and the norms. Like Iblis, they were drawn to this city to find a safe place to be what they were, but Iblis had no place among them. His body was hard, his muscles like steel wire from the drumming, but no one looked upon his face with desire. He was not welcome among the flashing lights and sweaty bodies. More people pretending to be Breed. And more people who would fear and hate and hunt if they actually saw one.

He passed through the enclaves of wealth and learning, those on the top, on their way up and some on the way back down again. He walked all the way to the ocean. He didn't know why, but this was where he needed to be.

He sat on the sand, head wrapped tight, hooded sweatshirt under jacket with baseball cap and scarf. One must always hide from one's public.

The ocean's susurrus was its own rhythm, and his fingers began to match it on his thighs. Slow, at first. Then going in rapid counterpoint to the waves. It was mindless to him, yet also comforting. It was his way of communicating with the world. Even if the Naturals didn't understand it.

That's when he heard something. It sounded like crying. Keeping his head down, he shifted and looked around. Twenty or so feet away was a dark lump. His eyes had always been good in the dark (one needs good night vision when one lives underground, after all—not all of Midian's gifts had abandoned him), and he was startled to see it was someone dressed like him. He stopped drumming on his thighs and just listened.

A sniffle. A low moan. A woman. Or more like a girl.

Against practice and instinct, he got up, walked over, and sat down five feet away from her.

"What?! Am I bothering you? It's a public beach, you know."

He could not see her face, but he could see her pain. She was hiding, too. It was cold out, but not enough to justify the layers of clothing, not to mention the hat and scarf. She could have been his twin, at least when it came to attire.

"What are you staring at, huh? What? You think I'm a Muslim or something? You want to make fun of me? Why don't you say something? . . . You want to see? Fine! *Fine!*" Her words were slightly slurred.

She pulled off the hat and scarf in one awkward motion and he saw.

There was a small hole where her left ear should have been, surrounded by whorls of pink scars and tissue. The eye on that side was milk white, the hair burned away as well. The disfigurement clearly went down her neck into her collar, and left a very distinctive border between the not-quite-pretty girl she once was and the burned, malformed features that she was trying to hide.

"Happy now? Now you know I'm a freak? Happy?" She sobbed quietly and began to wrap the scarf around her head once more.

He waited in silence. Iblis had found not doing anything usually resulted in people continuing to pour out their feelings and thoughts.

She sobbed for a while and he began beating out a rhythm on his shoes.

"You're not grossed out?" Quiet, but genuine.

He shook his head no and kept gently banging on the sides of his boots. It was almost hypnotic.

"I didn't always look like this. I was pretty . . . once. My stepfather was kind of a jerk, and was smoking in the apartment one night and fell asleep on the couch. My room was right next to the den, so I smelled the smoke and got up, but by then . . ."

Iblis nodded. Not Breed, but broken. She knew the pains he knew. Hide away from the eyes of others. Especially if you don't like what you see in them.

"It was over two years ago, but the doctors say this is what it's going to be like, and we can't afford . . . and sometimes I just . . ."

She cried some more.

He thumped some more.

"You want to know the stupid thing? I'm not even crying about any of that."

She picked up a handful of sand and threw it. The wind caught some, the rest fell to the ground again.

"Tonight Ray Bradbury died."

Iblis nodded. As if he knew who that was.

"You know who that is? . . . I know, it's dumb. It's not like he was my father or my friend or something. I never met the guy. I dunno. It's just when I read his stuff I'd forget myself. I'd disappear and the only thing left was a world he created. Better than this one, or the one I was living in back home."

She shifted on the sand and just sat. He stopped drumming.

"I didn't know him and it's not like I read his books and I was like, 'Oh, he gets me.' I mean I'm not in high school or something dumb like that. I just . . . I just read the things he wrote and they made me think we're not alone and the world is a pretty amazing place. It's like an amusement park closing for the winter. You drive by and you know it's still there, but somehow the life is somehow missing and there is a little less light in the world. A little less joy. Cotton candy won't smell as sweet ever again."

Iblis nodded. This time he knew.

"Okay, I'm just being stupid. So, what's under your scarf? You burned too?"

She reached toward him and he instinctively pulled back.

"It's okay. I won't hurt you," and she continued to move toward his face. Gently but firmly he grabbed her hand, suddenly moved it down, and she stumbled into him, landing on the sand next to him so they now sat side by side.

He held her hand with one hand and began to drum on her palm. He could feel the tension and shock of being manhandled in such a way drain from her.

"Not a talker? Okay." Yet somehow the rhythm began to soothe her. Not taking away the pain, but making it a familiar presence, so it lost its bite.

A few minutes passed. A hundred yards away, couples walked hand in hand on the bike path. In the distance in the opposite direction, large ships slowly moved through the dark water. They sat, not speaking, but listening to the drumming of his fingers on her palm, and for one minute, each knew peace.

She wiped away a tear and got up, but only to walk over to her backpack. She pulled out a tattered paperback and handed him the book. He couldn't read any of the words, but the picture captured him. It was a man, sitting with his legs crossed, facing away. His body was covered in tattoos. Iblis wondered if he was Breed. Wondered if she was showing this to him because she understood Breed.

"It's a buncha short stories called *The Illustrated Man*. It's about this guy who has tattoos that tell stories that come true, but the stories themselves are about all kinds of things. He's intense, but there's a truth to him." She looked Iblis right in the eye. "Kinda like you."

She stood up, brushed off the sand, and gathered the backpack.

"Keep the book. A gift. You made me feel better for a few minutes, and that is a rare thing. Maybe Ray here," she said, tapping the book, "can help you feel better for a few minutes. He's good at that."

She turned away. "Night."

He did not watch as she began to move from him, but then he heard her coming back again. As he turned to look, she was already standing over him, bending down. Her lips touched his forehead, brushed against his skin, and then were gone again.

"Thanks. I just wanted to say thanks. And you don't need to be so sad. Read the book. Maybe it will bring a smile to whatever it is you're hiding behind that scarf."

As she straightened up, he dropped the book and slowly pulled down the scarf. She looked at him, and did not scream. Did not wince. She just looked. And then whispered, "Thank you."

She turned again and walked away. Iblis sat for a long time. He sat until he knew he had to leave in order to walk back to his home before the sun rose.

As he walked, he looked at the picture on the book. The man faced away. You couldn't see his face, but his body screamed power. His sinews were taut and tight and ready, yet at rest. You could almost see the small images on his body changing.

As the sky slowly began to change from black to blue, he knew that someone or something had left the world. It wasn't like Midian had fallen again. Just that it had gotten smaller. The Naturals had grown closer. That's when he realized. He didn't know her name. He knew nothing about her but her pain and her loss. But he was able to lessen those.

He walked past the temples of the beautiful, now silent. No more loud rhythms enticing the crowd. They stood empty and abandoned, like Midian. He saw the homeless sleeping in the doorways.

He felt changed. Was this what Cabal had gone through? He shifted in his skin, under the scarf and the hat and the jacket and the hood. Sometimes the walk back to what passed for a home simply reminded him of how alone he now was. Not tonight. Tonight something had been lost, so something must be gained.

Instead of turning on Coldheart, he kept walking, back to Hollywood Forever. That was what was missing. He had been putting on the costume and mask and drumming for the band so much recently he had not been here in a while. He needed, before the sun was fully up, to drum again. Not for crowds of people pretending to be monsters, not for the beautiful to dance and seduce and judge, not for crowds at all, but for the lost and the broken.

He moved past the familiar marble. The lawns and graves were well kept here, unlike Midian. He was still at home among the dead, even the beautiful dead of Los Angeles. Even the name, Hollywood Forever, seemed a lie, but a lie with a promise. Among the familiar stones, paths, and crypts the real rhythms of the Breed began to return to him. Not what he played in clubs and bars, but what had come through him in Midian.

He drummed for her. He drummed for her dead friend. He drummed for himself and all the Breed. Not for those pretending, but those who were. When he walked, he was never alone. He was Iblis, and he was born of fire.

ANOTHER LITTLE PIECE OF MY HEART

A Story of Midian

Nancy Holder

The air belowground in Corazón was thick with the scents of incense, blood, and meat. Good scents, holy, but if they had a sound, it would be a closing door. A gate, shutting. A tomb collapsing in on itself. Separated, away.

From Cabal.

Other sounds clanged against Coeur's eardrums, but these were like slowing heartbeats. She had just received her three sacred words, her mantra. Her path, then, would be Dark. The chant had been chosen for her by the elders, and divulged to her by Jean-Marc, first elder, who was her father. This was her initiation into the holy work of the tribe: some rejoiced, others mourned, all sought to confuse.

Her words mourned.

They were not the three words she had longed to hear. They were words of the past. Of moving away from the Beloved:

Invasion.

Diaspora.

Exile.

Coeur's vocation required her to think the words until they were a part of her. To find her own darkness and increase it, to send her thoughts out to the night on behalf of the tribe. Corazón must never forget that they had been and still were in mortal peril. Decker, the Antichrist who had led the human attack on Midian, was forever dead. Ashbery had been his disciple, and in the fighting had been made an imbecile who was some-how privileged to hear the plans and dreams of the Nightbreed, which he could relate to Eigerman. Eigerman, his minder, was Decker's other aco-lyte. And Eigerman had sworn not to die until he could put an end to the Breed, forever.

Because of the imbecile, each of the tribes silently chanted words to clog Ashbery's mystic channels—to confound and deceive their mortal enemy. All of the tribes, each with their own mantras, whispered such barriers into being. It was marking time, in a way. It was waiting. Stalling, some said. But it was a life.

Sange, who was exactly Coeur's age and so was initiated at the same time—they were both eighteen tonight—smiled when Jean-Marc whispered his three words into his ear. Coeur knew then that he had been given the words of the Light:

Rendezvous.

Rebuild.

Restart.

The words of hope, and also of defiance. If Ashbery heard them, he would translate them like this: *When Midian is rebuilt, we will dance on the graves of the human race. You will become dust, and you will be utterly forgotten.*

Only the elders could utter the Prophet's name aloud:

Cabal.

His human name was Boone, and he had been chosen by the Divine Creator whose name no one but Cabal was worthy to speak:

Baphom-t.

Cabal was to lead the people while they were scattered over the North-ern Hemisphere. Cabal had caused the fall of the Nightbreed, but Baphom-t had decreed that Cabal would also bring them together when the Moon and stars aligned, and Midian rose again in glory. When the crass and bru-tal sun burned the human race away, and the Moon regained her lumi-nous dominion. Then the Nightbreed would caper and dance over the world made new.

And then she would see Cabal.

Until that time, the Nightbreed must hide below, as they had done in Midian. In simplest terms, they must outlast their enemies. As it had been written: *"Keeping the children from the roofs at night, the bereaved from crying out too loud, the young in summer from falling in love with a human."*

And on the night of her initiation into the tribe, and the receipt of her three sacred words, Coeur knew that she was in terrible trouble. Her sin was grievous. Because other words filled her head:

Let's

Run

Away.

The tears that she shed during the ritual weeping of every initiated Dark member were genuine. The pain that coursed through her body as she knelt in the dirt and her wings were sewn together was real. But as the elders cut her hair and burned it with the incense that clogged and choked the passageways of their village, she wasn't meditating on the suffering of their sundered god, Baphom-t. She wasn't mourning the flight of a dozen tribes hastily formed as Midian fell, each given a piece of the One to protect until He could be made whole again. She wasn't showering Cabal with filial love and obedience.

She was thinking of the human boy aboveground who was waiting for her. Because it was summer, and she had fallen in love.

After she had put on her black robe and the music started, she stared at the chunks of meat and told herself over and over that they weren't Bobby. They couldn't be Bobby. Sange, in a white robe and feasting hungrily after the long fast, sidled over to her and smiled.

"Coeur, are you all right?" Sange asked. His dark eyes were set deep in a face of hollows and valleys, and fleshy lips that would now mouth three happy words nearly every waking hour.

Sange towered over Coeur. He was so muscular that when his wings had been sewn together (like hers: symbolic of their hobbling until Midian was restored), cords of muscle bunched along his shoulder blades. When they were younger, she had thought him the most beautiful of the Breed she had ever seen. And that was still true.

But then she had learned that beauty truly was only skin deep.

Yes, she had gone aboveground. She blamed it on the Internet, which of course she couldn't access deep in the earth. But the elders went upside to communicate with Cabal and the other tribes. They discussed the possible sightings of Eigerman. They debated whether or not it was safe yet.

They traded news about their tribes: births, illnesses, abundance of meat, lack thereof.

It wasn't hard to go up. She dug herself a little tunnel—it had taken only a month—and stumbled out into the night. Sweet, fresh air. Stars. The moon, which was the eye of the Creator. She whirled in a circle, laughing, and took off all her clothes. Her hobbled wings strained to flap in the breeze. She raised her arms, dreaming of flying.

No one caught her; there were no consequences. And she began to think that maybe the elders looked the other way as a matter of course, and others did what she was doing. She tried to hint to Sange, test him, see if he had gone up.

It was pretty clear to her that he hadn't. He had never even thought about it, as far as she could tell. And from now on, he would think only of *Rendezvous, Rebuild, Restart.* He wouldn't think about cacti and coyotes, as she did. Or about a boy who rode a horse and who sometimes rode with other humans. And who talked about *Albuquerque* and *the Balloon Fiesta* and other clues to their whereabouts—details that the imbecile could use to locate her tribe, and destroy it.

She shouldn't go. She couldn't.

Or . . . she could go forever.

That was Bobby's mantra: *Let's run away.*

He had seen her one night; he'd been walking his horse because the animal had thrown a shoe. When she had spun naked in the moonlight, arms raised, laughing, he had shouted so loudly that the coyotes had yipped and the wolves had howled. She had rushed at him like a hunter, ready to make meat of him. There had been no hesitation; she was Nightbreed, and he was not. He was game.

But then she saw his eyes. Deep brown, enormous, and somehow familiar. She stood rooted as he found the courage to approach her, and then he spoke, *and she understood him.* She didn't know if his language was the same as hers, or if it was a mystical connection such as the one between the imbecile Ashbery and the Breed.

He spoke triplet words:

Who

Are

You?

Not *What are you?* For her, always, there had been no thought of "who" when it came to humans. The named humans were evil: Decker, Ashbery, Eigerman. The once-humans had been renamed: Cabal and his woman, known only as She. Breed names.

Except that when Coeur didn't answer, he said, "My name is Bobby."

Why, oh why had she fallen in love with him? Why did his name ring in her ears during her initiation? Why was it so hard to hear *Invasion Diaspora Exile?*

Bobby had seen, and she had told him only a little. Only that she wasn't from outer space (not really), or a strange Native American angel, or a goddess. And that there were others, and she was bound to them. That by meeting him, and stealing away to be with him, she was endangering her family.

"Then run away with me," he said.

Maybe he didn't know that if she left her tribe she would be in worse danger. There was safety in numbers. A Breed alone was a walking target. Unless Eigerman wouldn't bother with just one.

Maybe Eigerman would hunt her down and torture her for information. Cabal had told them that the human devil had followers now, who sat at the feet of Ashbery and listened, rapt, as Eigerman translated what Ashbery was saying. They had pledged to rid the world of the abominations. To them, Decker was a saint, not a serial killer who had driven Cabal nearly mad. But who, in his way, had contributed to Cabal's transformation.

Would Bobby contribute to her transformation? Was her transformation important?

Cabal. She wanted to see him, hear him. She wanted to know the path she must take. Cabal would tell her her fortune. He would give her the answer. How else to explain her obsession with Cabal?

Unless all were so obsessed.

Bobby believed that he would be delivering her from horrible monsters who were torturing her—sewing her wings together!—and forcing her to live in servitude. She couldn't tell him otherwise. She didn't want him to know anything about the Breed. He already knew too much.

She didn't know if she could change him with a bite. No one in the tribe had ever changed anybody. She couldn't ask because she couldn't confess.

It was insanity even to think it. And a terrible betrayal. She was putting the tribe in danger every time she so much as thought of him. He was aboveground, waiting.

Once the initiation and feasting were done, it was custom to spend the night alone. It was the last night alone; ever after, one was joined in re-solve to protect the tribe.

And of course, to protect the piece of Baphom-t that the tribe guarded: in the case of Corazón, it was a fragment of His beloved heart.

Coeur had never seen it. She didn't know where it was kept. Only the elders saw it, and only on special occasions. Sometimes she wondered if it really existed. Or if Baphom-t was just a happy dream the elders had created to give the people hope.

If only she could ask Cabal.

She loved Bobby.

She hated her words.

But maybe they were the correct ones, because they would remind her that love could bring the downfall of the Nightbreed. Look at Cabal. His love for his woman had led to the destruction of their home.

But Cabal was going to make a miracle.

Cabal, not Coeur, was Baphom-t's chosen prophet.

But she *was* His child.

Bobby was not.

The odor of meat filled her nostrils but her stomach clenched. Sange touched her shoulder very gently.

"Coeur?"

"I'm—I'm . . . I hate my words. They're the Dark ones," she blurted. She was horrified. She hadn't planned to say that. It was sacrilege, she was sure of it, especially since her father was the leader of the elders.

Sange blew air out of his cheeks and took her hand. He hadn't touched her for years. When they'd been little, they'd roughhoused constantly. Her wings strained against their stitches and she had a sharp image of flying with Bobby. But Bobby had no wings.

"I'd hoped you get the words of the Light, like me," he said, "so we could chant together." His smile spoke other words. She'd always thought she'd wind up married to Sange. He was gentle and direct; she didn't think he knew what the word "duplicity" meant.

What am I going to do? What should I do? She wanted to ask Sange. Instead she smiled sadly at him and said, "I was hoping for that too."

He took her hand and laced his fingers through hers. "The right thing will happen."

"Do you really believe that?" she asked, and he nodded.

She reached up on tiptoe and brushed her lips against his. He growled with pleasure; then she darted away, grabbing a chunk of meat.

But she still couldn't eat. She looked at the faces of her tribal family, so familiar, yet changing with the years. Then she felt a gaze on her, and looked in that direction: it was her grandmother, who had been horribly scarred during the fall of Midian. She wore a veil over her face; she had once been a great beauty.

Coeur glided over to her and offered her the meat in her bloodstained hands.

"Grandmama," she said.

Her grandmother waved the meat away and Coeur set it on an empty plate. The old lady lifted her veil and Coeur didn't flinch as she kissed the deformed, crisscrossed cheek.

"Look at you, all grown up," her grandmother said fondly. "Initiated."

Coeur smiled falsely and nodded. "Ready to begin the work."

"I wonder." Her grandmother cocked her head. Her milky eyes bored in on Coeur; Coeur prickled with anxiety. "Walk with me, child," her grandmother said, extending her hand.

Coeur helped her to a standing position and her grandmother laced arms with her. Then she lowered her veil into place and together they left the feasting hall. Coeur looked over her shoulder at Sange, who was across the room, surrounded by his brothers and sisters. He was laughing with them, celebrating. Coeur was an only child. Her father was first elder, and her mother was always busy with the affairs of the tribe.

Her grandmother was revered; she could go anywhere she wanted in Corazón. Guards saluted her and moved aside from passageways Coeur had never seen before; together they descended a steep, dark tunnel.

The walls boomed and thrummed; the vibrations pulsated through Coeur as if she had walked into a gigantic living animal. As they went deeper, she saw rivulets in the surrounding rock that glowed then went dark, glowed-glowed, went dark. A heartbeat.

An arched wooden door maintained the rhythm, and it opened at the touch of the old lady's hand. She looked at Coeur and said, "Before we go in, I will speak three words to you: *Follow your heart.*"

Coeur gasped. Her grandmother smiled as gently as Sange and said, "I followed you up, child. I know about your human boy, and your plan. And you must follow your heart."

Coeur was speechless. She swallowed acid. Her wings strained.

"But I don't know my own heart," Coeur began, and her grandmother laid a finger across her lips.

"You love him. The Prophet has shown us that human and Nightbreed can become one. He was human. *She* was human."

Coeur gaped at her. This went against all teachings. *All*. This was blasphemy.

"I'm older than this tribe," her grandmother said. "I was there, Coeur. It's been forty years, and change must come. That is the lesson of Cabal."

She spoke his name!

Cabal. He was the apex, the centrum, the new thing. If only she could speak to Cabal herself, and learn what she must do.

"And, I believe, the wish of Baphomet," her grandmother continued.

And she spoke *His* name!

Coeur was nearly catatonic, unaware of movement as her grandmother led her into a dazzling chamber of visceral heat. Glowing, scintillating; Coeur had to shield her eyes. Her hands began to sear. She tried to turn away, but her grandmother planted a skeletal hand beneath her chin and turned her face to the fire.

"Open your eyes."

It was a struggle, but she obeyed.

A flash of an image: inside a charred box, meat, jewel-like and glistening, dripping and bloody; her mouth watering until the saliva turned to steam. Beautiful, beautiful.

The heart of her god.

The tribe created barriers with their thoughts; Baphomet created universes. Into Coeur he poured His thoughts, His mantra.

Follow my heart.

Her brain bubbled.

Follow my heart.

"Child?" her grandmother whispered.

She grabbed her grandmother around the neck and choked, and choked, and choked. The old lady struggled, her eyes bulging, her atrophied wings fluttering. She could not live. Could not know and say such things and live.

Cabal would agree.

Coeur let the body fall to the floor.

She left the chamber and shut the door. Stumbled up into the feasting room; then clawed her way up into her own little tunnel; emerging in the desert where Bobby paced. His cry told her he was there; his arms were strong as he embraced her. His mouth on her.

His promises.

"Cut the stitches," she whispered, turning.

He was ready; he had brought a hunting knife. He was not afraid or revolted. He cut through the thread, nicking her, apologizing. He didn't know that she saw nothing but light now. Some might say that she was blind. Others, that she was like Ashbery.

He kissed her, hard, murmured, "Fly us away."

Her wings flapped for the first time in the cold desert night. She saw Baphomet's eyes and all other pieces of Him in the planets and moons above them. His heart in the vast desert below. She flew and flew with Bobby against her chest; Bobby, erect and ready to meld with her and make futures, to begin a new race.

The tribes had hidden their god for forty years.

She soared up, up, to where there was no air. By then, Bobby was frozen; he held fast to her, his penis a length of ice, his words adhered to his lips.

I love—

She let go of the corpse and it dropped, where it would be pulverized. Never traced. Then she ascended, out of the atmosphere and into space. Following Baphomet's heart. Of which she was now a piece.

Revival

Resurrection.

Rebirth.

Through the door.

Beyond the gate.

Out of the tomb.

Taking flight on a shining path of light, to Baphomet's Beloved, His Prophet, and His Gatherer:

I am the carrier of the Light:

To Cabal.

THE KINDNESS OF SURRENDER

Kurt Fawver

She loved to stand in the field behind her trailer and stare at the night sky just after new moon. She would go out, naked and filled with wonder, and watch the shadows begin to recede from the vast cavern of space. Night after night she would steal away to the field, and night after night she would delight in the revelation that what gradually emerged from the cosmic darkness was a luminiferous set of bared fangs, pointed as an assassin's stilettos and ready to sink deep into the earth and all its inhabitants. Beneath that ominous crescent she'd laugh, tip her head back at an impossible angle, and let her own fangs—all one hundred ninety-six of them—shine against the stars. And for a few hours, while the corn rows brushed her barbed flesh and she could taste blood on the wind, she would feel freedom and security and she would remember a lost paradise for the damned, a refuge long burned away, and she would whisper, "Midian."

But, as with all things, the night would eventually end. Her head would snap back into place and her skin would again grow soft and supple and the world would return to the prison of banality it so dearly loved to be locked inside.

And it was then, in the bruised dawn light, that she would allow herself to miss her parents and her friends and, finally, cry.

"Can you believe it? Another one's gone missing. Chris Ritter. That's six in the past semester."

"I don't understand. So much promise. Why would they run away?"

"Well, you know, a lot of these kids are into drugs and s-e-x. I wouldn't doubt that played a part."

"No, no. Not boys like Chris. He sang in our church choir and Coach Kramer told me he was going to let Chris start at quarterback next year. No reason to run away. No reason at all."

"What do you think, Amy?"

The two women at the table stared across the faculty lounge to the eleventh-grade history teacher, Amy Radigan, who was curled into herself on the room's cracked-leather couch, nursing a mug of coffee.

Amy glanced up and shrugged her slight shoulders.

"Why do kids run away from anywhere?" she mused. "Probably because they're trying to escape what's inescapable. And in most cases that's people— people who judge them without understanding them, who despise them for their painfully marked differences, who'd like for all youths to be slaves or puppets or drones, standardized in the image of some ideal child that can't possibly exist except in the minds of the adults who designed it in the first place."

The women at the table sat in silence, mouths agape.

"Or maybe they're all out getting high and having a big sex party. Who knows?"

Amy slammed her mug onto an end table, leaped off the couch, and stormed to the door, muttering behind her as she went, "Excuse me, ladies, I just remembered something."

She flew to her classroom in a daze, palms clammy, heart beating in triple time. She wanted to punch the world. She wanted to smack the condemnation out of those women in the lounge. Most of all, she wanted to see if her room was empty.

It wasn't.

Through the little glass rectangle set in the door to the room, Amy could see a girl sitting motionless and unblinking in the back of the room. The girl stared straight ahead, at the dry-erase board at the front of the room, waiting for instruction that might never come.

Amy bit her lip and entered. The girl did not turn, did not speak. But her eyes, so blue, so like fire raging behind the curtain of the sky, somehow pinioned Amy from across the room.

Amy took a deep breath, shut the door, and locked it.

"So I'm going to assume you were with Chris Ritter last night?"

The girl nodded.

"I thought we agreed." Amy sighed. "I thought you were going to make an effort. I thought that's why we moved out here, into the sticks. Farms full of pigs and sheep and cattle, deer running wild. It's all for you, Asteria."

"It's not that simple," the girl, Asteria, answered, her voice stretched taut and flat. "I've told you that for years. But you'd rather not hear it."

Amy maneuvered around desks and crouched down beside Asteria. She rested a hand on the girl's shoulder.

"Okay. Fine. Then what do you need from me? What can I do to help you contain yourself? Please. Tell me."

Asteria again stared toward the front of the room.

"You know," she said, "that board up there isn't clean. Every time you wipe it off, you think you wipe it clean and new and fresh, but you don't. There's actually a perpetual buildup of residue. Every mark you make on it, every mark anyone makes on it, stays forever. And the harder you wipe, the more you scrub, the more you destroy the barrier between what you can erase from your vision and what lingers, unwanted. Eventually, you won't be able to clean anything off that board. Eventually, it will just be a chaos of scrawl."

Amy squeezed Asteria's shoulder. She could feel the girl's unyielding and surprisingly heavy musculature beneath her shirt.

"I'm always here for you, Asteria. We'll deal with your condition together. I know it's difficult, but you're not alone."

Asteria shivered and slid out of the desk in a blur. Before Amy had any real comprehension of movement, the girl was already standing ten feet away, gazing out a window, onto the gray miasma of snow and cinder in the parking lot beyond.

"I am alone, Amy. You think that because you read *Dracula*, you understand vampires. You think that because you watch *The Exorcist*, you understand demons. But you have no idea, Amy. For all your good intentions, you have no idea."

And then, suddenly, Asteria was gone and the window gaped open. Amy slumped into a desk and wondered if she'd been wrong to take in Asteria all those years ago, if the girl had been better off living on the street in anonymity. After all, how could she parent a girl that didn't age, a girl with bloodlust inscribed on her soul, a girl that was both more and less than a girl? How many deaths had she been a party to? How many times had she covered the grim truth with a sheet, only because Asteria was so very special, so very different?

Amy had always believed that the world needed as much diversity as possible, and that Asteria was a particularly pointed example of such diversity. On the basis that it was good to keep an open mind and spirit, she had always championed the weird, the unconventional, the outright freakish. That was as much a reason as any why she hadn't run screaming when Asteria first showed Amy her other face, her other body. She had looked on Asteria's nettled flesh and her unhinged, nightmare mouth, and seen the wonder of an infinite, if unforgiving, cosmos. She had loved Asteria for merely existing, for being a thing so crazy and unexpected in a world of people that tried, with all their neurotic energy, to cage and order and homogenize reality.

But that had been eighteen years ago, when Amy was just out of college, when she wasn't as fearful of the world or the consequences of living in it. Now, eighteen years on, Amy was simply scared so much of the time. She worried about Asteria, she worried about herself, and, most of all, she worried that loving monsters was wrong.

In the end, though, she had neither answers nor special wisdom—only doubt and hope. So she cupped her face in her hands and let the chilled wind from the open window numb them both as it raised gooseflesh on her arms.

"Asteria! Hey! Wait up!"

A tall blond boy with buck teeth and an impish grin cut across his face called out from the opposite end of the parking lot.

Asteria kept walking, head down. She did not need this. Not another one, so soon. Why did they clamor for her like ants on a sugar cube?

"Asteria! Hey! Stop for a second! Are you skipping out, too?"

Her stomach dropped away, down, down, below her knees, below her feet, into a place under the earth and within the earth, an unseen vortex filled with swirling blades and talons and thorns and, above all else, desire.

She stopped, not because she wanted to, but because she had to, like a shark invariably drifting toward a distant pool of blood or a viper striking out at a foot that steps too near.

"Because if you are skipping, maybe I can give you ride? Or we can hang out?"

The vortex crawled up from the deep, merging with her stomach, with the tunnels of her body, until she became it—the pit incarnate, the devourer of men and worlds.

Asteria turned, flashed a smile, and waved.

"No," she hissed to herself. "Stop it. Control it. Just keep walking."

The boy—Shane? Wayne? Asteria didn't really know his name and didn't particularly care to—ran to her side and threw a gangly arm around her shoulders.

"Did you say something?" he asked.

She shook her head and laughed. She didn't want to laugh. She wanted to growl. She wanted to roar. But roaring and growling were no way to satiate the pit, and she was at its whim.

She yanked on the boy's coat and bent his ear to her mouth.

"Why don't you take me back to my place?" she whispered, the heat of her breath promising ecstasy.

Asteria wanted to punch herself in the mouth and force all those words back into her lungs. She wanted to vomit the pit from her stomach. She knew she shouldn't take so many, so soon, one after the other. It was irresponsible, reckless. And yet, she did want to take this boy, she wanted to let the vortex shred him, body and soul. She wanted to introduce him to oblivion and its terrifying expanses. She wanted to feed.

The boy's eyes grew huge and his hands quivered.

"Yeah, yeah. Sure," he stammered. "You live with Ms. Radigan in a trailer out on Easter Valley Road, right?"

Asteria nodded and pressed herself to his chest.

The boy's grin grew wider, more confident, less imp than wolf.

"Then . . . yeah . . . let's go," he said, hugging Asteria tight.

He led her to his pickup truck and they hopped inside.

As he whipped around corners too quickly and sped down hills with hormonal abandon, he was sure he was going to get lucky. Sitting beside him, her hand playing along his thigh, Asteria was sure he was going to die.

———————

Amy returned home to find a truck she didn't recognize parked in her drive-way. The hair on the back of her neck stood at attention.

She jumped from her car and jogged to the trailer, curses already gath-ering on the edge of her tongue.

"Asteria," she called out as she opened the flimsy plywood door to their home, "Asteria, who does that truck belong to?"

No response. And no Asteria in the kitchen or the living room, either.

Anger rising, Amy ran to Asteria's room and threw open the door. And there the girl-thing was, splayed out on her bed, her mouth wide open and stuffed with a pale, bare leg. Her rows upon rows of jagged teeth gnashed and shredded; blood and saliva glistened on her stretched lips. Her eyes shimmered blue and yellow, green and red, like the wings of some tremen-dous dragonfly. She made no noise but for the rhythmic chomp and slurp of ingestion.

Amy gasped. She'd never seen the act before. She knew it happened. She knew what it must entail. But to witness it firsthand, to feel the heat in the air and to smell the many spilled fluids, was something she'd not been prepared for.

Asteria's eyes flickered back into humanity. She focused on Amy, disbe-lief and shock passing over her contorted face, then pounced from the bed, and, with a muffled shriek, slammed the door shut.

Amy backed away. Embarrassment, excitement, and rage colored her cheeks. She didn't know how to handle this situation. What was the proper way to approach one's ersatz daughter when one had found her shape-shifted into a vaguely reptilian form and in the throes of gastronomical delight? Should they talk about the incident? Should they forget it had happened? Or should Amy finally just let Asteria run away, back into the grime and shadows where she'd found her? No one wrote self-help books on topics like this. Even the Internet didn't have message boards or FAQs for adop-tive mothers of monsters.

Amy paced outside Asteria's room. She considered the myriad possible avenues of discussion she could take with the girl, but none seemed right.

Without warning, Asteria—now fully in her human vestments—burst from the room and shouldered past Amy.

"Come on," she said as she swept by. "We have to get rid of the truck before anyone notices it's here."

Amy followed, stopping only in the bathroom to pick up two sets of rubber gloves. Outside, Asteria was doubled over, retching in the driveway. Something fell from her mouth and tinkled to the ground.

Amy scowled at the bloody, shiny pile in the dirt and asked, "You swallowed his keys, too? Really?"

Asteria refused to respond. She tore a pair of gloves from Amy's grip, snapped them on, and picked up the keys.

"Ready?" she asked no one in particular.

Amy folded her arms over her chest and said, "I think we should talk about it."

Asteria blinked and smiled as if amused by some slow-burning joke.

"Talk? About what? Where we're going to leave the truck?" she asked. "I assumed we'd ditch it out by Pine's Mountain, near Route 45."

"No, Asteria." Amy sighed. "Not about the truck. About what you did in there. About what I saw."

The smile grew wider, almost clownish.

"What did you see, Amy?"

Amy struggled to find words. She'd seen death. She'd seen pleasure. She'd seen the inhuman heart of the universe beating strong and vibrant in one of its favored children.

"I'll tell you what you saw," Asteria said, preempting an answer. "You saw me. All of me. And you saw me doing what I do, what I have to do. It took ten years, ten years of you desperately avoiding what you knew to be true, but you finally saw it. And I know. I know. It's one thing to see the fangs, the spines, the crazy eyes and studded skin, and stand in awe of their power, their destructive potential, but it's another thing entirely to see how that power is used."

"Asteria, look . . . look." Amy stumbled over her thoughts. "You . . . we . . . need to find someone. To help you. To help you control it. This is all just . . . just too much."

The smile on Asteria's face vanished, replaced by a hard, freezing vacancy.

"I had people who could have helped me. A lot of people. In Midian. They were going to teach me when I was just a little older. But someone burned them all away, Amy."

Amy stood silent. She had no way to quench that fire from decades past and she wondered if it would ever stop burning.

Asteria gazed up into the sky. Dusk had settled over the firmament and stars had begun to poke through its darkening bowl.

"In monster movies," she said, more to the stars than to Amy, "nobody ever really likes the mob of villagers. They're not heroic. They're not villainous. They're nameless, faceless nobodies. They have pitchforks and torches and shotguns and riot gear, which you'd think would give them some sort of character, but, really, they're just a lumbering mass of anger and fear. See, they're angry that something has threatened the world they know and understand. Whatever that thing is, it's forced them out of their little routines, their safe assurances. And they're afraid—oh so afraid—that it will change everything for them and that their knowledge, their understanding, their routines and assurances, will be forever lost.

"Everyone who watches monster movies wants to be the hero . . . or the monster, I suppose, but no one ever wants to be one of the mob. Why? Because everyone already knows that they're part of it. Despite all the illusions of heroism or villainy most people cultivate about themselves, everyone knows that when a true threat enters their world, they'll glob onto a huddled mass and pick up a pitchfork, too. The mob makes everyone realize that they're not heroes or villains, but scared, powerless, inconsequential nothings."

Amy threw down her gloves and shouted, "No. No, Asteria. I am not like those people who burned your family. I care about you. I want what's best for you."

Asteria stared at Amy and held out her open hand, smeared in blood and bile.

"Then let's move this truck together, okay?"

Amy took a deep breath and nodded. She knew what she had to do, for her sake, for Asteria's sake, and for the sake of more young men and women.

"Yeah, okay."

She reached for her discarded gloves, fished in her pocket for her car keys, and tromped toward her car.

Asteria's upturned palm remained empty.

Later the same night, long after they'd dumped the truck by the side of the road, Asteria opened her bedroom window and crept outside. It was still full moon—a far cry from her preferred time for nocturnal roaming—but she wanted to adhere to Amy's plan. Maybe hunting the native fauna would satisfy the pit. Maybe a healthy deer would satiate the hunger.

She had to try.

Years ago, Amy had seen her panhandling on the street and taken her in. She'd given her a warm bed and a place to call home for the first time since Midian. An orphan herself, Amy had wanted for the two of them to be friends, if not family. And in return all she asked was that Asteria not heed the lamentations of the pit.

But, as was Asteria's refrain, Amy didn't understand what she asked. Asteria the girl and Asteria the monster could never be separated. The loving soul and the infinite void that pulsed within her were one and the same. Violence spun in orbit around the atoms of her being. She could no more stop killing than she could stop thinking, stop breathing, stop feeling guilty about ruining Amy's life.

"A devil with a conscience." Asteria sighed into the frigid darkness. "How can such things be?"

Amy had been good to her, even if Amy didn't understand. And so, for Amy, she would try to take the life of something that wasn't human and hope it pleased the pit all the same.

Through the barren fields she ran, faster than any human, faster than most of the small mammals that scurried in the darkness. She smelled caution in the air, fear of tooth and claw, but it wasn't the same as the nuanced terror that humans exuded.

She stopped dead and listened. Something grazed nearby, tentatively chewing at whatever remnants of corn or soy might have been left over from the autumn's harvest.

Asteria stalked her prey with the deliberate grace of a great cat. Body pressed low to the ground, she spotted her quarry—a young buck, head down, rooting in a field, oblivious to so much of the world.

She moved in. When she was close enough, she struck, and her strike was sure and lethal.

She crouched in the moonlight and tore the beast apart, swallowing it in massive bites, as she would any other sacrifice to the pit. But the meat tasted sour, bitter, and spoiled all at once. The flesh of a lower animal would not do. The void would not abide such a base offering.

The deer came rocketing back from the pit and flew from Asteria's mouth, a geyser of meat and blood spouting to the stars above.

"No," Asteria moaned. "No. It has to work."

Remembering all the smiles and the hugs and the kind words Amy had lavished upon her through the years, Asteria scooped up handfuls of the gore that had spewed from her stomach and downed them again.

She punched her abdomen and hissed, "Take it. Take it."

But again the organic miasma returned.

For what seemed hours, Asteria hunched in the field and force-fed herself the same sustenance that her body could not use. Again and again she regurgitated and again and again she swallowed, until, finally, she became too weak to swallow and the pit grew too enraged to ignore.

And when it was over, she lay down in the field and she wept, because she knew that she was destined to lose yet another family.

Just before dawn, Asteria, blood-slicked and exhausted, slid through the window that overlooked her bed and dropped onto her mattress. Immediately upon hitting that bouncy surface, several hundred pounds of muscle crushed down upon her and held fast her arms and legs. She felt metal encircle her wrists, binding them together. A mélange of voices shouted commands and the lights flicked on throughout the trailer.

Someone yelled, "Oh my God," and another blizzard of commands and legal rights engulfed Asteria. She picked out enough individual orders to realize her captors wanted her on her feet, so she stood.

She glanced around the room and her heart shriveled. Police surrounded her, and police could mean only one thing: Amy had surrendered.

An officer covered Asteria's nude form with an oversized blanket and two others marched her into the living room, where Amy sat, also handcuffed, beside a man in a navy suit—some sort of detective, Asteria guessed.

Amy looked up, but refused to meet Asteria's eyes.

"Where's the pitchfork, Amy?" Asteria asked as she was led through the room. "Where's the pitchfork?"

Tears streamed down Amy's cheeks.

"Asteria, I grew up. This isn't a monster movie. It's real life. You need help. You're too dangerous."

The officers shoved Asteria out the trailer's door. As she stumbled over the threshold, she called back to her friend, her sister, her mentor, and her betrayer.

"You grew old, Amy. And we all live in a monster movie every single day of our lives. The only question is how we deal with the monsters we encounter."

As Asteria was marched toward a squad car, she heard Amy shouting about Asteria needing extra security and medical care, about her not being human.

One of the officers that held Asteria firm laughed.

"Crazy bitch," he murmured.

The pit suddenly yawned wide open and Asteria felt her fangs sliding to the ready, her barbs shooting to the surface of her skin. She was a failed protégé, a broken child, but this was something she *could* do for Amy.

"Are you ready to meet the pit?" Asteria asked the officer as he pushed her into the backseat of the police cruiser. "Because it's ready to meet you."

The policeman laughed again, turned to his partner, and said, "Sorry. Crazy bitch*es*."

In this moment, for the first time in years, Asteria felt good about what she was, what she did. For the first time in her life, she was glad she would never grow full.

"Thank you Amy," she whispered, understanding that she would never know human kindness again.

And then she lunged and the blood flowed free and wild, as it was always meant to.

THE ANGEL OF ISISFORD

Brian Craddock

The restless heat blazed across the desert, pursued their vehicle and beat upon the top.

Despite the heat of the day, Upendra thought the desert looked lonely and cold. He wondered what trick of the desert—or the mind—could produce such an effect. The arid landscape was bare but for cornrows of saltbush, and the road was raised up off the desert floor as though to keep travelers from the lonely desperation of the barren landscape.

And Upendra was glad of it, too: nothing about the terrain invited his appreciation. It reminded him too much of his India, lost long ago to him now, where he was treated as something even lower than the untouchable caste, driven into the deserts and abandoned. He stretched his two sets of arms out over the steering wheel, as though to excise the memories.

The boy beside him—his traveling companion and, for want of a better description, his friend—smiled wistfully out the windshield up at the impossible vastness of the bright blue sky. Nhuwi, he called himself. His brown skin was dusted with the red earth of some Australian desert or another, Upendra couldn't remember which: every day, the boy would dust his face with a fresh palmful from a glass bottle he carried in his knapsack. The earth of his people, he called it.

In many ways, Upendra could appreciate the significance of the dirt in the bottle, given that he himself had now been driven brutally from two of his own homelands. He pined for the smell of both, for the hot and dry terrain of Rajasthan, and for the dank moistness of Midian.

The road hummed along beneath them. It had a rhythm to it that only long-distance travel can give, that lulls and soothes the soul. The landscape beyond the window looked mean and lifeless, and Upendra felt its concentration on them both as though it were waiting for the moment to open its maw and swallow them alive.

The wind from the open window ruffled a scrapbook of newspaper clippings on the backseat, the newest of which spoke of a remote angel cult. Nhuwi reached around and moved a box of leather shadow puppets across the seat and onto the scrapbook. The fluttering of clippings stopped. He turned back and raised his chin to Upendra, pensively.

"I would make a good meal, wouldn't I?"

Upendra was puzzled. He gave Nhuwi a sidelong glance, searching the boy's plain and smiling face for answers. None. The boy was a puzzle even to Upendra.

"We're going to see the angel," the boy added.

Upendra's grip on the wheel tightened.

"So it does exist, then?"

The boy nodded.

Their car raced over the Barcoo River and the desert gave way to deformed trees, and then to a township, where there was no road sign to tell them where they were or to welcome them to it.

John left off ministering to the hinges on his hotel's windows to watch the Volkswagen Variant cross the bridge and drive into Isisford. It passed by, and he saw in it an Indian man and an Aboriginal boy. His gut told him trouble had arrived; and if it hadn't, then it was coming.

The car continued to cruise slowly along Saint Ann Street, and John saw the dark windows of the storefronts and the homes blemish with the blurred faces of the townsfolk.

"Yep," he said to himself. "Trouble, trouble, trouble . . ."

They appeared first as just a few faces, silent strange things at their windows, watching him as he parked across from what declared itself the tourist center of the township. Upendra made a mental calculation as to how far from anywhere else they were, and was not assured when his mind placed them on a map in the middle of nowhere, in this place where streets were all named after the saints of Christendom, very far from anything else like civilization, and three days' drive from a metropolitan city.

"This angel better be worth it," he muttered to himself.

"Better wait out here, Nhuwi." He winked at the boy, who gave him a thumbs-up in return.

He donned his oversized jacket, with custom sleeves sewn inside for him to rest his extra set of arms, and stepped from the car.

Crossing the heat-stricken street in his scuffed boots, an Akubra on his head, his eyes kept low, Upendra saw each and every face follow his progress until he'd reached that confusion of timber and sheet metal that was the tourist center, and he slipped through the door and out of view.

Inside, Upendra was met with one more pale face, eyes smudged darkly into pits that watched him impassively.

He tipped his hat to the woman, gave a small smile, and gently made his way around the store, halfheartedly looking at the displays and the cheap merchandise. Rivers and crocodiles on mugs and fridge magnets. The dark pits watched him mercilessly.

"It's a mighty hot day, that's for sure," he established.

The woman didn't say anything.

"I like your wares," he lied. He picked up a rubber crocodile toy, turning it over without interest. "I was hoping to get something with an angel on it. . . ." He looked at her, looked for a reaction. Nothing. "You know, to send to the folks back home, something fun."

Now she did speak, this woman with the wet features.

"What's so fun about it?"

Upendra pushed his hat back, and gave her a cheeky smile.

"I'm sorry," he offered. "I didn't mean any harm. I'm just passing through, and heard about the angel—"

She cut him off, her voice like a bullwhip in the small shop.

"Horseshit!" She jabbed a finger at him. "You're just another big-city journalist come to dig the dirt. Come to spoil our good name!"

"Actually," said Upendra, apparently unaffected by the brutal force of her menace, "I'm here to do a puppet show."

The woman spat on the floor.

Upendra looked at the spit glistening on the linoleum and laughed, his eyes wide. "Are you serious? In your own shop?"

"Get out," she hissed at him.

He tipped his hat to her, and made his way very slowly from the store, idly scrutinizing the bric-a-brac on his way. But before he left, he noticed, up on one wall of the store, a large display informing visitors about the history of crocodiles in the area. Mounted on the wall, like some trophy kill, were two crocodile skulls. But one of them, the larger of the two, was radically malformed, its snout misshapen and snub-nosed, its brow higher and slightly domed. Upendra stopped and pointed at the skull, throwing the woman an incredulous look.

He scoffed.

"And what's *that* supposed to be?"

She threw a stapler at him.

He grinned and finally crossed the threshold and into the glare and ferocious heat outside.

Out in the street, Upendra saw that the townsfolk were still at their windows, but some had traded windows for doorways, their thick arms crossed over their chests and their mouths turned down. It amused Upendra, a little. But he had lived long enough to know that the promise of violence was in the air. Perhaps it was only the insufferable heat that quelled it?

Nhuwi wasn't in the car. The door was wide open.

Immediately Upendra looked to the people in the doorways, looked about for the telltale sign of some bully with revenge carved into a smile on his dull face. But instead he found the boy: he was levitating in the middle of the street, an illusion the heat gave, melting the asphalt at the boy's feet to make it appear he floated. He was staring at the sky, the full force of the sun on his face.

"Nhuwi! Let's roll!"

The boy dropped his head, and began running back toward the car, flipping his middle finger at one of the silent witnesses as he did so.

––––––––––

John brought them cool water, with ice, and a scotch each for himself and Upendra. True to his word, the interior of the hotel was cool and dark. They'd had too much sun for one day.

"I've put fresh linen in your rooms, and made the beds," said John, taking a place at their table.

"Thank you," said Upendra, "you're too kind."

"Pish posh," snorted John with a wave of his hand. "Don't get too many visitors. It's good to have customers. To have company."

He raised his glass and Upendra clicked his own against it.

"I thought this was a tourist destination, what with the tourist center and all."

"Sure, it is," said John, "history and all. Goes way back." He pointed to a wall where old photographs were pinned amid tracts of text. "You can read about it over there, even. But a lot of folks that visit out here have their caravans, their Winnebagos and whatnot. Not a lot of call for an old-fashioned room anymore."

"Shame," mused Upendra, "you've done this place up nicely." He sipped his scotch and considered the room, the high ceilings and red-painted beams.

"It's all I have now," John said sadly, looking up at the ceiling. "Since my wife passed, this place is what consumes me"

Nhuwi sat upright. "You should come with us, mister, when we go. Come traveling with us."

John laughed, a delightful laugh. "Ah, from the mouths of babes, eh?" And he tousled Nhuwi's hair and sat back grinning to himself. "It's okay, boy; I have my place here now. I couldn't leave her if I tried."

Upendra wondered who "she" was: the memory of his wife, or his finely polished hotel.

Nhuwi shuffled off his chair and padded over to where Isisford's history trailed across one of the walls. He peered closely at each photo, and rubbed his fingertips across their dog-eared corners.

"I assume," said Upendra, "that the angel cult isn't on the wall over there? Isn't included in the history?"

"No," said John quietly. "It's not."

Upendra sipped at his drink, not making eye contact with John. The subject seemed a sensitive one.

"Well, as curious as that all is, I can assure you, John, I'm here to do a puppet show."

John didn't look convinced.

"Scout's honor," said Upendra. "I travel around doing puppet shows for communities. I have whole boxes of them in my car. I'm thinking about doing one here, in Isisford."

A laugh burst from John, and as quickly as it came he recovered and kept himself in check. "Are you for real? You want to perform a puppet show? Here, in this godforsaken hole?"

Upendra was taken by surprise. Indeed, he hadn't thought much at all of the township: the homes had no lawns, just dirt with pits full of half-chewed bones and broken dog collars, driveways choked by shells of cars half pulled apart. There was nothing of beauty in the place, apart from the proud hotel owned by this broken man. Upendra felt a kind of concern for the man, could only imagine the anguish and loneliness that kept him pinned to the place of his wife's passing.

"I'm sorry," said John, and picked up his empty glass. "Look, it's not good here. You two, you and the boy, you shouldn't stay long. It's not good for children here."

And with that, John left the room and all was quiet.

Nhuwi gave a small chuckle, and Upendra glanced around at the boy, frowning.

He was pointing at a very old black-and-white photo of four small boys saddled to goats, with the desert as their backdrop. Their eyes were dark and angry-looking.

"Goats," snickered Nhuwi, and shook his head.

Upendra gave his performance. He set up a makeshift stage in a local park, where the dust blew across the ground and no grass grew.

His four arms worked tirelessly to bring life to his leather shadow puppets, to ring bells and shake rice in tins and create every illusion he could to tell his story. He looked out through his peephole, from behind the screen that hid him from view.

His audience had come not so much from curiosity, but as a show of force against him. Their children left at home, obviously, denied the joy of a live puppet performance. It was just a posse of angry adults. He paid no mind to it. Let them glare, shout their insults, kick dirt into the wind so it floated across his face. His story would be told, damn it.

And it unfolded. Act by act, he performed to these dull and blunt people, spilling out strange journeys of even stranger creatures, stories that held visions and mysteries and mayhem. Stories that, wherever he performed them, unsettled his audiences, because of course they weren't meant for them. His performances were a secret tale, something to reach out to the beast in the crowd, to that creature hiding among the humans Upendra was calling out, asking to be embraced, not by the witless crowds, but by that one who chanced upon his tales, who recognized their heartbeat, knew innately their core.

This day, it was none of these people. They shifted, restless and unsettled. And their conspiratorial chatter soon gave way to action, and a bull-necked man stormed the performance and the illusion was wrecked. The screen torn asunder, Upendra sat there in all his glory: an Indian man with four arms, two sets of hands manipulating several puppets and musical instruments at once.

The audience was horrified, stepping away. A mangy dog snatched away one of the puppets from the ground. Some people stepped closer, holding their hands over their hearts and squinting their hollow eyes in an attempt to uncover the trick.

But they all *knew*. This was no trick. This was something freakish.

And Upendra knew from experience that what would follow would not be fear, but anger. The crowd would slowly become enraged at the deception, at themselves for not having been more aware of such a monstrosity in their midst, for having allowed it to linger for so long: to learn their names and faces, to know their homes, their families.

It came quickly.

"Run, Nhuwi!"

But the boy was already off, and Upendra didn't have time to even face his audience before the first blow was struck. The bull-necked man was in quick, and once he was there, five more furious people followed. And then there was no stopping the tide.

The fires were low, many of them simply embers in braziers. They lit the room in a soft warm red. It was like being inside a womb.

But his body ached. Upendra was certain he had broken bones; maybe even parts of his face were fractured. He tried to sit up, but couldn't. There was talking, a deep voice, something not natural. Something he'd been looking for.

He could smell a barbecue cooking. He was salivating. His body longed for sustenance, to heal itself.

He let his head roll to one side.

He'd been brought to what looked like a church. Or a hall. There was a creature standing against the light, silhouetted, huge wings folded against its nakedness. And beyond it, the townspeople.

"It's real," he whispered, more to himself than anything. But he was heard. The intonations ceased.

The creature turned, and came toward him. It leaned over him, its golden face now in the glow cast by the embers behind him. The creature looked cruel, looked damaged. But Upendra knew its face. He actually recognized it.

"Vauiel."

The creature, Vauiel, cocked his head.

"You know me, my name?"

"Yes," Upendra whispered. "I knew you when we had sanctuary. You were Peloquin's friend."

The creature's big black eyes went wide and its mouth opened in a silent gasp.

The townspeople were restless. They began to murmur, and someone shouted that Upendra's throat should be cut now.

Vauiel turned on the crowd, and a roar came from him that was deafening.

The people went quiet, and fell back, gathering at the far end of the hall. In fear, noted Upendra. Not in anger, as he had always encountered.

When Vauiel faced Upendra again, his cruelty had softened. Upendra was in too much pain to care if this was a good thing or not.

"Come with me," Upendra whispered. "Leave these people to their useless lives, and come with me."

Vauiel frowned. "I don't remember you."

"You won't," confessed Upendra. "We were not friends, you and I. But I travel where I can, and my plays bring the Breed to me. We are lost, but I am reuniting some of us. We have a gathering here, in Australia. We are waiting for Cabal's call."

Vauiel scoffed.

"What call? He is no Cabal. And our god is as lost as we."

"But we can build a new home, to replace Midian."

"Upendra, you fool." Vauiel brushed the hair from Upendra's forehead. "You would hide away from the Natural world again? And they would find you and hurt you again? No, you must reclaim your place in the world."

"Like you? Like this pathetic angel cult in the middle of nowhere?"

"I have my reasons," said Vauiel quietly.

"There are no reasons for this."

Vauiel motioned to someone, and one of the townspeople stepped forward, carrying a bowl. The aroma of cooked fat and meat came from it.

"Here," said Vauiel in a soothing voice. He scooped some of the food from the bowl and pressed it to Upendra's lips, and Upendra ate of it greedily. Vauiel scooped him out some more.

"You went to the visitors' center?" asked Vauiel. When Upendra didn't answer, Vauiel asked again.

"What of it?" Upendra's voice was sour.

"The skull, the malformed crocodile skull hanging in there. They say it's a new species of crocodile found in this area alone."

"And?"

"It's my son, Upendra."

Upendra was stupefied. He looked at Vauiel, saw that the angel's eyes were deeply pained. There was such suffering in those eyes.

"What is the meaning of it?"

Vauiel rolled his head from side to side, some kind of soothing gesture. He placed the bowl of meat onto the table that Upendra lay upon.

"I lived in these lands before settlement. I lived here with my wife and then with my child. They were shape-shifters, crocodilians. But my son hadn't mastered the skill fully. His name . . ."

Vauiel faltered. He was crying, Upendra saw, but he made no sign of having noticed.

"His name was Kambara, and he was the pride and absolute joy of Kena and me. We lived in harmony with the local aboriginal people, the Malintji, and they even would call my son Ginga, after one of their own legends."

"What happened to your family? Why were they not with you in Midian?"

Vauiel stretched himself, his wings slowly spreading wide and then closing again. He sighed.

"The people of Isisford, the new settlers, they became aware of us living nearby. My family was killed. My boy, Kambara, he was chased down by boys riding on goats. They chased him down and finished him. But I escaped . . . only I. I flew into the air, where they could not follow. They thought me an Angel of their Lord, and that I was a sign that some evil had been vanquished. It's why they named their streets after saints: I am their own legacy. And I went to Midian, and when the Men of Hate came again, I felt something in me find itself. My resolve. I heard Cabal's words, and I rejected them. I knew Baphomet's laws, and I rejected them. And I came here, and I took my revenge on these people. And they praise me for it. I am their god now."

There was something in Vauiel's words that didn't sound right to Upendra. He was struggling to hold on to it, through the pain of his injuries and the revelations of the angel.

The doors of the enclave burst open, and John staggered in. He had been beaten. His face was swollen and bloodied, and barely recognizable. He fell to his knees inside the doorway, and struggled to get to his feet again.

Upendra was horrified.

"What have you done?"

"It was my followers," admitted Vauiel. There was little remorse.

One of the congregation spoke up, shouting gently across the room: "He was consorting with the outsiders, my lord."

"You let these people go," demanded John. His voice slurred, and blood dribbled down his chin.

"What does he mean?" Upendra searched Vauiel's face for answers.

Nhuwi steeped into Upendra's vision.

"I don't want to go anywhere, Upendra," Nhuwi said softly. He looked up at Vauiel. "I want to be like him. To fly. To see the land with my own eyes." The boy approached a brazier, his back to Upendra, and held something over the flames there. "No more Dreaming."

John continued his demands. "Let them go. The man and the boy. They haven't done anything to you."

Someone kicked one of John's legs from under him and he fell heavily onto his side, crying out from pain.

"Fuck you!" he yelled through clenched teeth. "Fuck you all for what you did to my wife!"

A large woman stepped forward and stomped on John's face.

"No!" screamed Upendra.

Nhuwi screwed his face up at the violence. He looked distressed. Gone was the happy child staring at the sky.

Upendra banged his head hard against the table, again and again. A knot in his stomach formed. His body craved more food, more of the meat that cooked and blistered nearby. He groaned.

"Upendra," said Vauiel. "Upendra, listen to me. Stay here, with me. Give up this foolish quest of yours. Stay, and eat. You must eat. You're weak."

Upendra eyed Vauiel suspiciously. The angel smiled, the cruelty from before edging back into his features.

"You're weak, Upendra. Eat."

Nhuwi stepped closer to the table.

Upendra looked at the child. There was something else here, too. Something he hadn't noticed before. He looked past Nhuwi to the congregation in the room. At all those bullish faces and fumbling limbs. Those feverish, frightened people, cowering before their angel. But something was not right.

"There's no children."

Upendra thought back to the puppet show in the park. Where were the children of this town. He hadn't seen any since arriving.

Nhuwi was mewling. He looked ill. Sweat beads were forming on his forehead and starting to run.

"Nhuwi, what's wrong?" asked Upendra.

Vauiel's voice was insistent. "Eat."

"Yes, eat," agreed Nhuwi weakly. He offered his arm up to Upendra, and it was burnt and blistered and more than that: there were bits of the flesh missing. "I saw this. It's okay."

"Eat some more," said Vauiel dispassionately. "Join me, brother."

A roaring noise was filling Upendra's head. The horror was overwhelming, and his body was aching. He was trembling, and everybody in the hall was watching fearfully, as little Nhuwi proffered his own arm for Upendra to eat some more from.

"They ate my child, Upendra," said Vauiel, his dark eyes sparkling in the glow from the embers. "They caught him, those boys on goats, and the people ate him."

Upendra groaned, and the smell of cooked meat was strong in his nostrils. Vauiel shoved Nhuwi closer, and the temptation overcame Upendra, and he began to eat of his little friend, his companion of the road.

"It is why I returned to this place," continued Vauiel. "As they ate of my child, so I eat of their children. Never again will they see their children grow, and have children of their own. And soon, their lineages will die out, and my revenge will be complete."

Upendra had stopped listening. His head was all noise, and his mouth was clamped to Nhuwi's arm.

PRIDE

Amber Benson

They were parked along the side of the bridge where the wind was most fierce, backs against the ticking steel of the red VW bus as they watched the last rays of burnt orange sunlight filter through the cloud-strewn sky. Sun-bleached, blond hair whipping frothy against their handsome faces, they stood on their perch high above the water, physiques chiseled as stone, the illicit hunger that swelled inside each of them—which had, in fact, brought them together—sated for the moment.

They'd cut a long slit in the girl's abdomen, filling her belly with limestone and quartz pebbles from the beach; then they'd wrapped her up in a cheap Mexican woven rug and pitched her off the side of the bridge. There was no splash as the body hit the water, just the lonely banshee-scream of the sea as it lashed itself, again and again, against the craggy rocks wreathing the pilings of the bridge like a sharp-toothed maw.

They were dressed in ripped, light blue acid-washed jean shorts with neon orange and yellow and lime tank tops, golden honey skin even richer against the garish colors. They didn't shiver as the chilled ocean air bit into their exposed skin, tearing into ripped torsos and muscular legs, and calling up gooseflesh that made the pale blond hair dappling their hard bodies stand on end, but they weren't impervious to the cold. They were just unmoved by it—as unmoved as they were by all the death they'd wrought.

Cal was the leader. Jeb was second-in-command. Sal and Dix were fraternal twins six years younger than the other two—though you'd never have known it from the look of them. In the glow of the late-afternoon magic hour, the four men stood out like a pride of lions—glorious to behold, but wildly unpredictable; four mercurial gods so bronzed and well formed it was hard to rip your eyes away from the sight of them.

"Sun's almost set," one of the twins said, raising his tawny head and yawning.

The others nodded. The deed done, it was time to ride.

———

Abra looked forever young. She could pass for human until she opened her mouth, but, after that, all bets were off. Not that she wanted to be human. Humans had taken away her sense of safety and burned her beloved Midian to a crisp, forcing her to flee the only home she'd ever known. Since then there'd been many wayward places—but it was the laid-back beach town of Solara, California, that'd finally stolen her heart, and it was here she'd stayed the longest.

It might seem counterintuitive that someone whose death was tied to the touch of the sun would seek refuge by the Pacific Ocean—especially in a town where *everything* was so ripe with sun and summer and surf— but one should never forget that even the sparkling places have their dark side and without the light, there would be no shadow.

Abra was not alone in her fascination for Solara. The tourists arrived in droves, flooding the little beach community year-round. They were an infinite tide of humanity washing up on Solara's shores, ready to spend their money and time then disappear, maybe never to return again. Of course, this suited Abra perfectly. She joined the crowds of tourists at night and burrowed in with the unwashed masses living under the Boardwalk during the day.

The underbelly of the Boardwalk seemed fashioned expressly for the homeless and disenfranchised. There were dozens of bolt-holes for Abra to hide in, recesses tucked away within the concrete girders holding up the wooden structure of the Boardwalk, disused entrances leading to cavernous rooms containing the massive electrical system that supplied power to the amusement rides and vendors.

The discarded detritus from the topside pleased Abra, and she spent much of her time playing with the trashed remains of summers past, the garbage sparking her childlike imagination like tinder. Anyone else would've found the place sad, but Abra liked living among the discarded lawn chairs; the old mechanical shark that lay on its side, half rusted through; the busted plastic cups smashed like flattened Chinese lanterns; the rotting flyers in a rainbow hue of colors; and the robin's-egg-blue tent whose canvas body had been tattered into ribbons by an unseen hand.

It was a burial ground of sorts and Abra was just another dead thing taking up residence there.

Night fell fast, dropping a heavy, black velvet curtain over the Boardwalk—not that anyone seemed to care. Like a herd of antelope on a grassy African savannah, the tourists were ripe for the picking, too wrapped up—in eating corn dogs and popcorn, in hooking shiny metal rings over milk bottles, in wriggling with delighted terror as the roller coaster inched up its first incline—to notice anything was wrong.

The four of them stood on the periphery, watching and waiting. Theirs was a mission of quality not quantity. Unlike a real pride of lions, they were not interested in picking off the weak or infirm. They were looking for something special, a glorious female with perfect, angelic features and a disposition to match. Once found, they'd catch her then share her body among them—and when they'd finally used her up, their prize would be discarded in a shallow grave, or the eternal depths of the ocean, forever theirs, marked and mated with for eternity.

"What about the girl over there?" one of the twins said, pointing to a tall brunette with skin the color of slightly burnt marshmallow. She was on a bench by the cotton-candy stall, texting someone on her phone, fingers flying over the screen, oblivious to everything and everyone around her.

Cal and Jeb shook their heads. As if she'd heard them talking about her, the girl looked in their direction, left eye drifting lazily within the confines of its socket. She didn't try and catch their gaze, or flirt with them like a real lioness would, but quickly returned to her phone.

Something about the intensity of their stares must've spooked her, because a moment later she stood up and wrapped her red sweater tightly around her shoulders before moving off into the crowd, unaware of just how close she'd come to an unhappy ending.

Sometimes it took only a few moments to lock on a target. Other nights they skulked back to the red VW bus empty-handed. The longer between kills, the more ferocious the hunt and capture of the next victim would be; the more titillating. They'd learned from experience it was better to wait for the right specimen than to take down substandard fare just because they could.

They waited now for the right woman to cross their path.

———

Abra smelled them before she saw them. She doubted if any of the humans noticed, but, to her, their scent was palpable: rank, animal musk that screamed danger. Then she saw them and knew her nose hadn't steered her wrong. These were human monsters and they were on the hunt.

Abra watched them, curious and strangely drawn to their raw masculinity, as they lounged against the Boardwalk's protective wooden railing, backs to the sea. One of them was sitting on the handrail, bare feet swinging, while the others stood, bodies relaxed, hands casually at their sides or in the pockets of their jean shorts. Abra wanted to laugh at their studied postures, an affect cultivated in order to appear nonthreatening.

With their tawny, tousled hair and ruggedly handsome faces, they looked like models. Many of the women who saw them did a double take, stared openly at them, or smiled so broadly it looked as though their faces might split in half. For the most part, these women were ignored. Once or twice, the one sitting on the handrail would hold a woman's gaze, but never for long—and never so one of the others could see.

Abra wanted to go to them, to see if they could sense in her some of the things she sensed in them, but she was shy. She'd been alone for so long that she felt awkward and tongue-tied. Instead, she watched them from afar, biding her time.

———

Jeb saw her first.

Still as a large cat, he flicked his lazy caramel-brown gaze in her direction, drinking her in. She was small and slim, but beneath her clothes he could see the gentle curve of hip and thigh, the fullness of pert, young breasts straining against the sheer, black fabric of her thin dress. She had tiny wrists and a delicate neck, the pale white skin at her throat throbbing with bruise-blue veins. She was angelic and beautiful.

He got hard, watching her breathe, and imagining the short yelps she'd make as he entered her, drove himself inside her over and over again until he'd covered her with his scent and seed. He wanted her badly and he knew the others would feel the same.

She had a striking face, symmetrical features in a sharp, heart-shaped frame. She tilted her head, a sheet of straight, honey-blond hair falling across one dark violet eye, causing her to appear aloof and mysterious. He didn't think she'd noticed him yet, which was good. No one wanted to tip off the prey too soon in the game.

"Three o'clock," he said, his voice smooth as cream, trying not to betray his excitement.

The others followed his gaze, and three more sets of eyes locked on the girl. Usually, the power of four male stares was enough to turn any woman's head, but she didn't seem to notice.

Without exchanging a word, they began to move, fanning out so their paths would eventually draw them back together, hemming her in place. Weaving through the crowd, they took their time, sinewy muscles flexing as they engaged in the controlled stalking of their prey.

Even though Jeb made the selection, Cal was in charge. He stepped up to the girl, his perfect white teeth flashing under the Boardwalk's fluorescent lighting.

"My friends and I couldn't help noticing how beautiful you are."

The girl lifted her chin, head turning as her blank gaze settled in Cal's direction, following the sound of his voice. Cal looked startled; then comprehension dawned across his face as he realized they'd missed the obvious—there was something wrong with her, a disturbance of the mind. He doubted she possessed the IQ of a small child.

He shook his head at Jeb and the twins, letting them know he was aborting. The others drew back, disappearing into the anonymity of the crowd, leaving Cal alone to deal with the simpleminded girl.

———

It was a wash. They'd waited half the night, but no other woman had piqued their curiosity. Abra followed them as they left the Boardwalk, keeping a safe distance behind, not wanting them to know she was there. One of her gifts was the ability to move in silence. She glided, her footsteps muted as she shadowed them across the asphalt parking lot and onto the wide concrete sidewalk that paralleled the Boardwalk.

It was early enough that there were still people out on the street, strolling couples holding hands, families with small children half asleep in their parents' arms, and Abra used them like human cover, hiding behind them whenever she felt vulnerable. As they moved farther away from the Boardwalk, skirting the residential sections of town, the crowd began to thin and she had to fall back even more. There was almost no foot traffic once they moved into the suburban areas, and so she used the long shadows in between the streetlights to hide herself away, tucking up close to the bungalows and cottages she passed, ready to step into a front yard or garden and disappear from view.

Up ahead, under a bright yellow streetlight, she saw them stop beside a red VW bus. The sound of the bus's side door sliding open carried across the emptiness of the landscape, and she knew if she was going to make her move, it was now or never.

They climbed into the car, the twins in back, Jeb shotgun, Cal driving. The night's search had been fruitless, but they were unfazed, used to such evenings. It was only a few weeks since their last kill and going without the feel of a woman underneath them for so long only built anticipation, heightening the next experience. Cal started the engine, the old bus knocking back and forth on its wheels as it came to life.

They pulled out into the street, the bus slowly gathering speed as it prepared to melt away into the night, but then the sight of a figure standing in the middle of the road, bathed in the glow of their headlights, made Cal slam his foot on the brakes.

It was too little, too late. They hit the figure straight on, the body slamming into the windshield.

When the bus finally came to a jarring stop, they were all silent. The front windshield was cracked down the middle, flecked with what looked like black blood spatter. Cal opened his door and climbed out, the empty street ahead of him lit by the car's headlights. He looked around, expecting to see a crumpled body lying in the road, but there was nothing. He felt a tap on his shoulder and he whirled around, expecting the worst.

The simpleminded girl from the Boardwalk was standing behind him, her hair wild around her porcelain face. There was black fluid running from her left nostril and the corner of her mouth, and her left shoulder was out of joint, hanging limply at her side.

"You," Cal whispered, unsettled for maybe the first time ever in his life.

He'd radically misjudged her. There was still a vacuous look in the girl's violet eyes, but she was *not* simpleminded. He realized this, too late, as she smiled in his direction, revealing two rows of utterly inhuman crocodile teeth and a forked tongue that flicked out in his direction, tasting the air.

"I want to play with you."

Her voice was soft and melodic, but frightening in the context of the black fluid and her injuries. She reached out with her good arm and touched his chest, her fingers smearing black fluid across the front of his neon-green tank top.

Inside the bus, the others watched as Cal took a step backward. The girl dropped her hand, her beautiful face scrunching up in a frown of confusion. With a violent shake of her torso, she snapped her disjointed shoulder back into place and smiled—but there was nothing happy about the angle of her lips.

————————

When Abra realized they were leaving, that her chance was slipping away, she didn't think. She just stepped into the road. There was no pain as she slammed into the glass windshield, cracking her head and tearing her shoulder from its socket, only the thrill of excitement, and knowing she was going to share herself with creatures that were as deviant on the inside as she was on the outside. But then he'd stepped away from her—the only one who'd been bold enough to catch the eyes of the women on the Boardwalk— and she realized he was scared, his fear a heady musk leaking from his mouth and his pores. Confused, she'd tried to touch him, to let him know she just wanted to play, but the fear smell only increased and he moved even farther away from her.

She wanted to be human, so she could cry and bang her head against something hard until the skin and skull split open and the brain inside was mashed to a pulp and she didn't have to think anymore—anything that made the pain of being so alone go away.

These men were supposed to embrace her. They'd come her way once, and she'd dropped the ball, so nervous she hadn't been able to talk. Now here she was again, ready to join them for the night, but in the space of a few hours something had changed. She was a pariah even to these monsters.

She howled in pain, her mind on fire with misery and anger—and then she stopped thinking at all and began to act.

The girl lashed out with her right hand, driving her fist into Cal's chest. With a wet, sucking sound, she extracted his heart and hefted it into the air so the others could see it in the glow of the headlight. Eyes rolling up into the back of his head, Cal pitched face-first onto the asphalt, where he stayed, unmoving, as the girl threw the bloody thing on the ground and stomped it into pieces with her bare foot.

When she was done, she leapt catlike over his body and raced to the driver's-side door of the bus, where the others were sitting in stunned silence, watching the action play out through the cracked windshield like a scene in a violent action movie. As soon as the girl made her move for the bus, Jeb threw himself across the front seat, hand poised over the door lock to engage it, but the girl was faster, grasping the outside handle and ripping the door out of its frame before Jeb could lock it. She reached through the empty doorframe and grabbed Jeb's left arm, tearing it from his torso then throwing the meaty limb behind her, where it landed on the road with a loud *thwack*.

Jeb screamed, and the girl punched him in the throat, compressing his windpipe until the scream became a gurgle. He collapsed against the passenger door, grasping at his throat with his hand as the girl placed her hands on either side of his head and twisted until it detached from his neck. Dropping the offensive head into the well between the front seats, she turned her attention to the twins, who were falling all over themselves to get out of the bus, hands scrambling to unlatch the door.

Grabbing a fistful of blond hair in each hand, she dragged them backward across the seat, pulling them into the front so she could get a better grip on their necks. Then she bent over each one in turn, and used her crocodile teeth to rip out their throats.

The police had blocked off both sides of the street, yellow crime-scene tape flapping in the chilly early-morning breeze, but the neighbors ignored the cordon, standing on their porches and out on the street in their pajamas and robes, eyes wide as they took in the procession of investigators and forensic technicians alighting on the crime scene.

Abra sat on the roof of a nearby house and watched as the coroner loaded the four mangled bodies onto stretchers and took them away. She wasn't sorry for what she'd done, only for what she was.

Not that any of it mattered anymore—she wasn't going to make it back to one of her bolt-holes before the sun came out, and she was glad for it. Besides, it was nice up here, the coolness of the slate roof radiating up through her back and head as she watched the stars wink out one by one above her.

It wouldn't be long now.

BUTTON, BUTTON

Ernie W. Cooper

Kathryn Miller wrinkled her nose as she dug into the damp mass at her feet. The breeze was cold, colder than she had expected when she first decided to haul the overflowing laundry basket to the small yard behind the modest house. Their dryer had broken several weeks ago, and she now had to hope for the weather to cooperate whenever the piles of clothing in her or Elliot's room approached critical mass.

At the other end of the yard, Elliot crouched in the grass. The stiff breeze tousled the twelve-year-old's brownish hair as he lined up a row of twigs meticulously in the soft earth.

". . . seven . . . eight . . . nine."

He nodded slowly at the ninth stick, and then knocked the collection to the ground. Kathryn sighed as, moments later, he began to line them up once more.

"Elliot!" she called to him, softly at first, and then again.

Her son destroyed his handiwork, oblivious to her calls. She sighed and shook out one of her work skirts. As she lifted it to the line, she swore softly. The three buttons that ran down the side of the garment were missing. She ran her fingers over the little frayed areas where they had been plucked off, and then strode across the lawn to Elliot.

He plunged the seventh twig into the ground, and then her shadow made him pause. He looked up, blinking. She held the skirt out to him.

"Did you do this?"

He stared at the skirt and then gingerly reached up, running his hand across the cloth.

"One . . . two . . ."

She pulled the skirt away. "Three, yes. All three buttons are gone. Why did you take Mommy's buttons? You know she needs this skirt for work."

Elliot's fingers slowly twitched in the air, still feeling for the third cloth nub. "Didn't," he replied sullenly.

Kathryn threw the skirt over her shoulder and knelt down in front of her son. She held him firmly by his shoulders. "Can you give me the buttons? I can sew them back on, I won't need to buy a new skirt."

Elliot looked away. "I don't have them."

"Please, baby."

"I didn't do it."

Her grip tightened on his shoulders. "Give Mommy her buttons."

His hands began to spasmodically reach out and snap the twigs in front of him. "Didn't."

"Why are you lying to me?"

Elliot stopped breaking sticks. His brow furrowed, and he whispered softly, "Why don't you believe me?"

There was a heartbreaking silence. They'd had this conversation before. It wasn't always about a button, but it always ended the same way.

Kathryn chewed softly on the inside of her cheek and ran her hand slowly down the side of his face. She could feel his slight shaking. Her stomach twisted. A mother's touch should not evoke such a reaction in a child. It was all just so frustrating. Two years. Two years and no end in sight.

Her hands dropped to the ground and she tilted forward, resting her forehead against his. "Why don't you go to the park? Maybe I'll meet you there when I'm done with the laundry."

Elliot knew he was being exiled. Rather than continue their discussion, his mother found it easier to just give up and send him away. It was happening more and more of late. Laundry would give way to dinnertime, and there would be no meeting him at the park. They would both find some peace apart from each other, their mutual accusations fading temporarily.

He brushed his lips against her forehead and turned without a word.

Kathryn watched his small, hunched back retreat from the yard. She went back to the clothes basket, unaware that the buttons in question were roughly twenty feet away, under her back porch.

The three buttons were laid out on the cold earth in the darkness. There were two holes in each dark blue button, and they ran perfectly in a line from one to the next. Five white buttons lay in a line that ran perpendicular to the blue ones. Six black buttons ran parallel to these. They were slightly smaller than the blue ones, with four holes.

A small figure lay next to the arrangement, his black eyes watching Elliot walk away. He was the same size as Elliot, but it had been a very long time since anyone had considered Simon a boy. One long-fingered hand hovered protectively over the missing buttons. They were his now. He had taken them from the woman's room the night before. Now he lay in the cool darkness, waiting to take his night's haul back to his new—albeit temporary—home. The sun would not be kind to his pale, almost translucent skin. In the days following the fall of Midian, he had learned to travel by night. Normally, he would have been in and out of a house long before the dawn, but the boy had been up most of the night again. Simon had stood in the hallway, listening to the soft counting on the other side of the boy's door. It had been hypnotic, comforting.

He began to count, quietly running through the fourteen buttons that kept him company. He rolled the numbers slowly around in his mouth as if he were tasting them. They did not soothe him as the boy's droning had, but he still felt his eyelids grow heavy. Sleep had been a luxury since he'd lost his friends and family, his tribe, on that terrible night.

As fitful slumber claimed Simon, Elliot was cutting across one of the neighbors' yards. Since he knew that his mother was unlikely to join him, he could freely skip the park. There would be other children there, and he had no desire to see them. Generally, they were cruel. Best-case scenario, they were confused by his behavior. He would rather be alone than face their taunts or pointed ambivalence.

His left hand absently plucked at one of the buttons on his shirt. Kathryn had planted the seed, and even though he had not ruined her skirt, he found his way to his own buttons. His thumb played around the smooth plastic. It was solid, comforting. It was an anchor.

The town's cemetery loomed ahead, and Elliot eagerly pushed the gate open. The headstones were neat and orderly, and that pleased him. The rows of white stone glistened slightly in the sunlight as they climbed up and back over the low hillside. Elliot breathed deeply as he caressed the first stone he came to. The name was irrelevant. Instead, he felt his eyes drawn to the date of death.

Elliot knew death. His grandparents and his father had all died. One set of grandparents and his father were in this very cemetery. He vaguely recalled their funerals, but had never found his way back to them on the days he came here to play among the headstones. Or maybe he had, but was so caught up in the numbers that their names had not registered.

1947.

He smiled and raced off among the stubby monuments, searching for 1948.

———

Back under the house, Simon twitched in his sleep. The nightmare came, like it always did. He was lost in a sea of noise and confusion. There were uncertain cries of terror ringing out down the tunnels of their sanctuary. Simon's brother, Alexander, had him by the hand and was pulling him toward the surface. There was smoke, there was fire, and when they finally reached the surface, there was the Button Man.

Alexander had turned toward him. He was outwardly calm, but the organs visible beneath his pale skin betrayed his mood. They pulsed and twisted like a school of fish, or perhaps a bloom of jellyfish, bunching and breaking in agitated waves. He looked as if he were about to speak, perhaps to say something reassuring, but he retched up black bile instead. A knife tip blossomed in the center of his chest.

The multitude of black organs attempted to move away from the invasive steel, but the knife plunged in again, and Alexander fell heavily, black blood continuing to gurgle from his mouth. A figure towered above him. In the orange glow of the flames, Simon could see the glint of two buttons staring down at him. The Button Man cocked his head, listening, and then casually opened Alexander's throat before striding purposefully away. Simon watched him cut down another one of the Breed before being swallowed up by the acrid smoke.

The smoke grew thicker in the dream, the screams louder. As they reached a crescendo, his eyes snapped open under the porch. The sun was still somewhere overhead. He had probably been sleeping for mere moments.

Every time he closed his eyes, the Button Man came for him. As much as it terrified him, he was always a little disappointed, though, that it was just in his head. In the confusion after the fall, when the tribe began to scatter, he had been told that the Button Man had been killed.

Simon knew better.

The thing that had taken his brother from him was still out there. While the survivors of the fall spread out into the harsh world, Simon began to move slowly from town to town. He would avenge his brother. When others called for reunification, Simon knew that he must strike out on his own.

He needed only to find the right button.

He had been here for several weeks now. Among the pristine white headstones in the cemetery was an older mausoleum. When he had first slid inside, he had unearthed a small tunnel that led to a tunnel that cut back into the hillside. Obviously, some of his people had been there, many years ago. For now, he would use the mausoleum as a way station. There had been three other towns before this one, but something felt right about this place. It might have been the familiarity of the graveyard, but over the last week, as his collection grew, he also found himself drawn back to the same house.

The boy always seemed to be searching for something with an intensity that matched Simon's own. And his affinity for the graveyard confused Simon. Sometimes, as the sun set, he watched from the safety of his crypt as Elliot ran about the graveyard with a sense of mysterious purpose. Did he know about the Button Man?

In the graveyard, Elliot was looking for 1971. His quest was interrupted by the arrival of Shawn Wells. Shawn was years older than Elliot, and lived three houses away. He'd spied his neighbor entering the cemetery three days ago, and now casually looked that way whenever he was in the kitchen, on the off chance his victim had returned. And while Shawn had always been an equal-opportunity bully, the more withdrawn Elliot grew, the more Shawn seemed fascinated with Elliot's behavior. No amount of physical or verbal abuse seemed to deter the boy from his collecting or his counting. It soon became a challenge.

This time, Shawn didn't say anything. He just slouched lazily across one of the headstones and watched Elliot scurrying about the cemetery. Elliot kept glancing up nervously, and soon abandoned his search. Shawn grinned triumphantly as the smaller boy retreated through the gate.

"That's what I thought!"

Elliot gloomily returned home. He went to the rear of the house, but his mother had already finished and gone inside. Simon followed his trudging footsteps as he clambered up the back porch, noting that he softly counted each step. The footsteps stopped, briefly, directly above him. Simon stared straight up, breathing in, exhaling. Repeat. He started counting the breaths to himself.

Finally, the steps continued on into the house. Simon continued counting each individual breath, and sleep claimed him. The Button Man stayed away for hours.

This time in the dark dream, Simon himself felt the Button Man's blade, and it startled him awake. One hand clutched at his chest, and the things within him pushed outward against his chest, reassuringly, like the beat of a chorus of hearts.

He slowly moved out from under the porch into the night air. He reached into the pocket of his ragged pants and felt the weight of the buttons therein. He cinched the rope that held the pants up a little tighter. The button that had previously done the work had been one of the first added to his collection.

He'd never been away from the cemetery tunnel this long. It made him slightly nervous. As he prepared to slink across the yard, he glanced back to make sure the home's occupants were asleep, or at least not anywhere they could see him.

His eyes fell on a single dark button lying in the center of the porch.

Simon stopped breathing. There was no question, it had been left for him. Was it a trap? Countless years of mistrust and words of warning told him it had to be. On the heels of the nightmare, he even pondered if it could have been set by the Button Man.

Paranoia was soon replaced by a stronger sense of conviction, though. The boy's footsteps had stopped overhead. He had come back while Simon slumbered. It wasn't a trap. It was a gift.

Simon stepped carefully onto the porch. He picked up the button and put it in the pocket opposite the rest of his collection. The mystery button could not mingle, and potentially taint, the rest. Not yet. He would somehow find a way to vet the button.

One of the porch windows was half open, and another button lay on the sill. It had clearly come from the same article of clothing. It quickly joined the first button in his pocket, and he stood in front of the window. Another button lay in sight on the hardwood floor of the dining room.

Simon's lips pursed, and his pale skin blackened as the ephemeral black shapes within him rushed to his face. Without even finding it necessary to compact his frame, Simon climbed into the house and advanced on the third button. Three buttons later, he stood in front of Elliot's door. He hesitated, took a long, deep breath, and then pushed the door open.

Elliot was awake in bed, knees pulled up to his chin. Waiting. Anticipating. Simon slowly walked into the room. He could hear the woman breathing noisily down the hall, and so he gently pulled the boy's door shut behind him.

One last button sat at the end of the bed. Simon crawled onto the bed, his slight form barely making an impression. He sat cross-legged and picked the button up, rolling it between thumb and forefinger.

Elliot stared at the boyish creature before him. His feet were bare, and his toes were slightly elongated, just like his fingers. In the dark, his skin almost seemed to glow. Dark shapes moved under the skin, swimming up and down his forearms. His eyes were shiny orbs of black, glistening curiously at the human boy in front of him.

They were both silent until Elliot slowly asked, "Seven?"

"Seven," came the reply.

Two days later, Elliot was crawling through a small hole in the back wall of the mausoleum. The dirt tunnel led away into a large chamber inside the cemetery's hill. In the center of the chamber, low flat stones ringed a black hole that dove deeper into the earth. Simon had not tried to search anywhere past the central chamber. Whatever Breed had lived there in the distant past, the dust and disuse in the central chamber proved they were long gone. No one else fleeing Midian had come upon the refuge.

Elliot was soon sitting in the dirt, moving buttons back and forth, counting diligently by the light of a single lantern. Simon had been busy. There were two small bags from the previous towns he had visited, and his newest buttons were in small, discrete piles on the stone floor. Over the last two days, Elliot had begun arranging them in various geometric shapes from one end of the room to the other. Simon was pleased.

Simon chewed thoughtfully at the roast-beef sandwich that the boy had presented him with. Each time he swallowed, dark shapes moved up and down his throat, ferrying bits of food to unknown locations hidden by his dirty T-shirt. Elliot was fascinated by the process, and having a difficult time splitting his attention between the button collection and dinner.

Simon noticed the boy intently watching him. "What is it?"

Elliot felt his face redden as he was caught staring. He fumbled mentally, and then finally asked, "Why the buttons?"

The crypt dweller answered by firing back, "Why do you count?"

"It makes everything quiet."

Simon nodded. It made sense to him. Ever since he had begun observing Elliot's behavior, the nightmares were getting better. The counting instituted some order in the mad chaos of the memories of Midian's end.

"Was there a time before buttons?"

"Yes. Why? Was there a time before counting?"

"Yes."

Simon thought of his brother. His insides writhed in sympathetic sadness. "Was it a happier time?"

"I guess. Maybe." Elliot sighed. "Not really."

Simon made an apologetic sound.

Elliot began segregating buttons by color. "I count everything, though. Everything. It makes my mom nuts." His face fell. "It makes everyone nuts. Why just buttons for you?"

Simon's eyes narrowed as he thought of the Button Man. "I'm looking for the right button."

"How will you know?"

"I've seen these two buttons before."

"What happens when you find them?"

What would happen when he found them, after he killed the Button Man? Or killed him again, maybe, if the rumors contained half truths. What then? Would he try to find the other Breed? Would there be another refuge? Or had Midian taught them a lesson. Was it better to live on the fringes, alone?

Simon finally shrugged as the thought of the confrontation caused the small black organs to race back and forth under his skin angrily. Elliot began to impulsively count the shapes running up and down his friend's left ankle.

"The nightmares stop."

────────

Days passed. Both Elliot and Simon found themselves looking forward to their visits. On a particularly gloomy day, though, Elliot crawled into their sanctum and immediately put his back to his friend. Simon crawled across the floor, eventually pointing to Elliot's face.

"What happened?"

His lower lip was split and puffy. Elliot gingerly reached up, fingertips coming away slightly bloody.

"Nothing."

"Did someone . . . hurt . . . you?"

"This bigger kid named Shawn. He was just fooling around. He's always . . . fooling around."

Elliot ground his teeth and suddenly flipped the button he was holding into the well in the center of the chamber. Both of them reached out, but it was much too late. The button had vanished soundlessly.

"Sorry," Elliot mumbled.

Simon leaned in, staring at the blood welling up and trailing down the boy's chin. He slowly reached up, two fingers extended. As they approached Elliot's skin, the fingers blackened, and Simon felt himself trembling. The things inside him all rushed forward. His digits became engorged, and the blackness started to ooze right from his pores. Simon gently poked Elliot's lip, and some of the dark liquid moved into the boy, suffusing across his ruddy face. Likewise, some of Elliot's blood soaked into Simon's fingertips.

Elliot rubbed at his face. "It itches."

"I'm sorry," Simon said sheepishly. "I think they like you, though."

"What are they?"

"I don't know, but they've always been with me. With me and my brother."

"You have a brother?"

Simon was silent.

"Oh."

Simon picked up a button and sent it into the well. This time, neither of them reached out after it.

Elliot cleared his throat nervously, and then asked, "What did you wish for?"

"What?"

"When you throw a penny in a well, you get to make a wish. I figured this was close enough."

Simon stared into the hole in the ground, and then whispered, "Monsters don't get wishes."

He sat down, and it was his turn to face away. The two sat silently, lost in their own thoughts. There was no counting. There were no buttons.

———————

It was three days later when Kathryn Miller's mind finally broke.

There are many things that a mother always hopes to never walk in on her son doing. As she stood in the open door and stared at her son staring up at her, a pile of buttons to one side, a pile of ruined clothing to the other, she vaguely wished that it were any of those other things.

Elliot looked fearfully up at her, but she just slowly knelt down next to him. In the last few seconds, she had officially become incapable of caring.

"What are you going to do with all of these buttons?"

Was this a trick? No yelling? No tears? He decided to be honest with her. "They're for my friend."

She began to pull all of the clothes he'd destroyed to her. "Oh? That's a relief. 'Cause if they were for you . . . Well, that would just be crazy, right?"

"Right," he replied, uncertainly.

"Why's your friend need all of our buttons?"

"He's going to stop the Button Man."

"Do you mean the Bogey Man?"

Elliot looked at her sternly. "The Bogey Man's not real, Momma."

She stood up and looked down at the earnest sincerity on her son's face. Nervous laughter spilled out as she walked away, dragging one of her dresses. "Of course he's not."

The next day, Elliot presented Simon with his grand haul. The two of them eagerly began to count and sort through the newest additions, as well as the ones that Simon had gathered from across town the night before.

Elliot stopped at one point, looking down at his hands and the buttons they clutched. "I think there's something wrong with my mom. She's acting really weird."

A voice spoke from across the chamber, near the tunnel to the crypt. "Of course she's acting weird, she knows she has a freak for a son."

It was Shawn.

Shawn had watched Elliot make his customary pilgrimage to the cemetery, and had followed him. He had hesitated in the mausoleum, at first because he overlooked the small tunnel entrance, and then because he was unsure if he really wanted to crawl into a small dark hole in a cemetery.

Curiosity won out, though, especially when he realized that nobody knew what either of them were doing.

Nobody would know.

Shawn soon made his way into the central chamber. He was initially disappointed at the spectacle before him. He didn't know what he would find, but Elliot ruling over a kingdom of buttons in the dark was not it.

"Shawn," Elliot whispered with dread. He turned to where Simon had been sitting, but there was only flickering light playing across the wall.

"Holy shit, kid." Shawn kicked his way across the room, scattering piles of buttons. Somewhere in the darkness, Elliot heard Simon hiss angrily, but Shawn could not hear over the miniature carnage he was creating.

"Everyone knows you've got issues, but man, this is just fucking nuts."

Elliot was shaking. He should have made sure nobody followed him. What was he going to do? And where was Simon? He dropped down and impulsively began to move buttons around, quietly counting them.

"Knock it off!"

Shawn pulled Elliot to his feet. Elliot reached out and started grabbing at the small metal snap buttons on the older boy's varsity jacket.

"Jesus, what's with you and buttons?!"

Elliot clung to the jacket, and Shawn spun him around. His feet entangled, Elliot suddenly found himself tripping over the low stone wall around the well-like hole that dominated the chamber. He gasped in fright before tumbling over the side. He frantically grabbed at the stones, breaking his fall before plunging into the darkness.

Breathing hard, Shawn stepped over and looked down. The lantern did nothing to light the black maw. It could have ended inches below Elliot's scrabbling sneakers, or it could be bottomless. He had no idea.

But he could find out.

Shawn leered down as Elliot made mewling sounds of protest, trying to pull himself up.

"So you like to count, huh?"

He reached down and grabbed one of the boy's fingers, wrenching it up and away from the stone. Elliot howled in pain as Shawn called out, "One!"

Shawn stood up, and howled into the darkness. "Man, you're right, that's good stuff! Now count with me!"

Elliot gritted his teeth, choking back sobs.

"Fucking count with me or I'm just going to drop a rock on your retarded head, kid."

"One," Elliot muttered.

Shawn went for another finger. There was a tiny snap, followed by, "Two!"

Elliot was crying now. He couldn't say the number. He wanted to be brave and strong, and to protect his friend. His fingers hurt so much, though. As Shawn leaned in again, Elliot called out for Simon.

"Simon? Who's Simon?"

The light in the chamber dimmed briefly as the lantern was lifted off the ground, and then dashed across the floor. Shawn spun around as flames began to claim button and bag.

Simon stood in the glow, black eyes wide, gray teeth showing in a rictus grin, hands reaching out for Shawn.

"What the fuck are you?!"

Buttons were melting and burning around him. His collection was destroyed, his sanctuary ruined, but Simon could only think of the horrible night that had claimed his brother. In the glow of the fire, Shawn's metal buttons gleamed, taunting. They flashed as Shawn twisted to run, a metallic sheen like the cruel knife of the Button Man.

Simon's finger bones pushed outward, rushing to join the black ephem-era. Bones elongated and poked through the skin, forming long talons. Simon's hissing grew louder, and he raked at his dirty T-shirt with his claws. The tattered cloth fell away, and his chest was a dizzying mass of zigzagging blackness and skeletal protrusions. Fountains of bone welled up against the skin, capped with large, organic buttons. Each button had four holes, with tiny knots of sinew that held them in place. As they broke free from his skin, dark ichor spewed outward. These were the buttons that haunted Simon's dreams, the impassive face of the Button Man that had taken his people from him.

"Kill the Button Man," Simon growled.

"Keep away!"

Somewhere in his frenzied mind, the shreds of Simon's rationality argued for mercy. This was not the Button Man. Cruel, yes. Human, yes. But deserv-ing of his vengeance? No. He couldn't kill this boy. He knew the old tales. Killing a human would bring other humans. Lylesburg had always been clear on this point. Better to flee. Save the boy, and run away.

Shawn was frozen, a terrified expression on his face. He batted feebly at the black liquid sloughing off his jacket. The black, gnarled claws were inches from his vitals.

As Simon warred internally, his body outwardly reflected the battle. The black organs began to grow lazier as he calmed down, though, dark bones pulling back inside of him where they generally belonged.

Yes, it was time to run. He would begin again, in another town. This fire would bring the humans. His buttons were lost. And his new friend, he was lost to him, too.

There was a guttural scream from behind Shawn, and then the older teen's eyes widened in surprise. Blood exploded from the top of his head and cascaded down his forehead and into his eyes, his mouth.

Elliot had pulled himself from the hole and hefted one of the large flat stones, moving silently up behind his adversary.

His eyes were wild as Shawn turned around, hands reaching up reflex-ively to ward off a second blow.

"Two!" Elliot screamed. Shawn was slow, stunned. The rock deftly ma-neuvered between his hands and caught him in the face. Teeth joined the buttons scattered across the floor.

Shawn crumpled to the ground. The rock went up and down, and Elliot continued to count out above the meaty smacking sounds.

". . . Eleven! Twelve!"

Chest heaving, he dropped the rock onto the teen's corpse. Simon stared down at the body, and then up at his friend.

Blood slowly dripped from each hand. Elliot burst into tears.

Simon reached out, and his hand blackened, stretching. Elliot reached back with his own blood-slicked hand.

"You'll come with me now," Simon spoke softly, matter-of-factly.

The darkness within Elliot answered.

I AM THE NIGHT YOU NEVER SPEAK OF

C. Robert Cargill

It's banging in my skull again. The hunger. It starts as an itch on the other side of the bone, behind the earlobe, just where I can hear it. Scritch, scritch, scritch it goes in the night. I don't notice it when it's just a tickle. I've trained myself not to. But when it's a scratch, I know I'm in for it. I know that it will get so bad it'll curl my fingers, curl my toes, paint my knuckles white and choke my fingertips red. It'll arch my back and make me want to bite my own tongue clean off. I'll start beating a balled fist against my skull, want to drive a knife or a screwdriver or a power drill—whatever I have on hand—right into the spot to scratch it.

But that's just how it starts. And it only gets worse from there. Next comes the pounding, a screaming headache like a hangover from three solid days of tequila and nothing else. My brain throbs against a skull full of exposed nerves and I want to tear my skin off my arms just to feel something else for a change. I want to pull out my hair in clumps, bits of flesh dangling from the ends, rip my ears off both at the same time. But that won't help. That won't be but a distraction, a momentary dalliance from the scratching and the pounding and the bleating of my hunger.

I have to feed. To eat. To devour whole the dark of night. Its sins. Its memories. I have to feast upon the guilt and glee of a hundred carnal pleasures, to drink and fuck and finger and sink low into a junkie sleep rich in the glow of a peaceful head and the taste of cock and quim and filth on my mouth.

Not that I love that shit. I hate it. It's fucking cotton candy for the soul. A second on the lips, a flash on the tongue, and then vapor—an unsatisfied memory of a moment you can't ever get back. You need more. You gotta have more. That's where it started, for me at least. And it never ends. It never, ever, ends.

I don't eat people, not like the others. Some of the others at least. I eat the sin. The act. I dine off the moment that the soul crosses the line from one side of morality to the other. But it ain't like you think. A sin ain't found in the lines of a book. It's found in the heart, the soul. A sin is found in shame. Or in that dark enjoyment of something made better because you think it's wrong. That's where I eat; that's where I live. That's where I come for you.

Getting people to sin is easy. Everyone wants to be around me. I'm fucking beautiful. Not hot. Not sexy. Beautiful. They can't take their eyes off me. You. You would fuck me. That's how beautiful I am. I haven't even told you if I'm a man or a woman yet, and I don't know if you're gay, straight, or married. But you'd fuck me. You know you would. You're starting to picture me now, see my features through the fog, feel the tickle in your groin as you rub your thighs together hoping no one else in the room notices how hot you're getting. That's how fucking beautiful I am. And that face you're seeing. That's what I look like. That's what I always look like.

And everyone sees me different. Everyone but the monsters. To them I always look the same.

In Midian they called me Bacchus, the god of lust and ritual madness, of ecstasy and wine and all the filthy fine fucking things folks love. Most thought I might actually be him, or at least the inspiration for the story. But I ain't him and he ain't me. I ain't half that old. It's just a name, good as any other. But now, now that they know me, now that the walls have come down and so many truths have been revealed, they don't speak that name in jest. They don't think about me that way anymore. Now I'm something else. Now that word has a whole new meaning.

Now they know that I eat sin and a monster ain't nothing but.

People think of psychopaths and equate them to monsters. They think of the cruel emotionless detachment and see the awful things they've done and scream *A MONSTER! A MONSTER!* But that's no monster.

A psychopath is just a thing that's broken. They're not men; they're animals—devolved brains that have ceased feeling and turned to instinct. Animals, those are the only things that will do something cruel without remorse. They'll bite their best friend for a morsel and never give it a second thought. You can smack 'em upside the head and they'll come back to you—if you've broken them right. That's no monster. Monsters know. Monsters feel. They know exactly what the fuck they're doing; they know the things they do are wrong but savor it anyway. Every. Delicious. Moment.

Until you've watched a monster eat a man, head and all, tear out its entrails, and dance beneath the moon with a delighted blood-smeared smile, you don't know. You can't know. They love it. They love the shit out of it. That's a monster. And that shit gets me harder than anything. A monster, a good and proper monster, will sate my hunger for a decade or two. I'll gut 'em like they would a human and gobble up every sinful morsel; I'll crack their bones and drink the marrow. Once I ate one so foul that I didn't get hungry for another thirty-four years. But that time I got lucky. A beast like that is craftier and more cunning than anything you've ever known. To get one like that you've got to catch 'em at their weakest. At their hungriest. When their insides pound as hard as mine do now.

But I ain't seen a monster like that for a very long time. Not since Midian. Not since the walls came down and we scattered to the winds. Midian was good to me. I could watch and wait and learn the routines of the worst of us. Then, when the hunger or boredom got to be too much for them, I'd follow them out, wait for them to break the law. And then I would break it myself. Only had to do that a few times. The rest of the time I could live in peace. Quiet. The demons screaming in my head sated for years. I could read, have real conversations in which I didn't have to pretend so much, maybe even watch a little TV. I never had to drink, to feast, to find myself throwing up in some back alley, needle in my arm, unshaven junkie on my cock working for his fix. Not unless I wanted to. Those were good days. But they're gone now.

So I have to fill the new ones. I have to feed. I have to gorge on whatever weak-ass human sin I can find, which means most of the time I have to make my own. It's awful. A single night of human debauchery is like a thimbleful of water after three days in the desert. It'll stop the pounding all right; it'll stop the itch. But it'll only buy me a few hours of peace, a few hours of quiet, a few hours without the walls of my sanity tumbling down. Just enough to sleep. But most days it's the itch that wakes me up.

So my life is a constant party. A night train of debauchery with no stops until dawn. Booze. Sex. Drugs. Gambling. Theft. Violence. Whatever your kick—your real kick—I aim to supply it. To be that silent dream drifting into the bar to grab you by the short and curlies and tug you into a smoky backroom corner to finish you off in the dirtiest, filthiest, most perverse way you can imagine. But don't get too excited. I ain't your fucking fantasy. No. That would be too easy. I don't get off being everything you wish I was.

Who the fuck am I?

I am the night you never speak of. The porn you jerk off to but could never tell anyone about. The tryst when your wife is out of town. The drunken night after five years sober that leaves you lying in a pile of your AA anniversary chips. I am the memory that makes you cringe in the shower, the lie that ruins your marriage, the truth that makes you put a gun in your mouth after midnight when no one is awake to take your calls. I am the dark deed that hollows you out and leaves you like a husk to be filled with booze or sex or love or excess or consumerism or religion or fitness or parenthood—whatever your vice may be. That's who the fuck I am.

And tonight, my head is pounding again. The sun is setting and I'm running out of smokes. It's time to hit the town. It's time to eat. It's time to ruin someone's life.

I'm staying in a shithole motel in a know-nothing town that is the pimple on the ass end of Texas. I've just finished a long run in Vegas—which I can only handle for so long. There's no night in Vegas, not inside the city limits. Not where the hunting and feeding happens. It's all lights and noise and six-dollar steaks, all day, every day, in a way that it eventually makes the sunlight feel wrong. It flips the whole world on its head. I lived underground beneath the dirt and graves for ages, and even I can't handle Vegas for longer than a month or so.

I hitched my way as lot lizard, blowing truckers in their cabs, feeding off the really dark shit they daydream about on the long hauls. It's not that I'm poor. Cars can be tracked. There are always people looking. Monsters looking. And I don't like anyone to see me coming. Or going. It's why I'm still here after all this time. Remember what I said about clever monsters? I was being humble.

So here I am in some shitsmear Panhandle town with my head on its way to making me cry out loud and I'm dying for a smoke.

I'm thinking there might be a bar nearby. I've been to this town before. That's why I hate it so much. I always forget its name. It's something stupid like Oatmeal or Friday or Happy or Paris—you know, one of those cute coopted bullshit names Texas loves. But I think there's a bar, and I think it should be open, so I hoof it across the dusty, yellow-grassed plains to cut an hour or so off of my walk.

And I'm right. There's a bar. And it's open. More or less.

It's one of those concrete box buildings that just looks wrong all by its lonesome. Sharp angles, whitewashed cinder-block walls, a sign hand-painted by someone with aspirations of leaving this town but lacking the talent to actually do so, a big black metal door and no windows to spoil the neon drenched insides. It's got one of those stupid lighted arrow signs out front with slotted letters falling off that no one gives enough of a shit about to straighten after a storm. Why bother, I wonder. It's not like you could miss this pathetic structure along the road with nothing but telephone poles and a gravel parking lot to keep it company. But there it is, inviting you in for CHEAP BEER and FRIDAY NIGHT POOL TOURNAMENTS.

It's Tuesday. But thankfully there are a half dozen cars and trucks in the lot. Probably the only alcohol for fifty miles.

The inside smells like stale smoke and dirty mop water. It's exactly as I remember it. Cement floor covered by a stained tattered rug—the thin, rough kind you find in cheap strip center offices. It's lit almost entirely by neon advertising, some corners brightened by beers that haven't been available for decades. It's not so much a bar as a coffin where a lonely few escape their somehow even worse lives.

I smell the guy right away. I can taste his longing on the tip of my tongue, the want lingering at the bottom of his heart, buried under ten years of single-position Saturday night sex. He wants a turn. He's waiting for it. The rest of the bar is slim pickings. You'd think that everyone could be broken by something, could be lured away with just the right offer, but I'm telling you now, that ain't the case. Some people want for things they'll never allow themselves to have.

But this guy, this guy has it bad. He's a stained T-shirt barely squeezed over a spare tire; salt and pepper stubble sprawling across two different chins. He's daydreaming over his beer, thoughts lingering over freshly dusted memories some fifteen years old. This guy's special. Sure he'd love a roll in the hay—a good, righteous fuck or even a quick handy out back. But that wouldn't even register. That'd be the pitiful highlight of his fucking year and he might go so far as tell his wife about it just to piss her right the hell off.

No, this guy is looking for something else, a different brand of vodka altogether.

I sit two stools down and don't make eye contact. That's the key. People get suspicious when they get everything they want without having to work for it. So I make him work for it. He nurses his bottle of beer for a while, checking me out in the mirror hanging on the wall behind the bar, mindlessly picking at the label.

I wonder for a second what I look like to him. I never get to know. I get an inkling, a few of the details—young, old, black, white, male, female—that kind of stuff. And I only know that because I know what they want. But I never see myself, not as they see me. I know he thinks I'm a man, I know I'm in my twenties. But I know shit else. Hair color, eye color, beard or clean shaven. None of it. I look across the counter at the mirror and see nothing but the monster, a withered old husk, partied out like a drooping, wrinkled party balloon. It's a good thing no one ever sees my eyes, my real eyes, bloodshot and yellow with a thousand-yard stare that'd just downright chill you to the bone.

"Can I get a pack of smokes?" I ask the frumpy, dumpy white-trash owner of this fine establishment. She nods and tosses me a pack from behind the counter. "My brand," I say with a smile. At this point, they're all my brand. I light up, the smoke only the faintest relief against the din in my skull. But I draw in a drag like it's fine wine, smiling and letting it roll over me. Headache or no, the show must go on, or else the headache will just get worse. And it will get worse. So I'm all about the show now.

In the mirror I see a flash of razor teeth.

I hate seeing myself in the mirror.

"You still play?" he asks, drifting back in from out of his daydream.

"What?" I ask.

"You still play?"

"Ball?"

"Yeah, ball."

"How'd you know?" I ask, already knowing the answer.

"The way you carry yourself. A guy who plays ball, if he's the real deal, if he gives himself to it, it gives him a walk."

"My posture gave me away?"

"Yeah. I'm guessing . . . running back?"

"Tight end. You?"

"Quarterback. Up through college." He lifts the sleeve from his biceps, revealing the number 27 in big block letters and local high-school colors. "Till I blew out my knee."

"Who'd you play for?" I ask, the lilt of my voice showing genuine interest.

Bam. He's on the hook and moving two stools down to sit beside me. He wants it bad. I can taste his thoughts, the stench of his desire reeking like a bloated corpse. Middle age is making him weary, sad, putting the creak in his bones and a layer of fat on his belly. He wants to be young again, but even I can't do that. So he talks about it. And he talks about it. And beer after beer he keeps talking about it, reliving every glorious moment.

His name is Bill.

It's an hour in and he's recapping the final quarter of the big state championship. I know when he's lying, but I don't mention it. The embellishments are the only thing making the story listenable. Otherwise it's the standard claptrap that I try to choke down with as much alcohol as I can stomach, half a pack of smokes, and the hope that this headache will soon be gone. Every once in a while I break in to tell my own lies, stories I've lifted from a hundred other guys just like him, details that sound right because they actually happened to someone else.

But none of this is going to chase away the hunger. It's all just foreplay. I gotta get this guy out of the bar so we can get down to business.

"Man," I say before killing the last few swigs of a beer. "I wish I weren't so far from home. I could really go for a round of shooting right now."

"Shooting?" he asks.

"Yeah. Me and the boys like to go out after a game, get completely wrecked then line up our bottles and shoot shit until we pass out. All this talk about playing has me wanting to shoot."

"I got a couple shotguns in the truck. Maybe fifty, sixty rounds."

"Bullshit," I say, pretending that I haven't been smelling the gunpowder on him for the last hour.

"Ain't no lie. You wanna shoot?"

"Yeah I wanna shoot." I look up at the bartender. "How much for the rest of that bottle of whiskey?"

Bartender shakes her head. "I can't let you walk out with anything open. Not so much as a beer."

"Then how much for an unopened bottle?"

"Ain't got a license to sell you that, neither."

Bill waves a fat finger at me. "Let's do a few shots now and it'll hit us just in time to shoot. Trust me. I do this all the time."

He was right. He does. The whiskey hits us just as we've lined up trash on a fence out in some disused field miles away. He's a good shot. I pretend not to be half bad. Truth is that I've spent an untold number of drunken nights getting hillbillies and rednecks to shoot at things that shouldn't be shot at. It's not all about college girls, struggling ex-addicts, and cheating husbands. I gotta dig deep to keep on keepin' on. Some nights it's getting spanked by a priest, others it's getting someone to cheat at cards, and yeah, others still are spent shooting cans out in the sticks, talking a drunk idiot into going down on his drunker sister or . . . putting some buckshot in his asshole neighbor.

So yeah, I've done this once or twice.

We shoot until we've almost run through his ammo. I get pretty close most of the time, but as the shells start running thin, I start nailing my shots one after another after another.

"Damn, son," he says. "You're getting' the hang of it."

"I'm getting sober is what I'm getting."

"Young man like you can hold his liquor. I'm drunk as hell."

"Well I ain't anymore. Let's go get some more to drink."

He looks at his watch. "Bar's closed. Missed it by ten minutes."

I make a pained face and look up at the wide dark sea of stars above. We really are out in the middle of nowhere. "There's a house along the road about a mile back. What do you say we raid their liquor cabinet?" I shoot him a playful smile, but cock my brows just so to tell him I'm serious.

"That's breaking and entering."

"Yeah."

"No way," he says.

"What? Do you know 'em?"

"No."

"Well, ain't you never raised hell, before? I thought you were cool."

That hits him like a fist to the gut. He tries to hide it but his eyes give him away. He thought he was cool, too. For a while there he was feeling like a kid again, just one of the guys.

"We ain't gonna hurt nothin'," I say. "Just peek in their liquor cabinet and take some for the road. You never done that?"

He has. But not in a long time.

I can feel it in my bones, smell it on his breath. He hesitates, temptation gnawing a hole so big in his gut you could drive a truck through it.

He smiles. "Fuck it. Let's do it."

Release. It's like that moment you stand up after drinking when it all hits you at once coupled with the tingling opening salvo of a full-force orgasm. The headache vanishes in an orgiastic rush, with even the itch banished to the back of my skull for another hour or so. If he goes through with this, I'll be good till sundown tomorrow. If not, I've got a few hours' reprieve to figure out my next move and find my next victim.

But this guy's gonna go through with it. I can tell. I can always tell.

But that ain't the worst of it, not for him.

This poor son of a bitch has no idea what he's walking into. You see, there are a couple of things I haven't told you yet. Firstly, I know exactly where we're going and I know who lives in that house. I smell 'em every time I end up here. Secondly, I didn't end up in this town by accident. Not this time. And lastly, we're not going there for booze. We're going there for peace.

Who lives in that house?

UHF and the FM Girl.

That's what we called them anyway, in Midian, behind their back. Their names are Humphrey B and Sylvia, but the first time you see them you can't think of them as anything but UHF and the FM Girl. UHF is a tall guy, six feet at the shoulder, with an old nineteen-inch black-and-white CRT television for a head. There's all this sinewy muscle wrapped around cables running up from his chest and neck into the TV, but the back of the set is blown out, like it was hollowed from the inside by a shotgun blast—jagged plastic surrounding a seven-inch hole. Inside there's nothing, nothing at all. But the TV screen is always lit, a disembodied head in fuzzy black and white, ever floating, reacting, just as you'd expect his head to react.

The FM Girl is different. She's lithe, willowy, easily five foot nothing, her skin wrinkled and desiccated, like she was mummified, her eyes and mouth sewn shut with ratty black thread. While she can't speak, she's always broadcasting her thoughts, and if you've got a radio nearby tuned to the right station—89.7! The screaming sounds of hell!—you can hear her just fine. So she carries around an old beat-up hand-cranked emergency radio that she'll wind to life if she ever has anything to say.

They're a fine couple, as married as us monsters can be. FM Girl needs flesh to feed; UHF just needs to watch. He can go a little longer than she can, but neither can go more than a year or two without a good, honest-to-God murder. I've been keeping track of them for a spell. They've been picking off truckers over the years, catching them overnight, murdering them in their cabs before driving their trucks off into oblivion. But it's been a while. And they must be getting hungry.

So I'm bringing takeout.

The windows of the house are blacked out for obvious reasons, but Bill doesn't notice. It's a run-down, single-story ranch-style affair with peeling blue paint and the rusted-out frame of a midseventies Oldsmobile oxidizing into nothingness out front. It is, as far as Panhandle homes go, entirely ordinary.

We slip in through the back door into a hallway that splits off to the living room and the kitchen. I point to Bill and then the kitchen, then myself and the living room. He enters the kitchen completely unaware that there's an open door to the cellar in there and that under this house there be monsters.

They hear him come in. He's about as silent as a raccoon in a trash can.

A pale blue light creeps up the stairs, but Bill's too busy picking through the cabinets to see it.

Behind him, not six feet away, is the FM Girl, her husband standing silently, ominously, behind her. Watching. The kitchen fills with the blue light of his flickering set and Bill turns slowly around.

His eyes go wide with fear. He's paralyzed, unable to process what he's seeing.

The FM Girl reaches up to her sewn-shut mouth and yanks at the thread, pulling it out in one slow, deliberate motion. Then her cheek splits, splaying her ear to ear, rows of needle-teeth glistening in slobber as her massive jaw unhinges. Her mouth is so wide it looks as if it could swallow Bill's head whole.

Behind her, UHF's head vanishes from inside the set, his display showing his view of his wife and her soon-to-be meal.

The FM Girl reaches down and cranks her radio, winding it up furiously. It crackles to life, thick static shrieking murderous thoughts along with the phrase "Wrong house, motherfucker."

My machete cuts her in half from behind before UHF can speak up to warn her, his flickering screen showing every horrible second of his wife's demise. Her body topples to the floor with two wet slaps.

I dive in like a rabid beast, razor claws rending her flesh into fistfuls of meat that I greedily shove into my mouth. Blood coats me in seconds, the floor growing slick with it.

I look up at UHF and smile. He's feeding. He's feeding watching his own wife devoured handful by delicious handful. He feels awful about it, can't decide whether to run for safety or stay a few seconds longer to taste the end of the love of his life. The thrill of his sin is the cream gravy on the chicken fried steak of my meal.

"You should go, Humphrey," I say through a mouthful of his wife.

His head reappears on the screen and his voice crackles through his tinny mono speaker. "Are you going to kill me next?"

"Do I have to?"

He shakes his head back and forth, the television remaining perfectly still. "No."

"Then go. Run. Before I change my mind."

He thinks for a second, knowing he should probably fight, should stay and defend the last remains of his beloved Sylvia. But he doesn't. He runs.

And I turn back to my meal, savoring every last bit of murderous sin that remains of the FM Girl.

Bill is slumped on the floor, staring at me slack-jawed, eyes as wide, unblinking.

So I turn to him. "You're not going to say a word about this, are you Bill?"

He shakes his head, terrified, a few seconds shy of pissing himself right there on the floor.

"Good. Now get the fuck out of here."

He stands up and scampers out the door without looking back. Frankly, I don't give a shit if he tells anyone. Who's going to believe him? He walked out of a bar drunk with a stranger and the next time anyone sees it, this house is going to be on fire. Telling stories about monsters in the basement will get him branded either a crackpot or an arsonist.

He'll choose neither. He's going to spend the rest of his life trying to forget what he saw tonight and maybe, just maybe, he'll stop trying to live in the past.

I don't have anything against humans, really. I don't ever make anyone do anything they don't want to do in the first place. Not really. I just give them a nudge. The interesting thing about doing this is seeing what comes after. My gift to them is they get to find out who they really are, deep down. And what they do with that knowledge defines them from that point on. Some folks can't handle the memories of their night with me, but others come out all right on the other side. They make peace with themselves. They become better people. But it's their choice. Everything is their choice.

So in case you were wondering, that's how I sleep at night.

And I'm going to be sleeping a lot better now knowing I won't have to be that guy for quite some time, that I won't wake up with an itch in my head that turns into a rumble that turns into a scream. All my drinking I can do for myself now, all my sins will be my own. At least for a while.

But now that my head's clear and I've got the taste of monster on my tongue, I'm wondering. Just how much more time can I buy myself if I run ole Humphrey down as well? I think I might do just that. He smells delicious.

THE DEVIL UNTIL
THE CREDITS ROLL

Weston Ochse

(Written while deployed to Afghanistan)

The silence was extraordinary as I stared into the darkness, waiting, knowing it would come for us. Like a nightmare scrambling across the desert floor, it would seethe into our midst. One or more of us would die tonight. I knew this better than the others. This was the second time I'd come to the monster. After the first time, I'd promised myself I'd never do it again and not just because the monster said the next time I'd die. There was something about the unworldly creature that brought out the primordial within me, cellular memories that evoked things in the darkness that needed to stay outside the fire, creatures whose existence preceded the idea of evil but nonetheless influenced humanity's idea of it.

"And you're sure it's up there?" Watson's dark shape next to me whispered. The sound of his boots scooting on the grit sliced at the Afghanistan night.

I tried to control my breathing. Each sound was like a rifle shot to my nerves. The monster would come when it wanted, but Watson couldn't wait. We were all Special Forces, but Watson had also been a Ranger, deploying six times in support of the advanced infantry force, and he was incapable of acknowledging that there was something he couldn't defeat with technique, courage, and steel. So he kept scanning the cave entrance with his night-vision, even though he'd been told the monster wouldn't show up in them.

To be honest, none of them really believed in the existence of monsters. I could tell they were reconciled that the entire mission was a lark and we'd be drinking scotch back on FOB Salerno in six hours. But I knew better and I felt more than a little guilt in bringing these five men to this otherwise nondescript cave in the Tora Bora Mountains.

The butt of Wisnewski's HK416 scraped the ground ever so slightly as he shifted, causing me to spin to the sound.

"This is bullshit," the big Polack grumbled.

"Keep your game face on," I ordered, my voice barely audible. I understood their doubt. I'd had it on my first mission to the cave three years ago. We'd been attacked and forced into the mountains, where a man pulling mules carrying scrap metal told us a terrified story of a creature living in the mountains who killed Taliban. What the old Khyber Pass peddler couldn't have known was the creature killed everyone. The Taliban were just its most recent victims.

I willed the silence to descend once again. The only way I'd hear it coming would be if everyone would shut the fuck up.

But Wisnewski wanted to be heard and simpered, "I still say this is bullshit."

Segrest shifted slightly on the other side of him.

Beside him sat Perez and then Dobler, the Agency man we'd picked up from the slick ten klicks north. The newcomer had made a career studying the Nightbreed. The incident in Midian hadn't gone unnoticed and eventually an analyst buried in the labyrinth of cubicles in America's secret palace latched on to it. Since then, Dobler had been peeling back the onion, trying to determine everything he could about the mysterious group. So this opportunity wasn't something he could pass up, especially when my after-action report hit his desk last year.

FORWARD OPERATING BASE SALERNO—SOJTF DETACHMENT
SPECIAL OPERATIONS JOINT TASK FORCE—AFGHANISTAN:
AFTER ACTION REPORT FOR MISSION 32-0073-12

EXSUM: ODA 32 ENCOUNTERED RESISTANCE ALONG ROUTE
YELLOW OF COMPANY-SIZED ELEMENT OF INS. DISENGAGED

PRIOR TO CONTACTING OVERWHELMING FORCE. UNABLE TO
MAKE ALTERNATE ROUTES. E&E TOOK ODA 32 ALONG TORA
BORA BACKBONE WHERE ADDITIONAL HOSTILITIES OCCURRED,
INVOLVING NON-COMBATANT CREATURE OF UNKNOWN
ORIGIN. MEDIVAC REMOVED THREE AC KIA, ONE KIA AND ONE
AC WIA. MSG JOHN HERSHEY GILLAM, ODA 32, SOJTF-A, SOLE
SURVIVOR.

AAR 32-0073-12 IS CLASSIFIED XX XX X XXX.
NON-COMBATANT CREATURE OF UNKNOWN ORIGIN.

After both the debriefer and I had signed nondisclosure agreements, three
Army colonels and a Navy SEAL lieutenant commander at Camp Integ-
rity had argued for hours about the after-action report, finally settling on
that term. They'd tried MONSTER, BOOGYMAN, FIEND, DEVIL,
even dallying with UNIDENTIFIED CREATURE. They'd finally settled
on NCCOUO, afraid that any other reference might bring undue attention to what otherwise had been a disastrous mission.

"Disastrous."

That was a word to describe it, I supposed.

In the end, I'd been forced to fight for my life, my thumbs pressing
through the pupils of my best friend's eyes as the Non-Combatant Creature
of Unknown Origin laughed and giggled and danced, using the entrails
of my other two soldiers as party favors for his own celebration. Ben had
almost strangled me before I was finally able to kill him. I'd pressed so
hard I'd bruised the soft parts of my hand between thumb and forefinger,
beating it against Ben's ocular bone as my digits sought to clear a deep
enough path so I could skull-fuck him. There were times when I could
hear the sound of my penis moving in and out of his head with sickening
clarity.

That hadn't made it into the report. But I had tried to explain things.
I'd tried to tell them what had really happened, but the psychologists got
involved and began making excuses for me that I never could have made
on my own. So I let them. I got some R&R and blew off some steam. Then
I came back, ready to become who I once was until Dobler contacted me
and had to remind me of who I'd been.

I stilled my mind. I closed my eyes and heightened my hearing. I felt it.

Any moment now.

My eyes shot open as a feeling descended upon me. A fear, born when the earth was young, enveloped me in a hollow grasp. I breathed but my breath went nowhere, sucked into the void growing inside of me.

Perez began to weep.

I wanted to do the same, but choked back my emotion.

"You come again," said a voice as close to my ear as the French hooker had been in Morocco when I was on R&R.

I dared not look. I didn't have to. A misshapen face materialized next to me, lingering like the smoke from a cigar before it dissolved.

Watson began to giggle. The slap of flesh on flesh came faster and faster as he unmistakably masturbated in the dark, his grunts of pleasure coming with metronomic frequency.

"We have a mission." My throaty rasp was calmer than I believed it could be.

"Children playing at war. Finger guns. Bang. Bang," the monster said, words surging in disjointed whispers.

Segrest whimpered. "Wha-at is ggg-going on, momma?"

I'd told them not to show fear. I'd explained how the monster fed on it. They hadn't listened.

Segrest screamed.

I rolled over and placed a hand over his mouth. I watched the starlight reflect in his feverish and darting eyes. "STFU, soldier." I glared at him, trying to explain with a look that Segrest needed to shut up to save himself, but he was staring at something not there.

The monster sighed. "You bring children to me."

My eyes watered as emotions seeped past, memories of my youngest sister dead in a post-prom car accident, my old friend Baker gut-shot and dying in my arms, the crying of my own sons on the telephone after my wife had stolen them away to some Montana farm, and Ben screaming at me to stop.

"We are all children to you, Rook," I managed to say, biting back the memories the monster sucked free.

Umbra, penumbra, and antumbra, the three distinct parts of shadow, coalesced into a dark figure sitting next to me. A single horn rose from its head like a rhinoceros's. I knew better than to look directly at the monster, instead keeping it in my peripheral vision.

"One of you will die tonight," it said.

"Then take me, but first let me tell you why I came."

I felt it regarding me. I was almost positive it couldn't read my mind, but I hid the truth behind memories, knowing it would relish these first.

"Tell me what it is that makes you want to die."

I paused, knowing that everything hinged on my next words. Then I said it, the culmination of too many ideas and my own desire to finally discover the truth. "We've found another of you and we want you to kill it."

The words had the desired effect.

Within minutes the monster had gathered us in his cave. Lined up as though we were the guests of honor at an execution, we were pitiful representations of humanity. I was the least affected. Still, I trembled a little, knowing that things could get much worse, and absolutely understanding that no one would be able to stop the runaway train called Rook if we let him get going.

Watson still pulled at himself, his face cut into a permanent leer.

Wisnewski's eyes fluttered, caught in the memories of a deed he hadn't told anyone about, telling us the tale over and over in a dead man's monotone. "And I took her face in my hand and held it before I shoved it into the dirt and then I ripped free her clothes and then I . . ."

Segrest shook, urine blackening his pants, the stench the only recognizable aroma in the monster's lair besides dead and rotting flesh.

Perez gripped his crucifix in his right hand so tightly his skin bled. He recited "Our Father"s and "Hail Mary"s in barely audible whispers, interspersing them with profanity and explicit descriptions of what he wanted to do with the holy mother, each utterance making him speak faster, trying to rid himself of the monster's terrible influence.

Dobler's reaction was the opposite of everyone else's. His face was fat with anger, red cheeks, creased forehead, and rippling sneer. Hatred bled from his eyes as his hands clenched over and over, invisibly strangling infants, the weak, and the infirm.

What I could see of the oval-shaped cave was lit by a small lantern that sat on a slat of wood balanced across several smaller rocks. From the ceiling hung several hundred heads, each one another version of the previous one—black hair, Caucasian features, head scarf, and an oval gash of terror for a mouth. Several Afghan rugs lay on the floor, creating a livable space. Their rich reds and blues made the room less a cave and more a parlor. A stack of pillows rested against one wall, and it was upon these Rook now reclined. The only piece of clothing he wore was a kilt, tartaned in red and blues. His body was long and well muscled. If a man hadn't seen his head, they might mistake him for tall lean human. But the horn atop his overly large and misshapen skull relegated him past the category of circus freak, firmly into the encyclopedia of monsters. Then there was the color of his skin. A dead color. The unmistakable gray of a cadaver.

Dobler was the expert. He'd studied the Nightbreed and had shared his doctoral dissertation on the subject of Midian, the last place they'd gathered in any strength. The CIA agent believed them to be Fomorian, the race that preceded humans in Ireland. I'd been forced to read passages of the scholarly supposition, and remembered a translation from an ancient Irish tome called *The Book of the Dun Cow*: "with the body of a man and the head of a goat, they were terrible in their beauty." Whatever Dobler thought they were, he'd have a chance to find out for real this night.

Rook wore spectacles and thumbed a well-worn book, its cover a glossy leather the color of old blood. He occasionally stared at the soldiers, who stood in a perfect line, seemingly incapable of shooting him, even though their weapons were loaded and at hand.

He let his finger follow a line in the book, then put it back down. "They called Byron 'sublime.' I like that word. Do you like it, Gillam?"

"I don't know that word," I said.

"The Greek poet Longinus compared it to establishing ecstasy. I know you understand *that* word. I do think that stuffy old Edmund Burke said it the best, however. 'Sublime is whatever is fitted in any sort to excite the ideas of pain and danger. . . . Whatever is in any sort terrible, or is conversant about terrible objects, or operates in a manner analogous to terror.' Am I not sublime? Am I not operating in a manner analogous to terror?"

I'd forgotten how much Rook loved to talk. "You are indeed sublime," I said, agreeing like anyone would to a preposterous question posed by a monster.

He smiled happily to himself, then put down the book. "So tell me of this other monster."

"He calls himself Jupiter."

Rook nodded. "I remember an old fat piece of sewage called Jupiter. I cut him up and left him to die in Midian."

"He's been sewn back together."

The idea of it startled Rook. "He has? Sewn back together, you say?"

I nodded, then leaned over and backhanded Watson across the face. When he didn't stop jacking off, I did it twice more. Watson let go of himself and brought his hands to his cheeks.

"Leave it the fuck alone," I said, then added, "I think you broke it anyway."

My activity caused the others to begin returning to themselves. The deleterious effect of our fear was still there, but it no longer seemed to hold them so terribly—not exactly a switch being turned off, but a rheostat being turned down.

"I warned you not to return," Rook said.

"I never wanted to." I shrugged and broke from the line. I carried an AK and laid it on the floor next to where I squatted. "But this other monster, this Jupiter, he's fighting us, supporting the Taliban."

"You know the same thing's going to happen again." It was a statement rather than a question.

I sighed at the memory of what had happened before. "We're prepared," I said. What I didn't tell him was that I *was prepared*, because as much as I wanted to think I was, I wasn't. Shit was starting to come back to me I'd thought long buried. My façade of being the good guy was tarnishing by the second.

Rook didn't seem to notice my indecision. Instead, he took one look at the group and let his head roll back as he laughed. "You're like a bunch of kids waiting for the principal to eat them. You're not ready. You're not even close." Suddenly Rook was no longer reclining and was instead standing eyeball-to-eyeball with Dobler. "And what is it with this one? He wants to kill me so badly I can taste it." He licked the side of Dobler's face with a tongue that looked like it was made from twelve inches of green and red velvet. "Delicious."

"He's a born-again Christian. He thinks your kind are all devils."

"He's probably right," Rook said, putting his arm around Dobler's head and petting it. "I'm the devil until the credits roll, then everyone scrambles to see who I really am."

"Doesn't make sense," Dobler said.

"Doesn't it? Think about it, my little Jesus freak."

"Which one of us is it going to be?" I asked.

Rook gave me the same look as a man appraising a new hooker. "We'll see how you all function, then I'll decide. So how does this work?"

"What do you mean?" Dobler asked.

Rook ignored the CIA man's question and asked one in return. "What's your plan? How am I going to kill old Jupiter?"

"What do you mean?" Dobler asked again.

Rook made a disappointed face and wagged his finger. "That's not good. I counted two 'what do you mean's and one 'that doesn't make any sense.' You're going to have to pay a penalty for that."

Dobler's eyes went wild. "What? What penalty?"

"A penalty. If you're not going to open your mind and pay attention there are sublime penalties that have to be paid." Rook glanced at me and grinned. "And God, but don't I love the sublime." Then he opened his mouth and clamped down on Dobler's left arm. Rook shook his head and twisted, coming away with a huge chunk of the CIA man's triceps, spraying blood across the cave.

Dobler screamed and screamed and fell to his knees. He stared at the blood gushing from his arm, unable to do anything.

Segrest rushed over to him. Kicking Dobler in the chin to get him down, Segrest pushed a knee on the left shoulder joint to slow the blood, then ripped Dobler's shirt free. It took a few moments, then he had a pressure bandage fashioned and the arm in a sling.

No one said a thing.

I'd seen it before. I'm not sure if it was a game or a test, but the monster had his way of doing things.

Perez had scooted beside me. He held his HK416 in a white-knuckled grip, the working end pointing ever so slightly toward Rook, while his crucifix dangled from his hand.

Wisnewski and Watson stood together, whispering to each other on the other side of the entrance. I hoped they weren't going to try anything. The plan was still in place. In fact, if Dobler could somehow keep from being eaten, we might just get somewhere.

Segrest splashed water on Dobler's face, waking him up. Then he worked his way back to me. By the time he was standing next to me, he was holding a 9mm pistol down in front of him, his left hand covering it.

Dobler seemed to collect himself, then glared at Rook. I have to give the CIA guy credit. He wasn't a shrinking violet.

"Where were we?" Rook asked, picking his teeth with what looked like a piece of bone he'd plucked from the floor.

"I was about to tell you the plan." Aided by his clenched teeth, Dobler kept his voice even.

"By all means. Tell me. How are you going to have me kill Jupiter?"

Dobler blinked for a moment. For a second I was worried he wasn't going to be able to deliver. Then he said, "Sunlight."

Rook smiled. With the blood staining the outside of his mouth, it was a terrible thing. "But that would kill me too. What do you think I'm going to do? Lead him outside for a chat? Me and Jupiter holding hands and walking through flower-strewn fields?" He glanced at me, then stopped as if he could read my mind. "But you knew this part, didn't you. It's how you escaped the first time. It's why I didn't go after you."

Hodges's and Mixon's bodies had already been near the entrance, their necks twisted, hearts eaten out of their chests, stomachs empty bowls of flesh. O'Bryant had been next. At sunrise, I'd knocked Rook free of where he was chewing on O'Bryant and had dragged my last soldier outside.

"How'd you explain to them that you weren't injured?" Rook asked. Everyone turned to me, making Rook realize. "Oh, you *were* injured. Of course you would be. You'd have to be, now wouldn't you? How were you injured, Gillam?"

SOJTF INVESTIGATION EXRACT FOR MISSION: 32-0073-12

EXTRACT: MSG GILLAM'S CONTUSIONS AND LIGAMENT TEARS
ARE CONSISTENT WITH SEL-DEFENSE AND EVIDENCE OF
EXTREME COMBAT. A 9MM BULLET MATCHING THE MANUFAC-
TURER OF ROUNDS ISSUED TO HIS TEAM WAS REMOVED FROM
HIS LEFT ARM. BALLISTIC STRIATIONS DO NOT MATCH ANY OF
THE RECOVERED WEAPONS, HOWEVER MANY OF THESE SAME
ROUNDS HAVE BEEN REPORTEDLY USED BY ENEMY FIGHTERS,
PURPORTEDLY STOLEN DURING SHIPMENT FROM PAKISTAN
TO AFGHANISTAN. RECOMMEND CLOSE CASE ON ISSUE AND
RESCIND DUSTWUN ON SFC BENJAMIN HAYNES. HIS BODY HAS
BEEN DEEMED UNRECOVERABLE BASED ON MSG GILLAM'S
REPORTS.

AAR 32-0073-12 IS CLASSIFIED XX XX X XXX.

"I was shot."

If Rook had been drinking he would have snorted. "And who shot you?"

"You shot me," I said flatly. It had been too hard to explain otherwise. It was no hard thing to push the barrel into my own arm and pull the trigger. God knew I'd tried to shoot myself enough times.

Rook raised his eyebrows. "Since when do Nightbreed need guns?"

Dobler glared at me. He was good at glaring. "I've always had a problem with that part of your story," he said, clearly trying to master a voice that was right on the edge of losing it.

"Shut up, Dobler, and get on with it," I said. Instead of standing, I shifted to a knee and folded my hands across it.

Perez whispered to me, his eyes wild as he took in the monster. "I can shoot him, boss. It would be too easy."

I shrugged. Why not? It wasn't like he'd do any damage. "Sure. Go ahead," I said.

Perez giggled as he opened up, firing three-round bursts into Rook, filling the cave with violently assaultive percussive noise that caused all of us to cover our ears. I closed my eyes as rock chips and pieces of pillow flew through the air. When his magazine ran out, Perez scrambled to load another one.

I opened my eyes and removed my hands from my ears. I worked my jaw to clear my head of the sound.

Rook laughed as he danced in the falling goose down.

"Seriously?" Dobler said, getting to his feet and staggering over toward Perez. "Why even try and shoot him, Perez—is that your name? We have this under control."

I looked at Dobler and knew otherwise. The monster had all of the control. The fact that Dobler thought he had the power to do anything just proved he had no idea what was going on. Maybe if we'd been outside we'd have stood a chance. Maybe. But here? In his cave . . . his lair? I didn't think so.

Dobler must have sensed my thoughts, because he rounded on me. "What? Now you have a comment?"

"Easy, Dobler," I said. "You've lost a lot of blood and aren't used to this sort of thing."

"Used to it?" he asked as his voice rose to breaking. "Like you're used to it? Does Special Forces have a new monster training ground I'm not aware of?"

I put my hand out. "Easy, man. This isn't done yet. We can still do what we came here to do. Stay on mission."

Dobler's eyes cleared for a moment. He licked his lips as his gaze darted momentarily to his arm. His movement had gotten it bleeding again, but he made no move to attend to it. Instead, he nodded. "Okay. All right." He turned back toward Rook. "You wanted to know how we're going to help you kill Jupiter. I said sunlight. That's true. But we have a suit for you. One which will protect you."

Rook rapped on his horn with the knuckles of his right hand. "Will it fit this?"

Dobler nodded. "Not sure if we have the dimensions right. We had to base it on Gillam's memory. But I'm pretty sure it will."

I was only half paying attention. I gestured for Perez to get behind me. Although the rounds hadn't hurt the monster, he didn't seem pleased at the destruction of his pillows.

"Watson and Wisnewski, check outside to make sure we're not going to have any unplanned guests." I glanced at them, and flicked toward the exit with my gaze. If we could get them out, it would be a start.

But Rook seemed ready. Just as the pair were beginning to move, he stepped into their path.

They raised their weapons, then looked at me.

"Come on, Rook. Let them do their job," I said.

He nodded, but didn't move out of their way.

Wisnewski raised his weapon and tried to slam the butt into Rook's face. The monster caught it, which seemed to be what Wisnewski wanted. While Rook's hands were engaged, the big Polack pulled free his blade from his thigh sheath and sawed it across Rook's unprotected stomach. Skin immediately peeled free, revealing a gash so deep I could have slid my hands inside.

But there was no blood.

Wisnewski hesitated, unsure what to do next . . . which was his undoing.

Rook became smoke and swirled around his attacker. Wisnewski spun too, trying to keep the bare hint of Rook's figure in front of him, but he couldn't move fast enough. Suddenly, he stopped, his body rigid. When Rook re-formed behind his target, he was once again whole and his fingers were inside the flesh of Wisnewski's back, wrapped around his spine.

Wisnewski tried to move, but Rook clamped down with his fist. The big Polack's eyes popped and his face showed the strain he was taking from the pain. He tried to scream, but all that came out was a whine.

Rook bit down on the back of the soldier's head and peeled back a piece of hair-covered skin. Wisnewski's eyes rolled back in his head and he began to scream, but Rook shoved him to the floor and pressed his face into the floor with a foot on the back of his head. The monster held him there as he pulled the flap of skin from his teeth and regarded it. "I'm not your cliché," he said, his voice wrought with sadness. He took a bite of the skin and chewed thoughtfully. "I'm not a creature from your stories. The idea that I exist, and therefore I am evil is a construct. If I live in a cave or under a bridge or in a mountaintop castle, it's because I don't want to be a part of your *humanity*. It's not because you're afraid of me. It's because I'm afraid of you."

"But that's ridiculous." Dobler was pale as he watched Rook chew.

"Is it? Did I come chasing after you or was it you who came after me? And for what? To weaponize me?"

Dobler gulped. "Maybe this is a mistake." He glanced at me. "Maybe we shouldn't be here." He gulped again. His voice became that of a child's. "Can we go now, Gillam?"

I shook my head slowly. I hadn't wanted to come here. I'd known how it was going to turn out.

"You asked the wrong person," Rook said. "Gillam is a far worse monster than me."

I couldn't help but laugh. In the realm of monstrous I was an acolyte compared to Rook.

Rook giggled and tore another piece of skin free. "When a monster is a monster he's being true to his nature. When a human is a monster it's far worse."

I wished Rook would shut up. I think it was all the time he spent alone. It made him want to talk. I opened my mouth to say something, but Rook interrupted, jerking Wisnewski's spine free with a mighty heave. He removed his foot from the man's head and stepped forward, holding the long meaty piece out for inspection. He regarded the spine for a moment, then tossed it at Dobler, who automatically caught it in his arms, before dropping it. Then Dobler bent over and retched.

"You're not a good person, Gillam," Rook said, licking his hand clean. "You try and be. You pretend to be. But you have thoughts, don't you? You have impulses. Crazy impulses. You see something and you want to do something bad to it. But then you don't and you pretend that everyone thinks the same things and that you're a good person for showing restraint. But you're not a good person, Gillam. You're not good at all. At least not how these people think. At least not how poor Ben thinks." At this last, he pointed toward the ceiling, to a spot where a single head hung, different from the others. This one had no cloth on its head. It had no beard. On its neck was tattooed A/9/2, Ben's first unit in Somalia.

I was shocked to see it. More shocked at the memory it evoked. Then of course I'd told everyone that Ben had been killed by an IED. No trace left. Nothing. Not even a piece of skin to test for DNA. And the others knew it too. They'd read the AAR. They knew my story.

Perez was the first to attack, but the sound of his knife sliding free was loud and gave me plenty of time to put my pistol beneath his chin and fire three times.

Segrest lifted his weapon and I brought mine around at the same time. I stepped backward and we found ourselves barrel-to-barrel. His eyes widened. Then I shifted slightly and pulled the trigger, catching him in the forehead. I threw myself down in case he fired, but he was unable to get a shot off.

"GILLAM!" Dobler shouted. "STOP!"

I landed next to Segrest. His dead eyes accused me. We'd drunk together. We'd killed together. We'd been friends. But I'd never really cared for him. I'd just played the part I was supposed to, doing the things I was supposed to do to get along. Cooperate to graduate, as they say.

Monique had looked at me the same way after she'd died. I'd told her I loved her. I told her I'd take her home with me. I told her I wouldn't squeeze so hard. It was her fault she'd believed all of my lies. Then as I took her from behind, I'd closed my eyes and remembered Ben, doing the same thing to his face after he'd died.

I spied Watson as he aimed at me. I used Segrest's body as cover and fired from the ground. I scored two hits center mass, but not before he was able to hit me three times in the back. I rolled over and groaned. The pain sent me away. . . .

I don't know how long I was out, but I awoke to hear Rook saying, "'Sublime' is a word I've discovered lately. It's a good word. Underused, I think."

Then blackness took me again.

I tumbled to a memory of me and Ben sitting and watching the television, some Armed Forces Network replay of a hero movie.

Ben asked, "Who would play you in the movie of your life, man?"

I remember wondering. I hated all the hero actors. I thought they were all a little too cocky and sure of themselves. I couldn't understand why people cheered for them. I was always ultimately disappointed when they survived to the end. I wondered why there were no movies where the bad guy survived.

"What makes you think you're a good guy?" I remember asking.

"Because I fight for the winning side," he said, laughing, completely unaware of the stupid simplicity of his answer.

Dobler was sputtering like a baby from somewhere off to my right when I next came to. "We have him in a box. We . . . we're studying him."

"Did he tell you what I did to him?" Rook asked.

I couldn't hear the answer, but I heard Rook respond, "I thought as much. So this was all a ruse? What would you have done if I'd come?"

Dobler mumbled something.

"Oh, you mean you thought I'd actually fall for it? What made you think that?"

I couldn't hear the answer again. I levered myself up, using Segrest's face for balance. I wanted to hear. I wanted to see Dobler as he was talking.

I saw him hanging from the ceiling, his hands tied and hooked. His skin was gone—completely absent from where it was supposed to be. How Rook had done it without killing Dobler I hadn't a clue, but I wanted to make sure and ask. It looked cool.

I straightened and arched my back. My shoulders felt tight so I rotated them.

"Why don't you answer him, Dobler? Why don't you tell Rook what I said?"

"He—he said you'd fall for it hook, line, and sinker."

Rook looked at me with those same appraising eyes he'd given me earlier.

This time I returned his gaze. "Sublime, isn't it?" It was a statement rather than a question.

Rook grinned. "Yes it is. Very sublime."

Dobler shook once, his body rattling savagely, then died.

Soldiers do things in war. Murder changes them. They can become monsters, torturing, raping, and collecting body parts as the animal part is begged to the surface. But this is only temporary. When it's over, we return home to a life where the only raised fists are at the television or against a bad driver. I used to believe that these things I did were like those things, an act of war meant to be left in the war. A souvenir meant to be left behind.

Rook had said it earlier: "I'm the devil until the credits roll, then everyone scrambles to see who I really am." It was the most sublime thing I'd ever heard and informed my inner self who I really was better than a thousand nights staring into the barrel of my gun.

Sometimes the devil plays himself, but most often it's someone else, someone you least expect, or someone you don't want to expect.

Sunlight suddenly streamed into the cave's opening like laser beams from an angry god. I took one look then stepped into the blinding day, and in that moment I knew who I really was.

My skin popped and sizzled.

My hair flamed like Johnny Blaze.

My ears blackened and burst.

I watched my hands turn to ash.

In the movie of my life I'd played the devil, but when the credits rolled, it was me all along . . . John Hershey Gillam, son of Marguerite and Frank Gillam, brother of Peter and Susan, soldier, warrior, believer in the cause, devil in disguise, Nightbreed in training . . . it was me.

It was me.

I stepped back inside the cave, glancing at Ben's head hanging with the others from the ceiling. Shadows lived where his eyes had been. He'd given me good memories all the way to the end.

Rook regarded me with a sad smile.

My hands re-formed.

And the credits rolled.

THE LIGHTHOUSE
OF MIDIAN

Ian Rogers

S he had many names.

The first one she got when she was born, the second she received when she was reborn. The others came after that.

She didn't remember her first name; she'd forgotten it, much as she'd forgotten the life that had gone with it. Her only memory of that time was a city of lights and cold winds that blew down mercilessly from the north lands. The second name—the one she thought of as her true name—had been given to her by Baphomet, the Baptizer, the one who made Midian.

Now Midian was gone, destroyed by fire and hatred, and she found herself, suddenly and inexplicably, back in that city of lights and cold winds. She thought it might be time for a third name but there was no one here to give it to her. No one except Causwell, and he wasn't giving anything to anyone these days.

So, for now, she remained Luna.

Luna of Midian.

Luna of the Nightbreed.

She was watching for the blue man.

Since returning to the city of lights and cold winds, Luna had discovered that if she sat on the sidewalk some people would give her money. Coins mostly. She rubbed them between her fingers, feeling a combination of cold metal and distant sympathy. It was, she came to learn, the sensation of an impersonal transaction. They paid her to ignore her.

One time a man offered her paper money, a pink bill with "50" printed on it. Unlike the others, he didn't leave the money on the ground in front of her. He held it out to her in his hand, and when she tried to take it, he gripped the bill tighter until she raised her eyes to his. She could tell what he wanted, but not from the look in his eyes. She knew the moment she touched his money. She let go, lowering and shaking her head in refusal. When she looked up again, the man and the money were gone.

There were a lot of people out tonight. She was stationed on the sidewalk in front of a large stadium. Larger even than the tabernacle in Midian. Inside, men in different-colored uniforms pounded away at each other in order to control possession of a brown ball. It was funny in a way. Also a bit sad. But it drew a lot of people, and some of them would give her money that she used to buy food.

She had to be careful, because a few times a man in another uniform, a blue one, would chase her away. She didn't let other people bother her, but the blue man was different. He wore a gun on his belt. Luna didn't know about guns until the fall of Midian. She had learned all about them, then. The loud, barking power they possessed. The damage they could inflict. Even a little one like the one the blue man had on his hip, always close to hand.

A couple walking past stopped suddenly. The man tried to pull the woman on, but she held him back. She looked down at Luna with something in her eyes that might have been pity. She held out a blue bill. It made Luna think of the blue man, and she didn't take it at first. The woman noticed her reluctance and held the money out farther. "Come on. It's okay. You can take it."

Luna reached out quickly and snapped the bill from her hand. It had "5"s all over it. She only had a little math, but she knew the bills were worth more than the coins. "Thank you," she said, with a small nod. "You're very kind."

The woman gave her a sad smile. "Do you have a place to stay?"

Luna responded with another small nod. She kept her head down, afraid to meet the woman's eyes. She stayed like that until the man succeeded in drawing the woman away.

Luna raised her head when she was sure they were gone.

It was then that she saw him. The blue man. He was sauntering through the crowd like he was the master of all he surveyed. Perhaps he was. He was the only one she'd ever seen with a gun.

Luna stood up abruptly, pockets jingling with the coins she had acquired that evening. She turned to put her back to the blue man and started away . . .

. . . and walked right into a wall.

At least that's what it felt like. Hard and . . . wet? Then the wall let out a grunt and a curse—"Fuck!"—and she realized she had collided with a man.

He was a brute, large and broad-shouldered, with a thick neck and a wide forehead. His face was a congestion of anger; squinting, unfocused eyes, sneering nose, and gritting teeth. He was wearing a jacket with a galloping horse over the left breast. He smelled foul, as if he existed in a personal cloud of pollution.

"You li'l bitch."

Her face was buffeted by his rank breath. She lowered her eyes and saw a plastic cup in his large hand, crinkled into a dripping, shapeless mess.

"You spilled my fucking beer. Li'l bitch."

The man's hand sprang open, dropping the mangled cup, and snapped out to clamp onto Luna's upper arm.

"Let me go."

She didn't scream, didn't even raise her voice above its normal register. There were two reasons for this. One, she didn't want to draw the attention of the blue man, who would surely side with the foul man and join him in this assault. The second reason was that she didn't need to raise her voice. She never had to.

With his grip on her arm, Luna saw everything inside the foul man. All the clean and all the dirty. There was so much more dirty. No surprise there. She held her breath reflexively so she wouldn't take it in, but it was all around her. She told herself she was clean, that this was the foul man's dirty, the two were separate, and she would be okay once they broke contact. But not yet.

With her mind, she reached out and took a piece of his dirty—she saw the foul man as a foul boy, almost as big in adolescence as the man he would become, wearing a jacket similar to the one he was wearing now. Luna saw him in a darkened room, tugging down the pants of a girl lying passed out on a bed, the muffled sounds of laughter and music coming from somewhere nearby. The foul boy climbed on top of the girl's supine body and began to thrust into her, moving with the beat of the music. Luna took the memory and turned it around and shined it back at the foul man.

Confronted with these noxious images, the foul man let go of Luna, his hand flying off her arm as if propelled by a powerful electric shock. He stumbled away from her, legs twisting around each other, and he tumbled over backward. He landed on his back and continued to push himself away from her, moving awkwardly like a crab along the sidewalk.

"Don't touch me!" he said in a high-pitched squeal that belied his massive size. "Keep your hands off me!"

Luna stared at him without expression. The foul man wasn't really talking to her. He was still inside his memory. He wasn't even himself right now. He was the unconscious woman he had assaulted. She had been passed out through the ordeal, but the foul man was very much awake. More awake than he'd been in his entire life.

As she walked off into the night, Luna knew he would never sleep soundly ever again.

The building had been a radio station at one time.

Luna knew about radio. Someone in Midian had one. It wasn't forbidden, but you had to get close to the surface to pick anything up on it, and the elders didn't like anyone spending too much time topside. The man who owned the radio—his name was Grazer—didn't seem to have much regard for Midian's laws. Luna snuck away to see him sometimes so she could listen to the music.

"Mostly country and oldies from the station in Peace River," Grazer told her. "Reception sucks, but that's the best you can get out here in the willywags."

Luna didn't understand "country" or "oldies," but she liked the sounds that came out of the black plastic box. Plucking strings and screaming horns. Sad voices, happy voices. She didn't always understand what the people were singing about, but it didn't matter. She loved to listen to those sounds from far away.

She had asked Grazer where they came from, those sounds, and he said they were sent out—"broadcast" was the word he used—from a great metal tower.

"How tall is it?" Luna asked.

"Very tall," Grazer said.

"Taller than the Strivent?"

"Yes, child."

Standing outside the abandoned building she now called home, Luna found that hard to believe. The tower that stood atop the roof was tall, but surely not as tall as the Strivent of Midian. She should know; she had climbed the Strivent on several occasions, had clung to the top as the wind screamed and howled and threatened to pull her off.

Of course, this was not the same station that broadcast from Peace River, but she imagined they were all the same. This one had gone quiet. It sent out no songs. The building was empty now except for her and Causwell.

———

She found him in the basement.

That was where he spent most of his time. Huddled in his blankets, wandering around in the darkness, yelling at unseen phantoms. Or at least at phantoms that Luna could not see.

Presently he stood in front of a tall metal box with a glass window on the front. Inside were rows of candy held in place by coils of metal. She had seen devices such as these before. You put coins in the little slot, punched the code that matched the one next to the piece of candy you wanted, and the coil would turn, causing the candy to fall to the bottom of the box, where you could retrieve it from a narrow push-door.

This candy box didn't work because there was no power in the building. Luna didn't know much about electricity except that many things in the city of lights and cold winds needed it to work.

Causwell wasn't about to let that stop him, though. He was hammering the window with a stick he had found somewhere. The stick wasn't very strong, and neither was the effort Causwell was putting into each swing; he had succeeded so far in only scuffing and scratching the glass.

He stopped when he realized he was no longer alone. He turned his sleek, hairless head toward her.

"Luna," he said in his hollow, breathless voice. "You came back."

"You say that every time, Causwell. Why do you keep thinking I'm going to leave you?"

"Everyone leaves," he said. "Eventually. It would be better for you if you did. This is a bad place."

"This is our new home."

Causwell sneered. "This isn't home. This is a foul-smelling pit." His eyes took on a dreamy look of longing. "I miss my old pit. This one doesn't hold a candle to it."

Luna nodded solemnly.

Causwell came shuffling forward, looking for comfort—Luna had held him through many a night since they'd taken refuge in this place. He stopped abruptly and sniffed at her.

"You smell like beer. Have you been drinking?"

"A man spilled it on me."

"Did he hurt you?"

Luna lowered her eyes and shook her head.

"Did you hurt him?"

"A little."

She expected to be rebuked, but Causwell scoffed instead.

"Serves them right." He looked away, deep in thought. "I came from a town much like this place—cattle country, it's called. Do you know cattle?"

Luna nodded. She'd seen pictures in books.

"They have an expression there: You mess with the bull, you get the horns. Same goes for anyone who tries to fuck with the Breed. Although in your case, I guess they get the eyes instead of the horns. We may not have a home anymore, but that doesn't change who we are."

The quiet strength of his words reminded Luna of the way Causwell had been in Midian. The tricks he could do with his body. Making cat's cradle with the veins in his fingers, drawing out the wet red threads to the delight of the children. The way he could extend his ribs out through his chest, the bones sharpened to points, and make them snap like a voracious mouth. He didn't do anything now except wander this dark basement and beat his stick against the candy box.

As quickly as it arrived, the conviction in his voice departed; his shoulders slumped, as if glad to be free of some monumental weight.

"Not that it matters," he said. "We're the last. They'll find us eventually and slaughter us. Drag our bodies through their pristine streets so they can show the world that the monsters are dead."

Causwell turned away from Luna, turned back into his sorrow. She reached out and gripped his arm.

"We're still Nightbreed," she said. "If we are alive, then there must be others."

"The Breed are gone," Causwell said despondently. "Like Midian."

She let go of him and he shuffled off into the corner.

When she wasn't sitting on the sidewalks for money, Luna walked the streets and back alleys looking for others of her kind.

After the fall of Midian, the remaining Nightbreed scattered to all points of the compass. Many had come here, to the city of lights and cold winds; their only wish to be ignored, to find the peace they'd once known before.

Besides Causwell, Luna hadn't seen any other Breed. But she could feel them, somewhere out there. Lurking. Hiding. She wanted to find them— she *needed* to find them—but the Breed were good at staying hidden, even from each other.

Her reasons were not entirely altruistic. She told herself there was power in numbers, but mostly she just didn't want to be alone. Causwell didn't count. He lived so much inside himself, inside his own melancholy, that it was like she lived by herself at the radio station.

So, every night she went out and searched. She moved like a ghost along the periphery of city life, drifting along the edge of crowds, losing herself in the smoke haze of bars and the frenetic light show of dance clubs. She explored abandoned buildings and stalked the city's few green places, which at night became black places. Occasionally she found traces of the Breed—a faint scent of tombs and spices, a sigil painted or on a wall.

She thought it was only a matter of time before she found them, just as she had found Causwell. But sometimes she wondered if they were the last. It didn't make any difference. No matter how much the dread in her heart might eclipse the hope, she knew she'd never stop looking.

No joy tonight.

Luna returned to the radio station empty-handed and empty-headed.

Her stomach growled; it was empty, too. Her pockets were filled with coins again, but she hadn't bothered to buy any food.

She felt bad that she hadn't at least got something for Causwell. She descended to the basement and found him in his corner. He turned away guiltily at Luna's approach.

"What are you doing?" she asked.

Causwell held something small and furry in his hands. He tried to hide it behind his back, but Luna saw it dripping on the concrete floor.

"Are you eating rats again?"

Causwell grinned a bloody, guilty grin. "I'm building up my strength."

"For what?"

Causwell looked away. "Always good to have strength." He changed the subject. "How is it out there?"

"Still dark," Luna said.

"No change?" he asked. "No call?"

"If there was, I didn't hear it."

"I told you. No one is coming. The Breed are gone. They're all dead."

"Not all," Luna said. "There is the one known as Cabal. He who . . ."

"Unmade Midian," Causwell finished. "He who helped cast us out." He spat on the floor.

Luna shrugged. "No refuge is forever."

"You sound like Baphomet. And where is *he* now?"

"Don't blaspheme."

"I didn't. I asked a question."

"I have no answers. I'm tired."

"Sleep, then. But don't dream. There is no comfort in dreams. If we're to find survival, it must be of our own making."

Luna smiled faintly. "That's the spirit."

"There is no spirit," Causwell said. "Only flesh."

He looked down at the dripping piece of rat in his hand and stuffed it into his mouth.

———————

Luna didn't know the girl, but she recognized her right away.

She found her under a stunted tree on the edge of a sprawling, empty parking lot. It was in the industrial part of the city, near an old warehouse whose roof was full of holes. The girl—younger than Luna, maybe twelve—

lay shivering beneath a pile of newspapers. Luna thought she was sleeping, but as she pulled the papers away, she saw the girl was bleeding. She was full of holes, too.

"What happened to you?"

The girl tried to shift away, and grimaced in pain. In a low, trembling voice, she said, "Please, let me be."

Luna touched the girl's cheek, smeared with grime.

The girl recoiled.

"You're Nightbreed."

The girl turned her head to look up at Luna.

There was no question. The girl's black hair was truly raven, not hair at all but feathers that curved down in a sleek wave to frame her porcelain doll face. Her eyes were small and brown; her nose was hooked, her mouth a lipless line that quivered with fear and pain.

"I don't know you," she said, but her imploring eyes held a glimmer of hope.

"My name is Luna."

The girl's eyes widened. "The Lighthouse! I should have known. Your eyes!" She tried to raise herself up, then slumped back to the ground, wincing. "It hurts. It hurts even to breathe."

Luna put her hand on the girl's shoulder, easing her down. "Tell me your name."

"Mordryn." She clenched her teeth, and Luna saw they were small and sharp, a mouthful of tiny fishhooks. "Mordryn of Midian."

"Midian is gone," Luna said.

"I know it."

"Who did this to you?"

"Men," Mordryn said. "Monster men."

"From this place?" Luna asked. "The city?"

Mordryn shook her head with a faint ruffle of feathers. "No," she said. "But they followed us here."

"Us? There's more of you? Other Breed?"

"Not now. The monster men got them. They hunt us." She reached out and gripped Luna's wrist with a yellow, reptilian hand. Talons lacquered with hot pink nail polish pierced her skin, drawing small pearls of blood. Luna barely noticed, her attention focused entirely on the words coming out of Mordryn's trembling mouth.

"They *eat* us," she said. "They tried to eat me but I got away from them."

"Who are they?"

"Monster men," she said. "They call themselves the Sugar Babies. They followed us from Midian."

Luna was confused. "I thought the men who destroyed Midian were killed."

"They were," Mordryn said. "These were the men who came after." She flung her head back and sobbed. "Our mistake was going back."

Luna shook her head. "I don't understand."

"After Midian fell, a group of us left. We didn't know where to go. We traveled north, into the Territories, but it was cold and we couldn't find shelter. So we went back." She closed her eyes and spoke the words like a mantra: "*Our mistake was going back.*"

"To Midian?"

"Yes."

"But Midian is gone."

"I know, but we were tired and hungry. We took refuge in the ruins. Then the monster men came. The Sugar Babies."

"I don't know who they are."

"They look like men in suits. Do you know suits?"

Luna nodded.

"The suits are as false as the men. They're monsters wearing other monsters. The ties they wear around their necks are alive! They move like snakes, and the men talk to them!"

"What happened?"

"We ran," Mordryn said. "We came here, to this city. But the Sugar Babies followed us. There are others of our kind here. We saw them. Tribes on the move. We warned them about the monster men, but they found us. They killed my friends. They were saving me for last. They called me their little treat, their dessert." She let go of Luna's arm and covered her eyes with her hands. "Our mistake was going back."

Luna cradled her and told her everything was going to be okay, but Mordryn died that night with the mistake still in her mouth.

The Lighthouse.

She never thought she'd hear that name again. She had gone by many names in Midian. To the trolls she was Li'l Luna. To the blind witches, the hagathas, she was Helper Girl. It was Wardent and his clan—a brave and foolhardy group of souls who went on raiding missions to Dwyer and Shere Neck for supplies—who called her the Lighthouse.

She had earned the nickname by climbing to the top of Midian's tallest structure, a towering obelisk that the Nightbreed had called the Strivent, to stand as lookout for Wardent and his raiders.

Every time before they left on a run, Wardent would curl one of his claw-tipped fingers under Luna's chin and tilt her head up to him. His pale yellow eyes, slit by triangular pupils, would stare into her glowing blue ones, and he'd say, "Keep a watch, little one. Climb to the top of the Strivent and show us the light. That's what you are, the Lighthouse of Midian. Show us the way home."

Luna was certain that Wardent and the others could find their way back without her, but she was glad to be included. With their excited howls still echoing through the night, she would climb the Strivent, digging her fingers into the cracks in the cold stone while the wind tried to pull her off and fling her to the ground. Once she reached the top, she would open her eyes as wide as possible, and even though she was far above Midian, and the Breed so far below the ground, she could see them, her people, her family, down past the graves and tombs, deep within the catacombs, thousands of darkling souls. She'd stay up there for hours, eyes blazing out into the night, until Wardent and the others returned with their pillage.

She knew they didn't really need her light. But they wanted her there, and that was more important. That was what made them family. What made them Nightbreed.

———

There was something different about the radio station.

Luna couldn't tell what it was at first. The building looked as decrepit as ever. A yellow-brick box with a metal tower sprouting from the roof. Smashed-out windows glaring like black, blind eyes. The pavement cracked and frost-heaved, sprouting weeds.

She stepped through the glassless front door and called out in a timid voice, "Causwell?"

No answer.

She started down the stairs to the basement . . . and froze.

Something different, right there. A ragged curtain hung across the entrance at the bottom of the stairs. Luna approached it slowly, warily, swept it aside—it was dry and thin, like very old paper—and stepped through.

As she stood there looking around, a series of emotions coursed through her; surprise, sadness, dread, and finally, fascination.

Causwell wasn't in the basement.

Causwell *was* the basement.

He had done something with his body, extended it, stretched it, spread it out across the walls and floors. His flesh and bones had been transformed into a structure that infused itself with the building's architecture. The previously sagging ceiling was now supported by beams of bone. The cold concrete floor was carpeted in warm, soft flesh. Luna looked over her shoulder at the curtain she had passed through. Not a curtain, she saw now, but a diaphanous sheet of skin.

This was unlike anything she had ever seen Causwell create before. And yet she knew it was him. His body, his smell, was unmistakable. But why had he done it? If he had grown tired of life, he would have killed himself. He had talked about it enough. But what she was looking at wasn't the result of suicide. Quite the opposite.

She found his head in the corner where he'd taken refuge so many times before. His skull seemed to grow right out of the Sheetrock, his blanched face peering at her like someone sunk almost completely in quicksand.

Luna leaned down to cradle his cheeks. "Oh, Causwell, what have you done?"

"I built it for them," he said in an airless voice.

"For who?"

"The others," he gasped. "The ones who will come."

Luna brushed her fingers across his forehead. "You said they were all dead. You didn't believe."

"I believe in *you*," Causwell said. "You've always been able see further than I can." His eyes darted around the room, admiring the sanctuary he'd made. "But it's not finished. I'll need more . . ." His gaze fell to the floor.

Luna looked down at the desiccated rat carcasses scattered about.

"I'll bring you more," she said. "As many as you need. And I'll bring *them*, too."

Causwell smiled. "I know you will."

She went up to the roof.

The cold wind caressed her, blew her hair around her face. The light in her eyes ebbed and flowed.

She went over to the broadcast tower and began to climb.

Her mind drifted back to the day of her baptism in Midian. The cold fire of Baphomet's touch, his enormous hands raising her up, his words searing into her mind, branding her brain.

You will light the way. When everything goes dark, when all ways are lost, you will be the beacon. You will guide them.

She reached the top of the tower. She couldn't tell if it was as tall as the Strivent, but it didn't matter. There was a light at the tip, but it was dark. That didn't matter, either.

She opened her eyes—opened them wide—and her light shone out across the night sky.

It was not a light for all to see. It was a private light. Only the Breed would see it. Only the Breed would know it. She hoped Wardent would be the first to come. If he was still alive. If he was out there, somewhere. She wanted to feel his claw-tipped finger tilt her face up to his. She was his Lighthouse. Now she would be the Lighthouse for all the Nightbreed. She would guide them here to the House of Causwell.

She clung to the tower with her legs, her arms flung wide, her eyes blazing.

And she waited for them to come.

LAKRIMAY

Nerine Dorman

I like the big house better than when Mom and I used to stay in the flat. There are lots more rooms where I can play hide-and-seek, and the furniture has dragon feet holding balls. At night I'm sure the tables and chairs go for walks. Mom says I'm silly but if I lie awake after the lights go out then I hear feet marching along the passage outside my room. Up and down they go all night. Sometimes someone calls a name, over and over again. It's a woman, and she says *Lilium, Lilium . . . Lilium.* So sad it makes my chest tight and my eyes burn.

I asked Uncle Rory about the people in the passages but he just looked at me funny. Mom told me to stop talking nonsense, but I know I hear foot-steps. I hear them every night but I don't get out to look because then the shadow thing under the bed will grab my feet.

Sometimes I want to call out "Here I am!" when the woman asks for Lilium, but I'm scared I'm going to get into trouble for waking Mom and Uncle Rory.

We live by the sea now but Mom hasn't taken me to the beach yet. It's walking distance, she says, and we're right by the big lagoon where the fla-mingos visit. I like the flamingos and I want to go look at them, and also go on the swings by the play park, but I'm not allowed outside the gate with-out Mom or Auntie Stella. Uncle Rory is always too busy in his studio so I mustn't bother him but I don't like Auntie Stella. She comes to look after me every day and she stinks like cigarettes and her perfume is too sweet. I can taste it when she hugs me or picks me up. I don't like it when she hugs me. The skin on her neck looks like wrinkly rubber and I think it's a mask. Underneath her skin is scaly, like in that TV show I'm not allowed to watch where the bad people are green and swallow rats.

Mom says I must be very quiet during the day because Uncle Rory works from home. He takes photos of the nice ladies who have bright red lips and wear panties. I know this because they come outside to smoke cigarettes when they have their tea break. They are always nice to me. Once they put some lipstick on me but Auntie Stella got very cross and made me wipe my mouth clean before Mom got home or Uncle Rory saw. She says they are bad ladies but how can they be bad when they are so nice to me?

Uncle Rory often has parties at the house. I'm supposed to be in bed then but I wear my blanket like a wizard's cloak and sneak around. The adults are always so busy talking and laughing and dancing. They listen to music so loudly they have to yell to hear each other. Sometimes the nice ladies with the bright red lips are there, like Sindy and Desiré. I want to talk to them but they are busy—pouring drinks and chopping white powder on plates with their bank cards. *Chop. Chop. Chop.*

Then they roll up money and stick the tubes in their nose and sniff loudly.

I tried the same the other day. I didn't have money so I drew paper money and rolled it up. I got some flour from the kitchen and Auntie Stella found me trying to make those lines. *Chop. Chop. Chop.* But I didn't have a bank card so I was using my fingers and I got flour all over the tiles in the hallway.

Auntie Stella was very cross and smacked my bum.

I'll be a good girl. I won't stick things in my nose again.

Not long after we move in I see the green lady. She stays in the room under the stairs that go to the basement. She has long black fingernails like claws and eyes like a cat. I'm scared of her but she's nice to me and whispers at me to come downstairs to talk to her.

"Look, little girl, I have a present for you," she says, and holds out her hand.

Her eyes gleam in the low light, but I'm scared of going down the stairs because of the shadows. I don't look too closely at her gift.

But I'll sit at the top, and the green lady will sing and tell me stories about a city under the ground called Midian, where all the monsters go.

"Will you take me there?" I ask her.

The green lady smiles and shakes her head. "I can't."

Auntie Stella doesn't like it that I sit by the basement's stairs so much. I hear her tell my mom, "Jennifer needs to go to play school to be with other children her age. It's not right that the child be inside all day. She's making imaginary friends."

"What is your name?" I ask the green lady one day.

"Lakrimay," says the green lady.

"Are you an imaginary friend?" I ask.

Lakrimay smiles and shakes her head sadly. Then she reaches into the pocket of her black dress and offers me a little bone. It nestles in her palm and makes me think of a long, thin finger. "I've got a present for you. Will you come downstairs and get it?"

"What is it?" I ask.

"It's an albatross bone," says Lakrimay. Then she tells me how the giant birds spend months at sea and never touch the land, always wandering, wandering in the wind. Yet every year they go back and meet their mates at the same place.

I want to go down into the basement but I can't. The shadows will pour down my throat and choke me. As it is, my heart is racing so much I'm scared it's going to end up in my mouth. Maybe that's why I sit at the top of the stairs—to see how long I can be at the edge where the day melts into night.

The next morning, when I wake up, the albatross bone is on my bedside table. The surface is creamy and smooth, and so very light. I think of the bird with the big wings flying forever, never resting, never walking, and I wonder what it must be like to soar like that.

"What is that ugly thing you got there?" Auntie Stella asks me when she comes to get me dressed for breakfast.

"It's an albatross bone," I tell her.

"*Sies*, that dirty thing? Give it here." She reaches out for it but I'm faster than her, and I run away to one of the rooms upstairs on the second floor where I'm not supposed to go.

"Jennifer!" Auntie Stella screeches. "Come back here this instant!"

I pretend I don't hear her and I go hide my albatross bone in the room Mom calls the spare room, where an orange quilt covers a big bed. This room scares me sometimes because I can hear a clock ticking and the air is always very thick. Sometimes I think there is a monster hiding in the cupboard, and if I keep my back to the doors, it's going to jump out with long, spider hands and snatch me into the darkness.

But no one goes here except for the time when there was one of the parties, and I saw the man and the woman wrestling on the bed. There's a little table with a drawer on the side by the window, and I hide the bone in the drawer where I put the marble I found in the garden. This is my treasure chest where I'm going to put all my special things, I decide. Magic things, like when I was grubbing in the flower bed and my fingers closed around the cat's-eye marble.

I don't like Uncle Rory. And it's not just because he is always telling me to stay out of his studio, but it's because he makes Mom cry. They think I don't know, that because I'm just a little girl I don't understand that he's horrible to her. Mom works so hard at the hotel and she doesn't like it when Uncle Rory's friends come have a party and she's not there. She doesn't like that the nice ladies visit when she's not here either. They always close the door and lock it and I can hear them giggling.

"Go play with your toys!" Uncle Rory growls.

It's summer, and the wind blows terribly. It rattles the gutter so it goes *brrrrrrrrr*, and Mom says we can't go to the beach when the wind blows but she's at work so much. I ask Auntie Stella but says she doesn't like getting sand in her shoes, so we don't go. Not even to the play park. The nice ladies are busy putting on pretty panties for Uncle Rory, so they can't take me.

So I sit by the big window in the lounge sometimes with my face pressed against the glass so I can watch the flamingos shivering in the wind walking on their stilt legs. The lagoon's water is a nasty bruised color, and the clouds are ripped on the mountain. People hold on to their hats. I once saw a man lose his newspaper. It flew away like a bird. I don't like going outside when the wind blows because it steals my breath and drives sand into my mouth. So I look at Uncle Rory's picture books and am careful not to tear the pages. He always says That Child will tear the pages.

"Tell me about outside," Lakrimay asks me when I see her again.

So I tell her about the wind ripping the trees, and the way the dust circles and gets up my nose. We sit and listen to the moaning in the roof, and I tell Lakrimay about the other monsters in the house.

She laughs softly. "Those are not the monsters you must be afraid of, dear."

I ask her if she can take me down to the beach but she shakes her head. "Not during the day."

"Why?"

Lakrimay won't say. Instead she tells me about Lilium, who is also a little girl.

"Where is Lilium now?" I ask.

Lakrimay turns her face into the shadows and won't talk to me.

The next morning a white mussel shell rests on my bedside table. Two perfect halves, the inside still moist with sticky grains of sand. They look like butterfly wings and I remember going to the beach with Mom where I filled my bucket with these shells. Sea butterflies that live underwater, I told Mom. She laughed and said the animals in the shells lived under the sand.

"But how can they breathe there?" I asked. "Aren't they scared of the dark?"

Mom couldn't explain it to me so I prefer to think of the sea butterflies and how their shell wings go from a bony white to inky purple where the two points meet. This time I don't wait for Auntie Stella to come yell at me for the shell. I get up and go hide the gift in the spare room, with my albatross bone and marble.

Uncle Rory makes Mom cry a lot more than when we first came to live here. I hide when they start shouting and when I tell Auntie Stella some of the words, like "slut" and "bitch," she slaps me hard through the face and says I must never use those words again. They are bad words. Dirty words. Go wash your mouth out with soap.

One day Uncle Rory gets so mad he slaps Mom like I've seen on TV. She starts packing up our things but then Uncle Rory comes and says sorry, he didn't mean it, and the next thing they're hugging and kissing and I must go outside the room.

I can hardly see because I'm so scared and my eyes are full of tears, and I go to the basement stairs.

"What's wrong, Jennikin?" Lakrimay asks me.

And I tell her as I wipe at my face and taste the salt of my own tears.

"Come here, and I will sing you stories," Lakrimay tells me.

I want to. She's holding her arms out to me and her eyes shine there in the shadows. I could go down to her. She'll keep me safe from the dark, and she's not an imaginary friend anymore, is she? So I get up and take that first step, but then the darkness creeps up the stairs to me and I remember what it feels like to wake in the night and have the shadow man press his tongue in my eyes.

"I can't," I say, and whimper.

Larkimay reaches up. She has something in her hands. It is orange and white, and curled like a giant snail.

"You must come down a little. I have something for you."

My fingers tight around the banister, I take a few steps, but not so many that I can't quickly turn around and fly back up.

This is the closest I've ever been to Lakrimay. Her skin looks like milk in a green glass bottle, all shiny. Her eyes are large and slitted, and her hair flexes and coils like the octopus I saw at the aquarium, only it's blacker than the shadows. It smells of fish down here, and like the sea.

Lakrimay hisses when her hand creeps out of the shadow, as if the light makes her sore, and her movement is quick, feather-light as she puts a shell on the step below my feet. Then she withdraws, her hand clasped to her belly.

Quick as a cat, I snatch up the shell and run back up the stairs with my gift pressed against my chest.

"Thank you, Lakrimay," I say.

"Every time you are sad, I want you to press the shell to your ear and listen to the sound. That's the sea in there."

I press the open end of the shell to my ear, just like she said, and it's true. There, faintly, *the hiss-hiss-hiss* of waves on the sand.

"Do you like it?" she asks.

"Very much!"

The shell goes into the little treasure chest with the albatross bone, marble, and white mussel wings. But almost every other day Lakrimay brings me another gift. Small cowries with little teeth; a mermaid's purse, all slick and black; delicate sea urchins like buttons; blue, brown, and green sea glass; and bits of polished driftwood.

Whenever Mom and Uncle Rory fight, I go hide in the spare room and pack out my sea treasures. I listen to the sea whisper in my nautilus shell—Lakrimay taught me the words for all the shells—and sometimes I can even hear my friend sing. She always sounds sad, like she lost someone. *Lilium, Lilium, Lilium.* When I'm playing with my treasures, I don't hear the slamming doors, the screaming or stuff being broken. I have the sea here, inside, and I make up my own stories about adventures Lakrimay and I have in the other place, in Midian where the monsters go.

"Take me to the sea, take me to Midian," I ask Lakrimay.

"Not in the day," she answers. "But if you come to me after the sun sets, and your mom's gone to bed . . ." Her white teeth flash, and hope burns fierce and bright in her gaze.

But at night I'm too scared of the shadow man and the thing under the bed, and I sleep with the covers pulled tight over my head so the skeletons can't stuff their bony wrists down my throat. If I open my eyes just a crack I will see the shadow man dance at the foot of my bed. I don't care if the air is stuffy under the duvet. It's better than the things waiting to get me, waiting for that one moment when I'm not careful and stick an arm or a foot out by mistake.

I want to keep Lakrimay's shell by my bed so I can press it to my ear when I'm scared but I worry that Mom or Auntie Stella will want to know where I got it and then they'll make me throw it away.

Mom and Uncle Rory have a terrible fight one day during lunch and it's all my fault. We sit at the kitchen table and I ask why big people like to wrestle without their clothes on. A sudden, terrible silence drops into the air, and Uncle Rory and Mom both stop cutting at the food on their plates.

I've got my bowl and my spoon in front of me but I'm not very hungry. I don't like the way Mom cooks when it's her turn, and it is her turn today. Auntie Stella is off, as Mom says, which means I don't have to see her.

"Where did you see them wrestling?" Mom asks, her voice very quiet.

"In the . . ."

Uncle Rory has gone ice-white and his stare is enough to make me want to shrivel up like a snail covered in salt.

"Studio . . ." I finish, that last word a whisper.

Mom's shriek makes me slip under the table, where I hide while plates and glasses go flying.

"Bastard!" Mom screams.

Uncle Rory says terrible things about Mom, about how she's a user, and he roars at her like an angry lion like on TV. But that's when I scamper out of the kitchen, tear-blinded. I run straight to the spare room. I would go sit at the top of the stairs by Lakrimay but it's too close to the kitchen. Once I have my treasures packed out across the orange quilt I can no longer hear the yelling. Or maybe it's because the yelling doesn't matter anymore.

I'm the princess who drinks tears. The albatross carries me across the moon to the land of Midian. We live in a chamber of mirrors with mother-of-pearl floors, and Lakrimay brushes my hair with a comb carved from bone. When the bad man tries to hurt us, the monsters rise up out of the shadows and they tear him into little scraps. *Rip, rip, rip.*

I scratch my fingers on the rough fabric of the bedspread and I imagine that they have little sharp claws hooking into Uncle Rory's flesh that scratch him like the time I hooked my leg on a rusty nail.

The door bashes open and Mom stands there. Her face is very red and she's breathing hard.

"Why don't you answer when I call you?"

"I—"

She notices my precious things, all lined up on the bed, and her face turns all ugly. "What the fuck is this? We've got enough shit without having to deal with you carting this rubbish up here." Mom strides forward, pulls me up, and delivers a hard smack on my bum.

I scream at the pain. She hasn't hit me in a very long time and the shock of it makes me blank for a moment.

"Go to your room, and stay there!" Mom yells. Then she mutters to herself as she scoops my treasures into the wastebasket next to the bed.

"No!" I yell, and try to stop her. "You're break—"

The albatross bone drops to the wooden floor and shatters into two smaller pieces and many splinters, and something inside me breaks too.

"Go!" Mom shouts. "We don't need more trouble from that man if he finds out you've been messing in the upstairs where you're not wanted."

I follow her to the dustbin down in the kitchen, screaming and screaming about my treasures, until she smacks me again, hard. This time through the face.

. . . where you're not wanted . . .

We stand, both of us still, and the house echoingly quiet. I touch my cheek that's so sore, and my eyes blur with tears. Only then do I run to my room—my bedroom this time—but I'm a big enough girl that I know how to lock the door from the inside. No one's coming in, not even Mom.

The house is very quiet later. I think I hear the front door a few times. A car leaving. Someone tries the door to my room but I'm not sure who; I'm too tired and sad to go find out. I don't have any more tears. The person stands outside the door, as if waiting for me to let them in; then the footsteps grow distant in the passage.

My pretty nautilus, my little cowries like baby toes, and the albatross bone—all the little treasures—they are in the dustbin outside now where it stinks, and their magic is gone because they are broken.

I lie on my bed and fold my hands over my chest like the pictures of the Egyptian mummy I saw in one of the books in the lounge. If someone could wrap me in bandages I would be hidden too, locked away in a room forever. I try to imagine what this must feel like. Perhaps waking up and being completely muffled in bandages, alone in the dark. I cry again, but this time the tears are an endless, slow stream that soaks my pillow.

The house is full of sighs and a pigeon is calling from the roof. I stare up at the ceiling, at how the room grows darker and darker, and still I can't move. Outside cars rumble past. Dogs bark. But the house is so empty, just like one of the pharaohs' tombs.

Tap-tap-tap at my window.

Immediately I sit up. It's dark now and I'm freezing. The orange of the streetlights spills into my room and outlines a figure looking into my room. How did they get up here? I'm on the second floor.

A small squeak escapes me. Maybe it's one of the monsters.

Tap-tap-tap.

Long fingers tipped with *tickety* nails against glass. Writhy snake hair. Lakrimay.

It's not a monster. I know her name and she gave me treasures.

I slide off the bed and run over to the window. Lakrimay is perched on the windowsill, where there's only just enough space for her to kneel.

"Hurry, Jennikin. We don't have much time," she says. *Tap-tap-tap.*

The brass fastenings are difficult for me to reach, and I have to pull up the bedside table so I can manage. Mom always says I'll be in so much trouble if I ever open the window or climb on the sill, but if Lakrimay can do it then it must be fine.

The window pops open and Lakrimay half climbs into the room.

"What are you doing out there?" I ask her.

"You are crying," she says, and reaches out.

Her gaze is warm but her fingers as they trace down my cheek are so cold, and my skin goes numb where she touches me. A small shiver runs through me but Lakrimay is so gentle, so kind, and I go to her and let her arms slip around me so she can hold me. Her smell is like the sea, and when she whispers in my ear I can hear the wind brush the albatross's feathers and taste salt on my tongue.

"Come with me, little one." She presses chilled lips to my forehead then slowly kisses the tears from my eyes. With each kiss, my sadness grows lighter. I'm with Lakrimay. Everything is going to be all right.

"Are we going to Midian?" I ask her.

"We can't go to Midian, but I can take you down to the beach and show you the sea."

"What about my mom? She's so sad and angry. I don't think she'll like me going to the beach without asking first."

"Your mom's broken, and there's only one thing to do when someone's broken," says Lakrimay. Her arms tighten around me as I look up.

"Fix her?"

Lakrimay smiles, and her teeth are sharp little fishes' teeth.

AND MIDIAN WHISPERED ITS NAME

Shaun Meeks

The ghost of the dead had called to him, brought him to the overgrown place that had once been soaked in blood. He stood at the gates and stared into the ghost town of a ghost town, listened to see if he could hear them call out again. For months they had spoken to him, whispered the name of Midian in his ear as he lay in bed and tried to sleep. From the shadowy corners he saw their pale faces, unseen to anyone but him, and they told him about Midian, the Nightbreed; begged for him to seek out what had once been.

Speaking to the dead wasn't anything new to Kaleb. Since he was eleven the dead had been a constant in his life. That was when his father went from room to room at the farmhouse he had grown up in. His dad put a bullet in each one of his family members before he shot himself. His mother, two brothers, and sister had died of their injuries, but Kaleb lived. He had passed at first, but something had pulled him back to the land of the living, and since then, he had been able to see and hear the dead. It was not something that was easy to get used to, but eventually he did.

His father had also lived, though he had blown away more than half of his brain and was to live the rest of his days in a hospital, strapped to a machine that helped him breathe. Kaleb was glad that he had lived. If he passed away but didn't move on to the hell that surely waited for him, there was a possibility that he would see the man who had taken everything. The thought of being haunted by the man he had once called Father, the monster that had nearly been his murderer, would have been worse than death.

He didn't want to think of his father, though, as he stood in front of what had once been the great city of monsters. Midian had been hidden from the world, a refuge for those who were nightmares to some and myths to others. Kaleb closed his eyes and listened to the echoes of the world that once was, able to hear the laughter, the joy of those who had been part of that world. There had been children who ran alongside fanged beasts with no fear, no hesitation. To them, werewolves and demons were as common as cats and dogs.

Then the true monsters arrived.

Mankind.

Humans showed up with guns and fire. They opened up the ground and burned the sky to kill the things they could not understand. Blinded by fear and religion, they followed the lies of an insane man. They showed that humans were the true monsters and destroyed the only home and sanctuary for the inhabitants of Midian—those once known as the Nightbreed.

Kaleb opened his eyes and looked around. He had been called to Midian, asked to come and help them, but he didn't know why. There was nothing left. Even the memories of the fire had been lost to nature. Grass and trees overgrew the damage and the carnage and made it look as though everything was just as it should be. He could see in his mind what had happened, but to his eyes, Midian had overgrown with the false sense of normality that the rest of the world had been painted in.

"What am I supposed to do? How can I help you?" he whispered to the old memories. The wind shifted, blew toward him from the ruins of the lost city. He thought the voices of the dead would speak to him and tell him why they had called, but there was nothing there aside from the scent of dust and rotted wood.

Then, he heard a faint rustle, followed by a strange rattle, and when he looked down at his feet he saw that the wind had blown small, frail bones toward him. The bones, delicate and gray, continued to come, and as they did, they came together and made a makeshift skull. It was warped and misshapen; looked as though it was from some sort of large animal, but it was impossible to tell. Once the wind stopped, a pale green light emanated from within the newly formed skull and Kaleb picked it up and held it in front of his own face.

"Help us," the skull whispered with the voice of many. Young and old; male, female, and things in between spoke to him in a chorus. "We need you, Kaleb. Midian needs you. You must help to save us."

"How can I?"

"Find the others. Help to bring them together. There is strength in numbers, but they do not know this. They have split up and need guidance. You must take them to Cabal and then he will help to bring back Baphomet."

"Where do I start?"

"Listen to the wind. Follow our cries. We will lead you."

And with that, the wind blew again and the skull came apart in Kaleb's hand, bones fell between his fingers. The ones that remained turned to dust and he watched the desiccated bone fly away from him. He turned back to the city that had once been. As the wind picked up again, he could hear more whispers from the dead and knew he would help them, just as he had tried to help those who begged him in the past. He had been given a gift as he saw it, one that allowed those who could not leave this world to communicate with him. Some asked for help, others for revenge. He offered what he could.

This would be no different.

When Midian's dead had first come to him, he researched what had taken place. There was little in the national news about what had occurred, but in the local papers and online, there was plenty to be found. It all started with two men. Boone and Decker. One was a monster, the other was his patient.

The way the papers told it, Decker had been a doctor who led a dark, double life. In one life he was a well-respected psychiatrist; in his other he was a madman, a serial killer that didn't just kill entire families, but utterly destroyed them. Kaleb scanned through some of the grisly pictures the papers and Internet posted after the doctor's life had been uncovered. After the incident in Midian, the locals focused not on the monsters that lived underground, but the one that had lived among them. There was speculation that the bodies in the fallen secret city had been nothing more than victims of the crazy doctor, that he had caused all the carnage and then disappeared, but things were found that could not be explained. There were reports of deformed bodies, ones that were inhuman and seemed as though they were trapped in a place between the real and fantastic. There were no pictures of Midian or the aftermath, but the ghostly figures that peered out of the shadows at Kaleb let him know that there was more to Midian than a mere psychopath.

He continued his research online and found bits and pieces on the fabled land of monsters. Midian seemed to be a rumor; an idea of what people wished were true. To some it was Oz, to others it was Nirvana, and those with a religious mind-set made it out to be the earthbound state of Hell. There was no clear idea of what it was, or once had been, other than a place where the monsters once went.

Kaleb finally gave up his research and went to find Midian, to see if he could help the ghosts that found him. He had asked them what they wanted at the time, but there was never any clear sense of it. Not until he showed up at the lost city did he find a hint of their needs. After he had gone to Midian and spoken to the apparitions, he knew what they wanted, but was not sure how he would be able to find the others. It had been years since the fall of the city; so many had passed that he wondered if the survivors were still alive. Since the papers and Internet had nothing much to say on the inhabitants of the underground world, there was no follow-up on what had happened to them. All he could do was hope the ghosts that led him to the town could lead him to a starting point.

A week later, Kaleb found himself at the end of a road just outside of Edmonton. He had traveled relentlessly most of the days, not wanting to stop and rest as the need to find answers pushed him forward. He was led through small towns, wooded areas, and bigger cities with nothing to show for it other than sore feet. On his way, he could hear the whispered words of the dead that pushed him on and saw the disembodied faces that stared at him from the dark corners as they asked for help. He never stayed anywhere long and then he came to the end of that road where a series of tents had been set up and he had hope.

Where would the monsters go to hide themselves in plain sight? Where would some of them go that didn't want to hide in the sewers or the abandoned farmlands? A carnival would be the perfect place for those who could never blend in with the rest of the world. Kaleb followed the dirt road to the entrance of the tent land, but as he moved closer, his alarms went up. He had been to a few carnivals, back in the days when his family had still been a family. In the life before his dad had snapped and decided he could no longer live in a world that offered him nothing and wanted to take his wife and kids, there had been days of happiness with them at the fall fairs and summer carnivals. The big tents full of mysteries and the unstable rides full of danger as his stomach tried to hold back the sugar and grease he had eaten were his first called memories. And although there were plenty of large, circuslike tents around, maybe fifteen in all, he couldn't see any rides towering above them. The place was lit up like a circus or carnival, glowed harshly in the dark of the night, but the air was quiet. No cheers. No ringing of games being won.

It was as though the place were a ghost town just as Midian had been.

Kaleb stood only a few feet away from the entrance and saw movement to his right. He turned his head and there stood a pale, decayed man who held a dog and shook his head at him. The ghostly figure looked at the tents, then at Kaleb, and continued the same head movements.

"What is it?" Kaleb asked, but the figure didn't speak. The small dog yipped at him, but the man stayed silent. "I have to go in. They are calling me. Don't you hear them?"

The man looked sad and bowed his head, and Kaleb saw that part of it had crumbled away and as his head tilted forward, sand poured out from the hole. The rest of his body turned to dust, piled on the ground, and blew away in the wind as the others called him from beyond the gates. He hesitated for a moment, wondered what it could have been that he was being warned against. In all the years since he had first been given the gift to communicate with the dead, none of them had ever seemed too afraid nor did they issue any sort of warning. Most of the dead only asked for help, and never offered anything in return.

Then, voices from inside the tents, those that belonged to the ones that led him to the carnival, called to him.

"They are inside. Help them. Save the Nightbreed in there. Take them to Cabal so that they may go find Baphomet."

Kaleb waited to see if the other one would appear, and when he didn't, there was nothing to stop him from going forward.

He passed the main gates and quickly learned that it was no real carnival. The lack of rides and games, the missing food and fair gave it away. What he did see were signs in front of each of the tents, ones that cried out CONFESSIONS, BAPTISMS, GOSPEL, and more. He walked through the city of tall tents, and found it wasn't a home for amusement, but a place of worship and fear: a church revival. There were no barkers at the openings, no fast-talking men to try to sway and woo people to enter. Instead, one or two solemn men in dark suits stood at each entrance and nodded as people entered.

Kaleb looked at the people who milled about, watched as some entered a tent marked REVELATIONS and wondered if he was in the right place. Why would anyone from Midian come to a place like this? Why would the Nightbreed be in a place of a false god? He thought that it might be best to leave, to turn and just disappear, but he saw something through the crowd that made him stop.

It was a child—a small, tan-skinned girl of six or seven years. She looked at him with dark eyes; her skin decayed the way paint will peel from old wood that has been water-damaged. She whispered the word "Here" and pointed to a tent that read THE DEVIL LIVES! It was then he realized he wasn't just there to find the Breed; he was there to save them from whatever was in the tent.

He took a step forward and the child became undone; her cracked flesh undid itself and faded to nothing. He didn't feel bad for her, as he knew she wasn't real, at least not anymore. Like his other visions of the dead, she had suffered in the past and only lingered in this realm as the scent of a fire will linger long after the flames have been extinguished. Kaleb looked at the two gaunt-faced men who stood at the entrance, gave them a nod, and entered the place where they claimed the devil lived.

The inside of the tent was more expansive and impressive than it had looked from the outside. There were rows of wooden benches that led up to a darkened stage, and on each side of it were two men who looked as though they had recently left jail and donned suits that could barely contain their muscular bodies, and both looked as mean as a rabid dog. They scowled at the crowd as strange organ music played from a source unseen. Kaleb took it all in as he walked down the row of benches and took a seat to wait for whatever show was about to take place.

He didn't have to wait long.

A man in a white suit stepped onto the low stage and the lights came on. He smiled out at them; his face ran wild with deep-set wrinkles, though he couldn't have been older than forty. He had a weathered look: sun-damaged skin, thin, brittle hair that matched his cold blue eyes, and yellowed teeth that were as crooked as a carny's morals.

"Welcome, brothers and sisters," he began. His voice had a slow, drawn-out quality to it and he delivered each word with an air of importance. "This is a celebration and a mourning of our world. We have all come here looking for salvation of some kind. And you will find it if you open yourself to it. Salvation is easy. What is hard, brothers and sisters, what is truly difficult is to see the evil in the world. To look out and see the devil that lives among us and to peer in the mirror and see the devil inside each and every one of us. For indeed, each of you, like myself I admit, have a streak of Lucifer somewhere in the darkest corner of our hearts." There were murmurs in the crowd and Kaleb saw many nod as what he said hit home. "But tonight, in this tent, it is not about the evil in our hearts and mind. It isn't about our addictions to sex, or drink; not about our lies and sins. This is about the very face of the devil that lives in the flesh; Satan's minions; the demon horde that walks, bound in skin and blood. Are you ready to see this, brothers and sisters? Are you ready to see the beast as the beast appears?"

"Yes!"

"Show us!"

"We must see!"

"God will protect us. Show us the devil!"

The volume of the crowd rose as the man onstage smiled and let them get more and more excited. Once they had reached a fever pitch, chanting "Show us" in unison, he held his hand up to calm them slightly.

"Very well, brothers and sisters, God shall see you as you are witness to the true form of evil!"

The stage curtains were pulled aside and onstage behind the man in the white suit were two cages. One held a pale, fat man who licked his lips furiously at the audience and the other cage held a blue-skinned monstrosity with a mouth full of fangs and ivory horns on his head. They both growled and hissed at the audience, reached through the bars as though they had a chance of attack, at which point the stern-faced men on either side of the stage pulled out pipes and struck the bars. The two hissed at them, but backed away, and the audience gasped at the sight. Kaleb didn't; he knew that they weren't demons in the sense that religious people thought. They were the lost children of Midian. The Nightbreed. They were the ones he had come to save.

The man onstage went on with more devil talk, but Kaleb heard none of it. Instead, he began to set a plan in his head of how to free them. He knew that there was no way he would leave without getting them out of those cages. They were his key to finding the rest of the Breed and eventually Baphomet.

As the overacted sermon by a man who was more barker than preacher ended, the audience was allowed to walk up and get a closer look at the devils in their cages. They were warned not to get too close to them, and Kaleb couldn't resist it. He thought he would go to them and let them know that he had been sent by the ghosts of Midian, whisper that he would save them to give them a sense of hope. The ex-cons were close, so he knew he would have to be careful, but at the same time he couldn't shake how terrified they must be, how relieved they would become once they knew that freedom was at hand. On his way up, the little girl appeared again, stood beside him, and walked with him on his slow approach to the stage. He didn't turn and look directly at her, as it could alert others to him, but he wanted to see what she was doing. Then, she spoke in her wispy voice that sounded more like leaves blowing than a human voice.

"You have found them. The big one is Leroy and the one with horns is Lude. Please help them," she said with sadness in her voice. He nodded as subtly as he could.

After nearly thirty minutes he made it to the stage and walked as close as he could to the cages. The two inside seemed annoyed, almost bored by the whole situation. They didn't look up at him as Kaleb checked to make sure the guards' attention wasn't fully on him. Then he whispered to the duo.

"Leroy. Lude," he said, and that got their attention. "The ghosts of Midian have sent me to help you. I'll be back later to help you."

"Oh, you already have helped us," Leroy said with a snicker, and looked over at Lude, the blue devil, who had begun to giggle. Before Kaleb could ask him what he meant, he felt a strong hand grab hold of his arms and turned to see that the stern-faced men who looked like prisoners had hold of him. "They've been waiting for you."

"Oh ladies and gentlemen, seems we will have to cut the festivities short," the man in the white suit said, and approached Kaleb with pure glee on his face. "It seems as though we have an interloper in our midst. Please follow the others out of the tent and I wish you all a safe journey home."

Kaleb struggled and the crowd followed their orders. The man in the white suit stood in front of Kaleb and placed a bone-thin hand on his shoulder. "Calm down, son. It's all going to be fine if you keep your head on straight. We have been waiting for you for some time. Oh my, it has been a long time coming. The Lord shines his smile upon us. Faith said you would come and here you are." The man in white turned to one of the men who wasn't holding Kaleb and told him to go get the others. They did as they were told.

"Does this mean we can have more of those delicious entrails? I'm famished," Leroy said as he stood at the bars and licked his lips.

"If this is what they were looking for, then I'm sure you can."

Kaleb looked at Leroy and Lude as they celebrated inside their cells and was confused. He had been sure the two had been prisoners, believed that he had come to save them from the overzealous religious people who ran the revival, but it appeared he had been wrong. They were part of whatever it was that was going on.

"No hard feelings, kid," Lude said with a shrug.

The man in the white suit brought a chair to the stage and instructed the two men who held Kaleb to sit him down. Despite his brief struggle, he was forced down, and within minutes, a small entourage entered the tent. There were more stern faces followed by a man with a misshapen head who wore the dirty, torn garb of a priest. His eyes were milky and pale; his hair was thin spiderweb-like wisps that floated about his bulbous head. He smiled when his eyes fell on Kaleb, and when he did, he revealed brown, partially rotted teeth.

Behind him was a tall man in a well-tailored suit who moved with grace and the presence of someone important. When Kaleb looked at his face, his heart stopped. His face was covered by a mask, but he knew the man right away.

"Decker," he whispered when he saw old Button Face.

"Ah! I see my reputation precedes me. I'm glad you know who I am, though I do not know you." Decker stepped up on the stage. "What's your name?"

"Kaleb."

"What a fitting name. Do you know what it means?" Kaleb shook his head and Decker was brought a chair as well. He sat down and as he did, Kaleb saw that the front of Decker's shirt was a mess. It was wet with blood, and an odor came off of him like old earth and death. "Kaleb is an old Hebrew name that means 'loyal dog.' Is that what you are? Are you a loyal dog, Kaleb? I would like you to be. You have a gift it seems, one that I would love you to share with us."

"I don't know what you are talking about. What gift?"

"Now, now, young man; there's no need to be coy with us. The Breed here, Leroy Gomm and Devil Lude, have told me about what is going on. The ghosts of Midian, those unnatural monsters that died, have been busy calling out for help. The fat slob there was the one that sent the little girl to you, the one you no doubt saw close to here. She wasn't a real ghost, just a little trick he can pull on some; especially on those with talents such as yours. It appears Boone was given a job to bring the Nightbreed back together, so that their so-called god can live again, but he is not doing such a good job. So the dead have taken it upon themselves to call out to people like you; psychics that can communicate with them. These two demons here used this to call you, or anyone like you, and now here you are."

"You turned your back on your own?" Kaleb asked them with disgust in his voice and neither Leroy nor Lude look ashamed.

"They are taking care of us. We help them, they help us. It's better than what Boone or Narcisse are doing for us right now. What do you expect from us? A growing boy has to eat!" Leroy laughed and rubbed on his ample belly.

"Shut up. Do not speak in front of the master!" the priest hissed at them and the two retreated to the shadows of their cages.

"No need for that, Ashbery," Decker said to the deformed priest. "Yes, Kaleb, they did in a way turn their backs on their kind, but only after they were left to fend for themselves. The cruelties of the world would have killed them if I hadn't come along and offered to assist them in exchange for their help. But that is neither here nor there at the moment. This is about you now. Are you ready to live up to your namesake and become my loyal dog?"

"Why would I help you?" Kaleb growled.

"Why wouldn't you? I'm offering you a spot at my feet as I rise above man and God." Kaleb laughed at that and Decker sat upright, clenched his fist as though he was about to strike. "You think that's funny?"

"How do you plan on rising above God?"

"I will let the Nightbreed reform, use you to help them. Once they have done so, created a new haven, a new Midian, they will call forth Baphomet. And that is when I will strike and kill their god. When I have drained the life from a living god, what will that make me? A killer of gods? A god in my own right? The heavens will fall for me and I will rise up as the new prophet, the new master of earth and heaven."

Decker stood up from his chair and took off his suit jacket. Kaleb watched as he opened his blood-soaked shirt and revealed the horrors underneath. Decker's skin had turned gray since his death, with veins of green rot which snaked across the necrotic flesh. The stomach area had been undone with a knife once and still lay open, wet with blood and hungry insects that swirled in the dark abyss. Decker reached inside the opening; his hands dug deep and made wet, smacking sounds as he probed. Kaleb felt sick as he watched, and it became worse when Decker pulled his hand out. Clenched in his fist was dangling meat. The foul smell of the dripping chunk found Kaleb and he wanted to puke.

"But every master needs his dogs. Every prophet needs his disciples. Every god needs his followers. This, Kaleb, is my body and my blood." Decker took the bloody mess that had come from his spoiled insides and jammed it into Kaleb's mouth. Kaleb choked and gagged on it, but Decker pushed it deeper inside him until he was forced to swallow.

The vile meat slid down his throat, and Kaleb was sure he could feel heat emanate from it, burn his insides as it went down. It didn't slide down as much as it felt as though it had small insect legs that crawled deep into him. He thrashed against the chair and the men that held him until suddenly a sort of peace fell over him; a calmness that seemed like a drug-induced relaxation. He thought that it must be how people on heroin feel.

"There. Isn't that so much better?" Decker asked as he sat back down. "You two can let go of Kaleb, my loyal dog." The men let go and Kaleb sat limp in his chair. He smiled at Decker, blood and saliva drooled down the front of him, and behind Decker, Ashbery laughed and clapped his hands. "Come here, Kaleb, and sit at my feet, where you know you belong."

Kaleb obeyed him and lay down on the stage in front of Decker. He nuzzled his face against his feet and licked the soiled leather shoes of his new master.

"Tomorrow we will find you a nice collar," Decker said, and stroked Kaleb's head. "Something special that will suit you. After that, we will find the rest of the Nightbreed and their god and show the heavens the face of their new lord and savior! Oh how the angels will weep."

CELL OF CURTAINS

Timothy Baker

Ozlet had secluded himself in his box, weeping, since they had hit the road. Beside him on the couch, Manda sighed. No coaxing would bring him out when he was like this, not even to enjoy the semiarctic air whipping around their small room in the back of the bus. The air-conditioning was new and worth every dollar she had saved posing as Mistress Miranda, the Amazing Oracle.

She stretched out along the couch, naked and lithe, her ivory skin glowing in the near dark. Through the parted curtains and the deep-tinted window, she watched the rain-heavy clouds roll and pass; the sound of the tires hissing through the rain made her eyes heavy. The cool air erected her nipples and she half dreamed of a man between her legs, writhing and satisfying her. *Feeding* her. It had been far too long and both hungers were growling. Her fingers combed through her white and sparse pubic hair. She would have gratified herself then and there had the fantasy not popped like a pin-poked balloon at Ozlet's loud, wet-sounding whimper.

Manda wasn't glad for his sadness; quite the contrary. She would give anything to take away his pain, but that wasn't possible. No one could. It was his to bear, even though it was pain stolen, belonging to some other soul now walking the world of day, grateful they no longer carried it, some memory of loss, shame, guilt of act or omission handicapping them from a better life. Ozlet had taken it from them, absorbing the soul-breaking emotion upon himself, at great cost to his body. He was stronger than anyone Manda had ever known.

Still, he wept.

For Manda—who had never cried—it was if he was crying for them both. The two of them had lost much: their friends, their home, their security, their *family*. A cataclysmic attack on their tomb-roofed home had sent them fleeing into the night, their companions scattering to the four winds. Refugees of the fallen Midian she and Ozlet were now, each all the other had left, torn from the cool embrace of family, hiding in plain sight among human freaks. Those who had once ruled the night lived in fear of discovery now even in the cloak of darkness.

Weep for me, dear one, she thought, *and for the children of the moon.*

The bus shook. Its worn shocks could barely hold them up let alone take a shallow pothole. Up front, beyond the curtains that kept them away from the burning light of the sun, someone cursed. It was Serge and he sounded drunk. When he was sober, his accent was light, but drunk he sounded as Russian as Khrushchev.

Come to think of it, he sounds like Khrushchev most of the time.

They hit a hard road bump and the back of the bus lifted and landed with a rattle, sending Manda's open suitcase to the floor. Ozlet's curtained box would have toppled to the floor had Manda not caught it with her foot. In a high-pitched voice, Ozlet cursed too. Manda sighed and sat up, bending over to pick up what few clothes she had, and tossed them into the suitcase.

She said, "Are you all right, my love?"

"Do I sound all right?" said the voice from the box.

Manda arranged her clothes, pressed them down, and closed the suitcase.

"No. Of course not."

A deep sigh from the box. "I'm sorry, my dear. Not a good day."

Manda stretched back out and laid her arm across her forehead. "I understand. I always do."

"Yes. I don't know what I would do without you."

"You would die." It wasn't true, but she said it anyway, not wanting to add to his pain. "As would I without you."

She could survive without him, of course, but the thought of parting never crossed her mind. Lovers since the Great War Between the States, they had never been separated. Ozlet had saved her from a burning stake, coming out of the dark and sending the mob to their knees, wailing and sobbing from unknown emotions. Her hair wilting and naked skin bubbling, she watched him walk through the flames, untouched, tall, lean, and as handsome as Stonewall Jackson. As he cut her bindings, he said, "You need to be more careful." He carried her in his arms through the fire, through the weeping mob, and deep into the forest, where he laid her down and healed her of her wounds with his touch. And later, when he saw her suffering past, he took that too. From then, they loved with the gravity of the earth and the moon.

There was a price to pay for his power and he had been too generous. Now he was a quarter of the man he was then, hiding in his curtained box. Though he was unable to satisfy her needs, she did love him with all of her soulless heart and would never leave him. But she *did* have needs, powerful and compelling.

A flash of lightning outside the window lit the room, making Manda flinch. She stood and moved to the shadow beside the open curtains and sat next to Ozlet's box. She slipped her hand between the slim parting of the box's vermilion drapes. A diminutive, fingerless hand lay in her palm, petting, too small to hold her hand.

"You are so beautiful," Ozlet said.

She closed her eyes and rested her head back.

"I know. Thank you, my love." Cool lips graced her palm. She felt his breath as he spoke.

"We need to get out of here. It's hell."

Manda squeezed his hand, swallowing it up in her fingers.

"But where would we go?"

"Somewhere. Anywhere but this circus."

A small smile passed across her lips. "It's not a circus, my dear. Far from it. It's a traveling freak show."

"It's fucking traveling hell."

"That may be so, but it's a hell where we can belong for a time."

Ozlet made a spitting sound. "They're Naturals, no matter how freakish they make themselves or pretend to be. We just blend in here."

"Precisely."

The roar and the wind from a passing semi made the bus shake and swerve. Even with the noise, Manda could hear socked feet, meant to go unheard, hiss and stop outside the curtains.

"These *freaks*," Ozlet said, "will turn against us too, eventually. Once they realize we aren't like them at all, *real* freaks. *Monsters*. You do realize that?"

Manda pulled her hand from the box and stood, taking her black silk robe from its hook, and slipped it up her arms. She didn't have to look to know there was an eye peeping between the room's curtains.

"That may well be," she said as the roar of the truck faded ahead. She pulled her robe open, pretending to adjust it across her shoulders as the watching eye widened.

She leaned over, closed the window curtain, and said, "Can I help you, Brigid?"

A suck of air beyond the curtains and the eyehole closed.

Manda tied her robe. "Come in, Brigid, I'm decent."

The curtains parted and let in a bit of cloud-filtered sunlight before Brigid filled the gap and passed through, snapping the curtains shut. Manda made a calm yet quick step back from the brief light that hit the floor. The sound of Ozlet's box curtains closing whispered in the dark.

"Sorry. Sorry," Brigid said.

For Manda, the dark was a cloudy day for Naturals, the world alit and bathed in blue-grayness. Brigid looked in her direction, unseeing, one hand holding the curtains shut and the other up as if feeling for something approaching. Dubbed the Girl That Plays with Fire, Brigid was young for a Natural, in her early twenties, but a toddler to Manda and Ozlet's years. She was spotted with mad tattoos about her arms and legs, wearing a plaid miniskirt and too-tight bodice that lifted her smallish breasts to eye-catching domes, and head-shaved and sporting metal piercings around every sense-catching skull hole. A row of black spikes adorned in a line the center of her scalp. She never dressed down, even in their downtime, always in character. Manda knew Brigid felt like a freak, and expressed it on her exterior, but inside she was just a scared little girl Natural. And Manda thought she was beautiful.

"Well? What is it?" said Ozlet.

Manda felt Brigid's nervousness at being caught. "Oh. Uh. Um. Not much. Really. It's just—"

Ozlet huffed. "Damn, little girl. Spit it out."

"Don't mind him," Manda said, "his hiss is worse than his bite. Go on, Brigid."

A nervous giggle and Brigid said, "Oh. Yeah. Sorry Ozlet. It's just that—" She paused, grasping for something to say. "Gosh, it's dark in here. How do you stand it?"

"Excuse my rudeness," Manda said. "I'm, *we're*, so used to it. And I don't know how you run flames across your skin and swallow it. I'm terrified of fire. I would burn to a crisp."

Manda watched her blush in the dark. "Oh. Well. Thanks. It's nothing. Doesn't hurt or nothing. I like it. Kind of a turn-on." Another giggle.

Manda reached into her robe pocket and put on her Jackie O sunglasses then pulled the high hanging chain. The fluorescent light above flickered on.

"Is that better?"

Brigid blinked and stared with girl-crush eyes. In the harsh light, Manda's skin seemed to emit its own. Brigid's eyes fell to the wide opening of Manda's robe and her deep cleavage. Manda pulled the robe only a bit closer and tilted her head, enjoying the sudden lusty taste in the air.

Brigid blinked again, her eyes cutting away only to come back. "It's just—"

"You said that already," Ozlet said.

As if brought out of a dream, Brigid jerked, and looked to the box.

"Right. Um, we'll be at the gig site in about an hour. It's gonna be big. All night heavy metal and all day tomorrow. Separate Souls are headlining then. I *love* Separate Souls. They kick ass. You like them?" She looked to Manda, as if trying to see behind the midnight sunglasses. "A carnival too. Is what Will told me. Another couple of hours and the sun will be down."

The Girl That Plays with Fire looked down at her feet. Her high-heeled boot pivoted on its ball. "So. Like. You can come out and set up. Or hang with me. Or not. You know. Whatever. The first band starts at midnight. We open, of course, at eleven. So like, no hurry or anything." She looked up at Manda with hope in her eyes.

From the box, Ozlet mocked, "Like, *whatever.*"

Manda smiled an honest smile, and Brigid managed a nervous one, seeming to melt on the spot.

"Thank you, Brigid," Manda said. "I didn't know our next event."

Brigid giggled. "Yeah. They're all kind of the same. Right?"

Manda kept her smile and nodded. "Yes." She stepped forward and cupped Brigid's cheek, making her eyes widen and her smile fall away. Brigid's eyes wandered across Manda's pale thick lips and rose to the bottomless black of the sunglasses.

"Again," said Manda, lowering her voice, "thank you." Manda stepped back.

Brigid's cheeks flushed and she only managed an "uh-huh" before she slipped between the curtains and back to the front of the bus and the world of light.

"You're going to get us in trouble," Ozlet said.

Manda killed the light with a tug of the chain and took off her sunglasses. "Don't worry, my love. I won't consume where I defecate," she said, licking the sweet sting of pheromone and sweat from her fingers. Brigid *would* taste so good.

With the falling of the sun, Manda opened a curtain and dropped a window. Even parked behind the dark box of the curtained stage, the roar of the whining gears of spinning rides and their cacophonous music punctuated by some shrieking girl wound its way among the multitude of buses. She breathed deep, taking in the rain-cooled night air. In the east, the clouds had parted and the full moon hung above the horizon, shining like a welcoming friend. She smiled.

She stepped away and parted the two-piece couch, shoving the sections to the side. The heavy blanket that hid the door, she pulled aside.

"You ready?"

Ozlet shifted in his box, making a thump. "I'm always ready to get out of here."

Manda dropped the sheer gypsy veil across her face, and with two hands, she pulled the lever across the stamped EMERGENCY EXIT, and flung the door open. A shadow of a wide-shouldered beast stood before her, its backlit bald head near level with hers. Manda gasped and startled back. Serge's deep staccato laugh filled the compartment.

"Did I scare you?" Serge's Russian accent turned "scare" into "scar."

Her composure back, Manda lifted Ozlet's box to the edge of the door. "What do you want, Serge?" Hidden behind her veil, she eyed him with suspicion and disdain. Serge was nice and protective to the entire troupe—especially Brigid—except her and Ozlet, keeping his distance and whispering to others behind their backs. Manda had felt a touch of hatred and mistrust leak from his walled-off mind. And sometimes, fear. Fear could turn even the best into monsters.

Serge took a step back into the light. Nearing seven feet tall, his already small Speedo looked swallowed by his bulging muscles. Bald and without a single hair on his face, his oiled body glimmered and rippled in the light. His arms were covered in a menagerie of tattoos and his chest was a billboard for a large-typefaced STRONGMAN. Below that, great brass rings pierced his nipples.

"Oh, no need to feel scare for Sergy. I may be *Strongest Man in World* but I am gentle as puppy dog. I am good guy. I am only here to assist you with your little man." He slapped the top of Ozlet's box a little too hard. "You okay in there, little Ozlet?"

"Hey," cried Ozlet, "watch the ape hands there. You about deafened me."

Manda set her hands flat on the box, holding it in place. "You never help us, Serge. What is it you want?"

Serge smiled without kindness. Brigid bounced out from behind his broad torso and waved.

"Sorry! It was me. I talked him into it. I just hate seeing you lug that b . . . I mean, *carry* Ozlet around all the time."

Manda moved around the box, her skirt rising up as she made the long step to the ground. Both Brigid and Serge eyed the long perfect lines of her pale legs before her skirt fell to her feet.

"We have done well this far," Manda said, turning her back to them and reaching for Ozlet's box. "And we will continue to do so."

Brigid slapped Serge's arm and he stepped forward, brushing Manda aside. He lifted the box as if it were empty cardboard and set it down with a *thud*. Ozlet made a muffled curse. Serge patted the box as if it were a tender kitten.

"Sorry little man."

"Yeah, right. Why don't you keep your stinking paws off me, you damn dirty ape."

Serge laughed too loud. "That is from movie *Planet of Apes.* Very clever." Serge's face fell to a grim menace. "For so small a man you have funny stinging mouth."

A high-pitched chuckle came from inside the box and the curtains barely parted. "Please disregard the warning on the side of the box, Serge. Let's touch and let me get to know you."

An uncertain smile passed across Serge's lips, and he glanced at Brigid then looked into the darkness of Manda's veil. He grunted and waved a dismissive hand.

"Enough," Manda said, and pulled a lever at the back of the box. It lifted on four worn rubber wheels. Her faceless veil turned to Serge and he stepped back, letting her roll the box forward and close the exit door.

"Thank you, Serge. I'm sure you've done quite enough for now." She turned to Brigid, who stood frozen in her faceless sight. "What way to our tent?"

"Oh yeah, let me show you." They left the scowling Serge behind as Brigid led them down the side of the bus, its side painted in broad carny colors declaring WILD WILL'S FANTASTICAL FREAKS, and into the maze of buses and trailers.

Even through the multilayers of hanging blankets in the tent, the thundering guitars and drums pounded into her sacred place. They had listened to the cheers from the outdoor venue as Wild Will, Master of Freaks, introduced the show's acts one after another, then the *oohs* and *aahs* and shocked moans as they performed: Serge the Strongman; Billy Blockhead; the Illustrated Hootchie; Black Saber, Man of Knives; Snake Girl and the Hypnotic Haboob; Dom, Whip Master; Chainsaw Cherri; Rubber Woman; Deep Throat; and the Girl That Plays with Fire. While they performed, Amanda performed too, without enthusiasm, reading the mundane pasts and sorry futures of the giggling, stoned young and debauched. When the music started, the customers ended.

Manda sat at her round, velvet-covered table staring into the glass orb at the table's center, idly shuffling her tarot cards. The single, handkerchief-covered lightbulb overhead spotted the crystal ball and splashed muted colors on the curtain walls. The smoke of incense layered flat above the bulb, turning in psychedelic swirls. She reached beneath her veil and scratched her nose. The emptiness she felt was not in her stomach, but in her loins and blood.

"I'm hungry," she said.

From behind her, Ozlet's box (its side stenciled WARNING: DO NOT INSERT

HAND BEYOND CURTAIN) sat on a shadowed table. Ozlet said, "Me, too. I can smell those deep-fried Twinkies from a mile away. Driving me crazy."

"That's not what I mean."

"Breathe, my love. It will pass. And remember the law of Midian."

She moved to turn to him, to chastise him for holding on to the past, and that burned dream. But she stopped, and laid the cards on the table.

"Midian fell and the law with it. I am free to do as I please now." She laughed without humor. *"Free."*

Ozlet let out a long sigh. "I've noticed."

From the distant stage, a power chord thundered and a demon-voiced singer screamed.

The entrance curtains moved, and in slipped the Girl That Plays with Fire.

"Busy?" She stepped in, hands held demurely behind her back. The hanging smoke parted and banked down in curls. She still wore her act costume: spiked high heels, torn and singed fishnet stockings barely held by frayed garters, silk panties that dipped far below her bared belly, and the nearly sheer red and black bra that lifted her breasts to a faux cleavage. The front of her panties held a grinning, flaming skull.

Manda smiled behind her veil and slipped her hands beneath the table to slide up and down her thighs as her legs parted ever so slightly.

"Not at all, my dear. How did your performance go? Amaze everyone with your fiery delights?"

Brigid giggled and Ozlet audibly sighed.

"Yeah, they loved me. I kind of pushed it tonight. Left the fire on a little too long in spots." She lifted a corner of the handkerchief to light her. She slid a pointed finger across her breasts and belly, tracing the bright red paths that marked the dragging fire.

Another fire lit between Manda's legs. Blood rushed and cried out in her veins. She leaned closer.

"Oh, my. Doesn't it hurt?"

"Hell no. Feels good, really. But I did kind of go too far here." She lifted each leg in turn, showing the deep red glow where fire met the skin of her inner thighs. Brigid rubbed at the minor burn as if she were putting out a flame.

"Crazy, huh?"

Dare I? She is so strange and beautiful and so willing . . .

"Indeed." Manda almost moaned. "But there's nothing wrong with pushing boundaries. Am I right?"

Brigid dropped her leg and dragged the tip of her finger across the smooth table cover. She grinned.

"'Pushing boundaries' is my mantra."

A sound of disgust came from Ozlet's box. "That's not a mantra. That's more of a philosophy. Not a healthy one at that." Ozlet's warning did not pass Manda by.

Manda lifted a dismissive hand. "Pay no attention to the man behind the curtain." She stood and moved to pull the opposite chair around the table.

"You know, I have never read you in all the time we've known each other. Would you like that, Brigid?"

Brigid smiled and clapped her hands and sat right down.

"Please, please."

Manda sat and reached out, clasping Brigid's hands in hers.

Brigid said, "Don't you need your cards?"

"Oh, no. That's just for the rubes. You get the real thing."

The girl's eyes went wide and she gripped Manda's long fingers. "Oh, wow."

Manda slipped forward in her chair, letting their knees touch. Brigid sighed.

"Quiet now," Manda said, her voice lowering. "Breathe easy and relax."

Manda closed her eyes and the images came rushing in. She spoke softly, careful not to react, telling Brigid of her torn past: the drunken father, the brutality of her mother's beatings at his hand, the dark shadow that entered her bedroom night after night, his wandering hands across her body and the pain as he lay atop her and entered her again and again, moaning and sweating; her mother turning away in silence, silent until he abandoned them, and silent still. Her high-school Goth years and the gang rape at a drug-fueled party as she lay incoherent and helpless. The cutting. The drugs. The burning of the school. The attempted suicide. Her running away and life on the streets. All laid out in Manda's dispassionate voice. Only when she heard Brigid's sobs did she break away, letting the brutal imagery fall away.

Manda pulled closer and cupped the girl's tear-strewn face. Tears streamed between her fingers and down the back of her hands.

"Oh, my dear girl. Such a sad life. So brutal and unjust. You are so strong . . . and tender."

Brigid gripped Manda's arms, and looked into the veil, searching for Manda's eyes.

"I'm sorry," Brigid sobbed, "so sorry. I didn't mean to break down like this. Let you see me like this."

Manda petted her cheek. "No, no, no. It's okay. You must cry. To let it all go and flow away with your tears. It will all be okay. I not only tell the past, but the future, too."

Her head tilting down, Manda took a hand away from Brigid's cheek and started to lift her veil. Far away a great calamity of thudding music and howling vocals rose with the cheers of the crowd.

Ozlet's voice went unheard. "Manda. Don't."

Brigid's eyes cleared and she stared into Manda's eyes. "What? Am I going to be okay? Am I going to die? What?"

Manda swept the veil over her head, revealing her quivering red-lipped smile. "No death for you, just bliss."

Brigid moaned in and out in a rush of breath as she stared into the mirrored pupils of one of the Nightbreed. Manda leaned in and pressed her lips to the girl's, sucking at her breath. As Brigid went near limp, her arms wrapped around Manda's neck as if she was drowning and feared sinking. With a quick sweep of her arms, Manda pulled her to the floor, pressing her body, parting Brigid's legs with her knee, her hand passing across breasts and belly and diving beneath the flaming skull. With mouth wide, Manda sucked in the eternal, life-animating force of the living. Her fingers massaged and dived between Brigid's legs, making the life force expand uncontrollably into her mouth and lungs, feeling it flow and burn into her cells, making Manda squirm and sending her to near orgasm.

They rolled on the floor and moaned.

"What the hell are you doing?" Serge stood above them, yelling above the musical din. He kicked Manda hard in her ribs, sending her sprawling and gasping to her back. Brigid moved as if drugged, trying to lift her head, eyes rolling into her head. Her skin was sickly pale and her lips blue. She gasped.

"No, no. Don't stop. Don't—"

With one hand, Serge threw the table aside with a splintering crash. The glass globe flew and slammed into Ozlet's box, toppling it to the floor.

Manda pressed a hand against her ribs and sat up, screaming. She turned her mirrored eyes to Serge and hissed. He took a shocked step back.

Grinning wide, Manda slung her hair back, pulled up her skirt, and spread her legs. She was too far gone and her hunger burned as a fire that needed quenching. Serge's eyes fell to her parted cunt and her glistening wetness.

"Come, *strong man*," Manda said, her voice turning velvet. "Take what you've wanted since you laid eyes on me. Come feed your lust. Come and *fuck* me."

Serge blinked and he staggered on weakening legs. "Yes," he whispered. Then his voice rose. "Serge will give you pride of Soviet Russia." He ripped his Speedo away and let the rising pride of Soviet Russia swing free.

Brigid rolled to her hands and knees, gasping for breath, and crawled to the back exit. She pulled at the curtains, found her feet, and stumbled through the opening between them.

Serge leapt between Manda's legs and she fell back, laughing and moaning, hands gripping at his back as he thrust into her like an invading soldier. Manda clutched his hairless head with both hands and pulled his lips to her wide-open mouth. She fed and her fingers lengthened across his skull, digging into skin and bringing blood.

Manda broke away from his lips and threw her head back. She arched her back, wrapping her legs around him, engulfed in orgasm. A lift of his head, and Serge shook and moaned in one final hammer thrust. Manda laughed, feeling his useless earthly essence spill into her.

Serge looked down at her, blinking and dreamy-eyed. His face had paled and tremors shook his body. Sweat dripped from his chin.

"You . . . you . . . are witch." He lifted his arm high, and clutched his hand into a massive fist. It came down like a hammer and smashed into Manda's cheek, making her head snap. Her legs fell from his waist and she went limp. He cocked his arm back for another blow.

"Serge will kill you."

"I think not," said a high-pitched voice.

Serge looked up. Crawling from the darkness, a contorted horror, hardly bigger than his pillow, grinned with twisted teeth, and bulging eyes. It was naked, skin loose and dragging as it flopped closer on a flipperlike arm. Drool dripped, escaping its darting tongue.

Serge tried to scream and move back, but an arm flung out from the thing, tipped with a crablike pincer, and caught his shoulder in a viselike grip. Serge the Strongman convulsed and rolled over to his back as the pincer pierced his shoulder. His skin turned gray and wrinkled as muscle deflated toward his deep bones.

"Hadn't you heard? Soviet Russia died long ago," Ozlet said.

The cool night-dewed grass felt good to his bare feet. It had been too long, too many deformed years had passed since he had run the night, bathed in the light of the lovely moon. Ozlet grinned into the moon's full face as he wept and ran naked across the open field toward the cloak of wooded darkness ahead.

He did not weep from the tortured memories from Serge; they were soldier's memories, violent and rage-filled. He had taken plenty of those onto himself, had even been one long ago. He packed those away like so many faded pictures in a trunk. No, he wept for joy at his transformation and the first burgeoning of hope since the fall of Midian. Full-bodied now, tall and lean as in his youth, he reveled in the power and length of his legs, the return of his arms and hands, and the strength to carry his love, his Manda, in his arms.

She stirred and her eyes opened to his moonlit face. Her confusion disappeared as realization dawned.

"Ozlet?"

He smiled. "Hello there."

She touched his face. Gone were the deformities. She wiped away his tears, then ran her hand across his bald head and returned his smile. "Ozlet."

"That's me."

Her confusion returned. "Serge?"

"A husk."

Manda bit her lip. "I'm sorry. It's all my fault."

Ozlet shrugged. "You are what you are. I can love you no less."

"Where are we going?"

"Oh, hell, I don't know. We run. We hide. Thus is our life."

"They will chase us."

"I'm sure of that. Didn't leave a pretty picture back there."

Manda laid her hand on his chest, feeling his muscles and the rise and fall of his breath. She smiled in amazement.

"Let's go far away," she said.

"We will, my love. But one thing is for sure."

"What's that?"

"I'll be carrying *you* from now on."

She wrapped her arms around his neck, and laid her head on his chest.

"I hope your hair grows fast," Manda said, smiling. "I hate bald men."

Their laughter ran across the grass and rose to the moon as they passed into the shadows of the trees.

TAMARA

Paul J. Salamoff

I am still haunted by the events that transpired at Midian.

It was never my intention to kill, but that is what I have done.

Baphomet help my soul.

When Boone arrived, it felt like a liberating time for the tribe of the moon. Even though there was immediate dissension in the ranks, he brought a newfound sense of hope. I could see it in Lylesburg's eyes. The way he looked at the young man. Was this the fruition of our age-old dream?

But our hopes were dashed when the world encroached into our sanctuary and our home was laid to waste in a pile of ash and rubble. Many of my brothers and sisters died that day, but I survived.

But at what cost?

I can still feel his warm blood on my body, a scarlet stain that won't scrub off no matter how often I wash or how hard I scour. My clawed hands thrust up inside his bowels. The gaping wound that I made led to an effortless evisceration. There was so much blood. It splashed against my naked form, coating my breasts, spikes, and stomach . . . warm crimson dripping down the cleft between my thighs.

I understood for a moment what Peloquin must have felt during his nightly hunts—the raw animalistic thrill of the slaughter. Face-to-face with my prey, witnessing as the light and life drained from his mortal soul. But that sensation was fleeting; a momentary thrill.

As my senses returned, what I was left with was the corpse of a man crushing me with almost two hundred pounds of dead weight. I am so small, so easily frightened. My lithe form is fragile. But Baphomet blessed me with talons and barbed protrusions to protect my physical self. These however do nothing to protect my soul. Even in self-defense, I cannot remedy my actions.

I am not a killer.

I was not a killer.

For the moment, I was safe. The fighting was long over, having ended in the early hours of the new day. As far as I could tell I was now alone in Midian. Left for dead underneath the carcass of a deceased man.

Using the cave wall for support, I used all my strength to heave the corpse off of me. He toppled over onto the harsh ground, eyes staring up through the blasted-out opening above us. Smoke still wafted on the surface, blotting out the morning sun and protecting me from its harm.

Wiping my bloodied hands on the man's clothing, I got my first real look at him. He seemed considerably younger than I thought. My first impression of him was that of a vicious old bear as he charged out of the darkness with a rifle leveled directly at me. Being petite makes me fast and I easily avoided the first shot as it whizzed by my torso.

He was moving at such a hasty speed in unfamiliar and uneven ground that he tripped himself up on a large rock and stumbled into me. The rifle was knocked from his grasp when we both hit the ground. It still lay where it fell.

Panicked even more so than I was, the large man punched and hit me. He was as desperate to kill me as I was desperate to live. I didn't know I had done it until it was too late. Human flesh is so delicate. It tears so easily. So much blood.

I cannot accept that I am forever damned. If Baphomet's teachings are true, then there is a way to make amends. A way to make peace with my heinous actions.

I studied his lifeless body. He was like Boone in many ways. Handsome and physically fit. Though he was dressed for killing, for the hunt. Curious to know the name of the man whose life I had taken, I rifled his pockets and found a handmade snakeskin wallet.

Flipping it open, I discovered his driver's license. I read through the words on it. Lylesburg taught me man's language and I had become quite adept at reading and comprehending it—so good that I would in turn teach the young Breed of Midian both English and our native tongue and read them stories found in books scavenged from the outside world.

Daniel Morrell was his name. Such an amiable name for a man filled with such rage and bigotry. He looked almost angelic in his picture. There was no hair on his face like there was now and he even wore a thin smile, a stark contrast to the angry scowl that came at me from the darkness.

There were some pictures among his credit cards. I wish I had not bothered to look. Then I wouldn't have seen their faces. A loving wife. A beaming son. So young. Too young to be without a father. But he would be without one—my talons still caked with his father's blood had seen to that.

I could make this right. I could ease the pain and ease the burden on my soul as well. Baphomet has blessed me with other gifts, gifts that made me unique among the tribe of the moon.

I was blessed with the *Becoming*. I discovered it at a very young age.

To know someone is to become them.

But the knowing was to devour their flesh, to consume them into my body so that I might join with them and become them.

Peloquin valued this about me, that's why he tolerated my pacifist chidings and reproaches against him and his hunts. He would on occasion bring me gifts fresh from the hunt, usually the heart of an animal, sometimes of a human, which I would devour like candy. I was young then and didn't fully understand the implications of the pieces of flesh that I simply regarded as nourishment.

He was very prideful and took great pleasure in imparting all the details of his hunts down to the most specific minutiae to the tribe. His stories were self-indulgent and boastful, and with my help, he could reenact the events of the evening as a bizarre Grand Guignol pantomime, with him as the noble hunter and me as his deserving prey.

You see, this gift allows me to transform my body, to change my appearance and become those that I *know*.

There's an address on the driver's license. Lylesburg kept maps in the library. Hopefully they have not all burned.

Just a taste is all I need. A small snack to aid me in my journey.

Covered in layers of heavy garments that provided shelter from the sun, the prolonged journey to Shere Neck was arduous. I kept mostly to the heavily wooded area, but the sun continued to beat down on me like a taskmaster's whip. The most demanding part of the journey was escaping the ruins of my home. Many came to put out Midian's fires and deal with the scores of corpses. Most were to be buried by grieving families. The others were to be marveled over, dissected and studied on metal slabs.

Who will mourn for them?

I got to the farmhouse on Crandall Road just before midday. I found safety and shelter in a barn among the animals that I felt more kinship to than the ones that kept them. From the hayloft, I had a good view of the comings and goings at the front of the house.

I was there when Daniel's wife was given the news about her husband. It ate into my core to watch her falter and slump against the lawman who delivered the tragic news. She was an attractive woman, even when her face was distorted by agony and despair. Her name was Anna. It suited her.

Eventually the man departed, as I'm sure he had more dire news to deliver to other families in the county. Anna stayed on the porch. She looked as though her life had vacated her body. A corpse cursed with the inevitability of having to go on living.

I watched her for almost an hour. Unmoving, she had no more tears left in her body to shed. *I truly am a monster.*

As the golden hour approached, a school bus pulled to a stop at the end of the long road and her beaming child exploded from the open doors. He looked to be no more than five years old. Running with the wild abandon of the young, he had no idea what grim news awaited his return.

My heart raced as I prepared myself. I felt it might burst at this very moment. It would have been a fitting demise for my crime, but I was spared the scene as Anna embraced her son with such fervor and then carried him in her arms into the house.

I hated myself for the feeling of relief that washed over me. I didn't deserve to be spared this, but thank Baphomet I was.

Lying down in the hay, I allowed myself to sleep. The events of the last twenty-four hours started to take their toll and my body, though strong, needed to rest.

It was many hours later when I awoke. I could tell by the placement of the moon that it was around ten p.m. Almost a full day since the siege and destruction of Midian. Its loss and the loss of my brothers and sisters were not real to me yet. My dreams saw fit to confuse me . . . trick me into thinking that reality was the dream.

While I slept, my brain concocted fantasies of a thriving necropolis where the forgotten and unwanted lived in peace. So many happy nights secluded and sequestered from the outside world. Those thoughts stayed with me as I woke and clouded my mind with erroneous hope.

It was the texture and smell of the hay bed that I slept on that brought me swiftly back to cruel reality. I openly wept. Not for myself, but for the others. The survivors. How scared they must be. *Where are they now? Did Lylesburg save any souls and lead them to safety? I wonder if I shall ever see a familiar face again.*

Looking out at the farmhouse, I saw that all the lights, save the ones on the porch, were off for the night. The house appeared still. The only sound was the grunting and clucks of the animals I shared the barn with and the insect life that sang their night songs.

Their melody soothed me as I initiated my *Becoming.*

It's a slow process, but there is no pain, just the ebb and flow of muscle and organs and the reshaping of my bones and cartilage. It always starts the same, with a tingle that surges through my body eliciting an orgasmic sensation. But after that, the physical alteration is always a new and unique experience. The process is never the same, especially when the *known* is human and in this case, a male.

This time my barbs were the first to go. Softening, they melted and stretched to accommodate the extra skin. My breasts recessed, as they too were absorbed into me.

My talons retracted as my hands traveled to my vulva still tingling from the initial surge. I gently caressed it as the delicate flesh moved beneath my hand, re-forming and extruding. I grasped the protrusion in my palm and coaxed the process along. It felt good and took me away from my cares for that brief moment.

As my hands moved up to my chest, I felt the mass of matted hair soaked from my sweat. I always liked the feel of hair and it brought back happy memories of when I used to embrace Raven at night as a small child. She was coated with the softest fur and it kept me warm during the winter nights in the bowels of Midian.

A few moments later and the *Becoming* was complete.

I'm always a bit shaky for the first few moments when it's finished, so I took my time getting up from the hay.

Once on my new feet, I surveyed my latest form. I felt dense and heavy. My body was stiff with skin stretched tight over muscles. As I touched my re-formed face, I could only imagine that it was a perfect match for Daniel's. There were no mirrors in the barn but I've never had a change fail and would be surprised if this one wasn't as flawless as the ones before.

I have read many of Lylesburg's books about the human body and about the genetic codes that dictate their forms. I may have what the humans call a supernatural ability, but science is science and the genetics of my body are anything but fantasy.

The moon and stars provided all the light I needed as I made my way down from the loft and out into the field that separated it from the house. I followed the dirt road that led directly to the front door.

———

I watched her as she slept. Anna. She was lovelier in person than her photograph did justice. Even though blindsided by tragedy, she slept serenely. As I inched closer, I discovered the origin of her peaceful slumber. A bottle of sleeping pills lay by her bedside. Still quite full, she had presumably taken only a dose to allow her to stave away the cruel news and allow her body to attain the strength it would need for the coming days.

I gently sat on the edge of the bed. The side once occupied by her husband. I made no sound, but the pressure on the mattress was enough to stir her from her drugged slumber. I froze in place as not to frighten her.

Her eyes fluttered open. Confusion on her face. Her bewildered brain further clouded by the sedatives. Neither of us spoke for what seemed to be several minutes. I could sense her brain processing the vision seated at the foot of her bed. Trying to work out the nonsensical nature of it all. A *waking dream?* Possibly. For reality held no rational explanation.

I then broke the silence.

"Anna," I said as sweetly as a summer breeze. It's always strange to hear my new voice for the first time and this one was particularly low and masculine.

Her brow furrowed at the utterance of her name. She stared intensely at me. Studying me. Gathering data. She then did something quite extraordinary. Shaking her head, she lay back on her pillow and attempted to fall back asleep. Within a few moments, her breathing slowed and she was once again in blissful slumber.

It was enough for the first night. I rose from the bed and exited the room. As I made my way to the front, I poked my head into the room down the hall. The sweet young boy slept like an angel.

I spent most of the next day in the barn with the animals. I remained in my new form, having already grown accustomed to it. I found out at a young age that I could stay in any outward appearance that I had *known* for extended lengths of time or indefinitely if I chose to. Once I had *known* the flesh of another, their body became one with mine and I could access them and *become* them as easily as one would change their clothes.

However, I rarely stayed in an alternate shape for long periods, as I was constantly in fear of somehow losing my own identity. But that was purely a product of my own insecurities. I am who I am and have always been able to find my way home no matter who I become or how long I keep up the façade.

I liked masquerading as Daniel. There was a certain thrill being this gender and size. He had a physical strength that I had forgotten I could wield even in my true form. I had become so beaten down by my life recently and allowed myself to become subservient to the tribe. It was entirely my own doing and I did not hold any of the Breed accountable for my lack of self-esteem or self-reliance. Maybe this time away from Midian and my own body would have a much-needed transformative effect on me. I suddenly felt a sense of renewal and hope that had escaped me for so long and I couldn't wait for the day to wind down to be able to share that with Anna.

I lay down to watch the outside activities from my hiding space. The hay was rough against my naked skin, but it reminded me how alive I was. I felt good and this feeling was physically manifested by my engorged and erect cock. I held the flesh shaft in my hands to feel its strength but I had no intention of bringing myself to orgasm, as I wanted to save that for her.

Every now and then there would be some goings-on outside. Friends and family stopped by to offer condolences and bring food. The Shere Neck mortician stopped by to make funeral arrangements, which took far less time than I would have imagined.

I was hoping to hear any shred of news about my exiled brothers and sisters, but none was forthcoming. Apparently they had disappeared into the night never to be heard from again. This did give me some comfort, knowing that they were still out there somewhere. I promised myself that as soon as I was finished here, as soon as I had made amends, then I would scour the land to find them. There were always whispers of the Nightbreed on the lips of those misplaced and abandoned by the world, so there was always a chance to be reunited.

As the day wound down my excitement grew for my nocturnal visit.

The minutes felt like hours as I impatiently waited for the lights to go out in the far rooms, signaling that Anna had tucked her son into bed and then turned in for the evening herself. I then waited another hour just to be sure, before I emerged from my hiding spot and exited the barn.

I must have smelled awful, having not bathed for over two days. I could even catch whiffs of the coppery blood smell that still clung to this transmogrified form. Fortunately there was a small creek nearby. I went there first to clean myself, letting the icy cold water cascade over me. It felt good. Revitalizing. I was wide awake for the first time in years.

The frigid wetness clung to me as I journeyed back to the house. It helped to slow my heart, which was racing with anticipation. I entered through the front door and made a beeline to Anna's room. I had no immediate plan, as I was going to let the night and Baphomet's will determine the course of my penitence.

In my haste, I swung open the door without giving forethought to anything other than to my own needs and desires. Fortunately Anna did not scream when she saw me standing in the doorway.

She was not asleep. She wasn't even in her bed. Anna sat in a chair by the window looking out into the night. A lit cigarette was gripped tightly between her fingers, but now threatened to slip from them as her mind went slack.

What must have been going through her head, I can only imagine. There before her, the naked form of her now two-days-deceased husband stood glistening in the light from the moon.

My first instinct was to run. But my feet held fast, frozen to the floor by a force far more powerful than Earth's gravity. This remarkable woman stood up from her seat. Stubbing out her cigarette in an ashtray on the windowsill, she walked toward me. No trace of fear.

"I thought I dreamed of you last night," she said. "Those pills can do that."

I stayed still, almost hypnotized by her calm. The moonlight shone through her nightgown, silhouetting her body with white light. She was naked underneath and I could feel my penis bolster.

"It is you, Daniel?" she asked. "You've come back to me."

She was mere feet from me. Reaching out, she touched my chest. My skin shuddered. Her hand moved to my face. Caressed it. "Say my name," she insisted. "Like you did last night."

"Anna."

Her hand found mine and guided it between her legs. "Say it again."

I obeyed.

She lay down on the bed and opened herself up to me. "I miss you."

I entered her. The sensation was indescribable. My cock was engulfed by a warmth that I have never known. Her hands grappled around me and pulled me deeper inside. There was an animalistic need in her that I struggled to match—a wildness to our lovemaking that would impress my kind. I never knew that the humans possessed this much passion . . . this I thought exclusive to Nightbreed couplings.

When we were finished, my body was beleaguered and drenched with sweat. I lay beside her as we both stared up at the ceiling. It was as if this moment would cease to be real if we looked at one another.

"I can't stay," I said.

"I know" was her unemotional response.

"Will I see you again?" she asked.

"If you'd like. But only at night. Only for a few hours."

I rose from the bed and headed for the door.

"Don't let Tommy see you," she requested. "He's having a hard time."

"He's a strong boy. Like his mother." I don't know why I said this. It seemed like the right thing to say to be comforting. I know I would have liked those words, had it been me on the bed. "Try and get some sleep."

I couldn't bear to look back at her as I left for the evening.

That night I transformed into a wolf and roamed the woods. The freedom I felt was exhilarating.

———————

It went on like this for the remainder of the week, almost becoming routine. I would bathe in the creek and then join Anna in her room to quench our passions.

She never questioned my identity nor asked for any explanation. My nightly visits were just accepted as a gift to a grieving widow. Over the course of these extraordinary evenings, I watched her come back to life and I, in turn, benefited from this most unusual penitence. I believed that I was making this right.

But when would this end? I must have attained my salvation by now. But then why did I find it a near impossibility to stop?

Every night I promised myself that this would be the last, yet when the sun set on the following evening, I found myself once again drawn to her bed. This woman truly cherished me. I could see it in her eyes as we made love. I had never felt desired like this before. I had been so lonely for so many years and now I wasn't anymore. I felt safe in her embrace and it was a sensation I was in no rush to abandon.

My selfishness stabbed at me like a dagger. Death by a thousand cuts. But it was a pain I could endure, because the few hours of bliss healed the wounds and made me whole again.

But we are the instruments of our own destruction.

I should have left. Apparently I am more human than I would like to admit. I sinned again and this was the sin of complacency. Baphomet abhors self-righteous satisfaction and for my crime of contentment I was to be punished.

I had grown too comfortable. Too safe. Every night it took me longer and longer to leave Anna's bed. This last night was especially passionate and I was so aggressive with my lovemaking that when I came, I expelled every last ounce of my energy. I was blissfully empty, body and soul. As I rolled onto my side of the bed, sleep came fast, too fast to stave off.

Before I knew it, I was back in Midian. Happy times as a child. Playing. Racing through the underground labyrinth. Days of wild abandon.

I remembered finding his room for the first time.

I had been told to never enter, but I was a foolish child.

His eyes were all I could remember. An infinite maelstrom of blackness and light. As if the universe itself dwelled within Baphomet's eye sockets.

Then there was his voice. It pounded its way into my head, each syllable a mallet strike. He imparted warnings. Admonitions to a foolish child. A sense of dread and foreboding cascaded through my core. Urine seeped down my leg as my bladder went slack.

My god cautioned that he is and will always be with me and that his laws are as severe and unyielding as the stones that mark the dead in the necropolis.

As these reminiscences swirled within my psyche, causing fitful unrest, I felt an unkind sensation, as if my body was no longer in my control. As if Baphomet's hands were re-forming me. Clay in his hands.

The next thing I heard was screaming.

It wasn't my voice . . . any of them.

My eyes snapped open. Anna was off the bed. Her face was a rictus of horror and dread. Confused, I reached out to her. Cruelly, the answer to her terror revealed itself. My scaled hands, spiked and taloned, stretched out before me. I immediately inspected the rest of my body as true despair washed over me.

Tears welled up in my eyes. A *fitting punishment.*

There was no point trying to explain to Anna. She would never understand. She needed to stop screaming. *Baphomet forbid she wake up Tommy.*

———————

I closed all the shades before the sun rose. I'd be safe for now. After I dressed, I headed to Tommy's room and woke him. He was groggy and needed some coaxing to get out of bed.

After breakfast I sent him off to school with a kiss. I looked forward to his return.

But there was work to do. A lot of blood to clean. A body to dispose of. And the weekend was coming soon. A perfect time for a boy and his mother to head out on a long journey together.

There's so much to tell him.

RAPHAEL'S SHROUD

Karl Alexander

The night wind had set me down atop yellow pollen on the pines at Twin Lakes, left me unhappy and afraid. I couldn't move without the wind, and the fucking sunrise already lit the top of the Sierras, changing me from all but invisible to iridescent. I find this annoying and wonder if it's the end for me or the beginning?

From the cabin below, I heard the black cat yowling. He was big and strong with a blaze of amber eyes, had a tail long ago broken at the end, but it was the utter despair of his yowl that got to me. I am a pushover for despair, having lived with it since the baptismal fires at Midian cremated me into a translucent rectangle of ash—a helpless shroud, yet a shroud filled with brain and purpose. *Don't disintegrate. Find a place for us.*

So when the breeze picked up, I floated from the tree to the cat and insinuated myself into him as a guardian angel. His name was Leroy.

He was a mess. His owner, Gale Jordan, a trust-fund TV actress, had gone camping for a long weekend with her new boyfriend, Brian King, who had just moved into the garage apartment at the cozy Malibou Lake house her parents had bought for her three years ago.

She had insisted that the cat come along on the trip. Given her career choice, the cat was the most important and stable person in her life. Indeed, Leroy was a person to her, not an animal, someone to come home to after a failed audition or a day with an abusive director. Besides, she was certain that—like her—Leroy had never been camping before. He'd be the perfect bridge between herself and this new guy, but if she spent the whole time with Brian, like, hey, they had plenty of chipmunks and birds at Twin Lakes. The cat would not go wanting into this long weekend.

She didn't know that Brian resented the cat. He also resented Gale's ex-lovers, her wealthy parents, their suspicion of him because he was black, bald, and buff—or so he assumed. I mean, he wore a pricey suit to work at the Gersh Agency in Beverly Hills and carried a fawn-leather briefcase with a laptop. Of course, Gale's parents didn't know that he carried them as props. He was a receptionist. His job description began with answering the phone, saying "Gersh" with attitude, and ended with directing the call.

He had led Gale and her parents to believe that he was actually an agent—just one major client away from hanging out his own shingle. He figured that if he could score her, well, then maybe he could score financing from her folks. That she was on the rebound from a hot young cinematographer who had dumped her for an *Ebony* cover girl was no secret. That in him she might be thinking image as opposed to love or commitment was no secret, either. It never occurred to him that Vegas or even Tahoe might've been a better call for the weekend instead of a cabin at Twin Lakes, but Twin Lakes was where his daddy had taken him when he was a happy little kid and the whole wide world was before him.

So after two days of the fish not biting, after two nights of premature ejaculation and vodka, the trip had turned sour. During one last sad coupling on the rusty, squeaky springs, Gale joked that she couldn't get off because the bed was too loud and Brian smelled like night crawlers. True, he hadn't washed his hands after being out on the boat all day—hadn't washed them after stinking up the john or before cooking hot dogs on the grill. He hadn't appreciated her humor, either, and called her a frigid bitch.

When she told him to get a life, he became enraged and jerked her off the bed. She took it sexually and thought that finally he was going to do her right and true. As she spread her arms for him, he drove his left into her belly. Her breath whooshed out; she folded up. His right smashed into her pretty face, and then he grabbed her around the waist and rammed her back and forth through the window. The glass sliced her carotid artery, and she bled out before he came to his senses and found the courage to call 911, but then he lost it and hung up on them.

Brian went from panic into automaton mode. He bagged Gale's body in his blue fishing tarp, then cleaned up the cabin, tossed her and all their stuff in the back of his old Expedition, and took off.

He left the cat behind.

Leroy had witnessed the violence and its aftermath from beneath the cabin's gas heater, paralyzed with fear. After Brian bailed, Leroy knew on a primal level that the one being in the universe he cared about was dead and that he would forever hate the man who had killed her. What to do?

One coherent answer came into the cat's brain. Go home. *Go home* consumed his twenty-pound, short-haired, four-legged frame.

And I accepted that challenge as I wrapped his presence and blocked out an awful indifference from the universe. I, too, had a goal, and face it, as a shroud alone depending upon the whimsy of the wind, I was not likely to lead the Nightbreed to the promised land. I'd never been a cat person, but teaming up with this bewildered feline seemed both smart and honorable. I recalled Cervantes. No, I wasn't huge on reincarnation, but maybe somewhere I'd tilted at windmills before.

So the cat and I headed south toward Malibou Lake, the cat's home.

We traveled at night, and if a moonrise hurt my sensibilities, I would guide the cat into shadow, whispering for him to stay on soft ground and conserve the pads of his paws. Though he didn't want to stop, I made sure he found water and rested. I didn't want my ride dying from exhaustion. I made sure he ate, too. Having lived with vermin, I knew where they were.

We found the first one kicked back in a storm drain, all bushy and fat from a steady diet of roadkill residue on the highway. The cat cornered the rat, cuffed him senseless, and was about to finish him, but then a scheme came to me, and I made the cat pause. Yes, the cat was a brother, but not yet in the bond. In the cat's pause, the rat lunged, but bit into me instead of the cat, and my fragile, dusty balm flowed into the rat. Then I released the pause.

In seconds, the cat had shredded the rat, and ate it as if it were filet mignon, its special sauce, of course, the balm. Then Leroy cleaned himself, and we moved on. Leroy was now a blood brother, and I was triumphant, certain that like any other small community not yet sanitized by routine fumigation, Malibou Lake would have insects. *Silent Spring* redux.

With the cat averaging twelve miles a day, the trip took twenty-four nights. So strong was his sense of home, Leroy ran the last few miles, then as the sun rose over the Santa Monicas, trotted up the dirt driveway and yowled at the door for his dead owner. When the cat heard Brian moving in the apartment over the garage, he hid in the bushes and watched him look out the window, the man curious about a caterwauling he'd last heard some three hundred miles north.

Soon, Brian came out on the landing. He was half dressed, shaving cream on his face and head. He scanned the yard, finally peered down in the bushes, and was astonished to see Leroy, a reminder, a witness to Gale's brutal murder. Not that the cat could talk, but the feline's mere presence freaked Brian out. Scowling, he went back inside and wondered how to get rid of the cat. The answer came quickly—a variation on what his boy-hood homeys had done to guard dogs when they wanted to hop fences and rob small businesses.

Brian got leftover raw hamburger from the refrigerator, mashed it flat on a plastic plate, then opened the china cabinet and looked for the pièce de résistance.

He set the doctored meat on the landing, thinking that cats were always hungry, so it wouldn't take Leroy long to find it. Then he finished dressing and left for work, actually looking forward to the hour-long drive and his boring, humiliating day. He didn't want be to around when the cat was puking blood and writhing in agony. Watching Gale die, he told himself, had put his sensibilities on overload.

No, I insisted, no way, don't touch it!

We were on the landing, and Leroy was sniffing the hamburger.

It's a glass burger, I told him. The motherfucker's left you a glass burger. You eat that, you die a horrible death, and I'm stuck in the goddamn bushes with no horse for my kingdom. Let's go find a field mouse.

The cat listened and obeyed. Within the hour, he had hunted down a sizable rodent under the house. We dined, then curled up and slept, the cat choosing a patch of sunlight coming in the door to the crawl space.

Gale's parents showed up a few days later in a leased Escalade, wondering what had happened to her. They unlocked the door and went inside, called out to an empty house. Full of trepidation, they crept from room to room afraid that they would find her body, were relieved to come up empty. They found her car in the garage, covered with dust as if abandoned. Next, they trekked up and down East Lakeshore Drive and asked the neighbors. Alas, no one had seen Gale. (No one kept tabs on Gale.)

Exhausted, they went back to the house, were overjoyed to find the cat yowling at the door. Mrs. Jordan let us in, hurried to the pantry and got a can of Fancy Feast, opened and set it down, then gave Leroy fresh water, going on and on about the poor, starving cat, Gale's best friend, and if only you could tell us where she's gone to. If this keeps up, I told Leroy as he wolfed the food, you're gonna lose your edge from a three-hundred-mile journey and become one obese fat cat.

Mr. Jordan opened the refrigerator, stepped back at the stench of rotting leftovers. Whew, and I thought the cat food smelled awful. He got a plastic bag and started slam-dunking the stuff, containers and all, then told Mrs. Jordan that they should go to the store, buy some food.

"We should call the police," she said.

"We're not calling the police," he replied, "not when the FBI wants to talk to me."

Apparently, Mr. Jordan was suspected of major financial fraud. His company had guaranteed seniors a forty-percent return on their retirement accounts, then paid them with stock from a corporation that had no assets. He'd recently wired all his money to banks in the Bahamas, and the Jordans were moving from Connecticut to Costa Rica when Gale went missing.

"Gale's your only daughter!"

"You call the cops, I'm gone."

Mrs. Jordan thought about that, and then decided to go to the store with her husband, making sure that he'd go to Gelson's and not LAX.

The window of opportunity had opened for us. I remembered the fire and my promise. I remembered the survival instructions, quite simply: Why, why not transmogrify? If you find a new Nightbreed turf, then no longer are we the scum of the earth. Why, why not transmogrify?

I pictured Leroy's bed—plush pillows in a wicker basket next to Gale's in the master bedroom—and he was there in a flash, having found his home within a home, very important for a cat who'd lost everything. I asked him to roll over a few times. When he did, me, myself, and I came off on the pillows and began shape-shifting into a dirty-gray angel. As I ballooned in size, I inadvertently dumped the cat on the floor. Unhappy, he growled and hissed at me, then headed for the sofa in the living room, his tail switching. Jesus, give a cat smelly food and a bed, and he gets an attitude.

I glanced in the mirror and snorted with disgust. I hadn't figured on reformulating as an angel and looked like one of Raphael's cherubs, my bad complexion suggesting cancer. Maybe the fire intended the new "me" as a symbolic gesture, except I had planned to arrive as a male humanoid so that I could take out Brian, and being four feet tall with excessive baby fat—well, taking out Brian was not likely.

The cat scratched his belly frantically, then started licking his balls, then went back to scratching. Oh, shit, of course. He'd brought in fleas. Blood-sucking fleas. Yet as an angel, so-called holy water ran through my veins, so I didn't have to worry. In fact, if I was an angel, why not try flying?

I did, and my wings worked fine. For once, it was nice to be up in the air without being held hostage by the wind. I gained some altitude—not to mention, attitude—and glided above the lake. Hey, everybody, I'm beautiful like an eagle, fierce and fearless—except deep down, I knew I resembled a flying pear.

Another circle above the lake—people were staring at me at and aiming their smart phones—so I had to zoom back to Gale's and make an awkward landing behind the house. When I came inside, the cat blinked at me, then the clock, and went back to sleep. Like he knew it was six o'clock and Brian would be coming home soon, and that made me a total loser, without a plan. I'd thought about leaving a note for the Jordans except I had no hands. I couldn't write.

Wait a sec. The refrigerator! Gale had those magnetic letters all over it. Using my wings, I arranged a sentence with them: "BRIAN KILLED GALE." I'd wanted to write, "Dear Daddy, Brian killed me. Love, Gale" but I didn't have enough "D"s.

Then I curled up in a pious, self-righteous ball beneath the sofa and waited.

"Joe! Somebody broke in," said Mrs. Jordan as her husband put the groceries on the counter.

"What are you talking about?"

She pointed at my message on the refrigerator.

Mr. Jordan frowned thoughtfully.

"Maybe a neighbor saw something and was afraid to tell us." She dissolved into tears, mumbling about her precious daughter. "Will you call the police now?"

"I'll kill the son of a bitch myself."

Well, okay, we could use the help.

Mr. Jordan went online and searched for sporting-goods stores and found three in the area that sold firearms, but Mrs. Jordan warned him that buying a gun would go straight to the FBI's network and set off alarms, not good for Joe Jordan in the age of GPS. So Mr. Jordan searched Craigslist and found a dude in Thousand Oaks who was selling an AK-47. He sealed the deal with a phone call, then told Mrs. Jordan to call him if Brian got back before he did. He took off.

Still angelic under the sofa, I resisted the urge to make small talk with God. Then—I don't know if it was Him or the fire—a message came through loud and clear: *The refrigerator isn't enough, boy. You can't rely on an almost-convicted felon, either. Get off your fat ass and do something. Brian King is on Lake Vista Drive—like right now.*

Okay, okay, who am I to hesitate when it comes to Them.

I took off from the bedroom window and slowly gained altitude, my breath coming hard, my wings redlining it, what with the goddamn low humidity. At a couple of hundred feet, I leveled off and circled the lake, let the wind do its work. The gawkers were gone, so I didn't have to pretend I was a Canada goose or an overweight seagull.

Finally, I saw Brian's SUV turning on East Lakeshore. Before Gale's house, there was a sharp curve and a twenty-foot drop to the lake, and he was going way too fast. Perfect.

Wings flapping, I climbed higher, then banked and dove. I was going to come in straight for him at eye level, figuring he'd react instinctively, jerk to the right and drive off the cliff as I veered over the top of his car, home free, but I fucked up and came in too low.

He didn't even see me. I hit the ground ten feet in front of his Expedition, and he ran over me. If I'd been a human, I'd be dead. Instead, I got up, brushed myself off, and trudged for the house, humiliated by the tire tracks on my wings. They looked like something a tattoo artist on meth would do.

When I got back to the house, Brian was already inside his apartment. Jazz was mewling from his entertainment center, and I imagined him kicked back with a vodka martini. Pissed off, I went in the house, banging the kitchen door.

"Joe?" said Mrs. Jordan.

"No," I replied, "not exactly."

She shrieked at my angel body and beat-up wings, her hand going to her mouth. I figured she was dumbfounded that I didn't have rosy cheeks, as well.

I brushed past her and went to the sofa, swept the cat off, my wings feeling surprisingly strong. Annoyed, Leroy hissed at me, but I ignored his puffball threat and kicked his ass out the kitchen door.

He paused and blinked at the late-afternoon sun, but finally seemed to get what I had in mind. Tail switching, he trotted down the steps, stretched at the bottom, shook himself, and was ready. He looked up at me: What *did* you have in mind, anyway? Consider Brian King a two-legged rodent or a cockroach, whatever you're in the mood for, I responded.

I knocked on Brian's door with my head.

He opened it and was surprised. "What the hell?" He stepped back. "Ain't no costume party here, kid. You got the wrong address."

Leroy bolted in the apartment.

"Hey!"

The cat leaped on top of the entertainment cabinet, a good seven feet off the carpet. (Well, goddamn, the cat can fly, too.) Centered on it was Brian's huge seventy-five-inch Samsung TV.

"Hey, get outta here!"

He went for the cat, and using the old two-against-one maneuver, I dropped on my hands and knees behind Brian.

Leroy dropped on Brian's head and dug in his claws. Brian shouted in pain, stepped back, tripped over me. The cat sprang off, and I was up fast and used my wings to push the TV off its shelf. All seventy-five inches of screen and plastic came crashing down on Brian, pinning his arms.

Leroy sprang onto his face, and in the seconds that it took Brian to free his arms, the cat ripped out one eye, was digging at the other when finally Brian pulled him off and threw him across the room.

Blood poured from his face. He got up screaming and staggered after the cat, cornered him under the cabinet and started kicking him. The cat yowled in pain.

I figured it was as good a day as any to die—or at least get seriously hurt—so I threw myself between Brian and Leroy. He swung. I ducked and head-butted him in the balls. He yelped and doubled over. I was laughing triumphantly when his second swing caught me full-on in the face, slammed me against the wall. Out cold, I crumpled to the floor.

A gunshot woke me up. I lifted up on one wing just in time to see Mr. Jordan switch the AK-47 to full auto and empty it into Brian's back. Like a puppet cut loose from his strings, Brian flailed and jerked, then fell into the cabinet, dead.

As Mr. Jordan absorbed what he'd done, I automatically looked around for Leroy. Not seriously hurt, his attitude back, he remained under the cabinet, chewing on Brian's eyeball. Damn cat will eat anything.

Time for me to bail. (Avoidance therapy.) I jumped on the kitchen counter and went out the window. I lifted off and flew up blindly, but didn't see the power lines until the last second. A quick and desperate maneuver: I backstroked, did a somersault intending to glide under the high voltage, and almost made it except for the oak tree.

I flew into its top branches, flailed mightily, but fell anyway, ricocheting between the limbs, wishing I was a shroud again. I hit the ground hard, was down and out for the second time in minutes.

This time I woke up to the cat licking dirt off my face. Instinctively, I rolled away in case he'd developed a taste for eyes. He purred and rubbed against my wings, which I guess was his way of saying thank you, brother, even though he'd been the point man in the assault and Mr. Jordan, the artillery.

The Jordans were gone the next day. Mrs. Jordan had wanted to take the cat, but Leroy made himself scarce, and eventually they left without him, which made Mr. Jordan happy. He blamed the cat for the flea bites on his ankles. Later, when the balm had done its work, he would wonder why he was staying up late and didn't like to go outside in the daylight when he'd always been a morning person. He would blame it on the decadence of Costa Rica.

And me? Oh, so proud, I put out the call on the wind, and the Night-breed answered, their tom-toms beating in my brain. Since I know they've always been more comfortable beneath something, I've left the door to the crawl space open. Once in that dank and musty darkness, they will pick their spots, huddle, and wait for further instructions.

WRETCHED

Edward Brauer

You keep looking over my shoulder, Chuckles. Getting me edgy."
Owen shoved a lightly seared piece of bonito into his mouth.

"Don't nitpick him, darling," said Lydia, tapping Owen on his
arm. "Charlie can look wherever he wants," she said, emphasizing my name.

"Just keeping an eye on our old mate over there." I pointed across the
bay to the rocks, where the fisherman I'd been watching danced with his
rod. Owen, Lydia, and Shannon twisted in their seats for a look.

Our boat was a good distance away, but we could see that there was something wrong with him. He wore a black raincoat with the hood drawn over—
covering his face—but occasionally he'd twist toward us as he cast his line
and we'd get a flash of something pink and haggard hiding in the veil.

We watched him move for a minute. There was a romance to it, like a
martial art. He stood unshifting as the ocean drew back its strength and
came at him, again and again.

Owen scoffed and turned back. "It's his own fault if a wave gets him,"
he said. His fork was pointed at me and he shook it for a moment, twid-
dling his fingers on his chin. Then he shrugged and returned to his fish.

The three of us adults were very hungover and slumped about in our
seats, the sun and the white of the deck glaring off our sunglasses.

"Dad, you know I hate fish," said Shannon, arms crossed over her lunch.

"Just eat it, it's good for you," grunted Owen.

"No! I swear I'll vomit if I do!"

"Then that's your problem!"

"Sweetie, go and make yourself a Vegemite sandwich," said Lydia, trying to fix Owen a stern look.

"Yeah great," said Shannon, slinking off to her bunk bed, which was right beneath my own.

We'd each had it rough the night before. Owen and Lydia, full of booze and holiday fervor, had gone at each other in the bedroom like they were getting paid for it. I'd escaped to the farthest edge of the boat and sat there with my legs over the edge, strangling the neck of a port bottle. Poor Shannon—too young to drink—had run out of batteries on her iPad and could only lie there and wait for it all to end.

"I tell you, Chuckles, if you ever have kids you should raise them in a tougher part of the world. That little sh . . ." He glanced at Lydia. "That kid has no idea what doing it hard is like. She's just like this damn country. Young and spoiled."

I grunted. Owen was a painful a man to debate with.

I'd traveled the world when he and Lydia first became an item, disappearing for five years in the hope that it would all blow over by the time I got back. All through Europe and Asia, civilization was inescapable, its roads and buildings dotting the continents like a pepper spill.

People thought of Rome or the Taj Mahal as ancient places, tiptoeing about them with this puppy-dumb sanctity in their eyes. But what's a few hundred years of human civilization, compared to the millions of years of jungle that came before? Only when I got away from all the people and the concrete and deep into the beastly wild could I feel in the presence of something truly ancient.

I realized, riding a train somewhere between Berlin and Madrid, that most of the country I came from was still enveloped by that oldest of kingdoms. It still breathed, rustled, and screeched all around us. Even the Illawarra coast that sat as the backdrop to our brunch—not a hundred kilometers from Sydney—was a looming entanglement that could contain all manner of creatures in its gums and ferns. It was anything but young.

"What do you say, Chuckles? It's past midday." Owen was brandishing two bottles of draft, their tops already popped off. It was the last thing I was craving, but I accepted.

My one job for the entire trip was to be Owen's friend—the guy he could bitch and moan to when his wife and daughter got him hot under the collar. Lydia had begged me to come along so that it would be someone she knew instead of one of Owen's regular asshole mates, and I'd agreed as a favor to her.

It was a simple enough gig. It just needed a lot of booze.

"Come play Uno, sweetie," Lydia said, giving Shannon a hopeful smile. The kid rolled her eyes and went back to staring at the roof of her bunk bed. I was impressed by how long she could do that.

"She thinks we're lame, sitting here enjoying ourselves the way we do," said Owen, taking a big slug of beer and placing it between his knees so it didn't go flying off with the next wave.

The sky had darkened as the afternoon wore on, accompanied by an angry swell. Our vessel rode harmlessly over the lumps of ocean that moved underneath it, but below deck was chaos. We'd stumbled all over the place in a half-drunk tidying frenzy, getting everything strapped down and behind a cupboard door before the rocking of the vessel sent more crockery and food flying everywhere.

I'd watched Lydia grabbing for the Vegemite jar Shannon had used earlier, a plate held against her small breasts, laughing so hard she had to sit against a wall and regain herself. A moment before I could turn away she'd noticed me staring.

We'd tidied the rest of the cabin in silence.

"Draw two, bubble-butt," said Owen, dumping a blue card onto the pile and leering at his wife.

"Sorry, Charlie," she said, biting her bottom lip and putting another draw two on top of his.

"Ah . . ." I began as I took four cards from the pile, not really knowing what witty thing I hoped to spit out—but not having to in the end, because we heard screaming coming from outside.

Owen and I exchanged a glance before I was on my feet and pulling myself up the stairs to the deck. Behind me I heard him swear as he dragged himself out of his seat to follow.

Rain spotted my shirt as I ducked outside and made for the bow railing,

securing it in my hands as the boat rolled over a large wave and tilted, pulling me backward.

Again I heard someone cry out; the beginning of the word "help," muted
by submergence. I looked to the choppy water but couldn't see anything.

The boat tilted as a wave picked it up again, pushing me against the railing and sending Owen crashing into it, his hands scrabbling for grip until
we hit the next crest and evened out. It was then that we saw a human arm
rising up out of the water, the body it belonged to instantly recognizable.

It was the fisherman I'd been watching earlier that day, garbed still in
his black raincoat. Only a strong current could have dragged him this far
out, and it looked as though he was on the verge of succumbing to his mis-
fortune. His motions were feeble and his head—a pink spot in the dark
blue—gulped just above the water.

Owen looked to me with wide eyes, his mouth puckered and eyebrows
wrinkled.

"Life jackets?" I said. "Where are your life jackets?"

His frown suggested that he couldn't remember. Lydia, though, had had
greater foresight than either of us, appearing at the stairs with three of them
tucked under her arm as another wave tilted the boat.

"Charlie!" she called out to me, bowling the life jackets across the deck.

I was struck for a moment then, by her pathological tragedy. With no
time to think she'd known exactly who the better of us was. But in the day-
to-day world of boredom and festering neurosis, she'd been compelled by
her dumb blood to choose Owen.

I slid my arms into the life jacket's holes and didn't bother to clip it up,
grabbing the second one that Lydia had tossed me and leaping over the
railing into the surf.

My vision was blurred as I came up, the veil of salt water burning my
eyes. I was already swimming overarm as I hit the surface, my clothes dragging in the water and the second life jacket clamped in my teeth. The sea
splashed my face and I could scarcely make out a thing.

I almost ran into him, disguised as he was by that black raincoat. He
responded to my presence in a manner contrary to the typical thrashings
of a drowning man, relaxing and allowing me to take his wrist and guide
it toward the life jacket I'd been carrying. He nodded when he felt it and
hugged it to his chest.

"Swim with me!" I yelled, grabbing him by the scruff of his raincoat and turning my back to the boat.

Getting back to the boat was an arduous journey. My kicks were blunted by the joggers I was still wearing and the waves remained fast and frequent. Despite the buoyancy of our jackets we went through them instead of over, coming up with stinging eyes and salty mouths.

Owen was waiting at the back of the boat, pacing like a hound in a yard. He pulled me up by the wrist, calling me a stupid bastard.

Then it was the fisherman's turn. We each extended a hand to him and he reached up to us.

As we took his wrists and pulled, a gust of wind got underneath the hood of his raincoat, flipping it open. The face that had been hidden underneath was, I knew at that moment, the most awful thing either of us had ever seen. As we hauled him aboard he let out a scream so wet and animal that we nearly let go of him then and there.

God help us, though, we didn't.

———————

The sun had fully set behind the escarpment and with it had gone the full force of the ocean. In the darkness outside, ripples lapped soft against the hull.

My wet clothes were stretched out in front of the heater in Owen and Lydia's room, next to the old rags that the fisherman had been wearing under his raincoat. The raincoat itself he'd patted down with a towel and put straight back on.

Gideon Skillet was his name.

He chewed the fish we'd served him like a cow chewing cud, the flaking skin around his jaw folding and stretching as it worked its circles; small flecks of skin detaching themselves and floating into his lap.

The man was a dermatological nightmare. Where his skin wasn't scaly and flaking, it was marked with jagged fissures and heaving boils that were either scabbed over or oozing with congealed blood. I thought of the tectonic maps we'd studied, long ago in geography class at school. Gideon Skillet's face was how I imagined the crust of the earth would look if we stripped away all the water, soil, and rock and were left with shifting plates atop a molten ball.

He apologized to us in a crackling old English voice for screaming when we'd hauled him in. "The shoulders get awful crook if you pull on them," he said, tapping himself where it had hurt and baring incomplete rows of browned teeth.

He was an ancient man. A widow of decades now, married again to the sea like so many woolly-haired geriatrics before him. His locale was a tiny beachside community nearby called Burning Palms.

We knew of the place, though never suspected anyone lived there full time. It was one of those weekend retreat destinations that regular visitors preferred to keep hushed about. No roads led to or through—it was only accessible by boat or a long hike down the escarpment. I couldn't even remember having seen power lines or a generator among those few salty cabins.

"So Gideon," said Owen, now into his fifth scotch, "the fuck is an old bloke like you doing rock fishing?"

Gideon chuckled, showing those terrible teeth again. "Long time looking at the lid, Captain."

He would punctuate a sentence by keeping eye contact with whoever he was addressing until they'd looked away, and he did this now with Owen, who flinched.

We exchanged glances while our guest busied himself with removing a bone from his fish. He had a remarkable dexterity when he did this—sawing around the tiny bone with the serrated tip of his steak knife and flicking it out of the meat with one swift gesture when he was done.

Shannon was staring at him from her spot on the bottom bunk bed, frowning. He became aware of her as he chewed, turning to her and poking out his purple and white tongue, bringing his thumb to his nose and wiggling his scabby fingers. She smiled weakly in response and flopped backward onto the bed again. He chuckled and returned to his fish.

Lydia fixed Owen with a wide-eyed stare. He mouthed *What?* at her, then looked at me and shook his head, downing the rest of his scotch.

"I'm afraid we can't drop you home in the dark," said Owen. "We didn't really plan for this eventuality when we left. But we'll put some sheets down and you can make the most of the couch." He referred to the built-in bench that ran along one side of the table. It was padded but short—the sort of place I could have easily crashed on during my twenties, but wouldn't dream of using now. "We'll get you home first thing tomorrow."

"You're all very kind," said Gideon, staring us down in turn as he spoke. "Samaritans at sea. The rarest. Very kind." He chewed, smiled.

———————

I dreamed that the ocean breathed as it smashed against the cliff faces; a lusty breath that came from its deepest throat.

When I woke, Gideon Skillet was there by the bunk bed I shared with Shannon, breathing hoarse and lusty as the sea had breathed in my dream, staring at Shannon's bunk beneath me and rocking his pelvis.

She woke and screamed, instantly rousing me out of my confusion. When she ran out of breath, she inhaled deep and screamed again.

I threw off the covers and leaped out of bed in my pajamas, left heel twisting slightly as I landed.

Gideon held his hands up and backed away. His pelvis continued to rock. "No harm meant at all sir, nothing to fear," he said.

Owen erupted naked from the cabin he shared with Lydia, his half-erect penis bouncing around like a dredged-up fish. He seized Gideon Skillet by the front of the raincoat and hurled him to the ground.

The old man went sprawling backward into the cabin, his arms and legs flailing in the air.

"A misunderstanding," he was saying as he scrambled to his feet. "Misunderstanding is all, and all will be cleared up."

"You're too right it will. Get the hell out of here."

"Oh, yes Captain," he said, flashing Owen a smile before he turned to climb the stairs.

"Get into bed with your mother," Owen said to Shannon. She nodded, her eyes wide. She moved slowly, her blanket wrapped around her. From within I could hear Lydia. "It's okay, sweetie, come here, it's okay. What happened? What happened, Owen?"

"Shut up and stay in there. Me and Charlie are going to sort this out."

After quickly scanning the kitchen for something to wear, Owen wrapped a towel around his waist and went up the stairs after Gideon. I followed a few paces behind, conscious in that moment of not having his ass too close to my face.

Outside, the air was quiet and the world was colored by that dimness that comes in the hour before dawn. Owen held Gideon by the front of his jacket and had backed him right up to the edge of the stern railing.

"What the fuck was he doing to my daughter, Charlie?"

I held back a few paces and patted the top pocket of my pajamas, knowing there wouldn't be a cigarette there. "I don't think he touched her. He was just kind of standing there panting when I woke up."

"An old man's got to catch his breath sometime, Captain," said Gideon, both his scabby hands caressing Owen's balled fist. I felt on the verge of throwing up.

"Was he catching his breath?" Owen turned his head to look at me. Over his shoulder, Gideon was staring at me, too. "Come on Charlie. Speak up."

"I think he might be a pervert, Owen. He was kind of . . . humping the air as well."

Owen's head snapped back to face the fisherman, his index finger hovering right underneath the man's nose. Spittle flew from his lips. "What the fuck, old man? That's my daughter!"

"And what quarrel if she is then?" All at once, Gideon's sincerity vanished. His teeth savaged the air as he spoke and his top lip twitched between words. "Can't a man long for the forbidden sea on your vessel, Captain?"

"The sea? What are you talking about?"

Owen was holding the man over the edge of the railing, both hands gripping the front of his raincoat.

"I think we need to take a step back here, Cap . . . er . . . Owen," I said. "Let's just get him to shore and work it out from there."

Gideon winked at me from over Owen's shoulder, revealing a scab on his eyelid.

"I'm talking, Captain, about the young, young sea between your daughter's legs," he said. "What a fresh salt!"

Owen drew back his fist and hit the man, three times in the face. The frail old body shook with each blow, flopping about in Owen's grip. The crunching of brittle bones filled the morning.

Then Owen shoved him over the railing and into the water.

"Oh no," I said, darting forward to the edge as the splash came.

Owen put the back of his hand to my chest and we watched the ripples clear. Gideon's body was about a foot below the surface, staring up at us and smiling, still. Blood had darkened the water around his head and his face looked shattered, as if all the cracks and boils had erupted at once. His raincoat rippled around him like the boneless fins of a ray, its edges bleeding a black smoke. A spasm went through the coat and it billowed up at us.

Then he sank into the deep.

I stood at the front of the boat as water rushed underneath, the midmorning sun cooking one side of my face. I took big, burning gulps of whiskey in place of the cigarette I was craving.

Nobody was talking. Lydia was sitting at the table inside, clutching at a royal-family tabloid magazine with white fingers. Shannon had locked herself in the bathroom and answered every knock with silence.

Owen I could see every time I turned my head. He was on the upper deck, at the wheel, frowning into the horizon. I decided to go and talk to him—for my sake more than his.

"Chuckles," he said, as I reached the top of the ladder. He didn't turn around. I walked over and sat in the spare seat next to him.

"Hey mate. I thought I'd come and see how you were holding up."

"Oh I'm great. I'm a fresh pack of fucking Juicy Fruit."

"Yeah." I tried to smile. "Stupid question I know."

"But seriously, good job Chuckles. You and that old fuck made a hell of a team." He turned to me then, predatory smile across his face.

"Come on Owen, what the hell?"

"You trying to get your dick into my wife, him trying to get his dick into my daughter. Hell of a team."

"Jesus Christ."

I left him there, returning to the front of the boat with my bottle of whiskey. Far ahead in the distance I could see the docks. I thought about all the cigarettes I'd smoke when I finally got off.

"Can I have a sip?" Shannon appeared next to me, her long hair tossing about in the wind.

"You realize your dad is just there?" We each glanced up at Owen, who was scratching at one of his wrists. I turned away quickly.

"I wish I could get drunk so bad right now," she said.

"How do you know it'd fix anything?"

"Well, you're doing it."

I looked at the bottle and grinned, in spite of myself.

"We all just have to pretend like nothing happened, don't we?"

I took another swig. "You know, it's actually easy to pretend. Especially when it's something you'd rather forget."

"Like you and my mum?"

I frowned. "Get out of here will you."

She started to leave, then paused and turned back to me. Her brown eyes were like perfect marbles catching the sun. "What was the deal with that old guy?"

I took another swig and paused, thinking about what I should tell her. "Look Shannon, I'm just trying to get him out of my head, like everyone else. He was a bad man. That doesn't make what your dad did right, but it kind of does make it righter. Is that what you wanted to hear?"

She shrugged.

"Give me a clue?"

She rolled her eyes. "I already know he was, like, a pedophile, so you don't need to shelter me."

"Yeah, all right. He was a dirty old pedophile."

"But there was something else."

I replayed the memory of Gideon Skillet in the water, his coat of smoke flapping and his body sinking into the deep. I took another swig.

"Well, I'm sure he's not the only ugly old pedo with nasty vibes."

She examined me for a moment, nodded, and left.

———————

Two weeks later my phone came alive with Owen's number on the screen.

"Owen . . . hi."

"Hi Charlie." It was Lydia.

"Lydia! How are you?" I cursed my enthusiasm as soon as I'd spoken.

"Charlie, I . . . we're in some trouble." She was in tears.

"Oh Lydia. Oh no. What's going on?"

She tried to speak, but she was all at once crying so hard that I couldn't make her out.

"All right Lydia, I want you to take a deep breath and just say yes or no— the rest can wait. Do you want me to come over?"

She sniffled a few times and then said, "Yes."

"Be there as quick as I can."

I hung up and got straight into my car, only realizing when I was more than halfway there that I hadn't done up my belt.

———————

Lydia answered the door and collapsed onto my shoulder, shaking with sobs. I put my arms around her and stroked her back.

"We'll sort this out, whatever it is," I said into her ear.

She pulled away after a moment and walked down the hallway, her socked feet silent on the wooden floorboards. I took my shoes off and followed her, noticing at once the smell of old cigarette smoke penetrating through the lavender air freshener.

She led me to the kitchen, where several bottles of red wine sat on the counter—one of them half full of cigarette butts.

"You're smoking again?"

"Don't, Charlie." Her eyes were red-rimmed and deep-set.

"Where's Shannon and Owen?"

She reached into her jeans and took out a pack of smokes, shaking one loose and lighting it off the stove. "Shannon's at her grandmother's," she said after a long drag. "Owen . . ." She shook her head and her lip trembled.

On the bench was a folded-up piece of paper. She slid it toward me with trembling fingertips and then looked away.

Nausea crept up on me as I unfolded it. I recognized Owen's scrawl.

Chuckles,
If you're reading this it means that I'm screwed and you're not.
That's hardly fair, but neither is what happened to Ned Kelly.

There'll be nothing left of me when you read this—that old cunt you dredged up from the ocean put his eggs in me or something. I'm itching, flaking. It's not just my skin, it's my mind. I have such thoughts, Charlie. Dreams of old places like wombs in the earth, all dug up now and made barren.

I'm sure you'll realise why calling the cops is a terrible idea, once you look through the garage window. I'm sure you'll realise exactly what has to happen. I'd have done it myself if I'd have known earlier, but now I can't—I'm too much gone already.

I don't have much else to say to you. I begrudge you the opportunity to look after my wife and daughter, but I'm not the fucking idiot you think I am. I know you're the best man for the job, so do it right, asshole.

—Owen

I frowned and shook my head at Lydia, handing her back the note. Her lips were pursed tight. She pointed to the high kitchen windows that opened out into their garage.

I took a deep breath and hoisted myself onto the bench between all the wine bottles, rising cautiously and standing on my tiptoes to look through.

In place of the four-wheel-drive that the garage usually housed were a futon mattress and a jug of water. Gideon Skillet sat on the mattress edge, looking up at me and smiling with his broken rows of rotting teeth. Draped around him was his black raincoat.

"Hello, Chuckles," he said, and laughed for a long time.

He called out to me as I worked.

"We can each get our own now, can't we, Chuckles? You take the old salt and I get the fresh."

I'd taken Lydia's smokes off her before I sent her to her mother's place and was chaining them down with big gulps of wine, scrawling out a step-by-step plan. I went through pages and pages of drafts and couldn't help but think of eggs when I looked at all the scrunched-up balls of paper around me.

"Why don't you throw me a fish, Charlie? I'll fillet it for you good and fast. Gideon Skillet's famous Midian fillet!"

I ignored him.

Hours passed before I had a plan. In the backyard I burned all the drafts, mixing the ashes well with the garden soil. It had grown dark.

I took a roll of duct tape from Owen's shed and unhooked their garden hose, bundling it into loops and bringing it out to the driveway. Using the full roll, I taped one hose end to the exhaust pipe of my car. Then I ran the other down the hallway, into the kitchen, and poked it through the high window that overlooked the garage.

Gideon looked up at me. "Hose me down will you Charles? Clean the dirty man up?"

I thought about it for a moment. Then—unable to deny myself those parting words—told him, "Thank you."

I sat in my car, in the dark, engine softly rumbling beneath me. Faintly, I could hear him calling out.

"Clever you, Chuckles," he said, over and over until he choked. "Clever you."

———————

I waited an hour before opening the garage door, to be certain. His body lay comfortable on the futon mattress, a three-dimensional shadow in the gloom. Without touching him, I rolled him up—raincoat and all—in a few blankets from the linen cupboard, then lifted him into the boot of my car. He weighed almost nothing.

The next day I rose early and got in the car and drove west for about twelve hours, out to where the desert begins and the earth is the color of rust. I took the loneliest dirt track I could find, abandoning it in the late afternoon and turning off-road. On a northern bearing I drove, for another three hours until the sun had gone down and the stars lit every arc of the sky.

I burned him there, wrapped in those blankets, in a nowhere place where the ground ran flat to all of the horizon's edges. Each time the fire died I poured more gas and lit it again, holding vigil through the night.

By the time dawn came there was nothing but fine ashes left, which I trampled and kicked until they were blended with the desert soil.

I'd left my phone and GPS at home, instead jotting down all the turns I'd made onto a notebook in my lap. I followed these back, driving in silence for another whole day and arriving home as the afternoon shadows became bloated.

Occasionally I'd scratch at my wrists.

———————

"Two days," I'd told Lydia before she left for her mother's. "Give me two days and then report Owen as missing."

It's been ten now and I've not heard a thing. No police with questions, no phone calls from Lydia, nothing. The drama of Owen's disappearance, playing out somewhere on the other side of my front door, is as unable to cross the threshold as I am.

Worse than the face that my own is becoming is how well I now understand its owner. Eggs he lays, yes, but it's the murder that makes them fertile, that gives him new life in his killer's body.

"Salt of the earth" he calls me. His voice gets louder in my head as he rises, up from the oceans of my mind.

God, but he itches.

A MONSTER AMONG MONSTERS

Stephen Woodworth and Kelly Dunn

It's Vagamel, all right," Burdock declared. "Or it *was*, at any rate." He peered at the scattered ash first with his right eye, then with the left. Placed on opposite sides of his head, the lidless eyes permitted Burdock a constant, 360-degree view, but they could never see the same thing simultaneously.

Hemmel scratched at his flabby chest, the ropelike curve of the Sickle coiling beneath his grubby shirt. He was scared, and that made him hungry. It didn't help that, since he was one of the few Nightbreed among them who could withstand daylight, they'd made him stand guard over the remains until they could convene an inquest after dusk. He hadn't fed all day.

Only one shaggy leg of Vagamel remained intact, from cloven hoof to heavy haunch. He had come to this dismal flophouse the previous night to feed on the homeless and drug addicts who sheltered there. Yet, for reasons unclear, he had stayed there past dawn, thereby dooming himself. Sunlight had streamed in through the flophouse window and severed his hind limb right at the crotch, leaving the enormous furred genitals unharmed.

Hung like a horse even in death, Hemmel thought.

Amalek crouched on all fours, his elongated snout sniffing the cracked linoleum of the floor. "I don't get it," he said. "There's no blood. No restraints to hold him down. How did the Naturals—"

Gisella leaned up against the peeling wallpaper, filing her talons between the spikes of her pointed teeth. "The Naturals had nothing to do with this."

"Vagamel wouldn't go without a fight," Amalek insisted. "He could easily have crawled into the shadows."

"He did not fight." The glossy sheen of Gisella's nude body shifted from indigo to maroon to ocher as she brooded. "And he didn't crawl into the shadows. He crawled out of them."

"She's right." Burdock pointed to five-fingered gouges in the tiles where Vagamel must have sunk his claws into the floor, holding himself in the searing sunshine as he convulsed in agony until he finally, mercifully exploded.

Amalek cocked his jackal's head in puzzlement. "Why would he burn himself?"

"For the same reason Jenya impaled herself, or Dandridge cut his own head off, or that Natural threw himself onto the Metro tracks." Gisella's skin turned to polished obsidian, but her eyes blazed orange. "Because *that* found them."

Hemmel abruptly lost his appetite. The Nightbreed used the usual pronouns to refer to one another with mutual respect: *he* or *she* or even *it*, for those among them who possessed no identifiable gender. Only one creature, however, merited the loathsome pejorative *that*.

The Pariah.

Every race has its legends, and the Nightbreed were no exception. All of them had heard the story of the Pariah, though they seldom repeated it, except to frighten their children into obedience to the laws of Baphomet. That was how each of them had learned the tale—through fear.

Down at the lowest depth of Midian—below the graves of the dead and the warrens of the undead, beneath the chambers where the Berserkers had been confined—lay a solitary oubliette, home and prison to a creature both pitiful and abhorrent. Its true name, if it had one, had long been forgotten, and no one but the Dark God knew what it looked like, for any who encountered it either lost all reason or spiraled to self-annihilation. Whatever the beast's nature, it engendered nightmares in the Children of Nightmare, drove even the inhabitants of insanity to madness.

It was not always so. In times distant, when the Immortals were young, an entity existed that could change its form with more divine skill than any Nightbreed before or since. It molded and reshaped itself into incarnations of such extraordinary art and beauty that one day it achieved a perfection that inflamed the lust of the great Lord Baphomet Himself.

He appeared to the shape-shifter as a thunderhead with eyes of lightning. "You are favored above every creature that walks or crawls or flies," He announced in a voice that resounded like planets colliding. "For I have chosen you to be My consort."

"Great Lord," the shape-shifter replied, "I am humbled by Your honor. But I cannot give myself to You, for I love another." And with that, it turned into air and fled.

But one cannot hide from Baphomet, Who sees all. The Dark God followed the shape-shifter to its lover. To an amorphous being, all forms are equal, and so the shape-shifter did not have the prejudice of beauty. Its beloved turned out to be a hog-sized, ratlike thing, and Baphomet became enraged that His chosen one had spurned Him for such an inferior being. Although the shape-shifter attempted to shield its beloved from the Dark God's wrath, Baphomet struck the rat thing with a beam of blinding radiance that shattered the creature into a thousand fragments, a horde of tiny, pathetic rodent replicas that immediately scattered in terror.

Baphomet turned His baleful gaze upon the shape-shifter. "Since you have denied Me," He said, "you shall have no one. You who have rejected your god shall be rejected by all, yea, even the lowliest of the low. Shunned by the shunned, loathed by the loathed, you shall endure alone forever. So have I spoken."

And with that, Baphomet cursed the once-enticing shape-shifter, changed it in some unimaginable way that made it repulsive to Natural and Nightbreed alike. Or so the story went.

"A bunch of hogwash, you ask me." Burdock scowled at Gisella, the brow of the eye at his right temple slanting downward severely. "The Pariah is a myth, a bugaboo for toddlers and fools!"

Gisella flushed crimson. "I tell you, *that* has escaped! When Midian crumbled, *that* got out, and now it's come after us to claim its vengeance."

"Nonsense!"

"Then what do you think drove Vagamel to this? Or Jenya and the others?"

Burdock had no ready answer. "Some mischief from the Naturals, you ask me. Maybe they're on to us."

Gisella gave an arch smile. "Then let us catch the thing that did this and see who is right."

The others all looked at one another, each waiting for someone else to object. Even Burdock paled and seemed less sure of himself. "I don't see how that's necessary. . . ."

"So we let *that* take us, one by one? Or let it slay so many Naturals that they come hunting for all of us?"

Amalek drew himself up to his full seven-foot height, tattooed hieroglyphs undulating as he puffed out his chest. "No! Natural or Nightbreed—we find it and kill it."

"There is no need to seek it. It will come to us. *For* us. And I will be waiting." Gisella grinned, the pointed teeth interlocking in a jigsaw of ivory. In the wan illumination of Burdock's flashlight, she seemed to disappear, for her skin altered its pigment again until it exactly mimicked the faded floral wallpaper behind her.

Hemmel licked sweat from his upper lip, fidgeting with the Sickle beneath his shirt. "Wh-what if it is the Pariah? Baphomet cursed it. If we kill it, won't He be mad?"

Only Gisella's orange eyes remained visible. The glare they gave Hemmel made him wish he hadn't spoken.

Burdock seized on the argument. "He has a point. If this Pariah does exist, it's still Nightbreed. To kill it for being what it is makes us no better than the Naturals."

"Then we shall try to capture it," Gisella replied. "And if that fails, we kill. Either way, it shall be Baphomet's will. Now let us return to the Enclave and prepare."

She shut her eyes and vanished.

As they departed the flophouse, Amalek took Vagamel's singed hindquarter and slunk down the nearest manhole to seek the secluded passageways of the sewers. That left Burdock and Hemmel to meander back to the Enclave at street level.

"D-do you really think it's the Pariah?" Hemmel stammered when they were alone, waddling to keep up with his companion. "What if it does to us what it did to the others?"

Burdock snorted and put on the dark glasses he used to hide the smooth, featureless brow above his nose. "Don't be such a dullard. You ask me, some blasted Natural is at the bottom of this, and we'll make him suffer for it."

He pulled on his shabby stocking cap and adjusted it so that his eyes could peek out through the holes cut in the sides. In the night-drenched streets of Skid Row, the cap's snowflake pattern camouflaged the staring orbs.

Hemmel sighed and trudged along in silence past shops that had rolled their steel doors down at sunset. Hardly any streetlights illuminated this part of town, so he navigated as much by smell as by sight. A pleasant background reek of rotting garbage from the burst trash bags that slouched on the sidewalk mingled with the pervasive undertone of human urine and feces that saturated the pavement. And here and there, the delectable scent of Meat whenever they neared a comatose vagrant slumped in a doorway. More than once, Hemmel had to restrain the squirming Sickle beneath his shirt. It wanted to feed.

At last, they arrived at the entrance to a dilapidated movie palace that dated to the Roaring Twenties. THE ELYSIAN, its marquee announced, every bulb in its curling script either blown or broken. Skewed letters promised that the theater was only CLOSED F R REMOD LING. Burdock strode beyond the boarded-up ticket booth and rapped on the cinema's double doors: four quick knocks, three slow.

Hemmel jumped as a voice spoke from the vacant foyer behind them.

"Took you long enough," it said.

Gisella rippled into visibility like a mirage.

Burdock harrumphed. "Let's see how quick *you* are after a couple more centuries."

He and Hemmel followed her into the lobby, where Amalek squatted, solemnly devouring Vagamel's severed flank as if it were an enormous joint of raw mutton. Among some Nightbreed, consuming one's dead kin was considered far more respectful than burying them. They became part of you—remained one with you forever.

Another set of double doors led into the auditorium itself, current lair of the Enclave, one of the wandering tribes of the Midian diaspora. The theater was perversely apropos to house the Nightbreed: gilt-edged glamour gone to seed. Faux Egyptian pharaohs flanked the proscenium arch. A stage that had once hosted vaudeville performers now stood deserted except for an enormous torn film screen. Pigeons roosted in the dying galaxies of disintegrating chandeliers, and the atmosphere sagged with the musty stink of their droppings. If Midian had been a cemetery for the dead, the Elysian was a mausoleum for dreams.

The Enclave had adapted the interior to suit their needs. Sconces that once sprouted electric candles now held burning torches. Rows of folding seats had been ripped out and rearranged around cooking fires and card tables. In the cleared spaces, velvet draperies had been refashioned into Bedouin-style tents on the gum-encrusted carpet of the theater floor. For a brief time, this place had become their home.

But now, the tents were being dismantled. Even as the tiny community's children still chased each other up and down the center aisle—some on two legs, some on all fours—their parents grimly packed up their makeshift shelters.

"We need this area cleared," Gisella explained. "For the trap."

Having finished his meal, Amalek strode up to Gisella, eyes gleaming in anticipation. "Tell us."

As the other Nightbreed completed their preparations, they too gathered around. Gisella held out her clawed fingers to indicate that all of them would be included in her instructions. "I've had Calay take the children away to hide them. The rest of us shall stay here, together. When *that* comes, we follow the plan." Gisella snapped her fingers in the direction of a velvet curtain that had been tossed in a corner. "Crocus."

The curtain undulated, rippled, and flipped back like a hood to reveal what appeared to be a girl in her late teens. "I'm here."

Crocus had a moon-shaped face and white hair. As she stood up, freeing herself of the curtain, a roll of fat around her belly flopped over her hips, hanging downward to midthigh like a miniskirt of flesh. Under the fat roll peeked Crocus's extra leg, which grew out of her groin, its foot planted forward between the girl's two normal legs.

Gisella indicated the auditorium doors. "We will leave the center door open. Crocus, you will stand just in front of those doors. When the Pariah comes in, that monster will see you. The second it does, what will you do?"

"I'll jump!" Crocus's extra foot snapped to the floor as if spring-loaded, vaulting her whole body upward in an arc as if shot by a catapult. For a second, Hemmel lost sight of her. Then he spotted her standing on the other end of the theater.

"Good." Gisella nodded in satisfaction. "Go straight down the center aisle, and then off into the wings with you." She gestured to a decorative arch near the right of the stage. "The fastest you've ever gone."

Crocus's luminescent paleness paled still more, a mixture of fear and determination. "That thing won't catch me."

"No, it won't." Gisella moved to the arch and faded into it as her skin matched its color. "I will be here in case. And Franchesco will know what to do. Franchesco! Are you prepared?"

A voice from overhead whooped, "You bet I am!"

Hemmel craned his neck toward the sound, which came from one of the decrepit chandeliers near the stage. The crystals clattered together musically as Franchesco shifted a little from his perch on top of the chandelier. He had the stocky build and broad shoulders of a bodybuilder, but a down of vestigial feathers plumed the skin in brilliant shades of tropical green and iridescent red. His nose dipped, sharply and cruelly, into a beaklike bend, giving him the visage of a bird of prey.

"The *monstruo*'ll be chasing Crocus, right? But my friends will drive him back, just where we want him." Franchesco let out a high, piercing cry. Suddenly the air filled with feathers: not only the pigeons that had claimed the theater before the Nightbreed had, but also crows, parrots, and even a seagull or two. Quickly falling into formation, the birds formed an arc, diving toward the arch and turning abruptly toward the orchestra pit. Franchesco gave out another cry, and the birds scattered, disappearing with such dispatch they seemed to melt into the air. "The *asesino* will fall right in!"

Burdock snorted. "And if it doesn't?"

"And if it doesn't . . ." From the far side of the orchestra pit, Lantana stepped forward, an ancient pixie, freakishly thin, her nightshade-purple hair spiking around her wrinkled face. "And if that doesn't, we might just cloud the issue, so to speak."

Lantana heaved, then vomited billows of an opaque violet mist into the auditorium. Hemmel suddenly felt off-balance, no longer sure of his footing. He took a shaky step forward, then another, and another. He couldn't see anything now but the hues of the mist: tints of sunset and the promise of fine hunting in the darkest hour of night. Voices seemed to float to him from several directions at once. "Gisella? Burdock?" he called uncertainly.

His head abruptly cleared as Lantana's rough laugh pealed out and the mist evaporated like a popping soap bubble. Hemmel realized that he had unwittingly advanced to the lip of the pit. One more step, and he would tumble down into it. He saw that all the other Nightbreed stood on the orchestra pit's edge, too.

Lantana smiled wickedly. "If I can entrance you to step forth to the pit, I can lure *that*, too."

Hemmel considered. "Okay, you get the thing in the hole. Then what?"

From deep below him, a smooth, deep voice replied, "What happens next, my friend, is also what happens last."

Hemmel looked into the blackness of the pit. Something shuffled into better view, and Hemmel gasped in surprise. "Desai?"

"None other."

Desai rarely showed himself. In fact, Hemmel had only met him once before. Desai preferred to live below the stage, where a decayed warren of dressing rooms, long since half buried in dust, provided the dark, cool hiding place he craved. Dozens of hands sprouted like cilia from the sides of his unclothed body, extending and retracting at will. Six of Desai's hands were out at the moment, reaching around on stubby, rubbery arms to frame his back as he slowly did a pirouette for the Enclave's benefit. He had many hands, but only two feet, and these supported him awkwardly.

"You see, my friends, I am fit as ever where it matters the most." As he turned, the hands, deft as a game-show model's, pointed to the hard ridges running down Desai's spine. At the small of his back, a jointed tail whipped upward, its sharp stinger dangling just above Desai's head. "When our tormentor falls in here, I will give him a taste of my Sleep."

"You're going to stun the Pariah?" Burdock asked.

"If possible. Keep in mind, I may have to use all my poison, and then I cannot guarantee that creature"'s safety."

Hemmel felt absurdly touched. Desai's mother had used all her poison in the fight at Midian, and it had killed her. Yet Desai was willing to risk his own life for other Nightbreed, with whom he seldom interacted.

Gisella flicked out her talons. "We understand. The Dark God's will be done. We appreciate your sacrifice."

She surveyed the semicircle of Nightbreed. "Everyone, get to your places. Someone must keep watch and warn us when *that* is near."

Burdock squinted at Hemmel. "That would be you, of course. You're practically a Natural."

"Yeah?" Hemmel raised his shirt and let the Sickle coil forth in all its hunger.

Burdock was unimpressed. "You look a whole lot more Natural than any of the rest of us."

Hemmel glanced around. He couldn't argue with that one. "Fine."

"You got your cell phone?" Burdock asked.

"Of course." Hemmel absently felt the lump in the breast pocket of his overcoat to be sure. Since leaving Midian, the Nightbreed had adopted many of the Naturals' technological conveniences.

"And you remembered to *charge* it this time?"

"Yeah! Yeah! I'm not stupid." In fact, Hemmel had recently walked over a mile to an all-night doughnut shop to find a working outlet where he could hook up the damned phone.

"All right then. Be ready for further orders." Burdock pivoted his head to glower at Hemmel through the hole in his stocking cap. "And keep an eye out!"

Hemmel grunted acknowledgment, and reluctantly left the auditorium to take up his post outside the theater.

Standing alone beneath the Elysian's marquee, he shifted from foot to foot and pulled his coat more tightly around himself even though he didn't feel cold. Beneath his shirt, the Sickle hissed like an asp. In all the fuss over the Pariah, everyone seemed to have forgotten about food. Everyone but Hemmel. He'd actually been tempted to ask Amalek for a bite of Vagamel's leg but thought that might be rude.

He sniffed the chill air. There was Meat nearby, no doubt about it. Hemmel glanced up and down the desolate thoroughfare until he spotted her—a plump, solitary bag lady, shambling in distraction along the opposite sidewalk.

Hemmel's mouth twisted in hesitation. She was just across the street. He could still watch the front of the theater from there, and it would only take a minute. . . .

The Sickle would not be denied. Hemmel unbuttoned his shirt as he moved to intercept her.

The old hag must have been demented or delirious or both. She tore at her gray hair, waggling her head, peppering the air with frantic mutters. "No, no! I can't—it mustn't. Horrible, horrible."

Hemmel opened wide his arms. "No need to fret, Granny. You won't feel a thing."

The Sickle sprang forth from his exposed abdomen. He pulled her against him, and the cartilaginous point of the arced proboscis pierced her thread-bare clothing and penetrated her midriff. The appendage oozed a numbing, coagulant pus as the three-pronged point opened inside her, questing for an organ to harvest.

The bag lady slackened in Hemmel's embrace as she succumbed to the narcotic effect of the ooze. A casual observer would have thought they were hugging. He patted her back. "That's it. Just relax."

There was a time when Hemmel might have treated himself to a brain or a heart or a lung. Now that he was forced to coexist with Naturals, though, he found it better to use more discretion when selecting his snacks. An appendix for an appetizer. The bonbon of a gall bladder. Half a liver—no more! Or in this case, one of a pair of nice, juicy kidneys.

"Never even know it's gone," he whispered, as the prongs of the Sickle closed around the chosen meal. The proboscis pumped in stomach acid to digest the kidney inside the bag lady, then sucked the dissolved organ into Hemmel like soda through a straw. The coagulant would seal her wounds and keep her from bleeding to death.

Before he could finish, however, a new agitation seized the bag lady, so strong it overcame the sedation of Hemmel's pus. She flailed in his grasp, shrieking. "Oh, God! Oh, God! *That* is here! Stop *that*! Stop *that*!"

Her odd use of the pronoun chilled Hemmel. She was a Natural. She couldn't possibly know about . . .

He loosened his grip, and she wrenched loose from the Sickle's impalement. In the struggle, the proboscis ripped wide the wound instead of sealing it. Entrails bulged from the red maw, blood speckling the pavement as she stumbled away in a haphazard delirium.

As if forgetting to zip his fly, Hemmel stood there, dumbfounded, with the blood-smeared Sickle hanging out in plain sight. He glanced over his shoulder in the direction the old lady had gaped—toward the theater. No hideous monstrosity there. The only thing moving was a haggard-looking black man in an Army-surplus jacket limping along the sidewalk.

Yet when the man looked at him with his sorrowful eyes, Hemmel sickened with an overwhelming revulsion. A revulsion that metastasized into terror when the man turned and entered the Elysian.

Hemmel fumbled the cell phone out of his pocket, fought to steady his finger long enough to push the right contact number.

"Burdock!" he babbled before the other even had a chance to speak. "The Pariah—it *is* a shape-shifter!" He grimaced at the stunning obviousness of the statement. "The black guy that just came in—"

"Hemmel?" Burdock interrupted. "But *you* just came in. Great Baphomet—what is that smell?"

Shouts of alarm sounded in the background, and Hemmel snapped his phone shut to cut them off. His instinct was to run away, to let Gisella and the others deal with *that*. But he knew their plan was doomed, for they could never have anticipated what they were up against. They had never expected that the enemy could so easily masquerade as a friend. The Pariah was far worse than any of them had guessed.

Hemmel could have abandoned them, but for what? He had never been without Burdock and the others. A life without the Nightbreed was no life at all. Better to perish with them than survive alone.

He waddled back across to the theater, the Sickle bobbing in front of him. As he charged through the lobby, he nearly collided with Amalek, who lurched out of the auditorium with his arms wrapped around his head.

"It touched me! Oh, dear Vagamel, now I understand—*that* touched me!" Amalek flattened his ears back miserably and yowled, pawing at his snout with his man-hands like a dog that's been sprayed by a skunk. He collapsed and writhed on the marble floor, whining.

And there *was* a smell. The odor hit Hemmel like an arctic draft as he advanced into the inner sanctum of the theater.

Few scents can appall creatures who regularly revel in the miasma of the swamp, the stench of the charnel house, the reek of the grave. But this one curdled Hemmel to his marrow. It smelled antiseptic and bitter—a gust of wind across the glacier left by a nuclear winter, tasting of nothing but ash and ice. It blew from a world in which there would be neither blood nor flesh, ever again. An absolute desolation unknown even to the dead that lay in Midian.

The citizens of the Enclave stood in a circle in the center of the theater.

They had surrounded *that*. But Hemmel blanched as he saw, in the center of the circle, the mirror image of himself. The Pariah had duplicated him perfectly, even down to the slight bulge of the Sickle beneath his shirt. Hemmel's gorge rose, and his skin broke out in a feverish sweat.

But he did not have to endure the sight of himself as Pariah for long.

It was apparent that Gisella's meticulous battle plan had already unraveled. Caught off guard by the Pariah's deception, Crocus had not jumped until the disguised intruder had come close enough to lay hands on her. The girl had since leapt to the far end of the theater and ran in circles there, gibbering hysterically, disordered by fright.

Now, while Hemmel watched, Franchesco marshaled his avian squadron against the enemy. As the flock swooped from the rafters, though, the birds seemed to hit an invisible barrier, an impenetrable bubble around the Pariah that sent them glancing off, fluttering and squawking, in every direction.

The attack only succeeded in drawing the intruder's attention to Franchesco's perch. The impostor Hemmel looked upward and shook itself. It lost shape for an instant, then shivered into feathers of gold and silver and bronze, coalescing into the most glorious bird of prey imaginable. The false phoenix took flight, soaring up to circle around Franchesco's chandelier. When it dove toward him, Franchesco batted it away with disgust, flailing so much that he lost his balance and tumbled to the theater floor with a bone-breaking *crack*.

As he lay there, helpless and gasping, the majestic bird glided down to land beside him, craning its beak forward to bill Franchesco's cheek and coo in his ear. Paralyzed from the fall, Franchesco could barely lift his head, yet he so dreaded the Pariah's affection that he pounded the base of his cracked skull against the floor until it spilled grayish-blue cerebral jelly.

Before Franchesco's body twitched to stillness, a vague blurriness, like heat vapor, darted from an archway and assaulted the bird creature from behind. As it flapped and shrieked, Gisella crimsoned to the color of war paint and dug her talons into its hide.

"We know what you are," she shouted. Hemmel had never seen her tremble before. "How dare you violate our Enclave! Murdering your own kind! Accursed thing, now you will die!"

She snapped her wolf-trap jaws shut on its neck and clung to it as it began to change. It melted out of her clutches, then re-formed in front of her.

It opened arms with taloned hands like Gisella's own, enfolding her in its embrace.

Gisella screamed, a sound that made the chandelier crystals resound in an unbearably high frequency.

Heads formed with faces that were the male counterparts of Gisella's own. Their many colors, which changed in exactly the way Gisella's skin could change, pulsed around her as multiple mouths kissed, sucked, licked, seemingly on her everywhere at once in their ardor.

Gisella screamed again, her body convulsing, her skin rapidly losing its color until it turned a lifeless gray.

With their general dead, the rest of the troops fell into disarray. Even the great Desai had clambered out of the pit and was now skittering toward the nearest exit on all hands like a frightened roach.

"*Retreat!*" Lantana yelled. She exhaled gouts of purple smoke that clouded the entire room for nearly a minute. Under the cover Lantana had given them, Hemmel heard a stampede of feet and paws and hooves, and someone roughly shoved him against a wall in their haste to leave.

When the violet mist finally dissipated, Hemmel realized that, other than the bodies of Franchesco and Gisella, he was alone. The others had escaped, or else gone elsewhere to die of the Pariah's darkness.

But the monster's sickening miasma remained. Out of the air, the Pariah's energy gathered up into one brutal mouth, its corners turned down as it opened in a hideous, pitiable, earsplitting wail. Even from a monster among monsters, the noise could not be mistaken. An anguished sob filled the abandoned auditorium, the sound of utter despair.

Desperately wanting to flee and yet unable to look away, Hemmel stood transfixed as the Pariah's shape altered again. Out of one half materialized a shape Hemmel had never seen before. This new form had two faces looking Janus-like in opposite directions. The single body beneath possessed supernal symmetry, at the same time glowing with two separate facets like a jewel: on the left a male, its muscles rippling and sex organ thrusting in powerful display, and on the right a female, with soft curves and one lush ripe breast. Though every nerve in Hemmel shrieked and his stomach writhed in abhorrence, Hemmel could still gasp with awe at its beauty. Such a creature could certainly captivate Baphomet, could seduce the darkest of gods.

Yet as Hemmel marveled, the Pariah's other half began to take on a very different shape. It shrank, forming a sort of hairy oblong close to the ground, long and bulky like the body of a pig. A rodent face emerged from its awkward bulk, whiskered, with small ears and teeth so long they propped the mouth partially open. The thing seemed the utter opposite of the Pariah's perfect other half.

Hemmel remembered the legend, the ratlike thing that had so enraged Baphomet that He had split the hapless creature into a thousand fragments of itself.

The Pariah's lover.

The hairy creature cozened up to the godlike androgyne, snuffling in evident delight. And the androgyne wrapped its male and female arms around it in frantic passion. The hog-sized thing, with its ratlike face, suckled madly at the female breast, nibbled the areola with its ludicrous long teeth. The male Janus face nuzzled the hoglike thing's furry neck, while the female face moaned in rising ecstasy. The Janus's male organ penetrated its lover as the creature reciprocated, entering the androgyne's female sex. As the two halves of the Pariah's body stroked one another, writhing desperately, approaching a single climax, Hemmel sensed he was witness to an oft-repeated dance. Tears streaked the androgyne's two faces, and its rodent counterpart whimpered in distress.

How many times had this happened over the centuries as the creature agonized in its oubliette? Perpetually isolated, the Pariah's sole comfort lay in its own illusions. Only its own cursed touch could grant it release. Yet this could never truly satisfy. For even in the gifted multiplicity of its form, the Pariah remained alone.

At last, Hemmel understood. The Pariah did not wish to bring death. As it had in times beyond, it sought love. But it could only offer a love that utterly destroyed the object of its desire.

And any second now, Hemmel realized, he would be next.

He had nothing more to lose—no shelter, no safe hunting ground. Worst of all, his companions, his kin, the only friends he would ever have on the earth or under it, had either died or abandoned him.

And the Pariah—what did it have to live for? He'd be doing it a favor to end its miserable existence. It would not be merely revenge—it would be a mercy killing. But how? Strong as the others had been, they had proved no match for the Pariah's power.

The Sickle stirred, reminding Hemmel of its presence. Of course! Even shape-shifters had hearts. If Hemmel could find it, the Sickle would take care of the rest.

Hemmel felt the Pariah's attention turn to him. The faultless Janus and the glorified rodent dissolved as the Pariah, once again, molded itself into Hemmel's own likeness.

It had to be now. Unleashing a primal yell, Hemmel charged forward with all the speed his ungainly body could muster. For a split second the nauseous smell and the overwhelming urge to flee nearly overpowered him. Then the Sickle plunged directly into the false Hemmel's chest, its proboscis probing for the heart of the monster.

Instantly the Pariah's form softened and expanded, engulfing Hemmel completely. Hemmel panicked. He felt as if he were drowning, being smothered, being drenched in wretched muck. The Sickle, usually infallible in seeking specific organs, foundered. The Pariah's anatomy was unlike any Hemmel had encountered. Its innards melted and flowed and reconstituted themselves in new configurations, easily avoiding the Sickle's prongs.

Hemmel no longer cared about killing the cursed being. Whatever the cost, he had to escape.

At the same time he sensed that escape would be impossible. Already he could feel hands and tongues on his body, a rain of kisses and caresses that made him want to die. Withdrawing the Sickle from its fruitless quest, he turned the cutting tip toward his own chest. Better to end it now, himself, than die as the others had. The Sickle hesitated, then plunged into his chest. The pain made Hemmel cry out, but at the same time he could only feel relief at the thought of ending his proximity to the Pariah.

"Never even know it's gone," he gasped as the three-pronged claw cleanly severed his arteries. Hemmel felt his heart beat its last as it liquefied.

But the expected oblivion did not come.

Instead, a viscous clamminess seeped like bilgewater through the incision the Sickle had made and filled the empty cavity in his chest. Hemmel felt the substance congeal within him, knitting itself to his aorta. A moment later, it began to beat.

He looked down at his chest and saw that a network of stringy veins now fanned out from the sealed wound, gently pulsing as they circulated blood from him to the Pariah and back again. The monster had replaced Hemmel's heart with its own, entwining them forever.

Burdock stared out at the night, the eyes on the sides of his head straining to catch the slightest movement outside the abandoned warehouse where he and the other refugees of the Enclave had fled. He hadn't been able to rest in the intervening days since the Pariah had driven them out of the Elysian.

If his eyes had had lids, Burdock would have shut them. He was so weary.

Determined to fulfill his self-imposed duty as sentry, he sat on the floor beneath the window and leaned back against the wall, hoping at least to ease the tension in his body. Almost as soon as he reclined, however, he shot bolt upright again.

There was a scent in the air . . . a whiff of pungent, flesh-freezing coldness, as of steaming liquid nitrogen.

"Don't be stupid," he muttered to himself. To his shame, he often imagined he smelled the Pariah's vile odor.

He was about to relax when the locked warehouse door nearest him burst inward, swinging with the force of whatever had rammed it. Burdock jumped to his feet and snatched his cell phone from the pocket of his jacket, ready to alert the others. But something about the shuffling footsteps he heard next made him stop. He recognized that shambling gait as if it were his own, but at the same time it seemed totally alien.

The biting stench became unbearable as a misshapen silhouette clumped through the door and approached him.

"*Who are you?*" With his phone still ready in one hand, Burdock pulled out his flashlight with the other and flicked its beam over the intruder.

The circle of light darted from one cameo of abomination to another. Here, a pair of hands—one masculine, one feminine—fondled sagging male buttocks. There, male and female faces on a single head took turns languidly fellating the proboscis that jutted from an obese abdomen. Higher up, a chittering rodent nipped at the nipple of a pendulous male mammary. And, above this horrid mishmash of forms, the miserable image of Hemmel, blubbering in desperation.

"Burdock! You have to help me." The lumpy, misbegotten figure tottered toward him.

Burdock stumbled backward. He had loved Hemmel, but now he couldn't stand the sight or smell of the thing his friend had become. "Don't you touch me! Don't you come near me!"

Hemmel wept as he reached out to Burdock. "Please! Don't leave me alone with—with—*this*!"

It was no use. Burdock ran to the nether parts of the warehouse, stammering warnings into his cell phone.

Hemmel collapsed to the floor, sobbing in resignation. United to him by love and loathing, his new companion snuggled within him like a conjoined twin.

Amorphous, yet formed.

Shunned, but no longer alone.

Together, they were, and would always be, the Pariah.

THE JESUIT'S MASK

Durand Sheng Welsh

The trailhead wasn't signposted, was just a clot of shadow off the road's crumbled shoulder. The Mongrel almost missed it, even with the headlights on high beam. The lack of streetlamps or houselights—he'd passed nothing but bushland for the last two miles— didn't help, nor did the fact that the map on his phone had lost its connection during his low-gear ascent up what amounted to an asphalted goat track.

Driving on the left had never agreed with him at the best of times, not to mention he'd embarrassed himself at the car-rental yard by hopping into the shotgun seat before remembering the steering column was on the other side. Admittedly, Rome had been far worse. At least in Australia there weren't mad Italians shedding blood for a hair's width of lane.

He hit the anchors and threw a hard right, watching the high beams sweep across close-packed eucalypts and then knife down the dark throat of the trailhead's parking lot. The shimmying Toyota chewed across the scrim of wood chips and leaf litter laid atop the lot's graded dirt. Then the wheels straightened and the Mongrel was riding moonbeams and a funnel of dust to a split-log parking bumper. His final stamp on the brakes caused the metal case on the passenger seat to slide toward the footwell, and the Mongrel arrested its momentum with a light touch, like a man stopping a child from crossing a busy street.

Be still, be still partner. We're here.

The moment he clicked the engine off he heard the ocean. When he got out, a sea breeze raised gooseflesh along his arms.

From inside the metal case came screams of hilarity. The Mongrel ignored them and hid the car key behind the back tire and laid his copy of the New Testament onto the car roof alongside his machete. He turned his pockets inside out. There was nothing else.

Carved into the bedrock, stairs fell off the edge of the ridgeline to the west, winding down through eucalypts and semitropical ferns toward the tarnished plate-metal of the Pacific. A timber signage board held a map under a pane of Perspex. According to the posted blurb, the Bouddhi National Park was the eager naturalist's go-to locale for reef egrets, peregrine falcons, and marsupial rodents. Some people had too much free time.

The Mongrel sniffed the breeze. Salt. Eucalyptus oil. The fearful musk of native animals—just as advertised. And beneath those scents, the rank taint of his quarry, the Jesuit. A stench robed in spoiling offal and bloody stool, steeped in the territorial piss-stink of Midian.

The Mongrel had never known Midian. He didn't feel the pull of old vows and ancient rituals. He was of the new order—a child of that yet to come, not that which had been. He'd heard tales, of course, but who hadn't? *There are truths, and there are lies, and then there is Midian.* So he owed Midian's memory nothing at all. Yet here he was. What a farce.

The steel suitcase rattled. The Mongrel went to it and bent his ear to the cold metal. *"We're close, aren't we?"* a voice said from inside. It was muffled by the velvet padding and scratchy where Button Face's zipper clicked and clacked with the bruised exhortations of a stolen larynx.

"Yes," the Mongrel said. He inhaled. His lungs bloated themselves with the moist night air, became fat and pregnant in his rib cage, and then he exhaled, expelling the night shroud between his skinned-back lips, swaddling himself in the unholy. His sinews thickened, his jaw crafted itself anew. His anatomy reshaped itself as a bastard hybrid of the ichthyic and the reptilian, evolution toward, rather than away from, the primordial broth. A transformation he both craved and abhorred.

When he was done, the tatters of his mortal clothing shucked, he went back and collected the machete, the keys, and the Bible. *Forgive me Father, for I have sinned.*

He opened the steel case and placed them inside, next to Button Face.

Button Face snickered at the Bible. "Don't let your real father catch you at that blasphemy."

Conceived in a jail cell, the rotten fruit of the dead fucking the living—his very existence was blasphemy. Half the man and twice the monster was the Mongrel's private, self-deprecating joke.

To hell with his father, Boone, or Cabal, or whatever appellation was today's fancy.

The Mongrel shut the lid on his leering detractor and the worn Bible and descended the stairs. "My father is half a world away. If Aaron has a problem sending me to the corners of the earth to solve his problems, he's never said so before. The least he can do is let me worship my own god."

"Stubborn fucker, aren't you," Button Face said.

The Mongrel imagined swinging the case into a sandstone cutting, silencing the mockery. But he did no such thing. Like the faithful lapdog he was, he even let the elasticity of his muscles smooth the jolts as he descended to the accompaniment of the meekly shifting leaves and the seething ocean.

———

Baphomet, holiest of holies, vivisected relic of Old Midian's mythic splendor. At the outset of this job, Aaron gave—gifted, the lordly one would have called it—the Mongrel with a tender cut of the prophet: tongue and voice box cleaved from the revered flesh.

The last located relics, Aaron had called them. "A weighty trust, my son. They shall light your way to the heretic's lair."

Then his father had unveiled his second entrustment: a patchwork mask of blackened sackcloth. The mask displayed buttons for eyes, a zippered slit for a mouth. The zipper was crooked where the cloth had been restitched around its steel-toothed line.

Ol' Button Face himself, reclaimed from the fired graveyard earth, from ashes heaped upon ashes, a burned scrap salted with the sweat, the toxins, the heat-liquefied fat of its former wearer, Dr. Decker. The mask's torn fragments had been passed from shadowed hand to shadowed hand along the trafficking night lanes, back to that same hand that had destroyed it. Then that same hand had rebirthed the monster. *Needle and thread, balm and blood.*

Aaron, though, had wanted the Mongrel present for the final act of reconciliation. While the Mongrel watched, Aaron himself stitched the vocal apparatus of the prophet into the mask. Ol' Button Face was sewn around the Baptizer's larynx, lips, and tongue. This new relic, this freshly whelped child, junction of primeval power and modern terror, seared in the baptismal flames, anointed in Decker's blood and Boone's seed, was appointed the Mongrel's overseer.

Button Face had been curiously passive since they touched down at the northern tip of Australia, that prehistoric, baked slab of rock sundered loose millennia ago from the tectonic ridge of Gondwanaland. In fairness, though, the Mask had steered them true enough as they cut for sign along the northern provinces, had uncovered the first clues that turned them south through the rain forests of Cairns and motel rooms become abattoirs, then farther south, through gutted railroad towns and carcass-filled whorehouses.

The Jesuit has his appetites, that he does.

Now, on the temperate eastern seaboard, at the bottom of a bushland staircase, the trail was near its terminus.

The Mongrel stepped off the stairs and out into the moonlight. Against the sand beat the mighty Pacific. Its tempo was as slow and steady as the Mongrel's own heartbeat.

Button Face laughed using the Baptizer's vocal cords. "Hurry, hurry."

A boat bobbed in the bay, lightless, sail unfurled from the mast and flapping around the moon like a willful scarf. If the Jesuit was here, then there was no hope for the boat's occupants. They were already converts or dead.

"I smell him," Button Face said.

The Mongrel found himself wishing for the sun, the bronzing splendor of daybreak, and again he wondered if he was the right person for the task. He was tired of toiling for his father's dreams.

"Follow the estuary," Button Face said. "Even locked in this case I sense its fetid water. It is polluted with the ablutions of the Jesuit and his Breed."

"Ablutions?" the Mongrel said. "You spent too much time with that psychiatrist. A dictionary is a tool, not a calling."

"Fuck you."

"Not even if we find the Baptizer's stolen cock amongst these rebels."

"Graft his majestic thews onto me, would you, Mongrel? Wouldn't Daddy love that?"

"There are nights I get weary of your madness. Where's this estuary?"

he said, but he already smelled it. The beach was a scimitar of yellow sand, encapsulated by a tree-wreathed bluff. Halfway along the beach, the bluff fell back from the beach a ways, and all that fronted the tree line there was a berm of sand. The berm was cut through by a channel of water that trickled from a font hidden behind the tree line.

The Jesuit had broken the truce, had the hubris to think of making a dark Eden here in the south. Button Face and the Mongrel had trailed his boot prints through scores of riven towns and desolated rest stops. Whole municipalities given to the midnight power of the balm. A plague, an epidemic. Already the day world was stirring. Mutterings and chatterings in the synagogues, the churches, the mosques, in the city halls, the tiers of Parliament. The gluttonous armature of the establishment was rousing itself, and Aaron Boone was worried.

So, he had sent the Mongrel to make good on his promises of damnation for transgressors. But talk was cheap, and as always, the real work, work that was not so cheap, fell to the Mongrel.

"What would your god say about our mission?" Button Face said. The Mongrel scowled and started the hard slog along the beach toward the trickling channel. The machete swung with each step, its blade near keen enough to part the moonbeams from their heavenly fountainhead.

"The Holy Christ has no love for monsters," Button Face said. "No love for you or I."

"I'm no monster. And you're a sackcloth rag stuffed with a dead man's breath."

"O cruel world, to put me under your dominion. Alas, alack." More laughter. "Still, your choice of god is flawed. Why not be your own god?"

"Like my father."

"These daddy issues. They're growing old, Mongrel. I talk of God. You talk of your father. What would Dr. Decker have said about that, I wonder?"

They had neared the channel, and around its mouth, where fresh water burbled through the berm under a glaze of moonlight, the Mongrel saw footprints. The footprints weren't human. They were too large, too deep, and divots marked the placement of talons. The Mongrel didn't spare them further study. He would meet the owner soon enough, of that he was sure.

He lowered the case and cracked the lid. From inside came a rich, ambrosial stink and the clacking noise of Button Face smacking his zipper lips. "Follow the estuary, Mongrel. Tarry not. The Baptizer's flesh pulls me west, further back behind the sand."

The Mongrel hefted the metal case and the machete, and ventured away from the open beach, back into the shuttered gloom behind the tree line, following the sandy edge of the tributary that wended back into the scrub.

"Stop!" Button Face commanded after they had hiked a short way. "Read the sign," he said.

Too involved in his own thoughts, the Mongrel had missed it. The sign was stenciled sheet metal and had the official look of government signage. That was to say there was small print at the bottom warning of fines and penalties and litigation.

The sign's header read:

WHALE GRAVEYARD.
Do not disturb.

Button Face felt the need to explain about the process by which beached whales were ofttimes bulldozed into shallow graves behind the dunes. What else to do with a fifty-ton corpse? Button Face, he knew all about corpses and disposing of corpses. As he put it, his former owner was a "practitioner of the art."

The Mongrel looked for gouged earth, excavated soil, the belly-drag scars of towed leviathans. Despite what the sign cautioned against, he didn't see much that he could disturb except banksia shrubs and nesting emu-wrens.

As he stood there, still and silent, he noticed the little girl. She was a ways into the scrubland, her mop of dark hair shading in with the shadows. It was her skin that gave her away. It was stark white; skin never kissed by sunlight.

She was Breed. Odds were she was a new convert. Children took easiest to the change, the trading of skins, day for night, light for dark, life for death. The Mongrel felt the rawhide straps of the machete's handle scratching against his callused palm.

She had to be a lookout, a "cockatoo" in the native lingo of this southern hamlet. She'd seen him now, would raise the alarm if given a chance. He cut across the stream, hooked sharply into the scrub. He moved fast, a loping run. His blood was up, the Breed in him boiling to the surface. The girl watched him, unmoving.

His heightened hearing discerned Button Face's breaths grow quick in anticipation. Soon, very soon, Button Face would start clamoring to be let out so he could watch. He'd ask the Mongrel to daub fresh blood against his zippered mouth. He'd ask . . . for many things.

The Mongrel dropped the case and continued running. Behind him, Button Face screamed his outrage. But this girl, she wasn't destined to feed Button Face's fantasies. The Mongrel would give her the mercy of a clean death. He was almost upon her, the machete raised horizontally, ready to begin a flat arc toward the girl's throat. That was where he was staring— her throat. Fixing the cutting point, measuring his angles, judging the tensile strength of her cartilage and bone. It was only for that reason that he saw the crucifix, and even then only because it caught the moonlight at just the right moment, silver on silver.

The girl just stared at him as his feet stuttered and halted. The heat went out of him. He knelt in the sandy ground. "They let you wear that?" he said.

"Wear what?"

He opened his mouth, and slowly, so as not to alarm her, he sucked back the night shroud from his face and torso. It was a peculiar talent of his, this duality. He laid the machete on the ground. The girl smiled and held up the crucifix. "This?"

Under the laws of Old Midian, she was holding up her own death sentence. She didn't know that, though. She didn't know Midian or the old laws. How the Mongrel envied her.

"Everyone wears one," she said. She gave him a funny look. "Except you. Who are you? Why haven't I seen you before?"

"I'm no one," he said, and then the ground slid out from under his bent knees, tons of dirt collapsing down into the cavernous earth. The little girl, standing at the edge of the pit, watched his descent with pale, curious eyes.

The trap sprung, the Mongrel could do nothing but ride the serpent, down into the bone-breaking abyss.

———————

The Mongrel could hold his breath for half an hour. His heart beat but a handful of beats in a minute. Still, at some stage during the descent he passed out.

The Mongrel awoke to the hammering of nails. The rhythmic beat rattled his teeth, caused a flagrant booming in his skull. He tried to squeeze the heels of his palms against his temples and found he couldn't move his arms.

Above him, ossified bones girdled the ceiling, gave the Mongrel the curious impression that he was looking up a whalebone corset. Torches guttered in the walls. The air was syrupy with burning oil and the muck of the grave. *Ill omens to wake to*, he thought, and tried again to shift his arms. Turning his head he saw why they weren't responding to his summons.

Crouched low at either side, corpulent humanoids, stripped to breechcloths and rich with the sweat of their labor, pounded steel spikes into his wrist joints. The beasts had shark-tooth mouths at the crowns of their hairless skulls. Their flesh had the gray consistency of potter's clay, and wormy things wriggled in and out of burrows in their backs.

The grievous injury being occasioned, that workmanlike nail-driving, was curiously painless.

Was he doped? Suffering a delusion?

The nails were affixing him to a driftwood cross. He lay naked. His night shroud had deserted him, and when he tried to regurgitate it he brought up nothing but dusty air and red spackle. His assailants tapped the nails in the final few inches and then withdrew themselves.

"Easy friend," a man said. He leaned over the Mongrel, face hidden in the cowl of a hessian robe. The robe's fabric billowed and bulged as if something writhed in ecstasy inside of it. "Hush." He held a veiny finger to the black oval of the cowl. "You know me by that ridiculous title, the Jesuit. My true name is of no consequence, so for now I concede that the lie will serve. I have already tested the limits of my mercy by giving you a nostrum to nullify the pain. But the crowd, oh the crowd, like the Romans of old, they demand a spectacle, so a spectacle we best give them."

The Jesuit took a step back and whirled his arm. "Raise him up."

The cross was raised. The Mongrel milled his feet as his weight depended down from the two pinion points at his wrists.

From his newfound vantage, the Mongrel saw a subterranean lake, and before the lake a congregation of Breed. These were new converts, reveling still in the novelty of their dead skins, eager to flex raw flesh and supple limbs, vent roars and show needle teeth, caper and rut. The Jesuit had raided every larder for his army: whorehouses and churches, day-care centers and infirmaries, business schools and asylums.

The Mongrel met their accusing looks with his flat stare. He saw that the rabble's constituents all wore the holy cross. Just as the girl had said.

"Are you surprised that we worship the Lord here?" the Jesuit said. "That is why your father cast me out. You think he needed greater reason than that?"

"He had greater reason than that." The Jesuit had put their secrecy at risk. Guilt over Midian's destruction, no doubt, had compounded Aaron's fury. *Never again* was something of a mantra for the old man.

"You still believe Cabal's lies," the Jesuit said from the breathy void of the cowl. His words smelled of wine and garlic. "Poor lamb. I warn you, we're more the Old Testament than the New down here. Think on that before you answer my next question."

"You're a mass murderer," the Mongrel said. "There's your answer to whatever question you have."

"These people are reborn, not murdered. Now and then some of my followers may have become . . . unruly. But can they be blamed? Fresh converts . . . you remember what it was like, don't you? The urges. The confusion. Your father cares not for the deaths of mortals, only for the ripples those deaths create."

The Jesuit reached into the folds of his robe, and his hand came forth bearing a familiar book. The Mongrel's copy of the New Testament. He laid the book beneath the Mongrel's suspended feet. "Join me and this, everything within it, shall be yours. No more skulking out into the sun to thumb through the Gospels during stolen daylight hours."

The Mongrel thought of the metal case and Button Face, and didn't dare tempt fate by asking the circumstances under which the Jesuit had found the Bible.

"I'm more partial to Revelation," the Mongrel said. "Revenge. Damnation. Divine retribution."

"Be careful what you wish for, Mongrel. All you need to tell me, to prove yourself, is where the Baptizer's relic is. I know you brought a piece of his holiness with you. A way to track me, your father would have said. As indeed it is. Like has an affinity for like. He didn't tell you how that is, did he? Didn't trust you enough, perhaps. You are ignorant of my rightful appropriation of all the prophet's parts. My flesh, my soul, my very essence gestates the prophet's rebirth. Now where is the final relic, so I might give voice to the prophet's words?" He leaned close. Whispered: "Scream a little for the peasants. Our discourse is too civil for their liking, and we need both play our parts if you expect to come through unscathed. I can only pacify the flock so much."

The Mongrel grunted. But in that moment, he took the measure of the crowd, and beheld his fellow assassin, Button Face, among the sea of faces, zippered mouth glinting, button eyes mirthful.

I'll be damned, thought the Mongrel. Button Face was wearing a new body, had shorn it of its original head, a bait-and-switch bordering on high art. The cuckolded body stood unnoticed among the menagerie of freaks. With the methodical single-mindedness that was Button Face's nature, he began to work his way toward the head of the crowd. The Mongrel's machete trailed tip-down from one gloved hand.

"I know the piece is near," the Jesuit said, hot breath lathing the Mongrel's cheek. "I can feel it." Another heavy breath. "I'm offering a place by my side. A chance to worship your god without persecution. To belong. Turn the last piece of the Baptizer over to me. Subsume the old within the new. Cannibalize. As religions do."

The Mongrel watched Button Face approach. The cords of his pilfered neck were etched bloody where they'd been grafted onto his new body. His path took him by the girl the Mongrel had earlier encountered aboveground. As Button Face passed her by, he casually drew the machete across the back of her neck; her curious expression melding with puzzlement, she toppled, a rag-boned doll, sprawled behind her murderer.

He's done no less than what I had earlier intended, the Mongrel told himself in hollow justification.

"Where is it?" the Jesuit insisted. "Tell me!"

"I . . ." What could he say? Perhaps, ironically, if his hands had not been so securely fixed, he would have chosen to point just then at the approaching form of Button Face. But as it was, all he did was gasp a little, flop and roll his tongue, and make the most exhausted of utterances.

Button Face pushed aside the twisted limbs and grotesque torsos that barred his way; stooped once to adjust some monstrous failure in his new anatomy—a vestigial third arm that protruded from beneath his undershirt—and then he was standing by the Jesuit's side. The Mongrel hissed air between his teeth. Waited. Button Face cocked his head, tapped the soft earth with the tip of the machete.

The Jesuit turned to face the interloper.

"Jesuit," Button Face said, "I'm here to offer you a deal."

"Traitor," the Mongrel said, but Button Face only laughed at him. "The Baptizer wants to be whole again. He told me so. Me and Baphomet, lip-locked as starry lovers, closer than the bloodiest of blood kin. So stop your prattle, mutt. You think you're the only one worthy of negotiation."

"You'd betray us?" the Mongrel said. The Jesuit held his hand up for silence. Hoots and whistles erupted from the congregation. They sensed the play of great forces, the momentum of history being made.

Button Face's crooked zipper-mouth twitched. "Us? What us? Whom exactly do you speak for, mutt? Your father's fractured tribe? Now you wish to claim them as your own? A fine time for that."

The Mongrel fell silent. What response could he mount to that truth?

The Jesuit regarded Button Face. His hands trembled. A palpable hunger seemed to billow from beneath his cowl.

"A deal," Button Face said. "The mask comes with the Baptizer's vocal cords. A package deal, like a furnished apartment, my friend."

"What's in it for you?" the Jesuit said to Button Face.

"A slice of the future. You'll wear me, yes, as you take this tribe out of the shadows and we pull down the sun itself and bring the earth into the folds of eternal night."

That melodramatic vision won the Jesuit over, and he traded pleasantries with his new pilgrim in the shadow of the Mongrel's pinned and broken body. Hands were clasped, pacts sealed. The world turned. The Mongrel bled. The congregation roared.

"We'll feed him to the crowd," the Jesuit said, tapping the Mongrel in the chest with a pointed fingernail.

"First, the deal."

The Jesuit peeled the sackcloth mask from the walking corpse; the Baptizer's vocal apparatus came loose from its insertion. The Jesuit clasped the whole reeking, dripping mess, held it high to the crowd, and then took it inside his hood to make congress with his hidden face.

The crowd fell silent. The liquid sounds of Baptizer, Mask, and Jesuit all bonding filled the cavern. The Jesuit reached up slowly and peeled back his hood.

"Oh, this is surely grand," Button Face said from atop the Jesuit's body. The robe fell open, revealing the jigsaw of grafts and joins where the Jesuit had remade Baphomet's body from its fractionated pieces. Beneath the mask, the Baptizer's imprisoned face contorted in orgasmic thrill, his body whole again.

He approached the Mongrel, leaned in close. "I guess this is where we part ways. Any last wishes?"

"I'd rather not die on the cross," the Mongrel said. "I'm asking for that, at least."

Button Face stood motionless, then finally nodded. He ordered the hairless hammer men to take the Mongrel down, and they obeyed.

"Some dignity, please," the Mongrel said. "A private execution. No spectacle."

Again, Button Face took his time to respond, but again, after a pause, he acquiesced to the Mongrel's request.

The hammer men carried the Mongrel around the lake and behind the rude huts clustered at the shore. They laid him down and left him alone with Button Face.

The place was a graveyard of sorts, but not for men or women, and not for the Breed, who left no mortal bones. This was where the whales had come to rest, their corpses perhaps finding their way into this subterranean chamber via a similar route to the Mongrel's. Was this a mockery of Midian's necropolis? Or was there some nostalgic whimsy behind the choice? Either way, in his madness, the Jesuit had infected their rotten corpses with the balm. Around the Mongrel, the whales expelled deep sonorous breaths and aligned themselves to the invisible tides of the invisible moon. The Mongrel wet his lips, and clenched his hands in the mud. His fingers curled around something, a comb of broken baleen. Its edge was sharp and splintered.

"Go," Button Face said. "Or are you so dumbstruck by my largesse that you can't think to save your own skin?"

"You're letting me go?"

"Of course. You amuse me. Your hatred of your father amuses me. In that we are alike. In our hatred, I should say, not our amusement. We'll meet again, at the end of days. Soon enough, then. Soon enough." He turned his back on the Mongrel. "The way to the surface is behind you. There is a hidden door. Stairs leading to daylight. I know how you love the daylight, Mongrel."

The Mongrel tightened his grip on the baleen. He lifted it from its bedding of dirt. Button Face gave the ceiling a lonesome stare and sighed through his stolen vocal cords. "You always wanted to wear me, didn't you, Mongrel? I would have let you, too, but you never asked. Go now, you fool."

The Mongrel struck. The baleen cudgel caught Button Face between the shoulder blades, embedded itself to the hilt. Button Face swooned, turned. The Mongrel and he held each other, clasped in a tense embrace, and then slowly, slowly, Button Face slid toward the earth.

The whales breathed softly around them. Their undead eyes swiveled balefully. The Mongrel crouched down. He pulled free the length of baleen, and with savage cuts, excised Button Face from the Jesuit's face and the Baptizer's vocal cords.

"Perhaps you'll get your wish," the Mongrel said, and pulled Ol' Button Face down over his head. The sackcloth stank of blood and sour breath. He took the Jesuit's robes and donned them.

He hid the bodies inside the gullets of the whales.

Resplendent in the entitlements of his new office, he returned to his congregation, his tribe. He hid his wounded wrists within his sleeves. At the base of the driftwood cross he stooped low and collected his Bible. He ordered the cross torn down. He told his people that their first task would be the construction of a simple church. They would have to work swiftly. Their enemies were legion. Had they heard of Old Midian and a charlatan named Aaron Boone? The zipper was cold against his lips as he spoke. The metal tasted of Baphomet, of the Jesuit's blood, of Dr. Decker's spittle, of the ashes of dead Midian.

"Imagine the look on your father's face when we return," Button Face said with the Mongrel's voice. The Mongrel raised his hand, and drew the zipper slowly closed.

ROOK

Rob Salem

And he sent forth a raven, which went forth to and fro, until the waters were dried up from off the earth.

—*Genesis* 8:7

Monsters.
      Monsters everywhere.
      But not like him.

As far as his eyes could see—and those eyes could see beyond the horizons of this world and into other, not so distant realms—there were monsters everywhere. Not that they considered themselves as such, he mused, not even the ones who knew and embraced their own inner darkness. Down there, running around in the labyrinth of the city living their lives, most were content to believe that the towering glass-and-steel structures they had created were symbols of their greatness and mastery over the world and the laws of the universe. It occurred to very few of them that there might be "something more" out there in the darkness, watching, waiting, but even they couldn't really grasp the truth of it all, even if they wanted to. No matter. In the end, they were all the same. . . .

Meat.

Rook loved the city. The sights. The sounds. The smells. The hustle and bustle of a constantly "on" world, where much of daytime life carried on into the night, appealed to him in a way that most of the Breed didn't understand. He was one of the few that truly missed the sun, not just for its warmth and splendor, but for the hope of life that it offered, a life that would never be his again. Looking up, he could see the waxing moon, her usually silver face glowing a sickly yellow-orange through the haze of the city lights and smog, offering only the small comfort of a pale reflection of the sun, a dim reminder that it was still there. For a moment he envied her for the view she must have of the sun, and of the world, a view that made his own supernatural vision seem human by comparison. He wondered what she saw down there that even he couldn't.

For as much as he loved the sun and missed its golden rays, he also loved the moon and the night. How could he not? He was Nightbreed, of the tribes of the moon, and one of her children. Her blessings had been bountiful to him; bountiful enough that the loss of the sun, while sad, was worthwhile, and no part of his swearing his oath to the Baptizer was regrettable. Lylesburg and the others had welcomed him in, and Baphomet had named him the Sentinel, charging him to keep careful watch over Midian.

Then came Cabal, He Who Unmade Midian. Rook had seen his coming, of course, sharing a touch of the Baptizer's foresight. During the conflagration that destroyed the Nightbreed's sanctuary, He Who Made Midian had spoken again to Rook, changing him from Sentinel to Seeker, tasking him with helping Cabal find a new home, a new Midian, and reuniting the scattered tribes of the moon. So many nights he'd flown over the black-cloaked landscape of the world, soaring here and there following faint echoes in his senses of Baphomet's visions, eventually finding himself in Chicago. What it was that drew him here, he wasn't sure, but he knew better than to ignore the subtle guidance to his intuition.

A scream echoed off the walls of the alley below him. It trailed off into the hum of the city night, but not before pulling him from his ponderings. There, in the shadows, Rook could see a woman slumped against the wall. Even up here he could smell the blood. A man stood over her, undoing his pants.

She was aware that her heart had only a moment ago been pounding furiously in her chest, but now its once familiar and comfortable rhythm was diminishing, and on the edge of consciousness she knew that she was dying; her only thought—a prayer, perhaps?—was the hope that she would be dead or unconscious and thus spared the experience of what came next.

"Yeah, bitch. You may not enjoy this, but I'm sure gonna!" the man grunted as he fumbled with his belt and zipper. His erection was straining against the material of his dirty jeans.

"Damn it!" he, or maybe it, swore in frustration.

Finally free of its denim prison, his hard-on demanded attention *now*. Kicking her legs apart before dropping to his knees and pushing her skirt up, he found himself stopped short at the sight of a long shadow suddenly cast against the wall he was facing. He turned, erection in hand, to see who was standing behind him. He immediately went flaccid at the sight of a pair of giant black wings framing a slender but wiry human frame. One hand holding on to his pants, the other digging in his coat pocket for his still bloody knife, he struggled to his feet.

"You—You gotta problem, man?" he said with no small amount of disbelief.

Rook smiled, a jagged glimmer of silver-white in the darkness, the sight of his mouth full of fangs catching the man's balls in his throat.

"In fact, I do. I'm homeless and hungry. Spare some food?"

Talonlike claws launched out of the shadow, ripping open flesh and sinew. The man blinked and gurgled before slumping to the ground. His head was left attached to his body only by his spinal column. Rook crouched down over the bloody mess, turning its head face up to look at him.

"Now, let's see what you've seen. . . ."

Working his thumbs delicately into the man's eye sockets, he popped out first one eyeball, then the other, taking care not to damage them as he did so. After severing the optical nerve, he held the first eye up in the faint orange glow being cast by the alley's single light and studied it for a moment before popping it in his mouth. He bit down hard, feeling the rubbery surface cave and give way with a *pop* that flooded his mouth with gelatinous fluid. It was sticky sweet and chewy, but he missed all that as a wave of images flooded his mind.

Rook witnessed the man's life as he had seen it, from street rat in the ghetto to would-be gangbangin' rapist, right up until the moment the lights went out not even sixty seconds ago. Rook always found it interesting to see himself through someone else's eyes. Among the flood of memories were petty crimes, various acts of theft, vandalism, and some minor violence in the form of assaults; apparently this was the man's first *and last* attempt at rape and/or murder. Nope, he thought, not really a monster. Nothing even that interesting. Just common filth.

Mindlessly chewing the eyeball, Rook had forgotten about the woman.

She had drifted into unconsciousness right before Rook killed the man, but came to just in time to watch through swollen eyes as he thoughtlessly popped an eyeball into his mouth. This had elicited a startled gasp from her blood-spattered lips.

The sight before her was frightening and unnatural: the man with big black wings hunching over a bloody and nearly decapitated corpse now turned to his attention to her. If she hadn't seen him eat the eyeball she might have entertained a momentary notion that this was an angel come to take her to Heaven, but instead she realized this must instead be a demon from Hell. Now her thoughts were of salvation and redemption through Jesus Christ, someone she hadn't thought much of since graduating from Catholic school several years earlier. The words of the Lord's Prayer formed on her lips as she watched her demon exhale a heavy vapor that surrounded and permeated him, changing him before her very eyes. A moment ago there was a demon in front of her, but now there was a man. She coughed before lapsing into unconsciousness.

Rook turned and studied her. He gently brushed aside golden strands of hair plastered to her cheek and forehead by a mortar of blood and sweat, allowing him a better look at her. She was somehow strangely familiar to him. Through the blood, the bruising, and the swelling he could see that she was pretty, with features softened in just the right places. He allowed his fingers to trace the outline of her jaw and up and over her lips. Instinctively, his fingers traced his own lips, and he licked her blood off his fingertips. It was sweet, laced with adrenaline and fear. . . . It was also innocent and pure. And it too was familiar.

A wave of compassion washed over him. Odd, he thought. He'd been Breed long enough that he generally didn't feel compassion for victims, whether his or someone else's. But something about this woman caused his chest to tighten and flood with a long-forgotten warmth. That she was familiar unsettled him and made him uncomfortable. Letting his gaze wander downward he caught the shimmer of streetlight on her exposed black satin panties between her splayed legs. The thought crossed his mind—it had been a long time, after all.

No. He stopped himself. She was an innocent, and though he was a monster, he wasn't that kind of monster. He might have just nearly ripped a man's head off and then eaten his eyes, but he was not a defiler of the innocent. "Fuck," he muttered, as he found himself rifling through her purse looking for some kind of ID or other indication of her name and residence. That's when he noticed the knife wound in her side, and the pool of blood beneath her.

Sarah's eyes fluttered open. Her head was pounding, and even the dim light of her apartment exacerbated the pain, the light lancing through her eyes like searing rays of the sun. She squinted, trying to get her bearings.

"Welcome back."

The voice was a velvet whisper, but rang in her ears like church bells, causing a groan to escape her cracked lips.

"You've had quite a night, Sarah," came the voice again.

Sarah's blurred vision began to clear, and she could make out the form of the eyeball-eating man from the alley. Struggling to sit up, she felt a strong but gentle grip on her shoulder and back assist her.

"Here, drink this. It'll help with the pain." She found herself cupping a coffee mug with both hands, instinctively raising it to her swollen lips. They were dry and readily welcomed the first sip of warm liquid spilling over them. It was bitter, some sort of tea, with an iron aftertaste. It was just the taste of the blood in her mouth, she assumed.

"Who—" Her question was cut short by a dry cough. "Who are you?"

"Eh . . . call me Rook."

She suddenly remembered the last sight she had of him and pulled away.

"Don't worry, I'm a friend." He pondered that statement as soon as it left his mouth. Friends. He didn't have any, other than among the Breed, and even those weren't much more than loose friendships. Rook was a loner, which suited him fine. He was flighty, tending to keep on the move and taking little more than passing interest in most people before being distracted by the next shiny new thing.

He realized then that his eyes were locked on hers. She was bruised and there was swelling, but even so a light seemed to emanate from the brilliant blue eyes holding him captive. Somewhere in there, he thought he could see the sun, warm and inviting.

"You . . . you killed that man. . . ."

Rook closed his eyes as he came back to the present moment, hesitating before responding. "Yeah. . . . He was about to do some bad things to you."

"Why did you help me?"

That was a good question. He still wasn't sure. Had it been compassion? Initially it wasn't, though it became that . . . and then something more. He shrugged it off.

"It was the right thing to do."

"But you ate his eyes!" There was obvious revulsion in her face, matching the tone of her voice.

He studied her a moment. After bringing her back to her apartment he'd cleaned her up and treated her injuries. Then, because his curious nature wouldn't let him do anything else, he snooped around her apartment, though he hadn't been invasive. It seemed she was a student, apparently studying theology, judging by the books strewn about her table and lining her bookshelf. The apartment wasn't messy or dirty, but it was obvious that she was a person with more important things to do than organize and de-clutter.

"You believe in God, don't you, Sarah?"

His redirect caught her off guard. Yes, she believed in God . . . in a way. Her faith had evolved and changed as she had immersed herself in the study of various theologies and world religions. Regardless of how eclectic her personal "religion" had become, she maintained belief in a Divine Creator. But what did that have to do with anything, she wondered? Then she remembered. . . . wings. Maybe he was an angel? Or a demon?

Rook picked up a book off the table, turned it so he could read its spine, looking down over the bridge of his beaked nose. A *History of the Knights Templar*, it read. He let it fall open and lazily thumbed the pages. He didn't wait for her to answer. He knew the answer.

"You love the sun, don't you, Sarah?"

She missed the play on words. "Uh . . . I don't doubt that Jesus lived, but I'm not sure about the 'Son of God' thing."

He chuckled. "No, Sarah, I meant the sun. You know, the big yellow ball in the sky during the day?"

She felt her face flush. She was so consumed with her studies that she filtered almost everything through a religious lens, often overlooking the obvious and the literal. Metaphor and mythology was the language of her existence, and because of that sometimes she lost sight of reality. Gently rubbing her bruised eyes she realized her headache was gone; she almost felt good now.

"I'm sorry," she started. "I—"

"Don't be. Each of us sees the world as we want to, not always as it is. Ten people could be looking at the same thing, and each of them will see it in a way that the others don't. Words are no different."

She watched as he set the book down, leaving it open, his fingers lingering on the page a moment. He was strangely handsome, his sharp features softly illuminated by the single lamp lighting her apartment. She wondered why he hadn't turned more lights on. He turned away from her, going over to the bookshelf, and she strained to see if there were in fact wings on his back; all that was there was a long black trench coat of heavy wool.

Rook's fingers traced the spines of the various books lining the shelves, an eclectic yet homogenous mix of theological treatises, occult tomes, histories, and more. They stopped on one, a thick brown tome with silver lettering on the spine. He raised his head slightly and took a sharp breath as if to speak; it seemed as if he was going to pull it off the shelf, but left it pulled just slightly out before turning back to Sarah.

"I think you'll be okay, Sarah. I should be going now." Rook turned and opened the apartment door, then stopped and turned to look back over his shoulder. Standing there, the pale white light of the hallway behind him, he cast an imposing shadow over the room. "I'd avoid those alleys if I were you."

The door closed behind him. Sarah was left there, uncertain of what had just happened. She didn't even know how long it had been since the assault. She leaned forward and pulled the open book from the table to her lap. On the page before her was an illustration of an androgynous devil-like figure. The caption read "Baphomet."

———————

Rook strolled lazily through the city, his hands in his pockets, his eyes cast to the pavement. The temperature had dropped sharply in the few hours since his encounter in the alley, and a frozen wind cut through the night. But he didn't notice, lost in his thoughts as he was. He didn't pay much attention to where he was going, letting his feet carry him forward without any intended destination. It wasn't until he stopped and looked up that he realized he'd walked completely around the block and was standing in front of Sarah's building again.

Something was obviously pulling him to her. His thoughts had never left her, and he couldn't really figure out why. She was pretty, and he was certainly attracted to her, but this—she—was different. The book with the picture of Baphomet. The book on the shelf that had "spoken" to him and flashed an image of Midian in his head. Those things, along with the images he'd seen in her eyes . . .

Sarah got up and went over to the bookshelf, reaching for the book the stranger had started to pull out. Her fingers danced hesitantly on the spine for moment. *Encyclopedia of the Old Testament,* the spine read. She pulled it out and allowed it to fall open in her hands, the yellowed pages giving off a slightly musty scent. A piece of paper near the middle of the book apparently serving as a bookmark allowed the pages to part near the middle of this sea of information, opening somewhere in the "M" entries. At the top of the page was the word "Midian."

The door swung open as Rook raised his hand to knock. Sarah stood on the other side, the encyclopedia in her hand, a slight look of shock on her face at seeing him standing there. They both started speaking at the same time.

"I don't mean to bother you—" he apologized.

"I was just getting ready to come after you—" She moved aside to allow him inside. As he entered he caught a glimpse of the encyclopedia's open page. He went over to the window, pulling the curtain aside to look outside.

"Nice view." He could see her reflection in the dark glass.

Sarah closed the door, set the book on the table on top of the Templar history so that the entry for Midian and the image of Baphomet were both visible, and moved up behind Rook. Her hand rested gently between his shoulder blades. He stiffened at her touch.

"I—" she faltered. "I didn't say thank you." He shrugged. "Those books. Those pages. That wasn't an accident. And I don't think you saving me was an accident, either," she said.

He turned.

"Maybe this was a mistake. I should go."

She stepped in front of him, blocking his path to the door.

"No . . . please stay. I think this is important. I think I can help you."

His effort to navigate around her ceased.

"Help me? You don't know anything about me. For all you know, I could have come back here to finish the job that guy in the alley started." His words were cold and sharp, and sent a shiver up Sarah's spine, but she stood her ground.

"No. I know more than you think, and if you were going to hurt me, you would have done it already."

He stared at the door, refusing to look at her.

"I know what you are. I know about the Nightbreed."

His head snapped over, confirming her assertion, and their eyes locked. In the crystal blue of her gaze he could see symbols and images, glyphs that he had only ever seen in Midian; he could also see the sun. In the ebony depths of his she saw a burning city, the conflagration giving way to the first rays of dawn. She could also see the questions in his eyes, and knew she would have to answer them in order to gain his trust; he already had hers.

The question was, what would he do with it? She knew what the Breed were. Her long years of studious immersion in religion, folklore, and the occult had made the Nightbreed no secret to her. But he was the first she'd ever encountered. She couldn't help but consider it more than blind coincidence.

"I know about Midian. . . ." Her words trailed off, and though she offered them as a sort of comfort, he found none in them.

Somehow, while he'd been caught off guard by the fact that she was aware of what he was, he was unsurprised. Baphomet had told him that he would find guideposts in his journeys. Rook just hadn't expected them to come in the form of mortals.

"I can help," she offered again.

He turned his head away. Her hand, soft and warm, gently rested on his cheek and turned him back to her. Their eyes met again. This time, he saw hope. Warmth washed over him, a warmth he hadn't felt since he'd last stood in the sun, so long ago.

He believed her.

———

The last rays of the day beamed through the skyscrapers, reflecting off the mirrored windows and setting the city ablaze with twilight fire. Rook stood at the window. Behind him, Sarah was still sleeping in the bed they'd shared since that morning. The colors of dusk, filtered through the city's haze, filled the room with soft yellows, oranges, and reds, reminding Rook of the night Midian fell.

Sarah stirred in the bed. Turning to look at her, Rook took in the sight. Something in him stirred, and it was more than just the curves of her body or her milky skin; it was something deep, something . . . old?

"Hey . . ." The word was almost a whisper on her lips, and it was offered with a slight smile. She reached out for his hand.

"I need to know," he said.

"I know."

Sarah got up, grabbing the bathrobe that was draped over the back of a chair and putting it on. Going into the closet, she pulled a cardboard box from the top shelf, then sat on the edge of the bed.

"It's in here," she said, digging through the contents of the box. He watched her silently, working actively to restrain his innate curiosity. After a moment, she produced an object wrapped in cloth. "Here it is. I found this in Saudi Arabia a few years ago on dig I did with school. There was more, but it disappeared before we could catalogue it and get photos or anything."

Unwrapping the object, she handed it to him. It was a piece of stone, obviously broken off of a larger piece, rough on the back side, but it was the smooth front that caught Rook's attention. Carved into the face was a set of glyphs, glyphs that he'd seen before: in Midian, when he'd spoken to Baphomet.

"I'm sorry there's not more," she said. "I got a look at the rest of the pieces before they disappeared, but not enough of one to remember what the other pictographs were."

Rook knew he needed to see the rest of the symbols. He knew how to read them, or rather, that Baphomet would be able to read them through him, but there was only one way he was going to be able to see what Sarah saw. . . .

The last rays of sunset illuminated her face. He suddenly felt guilty. She was innocent. But she was also beautiful, and familiar. But now he knew why she was familiar—he'd seen her in the visions Baphomet had shared with him. His heart sank as he remembered the Baptizer's words to him. "You must do what must be done to find the path," Baphomet had said.

"I'm sorry," he whispered, brushing his hand along her cheek.

The room slipped into darkness as Rook leaned in to kiss Sarah one last time.

COLLECTOR

David J. Schow

The colorful logo emblazoned upon the can fascinated her. *Pabst Blue Ribbon*, it read. At least she could read. It resembled a medal, a commemoration of some kind in white and red and brilliant blue, a blue that evoked her own special eyes, which were a metallic cyan hue, nearly chromium. They did special things to the light messages they captured. She could see in total darkness, as indeed she was scanning the beer can now. The container itself smelled faintly poisonous, the reek of a lost soul lingering there. The truncated memory stored itself—it was an incomplete story, begging additional input that was unavailable.

Another incomplete story. She crushed the can, stomped on it with her beast foot, which designation was a misnomer because her left leg featured nothing that could be called a foot, merely an almost rectangular plinth of solid flesh from knee to ground, largely nerve-dead, an unwieldy tool that crippled her stride to a halting lurch, gimpy, giving unknowns another excuse to avert their gaze, which was a good thing.

She consigned the compacted can to her shopping cart with its load of plastic bags, castoffs, recyclables, satellite bags pendulant from port and starboard, the weight of the load anchoring the defrocked basket firmly to the earth, impossible to tip over. It was the latest of several such carts, never without at least one bumpy wheel, the sheer heft of its cargo making curbs a threat. The cart was additional reason unknowns rarely looked at her or engaged her eyes directly, also a good thing.

For another, her garb—also cargo, of a sort. A stratification of layers; sweaters, old hoodies, torn discards that muted her shape to that of a hunched, tiny monk, her unique eyes cowled in shadows, hidden and safe from inquiry. Sunlight had the power to raise ugly brown welts on her alabaster skin. She kept to the nightside, moving in darkness, good shelter a priority for sleeping sunlessly.

Recycling centers stayed open late, another good thing.

No biography, and few memories, one of the most prevalent being her brief time on the limelight as "Missus Humpty Dumpty," before the rural carny shows were hustled toward politically correct extinction. Her hairless white head, indeed egg-shaped, had gotten her the job a long while back. Her special eyes burned hotly from the center of that head. Two punctures for a nose, a rude down-turned rip of a lipless mouth. People had paid to look at her, and some to touch her, and when they did, she collected their stories until the accumulated sadness was too much to bear.

Now, there was only sustenance. A life of continuing, little more, without strategy or goal, because the world in which she moved was not her world. She was the intruder here, the outsider, and she kept that knowledge as a shield. This was the land of the Upworlders, the reivers, the monsters who had destroyed Midian long ago, way back in the before-times. The "Naturals."

This much she did know: Sired of Avo, born of Matilda. They were merely blank names to her now, forever wanting a nurturing that never came because of the bad thing called the fall of Midian. A young life of running and hiding; learning the art of concealment in plain sight among the denizens of the Upworld. Running? Hardly, not with her special leg.

Years elapsed.

The larger cities beckoned with their anonymity.

Counting years was pointless, because the stars she could see at night had no cognizance of time. Upworlders had little concept of how fluid and malleable the human conceit of "time" could be. What mattered was perception, survival, safety. She had not been schooled in her own hereditary mythology, and carried no religious bias as a result. The crucible of her personal rules was experiential. There was a lingering feeling, more akin to stolen and truncated memory, that between human beings and her own kind, one of them was not meant to be on this planet. The few books through which she had labored without guidelines only offered conflict and confusion.

That all changed when she was gang-raped and set on fire.

———————

"Dare ya to fuck it," said Dane, his scratchy voice slurred by vodka. Fulton dealt the bag lady another wallop with a steel-toed boot. She—it—absorbed the kick and contracted like a hedgehog, making not a sound. "Stinks," said Brad, leery. The trio were predictable to the point of cliché. Surly, pissed off, too drunk, too young to matter.

"Pussy," Fulton shot back at Brad. "Virgin pussy. You've gotta lose your cherry, bust that nut, pop it or drop it, chickenshit."

Dane, the oldest (according to his fake ID), busily peeled back layers of clothing from the ragbag. "Jesus, this looks like some kinda freak! Holy shit, check out the stump!"

"Circus freak," said Fulton. "Still, better than fucking a clown." He kept dancing in to kick their victim again with macho certitude.

"No fucking way," said Brad. He searched his mind, his history, for a better counterargument, but all that came out of his pale and disbelieving face was a mumbled mantra of no fucking way, over and over, like the babble of, well, a crazy person.

Fulton chugged the dregs of flask bourbon and shattered the curved bottle as punctuation. "Tonight's the night, Brad-lad!"

"No fucking way," Brad said again, with anything but conviction.

"Tell ya what," said Dane. "We'll all take her."

"Yeah, we got your back, bro."

That was how it started. The particulars of the violence were not new or important to note, for in a violent world it was just one more incident no one would record, or so she thought as it happened, Dane first, then Brad, then Fulton, amid much cackling and bonding that served the purpose, for them, of both display and power ritual. Semen ejaculated and nasty verve thus temporarily muted, their embarrassment and potential future humiliation prompted the next event of the evening. It was Fulton who produced the squeeze bottle of lighter fluid, Brad who lit the book of matches, and all three who backed nervously away when the cooking smells first struck them. They fled while she smoldered.

It was only right; the goddamned thing wasn't even human. It was a monster, and they all knew what needed to happen to monsters.

She awoke exposed to the sun, which wreaked damage on her sensitive flesh she knew would take over a month to heal fully. Six months later she expelled a glob of tissue that had a single, brilliant blue eye, like her own. Her issue died before it could draw its first breath.

A world away, in China, a boy was born with similarly special eyes. As he matured it was discovered that he could see clearly in the dark—as in reading clearly in a complete absence of light. There came much speculation about the tapetum lucidum, "eyeshine," retroreflectors and ocular albinism, as assorted experts attempted to debunk what was clearly a mutation. Human beings, in their entrenched prejudices, still automatically adjudged mutation as a bad thing no matter what the benefits or portent. Human beings tended to ignore or dismiss the signposts of their own evolutionary process, as if they had always been the same and always would be. It was the fundament of us versus them, all the way back to cave dwellers. Human beings were so obsessive about their enforced sameness that they even managed to circumvent natural selection for what they callowly called a greater good.

But now, post trauma, she discovered a new irritant, a hard, black, oblong nodule, beneath her skin on each inner arm. She worried briefly that she might be calcifying, turning to stone for some indescribable sin. As far as transgression went, she lacked a moral compass. What was right? What was wrong?

None of these ruminations mattered on the street, in the shadows she crawled back to. She knew the darkness loved and would not judge her.

The next·time a human being touched her, she would be ready with the blade. It was not special either—merely a worn Buck lockback knife with a dicey hinge, scratched and scored by its passage out of the world of practical everyday use and into her possession. She had scavenged it from a landfill, and its disinterment held the allure of treasure. This was a practical tool. She used it many times daily but when she was attacked, the knife was out of reach, tucked safely in winds of clothing so it could not be lost. Hinge or no hinge, she had honed the edge to surgical sharpness and practiced how to deploy the blade one-handedly. Without knowing why she had also given it a name: Alevan.

If she entered a fast-food restaurant at the right time of night, when the Moon was smiling upon her, and once the minimum-wage earners had dismissed her as a threat (tempered by their reflex need to get her *out*, as soon as calmly possible), they would never really see her with their eyes, which was a boon since she enjoyed cheeseburgers. She was careful to keep on the move and not repeat venues too many times; the trick, as always, was invisibility in plain sight.

She was blindsided in the parking lot between the Dumpster and the more luridly stinky cache bin for cooking oil, which was recycled for rendering into "yellow grease" for livestock feed and biofuel use. The stranger simply appeared; not there one second and there the next, without tripping any of her usual skin alarms or her proximity sense. She lashed forward with the knife, Alevan, and hooked an extended pale palm, bringing bright red blood on the cut.

"Wait! Don't! Stop!" hissed the intruder.

There followed that uncomfortable combat beat of exploded time, in which they regarded each other. It was the stranger's burden to provide fast illumination, to avoid further injury, or a death struggle at worst.

"I am Jexelle," the figure said, fisting its wounded hand so the blood flow was stanched. "I'm a Collector, like you. You are Aurora."

No words in her entire history could have hit her with more impact. Someone like her, dressed like her. Someone who claimed an actual spoken name. Someone who claimed to know her name, which she had never known herself. She reeled back, abruptly thieved of breath, her vision spotting.

Aurora reeled back.

There is a dance to steel and thorn; edge must answer edge, and Jexelle's own blade was already extended in a holding display that Aurora could not recognize, but knew down deeper on the level of instinct. She had never seen the draw. The blade was onyx, ornate, sunk in silver abraded so as not to reflect as much ambient light.

But it was Jexelle's wounded hand that urged Aurora's attention. Now it was held open, in offering, closer to Aurora than the mineral blade. The meaning was clear. Responding by sheer gut feeling, Aurora impaled her own free palm on Jexelle's blade, flowed her own blood, and clasped Jexelle's encrimsoned hand in communion.

To her shock and surprise, the first news she realized was that Jexelle's blade was named Viloriun.

JEXELLE'S TALE

I am not going to tell you a human fable.

You are not the chosen one, the hidden redeemer, or the secret savior. Our culture has never worked that way; messiah conceits based on completely unfounded optimism.

To begin at the beginning: Your name is Aurora, born of Avo and Matilda.

I have traveled two thousand miles and six years to find you, for you are a Collector, like me.

We have a history, of course—heroes, villains, betrayal and redemption.

But very little of it is supernatural. In fact, most of the Nightbreed's unique capabilities are defensive, no more unusual than fangs on a serpent, or talons on raptor. As in the human world, there are exceptions, and those exceptions form the stories that have always threatened us with genocide. As for humans themselves, they are silly and trivial, deluded and crazy, filled with hate and hallucination. If their idea of a god actually existed, he, she, it, or they would actively hate them. If they did not outnumber us, we could almost pity them.

For some of them have learned that we are the nightside dwellers, the ones who come *next*—after them.

We have legends, too, and prophecies, but we have learned to ignore speculation until it yields fact. We know the difference between fiction and reality. We are painfully reminded of it every waking hour. We squandered time with oaths and oracles; we squandered dignity waiting for the tribes of the moon to be judged by never-seen deities. We sanctioned the delusions of a self-appointed leader and paid the price for believing in Baphomet. Neither leadership nor belief saved us. Midian was lost as foretold, but the truer thing is that no home is forever.

Godless now, we are stronger.

Your aura, too, was quite strong. It repelled most who came near. In that way, it hampered us from finding you. You had no way of knowing what you were broadcasting; to you it was always a matter of shield and defend, which is practical and logical. Even those who move about the city streets as you do, in the big urban areas where detection is diminished, could not approach you, nor could they have known what to do with you.

It takes another Collector, like myself.

You have come into contact with others and tasted their stories, drawn them into yourself. All those stories will forever be at your beck. That is what Collectors do—we are the repository of the history of our kind. There is no dark library, there are no musty tomes of arcana or forbidden spell-books of sorcery, there is no record of artifact except what the Upworlders confect about us in their fear and ignorance. There are only the Collectors.

This is what you have not been told, because Midian was ripped away from us. To the generation that followed the fall, Midian became as fanci-ful as Atlantis. Another danger—and this is one we never share with out-siders—is the hazardous length of time it takes many of us to mature, fully twice the number of years of the humans whom we outclass, but do not outnumber. You, Aurora, are still an adolescent. Your forearms have not yet even sprouted. You feel the difference in your flesh, but there was no way to know that you are entering puberty only now.

I know, a thousand questions boil.

As I said, you are not what bad fiction would call the darling of destiny.

But you were born to a place in our society, and serve a purpose within our scattered family. Very soon now you will begin to discover the breadth of your true abilities. After all, up until now you have existed as little more than a child.

I have a little saying I made up: Instead of screaming and crying, I pre-fer creaming and scrying.

What Came After

Aurora startled herself again by actually laughing at Jexelle's joke. But then Jexelle was gone from her sight, vanished. She had been hoping for a stew-ard, a mentor to guide her through her thousand questions, but had now learned the hard lesson that this was not the way of her people. She was not an apprentice. She was not even an adult. Her task was to earn her place, in whatever world came After.

It would not be the same as the world she had come to know—its limits and dangers. She had become complacent about, if not comfortable with, the mystery she thought of as her fate, which turned out to be another story, one she had made up herself, one that was untrue.

Her intersection with Jexelle had produced a calmer veneer, like a warm membrane enshrouding her perceptions. When the single claw broke the surface on first one forearm, then the other, Aurora regarded them dispassionately. At first they resembled dewclaws, but slightly hooked, with points meant for precise penetration. Possibly for defense, although they seemed too fragile for that purpose. She could extend them, make them retract; and they caused no pain.

They were natural. They were supposed to be. Another tiny furrow of her mind activated eager synapses, and she deduced their purpose.

She already had the stories of Dane, Brad, and Fulton. She knew their lives as a Collector. Where they could be found; how they lived. She had their DNA and memories. She knew Brad secretly wanted to make sweet love to Fulton. That Fulton had killed and skinned animals for pleasure. That Brad planned to murder his parents. Now, in her new skin, tracking them down was easy . . . because she had their stories.

She learned her misshapen leg had a purpose. It was strength and power, balanced by the maneuverability of her more humanlike appendage. Not an impediment; a hammer. This knowledge altered her stride. She could pivot and swing her hammer to head height on the boys who had assaulted her; it would be like getting hit in the face with a cinder block.

Aurora had inherited some other things, too. Things she carried inside her, like the stories of a Collector, which did not take up space or encumber her in any way. Things she could give back to the ones who attacked her, merely by scratching them with her special new claws, which would dispense at her will.

Things with melodic names—hanta, Lassa, dengue—that seemed almost like kinship names for siblings she would never have.

Things with less melodic names, like HIV, bubonic plague, H5N1.

After the fall of Midian, the Nightbreed prided itself to not suffer many human misapprehensions—made-up gods, fairy tales, morality fables meant to blunt the harshness of an indifferent cosmos. The concept of race hatred was harder to shed. More difficult still was the covenant of retribution.

A new flame had been lit, and Aurora was ready to party.

BAIT AND SWITCH

Lilith Saintcrow

U sually I stayed away from Pammy's work tent.

There's nothing good about me being near tarot cards, or crystal balls, or any of that junk. That's why Pammy took the Madama Illyria spot, intoning portentous "fortunes" to idiots and draining each one a little, a very little. Not enough to notice, and if they did, well, lots of people had headaches and lethargy after a carnival.

Me, I was a Continuing Attraction. The Animal Girl. The shifting was easy—sometimes scales, sometimes fur, always teeth. So easy, in fact, that it was my incognito form—what you'd call *human*—that took effort now.

Which explains why I was wandering around during setup, in the gloaming, hat pulled low and shoulders slumped, sweating and suppressing the tickle of tonight's form all over me like a wire brush just slightly scraping, when I heard that word raising little devils along the dusty alleys between the tents.

Midiaaaaaan, it breathed.

Pammy was running her mouth again. Was she drunk? Baphomet be praised, but each time she got incandescent she started babbling about . . . home.

Or what used to be home.

I cut into the alley between RVs and trailers for the punkers, thin metal coated with a layer of dust that would hide any sparkle. Summer in the asshole below the Bible Belt, with a nice long drought to make you choke on all the yellow dust, billing ourselves as a family-friendly show. Even Pammy had to pray loudly to Jesus before gazing into her crystal ball. The smart ones, maybe, could hear the sarcasm in her earnestness, but if they were that smart, they kept their mouths shut.

Especially if they noticed how thin Pammy was, and how hungry-looking, and how her teeth were just a *little* too sharp. She didn't have to take a mouthful, neither of us *had* to, but there wasn't much around to keep us from doing it.

Except each other.

Midiaaaaaaaan. Again, skipping through the lanes, snapping the tent ropes taut, rocking the trailers just enough to make them creak. I shivered, scales rippling up my skin but retreating when I took a deep breath.

They itched, especially around my ribs. Which stuck out more than they should. Meatskin stretched too tightly over bone, and sometimes the shadows underneath looked like claws rippling under silk, just on the edge of puncturing. Sometimes I made a supermarket run and came back with a bag of raw meat, and that held us for a while.

I hadn't done that for a couple of weeks.

The sign wasn't out front, so she wasn't with a client. I pushed the flap open, blinking against a sudden gust of grit-laden wind, and ducked in.

Sudden, balmy dimness. Even twilight hurts our eyes sometimes. She had incense burning, a sharp exotic bite that immediately made me want to sneeze. My nose wrinkled, whiskers trying to prickle out on my cheeks, and I saw her at the table with a sharp-faced man.

He wore a linen suit and a fedora, as if he were on an old black and white rerun. Nose like a knife blade, and cheekbones under stretched-tight parchment skin. He reeked of nervousness, and a thread of that other scent, like music in the dark.

Nightbreed.

He sat in the old wooden client chair, the angle of its back just a fraction too acute, forcing whoever was in it to lean forward a little. Which he did, elbows on the table, a cigarillo fuming in one limp, wax-white hand. It smelled sweetish, and nasty. He looked vaguely familiar, but only vaguely.

Pammy, her dark hair a rat's nest and her eyes—just a little too big, just a little too dark—heavily outlined with kohl. I don't know who made the rule that all fortune-tellers have to dress in Romany drag, but on the circuit it's necessary. So it was the peasant shirt and the long flowing skirts, the beads and bangles and glimmers of mellow gold, and the peacock-eye shawl she kept wrapped as high as she could.

Things went easier when she acted like she wanted to cover up the scars. And the stumps on her back.

"Cal." Pammy grinned, and the glamour slipped for a moment. With it on, she was just a frail, older lady with white, sharp teeth.

Without it, her essential *difference* shone out, and the teeth, while just as sharp, were nicotine-yellow.

"What are you doing?" I tied the tent flaps, my fingers glimmering as luminescent scales crawled over them.

"Come meet him." She drummed her claws on the tabletop, and the crystal ball wobbled uneasily under the hank of spangled velvet she used to keep its eye closed. "Our savior."

"We had one, remember?" I stalked over the threadbare rugs piled on the tent's faintly mildewed floor. "Didn't work out too well."

"Calpurnia." The man's head turned, a fluid, predatory movement. "I've heard of you."

"Can't say the same." I halted just short of the table and slumped there, hands stuffed deep in my pockets. "What do you want?"

"We're gathering again." He didn't look quite at me *or* Pammy, just at some vague point to my left. "A new city. A new flame."

"Keep your voice down." A shudder passed through me, and Pammy hissed out a rasping, rumbling obscenity. Two nervous steps away, sidling, before I could force the claws to retract. My hands tingled. "Are you from . . . *him?*"

"Cabal? No." He said it so casually, I sidestepped a little more, ending up almost behind Pammy. "He is no true prophet."

"I saw—" Pammy began, and I shushed her. She subsided, but only grudgingly. If she started telling that story again—the fire, the fleeing, the gunfire, the dying—she'd be off the whole night.

"Who are you?" I kept my hands in my pockets, aching and trembling with the claw-tingle.

He grinned, a death's-head wrinkling itself up with sheer good humor. "I come from Seraphine."

Another cold, dark thrill all through bone and breath.

Her. Of course she's survived.

I stalked to the curtain, pushed it aside, and dragged the other chair across the rugs, clumsy with the shift fighting me. He expected to see something other than normal, and fighting the current of that expectation was hard swimming.

Pammy whisked the crystal ball into her lap with a sigh. I spun the chair, settled down spraddle-legged, and rested my chin on the high back. "Talk."

That night, in the trailer, she exhaled a long satisfied sound, creaking and cracking as she stretched swollen joints and unfurled the wispy, scorched stubs protruding from her bare back. Thick, pearlescent salve gathered between my fingers, I worked it into leathery skin.

"I don't like it." Very quietly.

"You never liked anything to do with her." Pammy cackled, but softly. "That pretty face of hers."

Irritation rasped a flush of scales down my arms, but my hands stayed soft. Extra fingers sprouted, a sweet piercing sensation, the shifting reflecting exactly what would feel best. Still, fingertip-claws prickled, and I knew she felt it.

She sighed again, her hair writhing against itself with dry whispering sounds. The take had been good for her tonight. For me too—they paid at the door to see the Animal Girl, and it was easy to be what they expected. Some of their darker imaginings felt . . . familiar. While they were dazed by the pheromones my glands pumped out, Jimmy the hawker took up a collection for the poor Animal Girl.

Some crowds were better than others.

Still, there was the dissatisfaction. After dark, within Midian's circuit, any of the gawkers would have been meat. Chase them outside, and you could eat your fill. Some, like Peloquin, stretched the law to its breaking point, feeding darker hungers.

Some didn't.

Pammy scratched under her left breast, scraping with flat spatulate nails. "You're quiet."

What she meant was that I hadn't said anything about staying or going, one way or the other.

"We shouldn't have come down on this part of the circuit." I touched one of the ruined stumps; it quivered. Once, she had been able to spread a blanket of black feathers over both of us. Now, I kept rubbing the salve in, and the fading luminescence of Baphomet's blessing in its oiliness was the same as our starving by inches.

She had screamed when the fire took her, and I remembered very little afterward. They expected monsters, those who broke our home, and so the shifting made me . . .

No, not the shifting. *I* did it. Later, when I dragged her from the cemetery, stone angels garish-painted with orange and yellow, the screams of the armed men as some of us fought back echoed along with hers. *Leave me,* she had wailed. *Leave me to diiiiiiie!*

"The take is good." She moved, restlessly, and I knew she understood what I meant.

"We're always five minutes away from another burning, down here." *And no Berserkers to set free to save us.*

"Even praying to Jay-sus before every show." Her derisive snort steamed the windows. Under her skirt, her feathered haunches would be twitching, her horn-tough feet with their rings and claws working. Shoes for her were always expensive, and her claws sliced them if she got agitated. "Stupid."

We must remember, Lylesburg always said. *We were gentle, once.*

So gentle that most of the tribe hadn't even fought back when the militia came. Their guns, and the stink of their fear. It took *him* releasing the old ones, the mad ones, for some of us to survive, to flee.

"We could find Cabal." I worked along the burn scars, pressing in where she liked it. "We're still of the Moon."

"Will he take us in?" High and breathless, childlike. She shivered, and I remembered her spread ink-black and paper-sharp against a full moon, rising over Midian on a flurry of straining wingbeats. She was so light; it was how I had brought us both out of the fire. The shifting on me denied injury, because I didn't expect to burn.

"You, he will."

"And you?"

"I don't know." I had broken their fragile bodies, and snarled as the blood spattered. I had always been more of Peloquin's persuasion than Lylesburg's. But maybe that was only because of the orphanage and the chains.

"Will Seraphine? A new Midian, he said."

"Maybe she has Baphomet. Or pieces of . . ." Perhaps Cabal was even dead, and Baphomet's remains in Seraphine's slender white hands.

The nameless man had those hands.

"I won't go into any Midian without you." Flat and toneless. Muscle flickered in her back, the stumps twitching.

My throat filled with something scorch-hot. "Pammy—"

"I won't." She shook her head, and her rasping hair flickered into life for a moment, fat snakes writhing. "You saved me."

Do you remember what flying was like? I couldn't ask her that, so I simply worked more salve into the scars.

"Cal?"

"Mmmh." I added up our savings, balanced the likely state of the truck engine against them, and decided. "We should leave here anyway. We've stayed too long. Even Jimmy's getting nervous." *Maybe he even regrets hiring us.*

"He can't complain about the take." Pammy yawned, luxuriously. Now that I'd decided, she would settle into resting quiescence.

"Still." I capped the salve jar. There wasn't much left. "At least the Breed smelled right." *Even though he insisted he had no name. Who does that?*

"It could all be fake." She shivered, skin rippling as once again the burned stumps tried to flex further.

I shut my eyes for a moment, wishing I could be the one asking for reassurance. "If it is, we'll find something else."

Our truck engine roused in gray predawn hush, creeping past the sleepers on either side. A carnival obeys its own schedule; on nontraveling days you have an hour or two before the sun rises to vanish.

If you have to.

I drove, because Pammy's feet . . . well, the pedals were a bit small for her. Also, I'm less sensitive to that great glare the meatskins call day.

She was silent next to me, propped against the towels and blankets I carefully arranged around her each time. Dust rose in silvery plumes until we turned onto blacktop, still warm from yesterday. No air-conditioning, but both our windows down just enough to provide a breeze. Wet heat, the type that slicks the skin and makes the tongue thick, not the dry oven-bake of the desert. Pammy descended into her dozing, twitching sleep—she was more comfortable hanging in a hammock, still a poor substitute for her old perch.

I drove, and remembered.

Tunnels below the cemetery, a honeycomb of delving in crumbling stone. Lylesburg said the will of Baphomet kept the tunnels from collapsing, but where was the spirit when the invaders came? And he—Cabal, once *Boone*, the most hated syllable among the tribes of the Moon.

Or if it wasn't, it should have been. *Boone* was dead. Cabal was different, they said, for all that he was in the same body. Cabal had the bones of Baphomet and was looking for a new home for the survivors of the shipwreck his former self had brought upon us.

First the tribes were orphaned when the meatskins turned against us, long in the ago. Each new generation of us was cast out from their daylight world, in one way or another. For Pammy, it was when the feathers came.

For me, it was at birth. Then there was the orphanage and the chain, the dank basement so I wouldn't be seen by the parents coming to choose their children. For a long time I wished I were one of the chosen, wished I could be taken to a daylight home.

Until Seraphine told me about Midian.

A child with long inky hair and glass-fragile bones, she was thought attractive by the meatskins but too likely to require medical care for adoption. When she eventually had to use the long metal canes to walk, so tiptap carefully, the taunts and teasing sprouted like mushrooms. Her face turned round and doughy, her hands turned into limp wax-white gloves, and her dark eyes began to burn.

Midian, she whispered to me in the dark of the basement. *There, I'll be a princess. I'll walk.*

I was useful, so she would guide us. I never knew how she'd learned of sanctuary's existence, or of its location, but she did. We survived the trip and were taken in, and it was a shock to find that the shift made me more valuable to them than her fragility.

Baphomet did not mend her bones, either.

As soon as the sun rose, a white glare in the east, I slid dark sunglasses on. Pammy's snoring deepened, and by the time we crossed the state line I was already contemplating how Seraphine was likely to greet us both.

Long ribbons of highway, gas stations where we paid cash, bought junk masquerading as meatskin food, and hunched our shoulders against stares. At least with the carnival we were part of a herd *expected* to be strange. There was some comfort in hiding among a mass, even of *them*.

After the first day we traveled at night. The days we spent in the trailer, Pammy in her hammock and me in my narrow bunk; I would wake at dusk to her chirping as she fried eggs and ate them six at a time.

I never openly mentioned the irony of her gobbling so many.

No raw meat, none of the energy-charge from a crowd of gawkers. We were both hungry, in that way meatskins never know. At least in Midian Baphomet fed us. Though Peloquin and his ilk wanted more. Hot blood and struggling prey, forgetting what we had once been.

Did it matter? Forget or remember, we were hungry *now*.

It was dead midnight on the seventh day when I found the exit—well, "exit" was too kind a word. A two-lane highway, rolling through forsaken mountains, pines and firs pressing close on either side, and the turnoff looked just like a long scar of gravel for a desperate trucker to use. At its end, however, there was a sharp right-hand turn onto a rutted dirt track.

We jounced along this for a few minutes, the trailer rattling behind us, the headlights a white smear as more dust rose. This wasn't the yellow sandy cake the carnival had been swimming in, but a floury glittering screen.

He coalesced out of the dark and the headlights, between one moment and the next. The linen suit was *exactly* the color of the dust, his hands loose wriggling worms, but the hat was gone, revealing indeterminate, closely cropped hair. His eyes were holes of darkness, and beside me, Pammy let out a soft sigh.

"At least we're on the right track," I muttered, and she elbowed me.

He turned on his heel and set off up the dirt track. We inched along, his speed matching the truck's idle creeping, his back bisected by one large crease in the linen, a knifecrack of shadow. Up in zigzags, and up, and up. Each turn was hairpin, and soon the trees choked close, their branch-fingers brushing the trailer's side, a lover's caress.

It took a long while, maybe an hour, for the vegetation to draw away. We crept out into a wide half circle of more gravel and flour-dust, and on the other side was a large sloped barnlike shape. The moon had gone down, so all we saw was weatherbeaten wooden planks, a few boarded holes for windows, and the front door, its double leaves flung wide.

Behind it, the mountain rose, a dark bulk against a star-riven sky. The moon had gone down, and our doors slammed loudly in the hush.

There comes a time past midnight when even wild animals are silent.

Pammy's foot-claws scraped gravel as she scratched, luxuriously. Weeds had once forced their way up through the plain of crunched rock, but they were yellowed, blasted where they stood. I took my hat off, shaking out long, fine changecolor hair. Part black, part orange, part other colors, it was the one thing that never shifted.

I unwrapped my scarf, my sweat-damp neck breathing freely and flushing with little pinfeathers. You'd think scales would help me stay cool, but they don't. They just get itchy.

I slid out of my jacket, tossed it in through the open window. My tank top was ancient and yellowed, but it didn't matter. Prickling ran across my bare arms, the changes moving across them before settling on smooth honeybrown skin, even though I never tanned. Pinfeathers moved uneasily over my cheeks and throat, rising on little bumps. After so long walking around muffled except in the hot close confines of a tent or the trailer, the nakedness of exposure, however welcome, was still . . . disturbing.

There was a pale glimmer in the dark between the doors. The nameless man glided silently up rickety stairs you could pose an extended family on for an interminable photo on a sun-gilded afternoon.

I glanced at Pammy, who stared, rapt, at that shimmer in the door's cave.

The smear of paleness resolved into a too-tall, stick-thin womanshape. She stepped out, onto the porch, and starshine was lost in the inkwell of her hair.

Seraphine . . . *walked.*

"Welcome to New Midian," she crooned, and beside me, Pammy began to weep.

Stupid, and careless. I was stupid to not ask more questions. Pammy was stupid to believe so wholeheartedly.

I halted at the foot of the stairs. "Sera."

"Cal." A slight tilt of her head. She probably thought it looked regal, but really it just reminded me of the round-faced child she'd been, pasty and burning with sullen, slinking rage. "He found you."

The nameless man passed her without a word, vanishing into the dark maw of the house. It *was* a house, a large one. Who would build it up here? Who cared?

"Thought he was looking for any of the tribes." We locked gazes, again, Seraphine's dark and mine . . . whatever it was. The shift responded, pinfeathers and scales retreating, meatskin form settling on me with the weight of her will.

Did she expect me to look like one of them, or was it just that we'd been children together? Her with her glass bones and me with scales and hair and claws coming in unpredictable waves.

"He was. But I've spoken of you often." Her smile wasn't pleasant, but I suppose mine wasn't either.

Pammy scraped tears away with the flat of her hand. "Is this the entrance? To New Midian? Is it really true?"

"It is." Seraphine's smile was supposed to be gentle, maybe. It showed her teeth far too much for my comfort. "Come on in, Pammy."

Pammy's claw-feet scraped against the stairs. The blackened stubs on her back twitched, muscle flickering as she balanced. Up, and up again, and she passed by Seraphine without a look back. Which meant I had to follow, stepping on the groaning, worn-smooth wood. Holes in the porch roof let fitful starshine leak through, and the blackness through the door was a balm and a promise at once.

I stopped, shoulder-to-shoulder with Seraphine. She facing the world, me turned toward this New Midian. "Am I welcome?"

A slight, disdainful, chilling little laugh. "Very." Seraphine moved slightly, and for a dizzying moment I was nine years old again, listening to that laugh. "Very welcome, Calpurnia."

It smells wrong, I realized, just as a stunning blow smashed against my head. Seraphine laughed again.

"After all," she continued, Pammy's terrified scream echoing oddly behind the words, "I am *very* hungry."

"Cal." A sharp hissing whisper. Blood caking my face, everything hurt. "Wake up. *Cal!*"

I groaned.

A frantic jabbing at my ribs. My head rang. *What the hell?*

"Cal, wake the *fuck* up." Pammy sobbed in a breath, and I jolted fully into myself. Blinking away crusted blood, I scrambled up to hands and knees, searching for a wall to put my back to.

I didn't find one. I found iron bars as thick as my forearm, and a wretched stink, and sterile dirt that hadn't seen light in a long, long time. And Pammy in the cage next to me, the faint gaseous light from above painting shadows on her face.

No, not shadows. Bruises, deep and fresh.

I coughed, rackingly. Spat to the side—the shift twinged and ached all the way through me. Now that I was conscious, the pain was roweled spurs all over. Scales flashed up, fur too, then retreated.

No wonder she'd wanted me pink-skinned and soft.

"What." I coughed again, retching up something foul that might have been the last bit of meatskin food I ate, swallowed hard—*never* waste anything edible—and found out I could breathe. "The. What?"

"Broke her arm." Pammy had found a stick somewhere and used it to poke me; it dropped on the floor between our cages. "At least, I think so. There was another Breed down here, they took him—"

"Who? Seraphine?" I winced, my head pounding. "Who else?" *Who's working with her?*

"Those . . . the nameless. Cal, she *ate* them, she hollowed them out. She's halfway to being Titan. They all look the same, and they took another Breed away. He was worked over pretty good too, and she'd been draining him for a while." Pammy pointed off into the darkness. "He was over there."

Four cages, familiar iron bars with dappled radiance dying slowly along their edges. Berserker cages, the smaller ones. Nothing Titan-sized, but then, she didn't need those. How had Seraphine brought them *here*?

Probably only Baphomet knew, since it was *his* blessing in the iron, leaching away like the glow in the salve. Maybe Seraphine had been hunting for a while, since Midian fell, and the nameless shadows did all the heavy lifting. She would only need a few cages, because we were scattered to the four winds now.

I scrubbed at my face as Pammy babbled on, trying to think through the noise in my skull. Grabbed Pammy's hand to reassure her, and she finally

quieted. There were sounds overhead—wet creakings, slapping noises, muffled howls.

"That's him," she whispered. "Maldeane. He told me she got him the
same way—a nameless came and found him. They bring her fresh Breed.
He also said—"

"Shhhh." I took stock. Tank top and jeans; my boots were gone. They'd
probably searched me, and found the knife. Under the thin scrim of cellar
dirt on the floor was rock. Our truck and trailer were probably pulled off
into the woods—she'd probably go through it for supplies, too.

Resourceful Seraphine.

The cages weren't whole. The doors had been wrenched open, broken
when Midian fell. A heavy chain wrapped around the doorfront of each one,
locked with a padlock the size of a Berserker's fist. Snugged tight enough,
it kept the thing closed, and Seraphine probably kept the keys on her.

"I'm so sorry," Pammy whispered.

The noise overhead crested, and a choked cry spiraled up into nothingness. I'd never passed words with fish-gilled Maldeane; he'd been one of
the solitaries, swimming the underground rivers.

Now I never would.

"I'm sorry," she repeated, and I patted her hand.

"Shhh. It's all right."

"I wish we'd never left the carnival."

I don't. I exhaled, sharply, and forced myself to *think.*

Because if I knew Seraphine, they would come for Pammy first.

It was silent overhead, the silence of digestion. The shift burned, or maybe
it was the bars.

Didn't matter. I tried again.

Pammy's shallow, rapid breathing echoed. She huddled in a ball in the
corner of her cage, and it was hard to think with her hyperventilating.

Forcing the shift this far was dangerous. There were some things that
couldn't elongate the way I needed them to, so it was a geometry problem,
bone crackling slightly as I pushed further than I ever had. The skull was
trickiest, because squeezing my brain in certain ways might even make me
black out. Plus, I'd spent so long just showing off for the paying crowds,
my control wasn't what it—

"Sssa!" I hissed in pain as a bar scraped along my narrow, naked hip, scoring a weal along my flank. A sick, appetizing draft of roasted pork rose. My pelvis creaked alarmingly, torqued almost double. Naked, sweat-greased, grimly hanging on to consciousness, I shifted a little more.

Stealthy creakings overhead. The quiet had been so thick they were unnaturally loud, and I strained against the limits of bone and stretched-tight Breed flesh. My foot slid, nails scratching against bedrock, scrabbling for purchase, and I tumbled into a heap with a loud crackle, rolling in grit and a splatter of foulness.

There were no bathrooms down here.

Hands and knees, the shift retreating and my body shrinking back into normal dimensions, head pounding, the smoking burns all over me steaming and grinding with pain. I curled into a ball, and it was a good thing I'd already emptied myself in every possible way. Slick with effluvia, I rested.

Outside the cage.

Pammy scrabbled closer, retreated when the bars of her own cage fluoresced warningly. "Cal?" A shocked whisper.

I'm fine. My voice wouldn't work. Maybe I'd broken something. So tired. Soft black wings at the corner of my vision, beating in my brain.

Soft and black like hers, before Midian burned.

I spent a little while in a soupy kind of half consciousness, my burnt flesh smoking in the dimness. The cages hummed, and overhead the creakings took on new life.

Thud. Thud. Thudthud.

At first I thought it was my heartbeat, but Pammy made a tiny whining sound and I realized what it was.

Feet. On the stairs.

I strained to move, collapsed, strained again. *Get up. Get up now.*

———

She stopped to sniff the reek of roasting filling the cellar, and that was what saved both of us.

I fell on Seraphine from behind, from the dark, as if I were Peloquin hunting in the ruins of the daylight world, outside the bounds of the law. My teeth sank in at the juncture between her shoulder and neck, and smoky-spiced wickedness filled my mouth as she shrieked, flailing across the stony floor.

Hit the side of one cage, a fountain of blue-white sparks popping, and she howled as her own white flesh, bloated with her recent meal, seared. I tore a great mouthful of muscle free, spat, dug my claws in, tangling in her ribs. They had once been brittle; now, bolstered by the death of her own tribefolk, they were merely spongy-resilient.

Pammy shrieked too, her arms through the bars, wicked claws slashing air as she tried to help. Seraphine spun just like the Tilt-A-Whirl ride, the cellar smearing like grease on slick cheap cardboard. I clung to her back like a habit, monkeylike, just as she had clung to mine during our voyage to Midian, whispering in my ear.

In Midian I'll walk. I'll be a princess.

I did not whisper. I *bit*. Again and again, and there was a clattering as the key ring sailed in a high arc, hitting Pammy's cage with a heavy clanging.

But I was weak, and she was flush with cannibal strength. Seraphine twisted, and I was flung loose, thrown across the cellar. Fetched up against a stone wall with a sickening crack, and the coppermad scent of my own blood-filled mouth and nose and eyes.

"You *bitch!*" Seraphine raved, as she bore down on me. "*Look what you've done!*"

I'll do it again, too. My arms and legs wouldn't work. Her will, giant pale brooding thing that it was, pressed down on me, the savagely mistreated shift responding sluggishly to my own expecting.

She kicked me, once, and howled afresh, hopping back. She could walk, certainly, but she needed other hands to do her violence.

There was a soft, slithering commotion at the stairs—the hollowed-out nameless ones, pale and stumbling, responding to their mistress's call.

Then, out of the dark, a harpy descended.

Pammy leapt, her hands and feet smoking—she had clambered atop her cage once the front was open—and her foot-claws sank in with a heavy, meaty sound. Her hands were claws too, burst free of the facsimile of meatskin camouflage. Her head snaked forward, burnt stubs on her back twitching frantically. If she'd still had her wings, the buffeting would disorient her prey. Frothing, rearing back and striking again and again with snakelike speed, her teeth slicing effortlessly . . .

She was beautiful, in the way only one of the Moon's children could be.

I crawled forward as Seraphine thrashed. Her cries rent quivering air; her nameless servants fell in writhing heaps, noisome sand tricking through rents and gouges in their pale exteriors.

The cellar resounded with crunching and slurping.

We ate our fill.

———————

Night fell in great indigo waves across the mountain. At dusk we crept out to the well behind the house, and a sluicing of cold water woke me fully from post-gorging doze.

Pammy made a happy humming sound, clicking her claws and emptying the bucket over her head. Fine bones and leathery skin unfurled, the prickles of black pinfeathers blooming as her wings creaked and crackled, expanding. All that stolen life could work wonders. It let Seraphine walk, and we had eaten our share. Watching Pammy's wings spread and flesh themselves with feathers in the umber and blue of dusk, I shuddered. The burning crackled as it fell from my skin. Naked, honey-glowing in the dark, I dredged up another bucketful and washed away pain and roasting.

Finally, dripping and shivering, I let Pammy close her arms and wings around me. We stood like that for a long time, my forehead against her breastbone, and we slowly warmed. Her wings kept making little sounds as they grew back, and her humming took on a deeper note. Her claws flexed, and she could stand straight if she wanted.

Straight and proud.

When the shivers were gone, thin traceries of steam rising from us both as we dried, I sighed.

Pammy's humming stopped. "I'm sorry," she whispered again. "I'm so sorry, Cal."

Why? You've got your wings back. "Me too. I should've suspected she would . . ."

"We ate her."

"Yes, we did. She was almost Titan, though. It wasn't against the law." At least, I hoped it wasn't. There was no Lylesburg to tell us Baphomet's will, no Baphomet to speak. We'd come all the way out here just on the hope that something could be salvaged.

"If there's a New Midian . . ." Tentatively.

She was bird-timid, but not stupid. "There might be. We can look.

Seraphine kept everything that came in the door, there's probably cash hidden in that pile. Find our truck, too."

"I . . . I have my wings, now." She spread them, and the sudden chill forced answering fur from my back and legs. A lovely, glossy pelt, black instead of changecolor now. "They'll let us in. Both of us." Hope lighting her beaky face, her hair raveling into black feathers along her shoulders, Pammy shifted from foot to foot. She probably couldn't wait to get into the sky.

I shrugged. Stepped back. "First we have to find it, Pammy. How about you go up and look around, see if you can spot our truck?" If she stayed in the wild places, she could hunt. Meat could be had. She wasn't helpless now.

Pammy didn't need me.

She outright danced now, but stayed on the ground. "You'll stay? You won't look without me? You won't leave?"

Fur eased over my breasts. The night wind ruffled it, and I stretched, luxuriously, tipping my head back to hide the sudden welling in my eyes. "I wouldn't go to any Midian without you, Pammy. Go on, now."

She cried aloud for joy, and as I stood under the caress of the night, I heard her footsteps drum. She leapt, and the sound of featherbrush wings filled the clearing. Behind me, the house exhaled its stink of rot. I'd have to go back in there and scavenge for anything useful.

Now, though, I opened my eyes and watched while she climbed.

"New Midian," I murmured. We could look for it anywhere, anywhere at all. Seraphine, bloated and terrible as she was, had the inkling of a useful idea.

If all else failed, we could make Midian ourselves.

THE FARMHOUSE

Christopher Monfette

1

On the wind, a word of plenty; in the water, a warning.

There had never been a time in the history of the tribes when the prophecies had been so competing. *You will be blessed,* they seemed to say—or others still, in darker moments, *cursed*. It mattered little, largely because they had known both. Blessed with curses or cursed with blessings—the bones rolled either way—but there was little denying that the future held room for an equal measure of suffering and celebration. Let either come; the difference was little. Such had been their history.

On the second week of their flight from Midian, the small democracy of Nightbreed which had, strictly by design of the season's breeze, chosen *west* as their bearing, stumbled upon a small patch of earth which told them politely to rest. They'd carved an existence out of listening to every grass blade and tree root, and few things proved less vital to understanding the language of the ground than living beneath it.

Their great fortune along the way, of course, had been Allyaphasia— with her weave of living tattoos, the shades and lines of which were never quite entirely *still*. Their vague patterns formed the outline of beasts across her skin—mammalian constellations—some of which, until their sudden journey away from Midian, she had yet to discover. She had conjured dogs from those tattoos—and weasels and rats—animals suited to a life in the muck, but never a creature so much belonging to the sky.

And so when, on the third day, an unfamiliar pulling along her spine and shoulders began to stretch out across her skin, she was perhaps the most shocked to witness the eagle emerge from the ink. Its talons came first—a sharp pain, not without blood—followed by wings that descended from her shoulders, and by the time the creature had pulled away and solidified its form, Allyaphasia had begun to weep. They were the tears of a mother discovering some secret child—an expression of great joy in the aftermath of an equally powerful loss.

Of all the Breed, Allyaphasia alone had the most right to sorrow. The destruction of Midian had afflicted many with the loss of a home—others, still, of wives and husbands—but none among them had gone away absent a child. Prior to the attack on Midian, Allyaphasia had confessed to never having encountered a human; nor had she known of bullets before one pierced the eye of her firstborn, or the heart of her second. Even Xxyzx—the most cynical and ill-tempered among them—afforded her the right to mourn, but of her love for the eagle would commonly roll his eyes in protest.

It was not, he insisted, her child.

"What is it then?" many of the splintered tribe inquired of its first appearance—if only for the sad truth of never having seen one before—at which point the faux-feathered beast tested its wings, *cawing* with a shriek, and took to the air, away into the blue-tinted evening. That Allyaphasia could pass her vision to the creature's eyes—smelling the air, sensing the wind—had made her the group's de facto scout—which, despite her reluctance, was perhaps the only thing that kept her alive. While they walked beneath the moonlight, safe from the sun, the eagle pressed on ahead, searching for their next day's refuge, ensuring that daylight would never come without the promise of shelter from it.

And so it was, from the height of the sky, that the low-dwellers first discovered the barn.

2

At night, there were the death-dreams, or so he called them—but never to his mother, who rarely remembered them in the morning. From his bedroom down the hall, the muttered panic of the wasting woman, who tossed

and turned in a kind of ghostly pantomime, woke the boy often and always with the same hopeless thought pounding in the space between his
head and his pillow.

Finally, my mother is dead.

His ears had long since tuned themselves to the first signs of trouble,
and some nights, lying awake in the darkness, he wondered if they would
eventually discern the final push of breath responsible for sending the spirit
of Elizabeth Adler once again out into the universe. He had heard the stories of slumbering loved ones who dreamed some final good-bye, waking
in the morning to find themselves, by some degree, more alone in the world,
and he secretly hoped that such might be the case. It would be better, he
thought, to say good-bye to the woman he always remembered—fresh-faced
and smiling, rosy cheeks alight with life—than the still-beating skeleton
he tended to now.

He awoke the same tonight, setting his small, five-foot frame onto the
cold, wooden floor, and pushed through the remnants of the old, familiar
fear:

Finally, my mother . . .

It was the "finally," for all its implied relief, that disturbed him the most,
and despite the stirrings of his mother beyond the doorway, it was that small
sense of hope—for his peace, for hers—that grew like a tumor of its own,
beneath his skin, grown fat on memory and guilt and sorrow and despair.
It was never lost on him that his mother's cancer would kill more than
simply her.

Jonathan navigated the second-story hallway, trying desperately not to
wake the useless bulk of his otherwise well-meaning uncle in the room next
door. Albert had traveled from his home in Minneapolis—more out of sympathy, the boy suspected, or obligation, than any real desire to help—and
despite Jon's relative youth, he was old enough to know that the clumsy,
half-bald stranger who had visited only once every Christmas was here
now to audition for the eventual role of father.

The boy didn't have the heart to confess to his dying mother his intention
to flee after her passing. He'd grown up among the fields and farms,
tending their own slice of earth—just the two of them, until the sickness
came—and he had no desire to be packed away like so much luggage,
crammed into the old man's station wagon and carted off to some American
Midwest metropolis. No, he thought. He'd run—however long, however

far—and take up with whomever might have him. He'd be a gypsy and learn the part as he went.

Jonathan pushed through his mother's door, unworried that the creaking of the old wood might wake her, and stood among the discarded blankets and amber pill bottles which guarded her bedside like the Easter Island statues he'd once read about in school.

"No," she muttered to the thing in her dreams. "Please. Don't hurt me. . . ."

Tonight, it seemed, the figure was a demon—other nights, it was an angel—and the only true detail she'd ever remembered or chosen, at least, to share with him was that the dream was of a figure, washed in fog, motioning her forward and calling her name. Jonathan had surmised on his own, in moments like these—watching her privately as she smiled or screamed—that the face of the thing was unknowable, some nights terrifying, other nights beautiful.

Jonathan chose to believe that it was God, calling her home, and her fear was in the going, but the distance between the two was shortening, that much he knew. Whatever it was, it would find her, or she it and he knew with as much sadness as a ten-year-old boy could manage that it was a meeting not far off.

She muttered as the wind blew in from the window, curtains tossing like gossamer fingers, like breath in the air. Albert, he thought. Stupid Albert. Who else could have left them open?

He crossed the room and parted the curtains, looking down at the shape of the barn outside as he reached for the latch. Lord, how he loved that place—from rafters to basement, a paradise for pretending. The bank, of course, had already come around sniffing, before his mother had lost the strength to fend them off. She had joked once to Albert that her worst fear in dying was that she might eventually meet the figure in the light only to find him an employee of the bank.

"Heartless bastards," Albert had offered. "God, the Devil. Repo men, all of 'em."

Jon fumbled about the sill, feeling his way along, thinking that for all the brightness of the sky outside, it might as well have been day, when suddenly a shadow cut the evening, silhouetting itself against the moon and then vanishing. He strained his eyes against the night and after several moments, caught the shape again. It was massive, nearly his own size—beak to tail, wing to wing, a bird as big as any he might have imagined. And when, for an instant, it turned to catch the light, he noticed that what he had mistaken for feathers weren't feathers at all.

They didn't flutter; they didn't flap.

They were painted. Tattooed.

And then the creature turned, spun, arched around the spire of the barn and *down*. It dove for the tallgrass below, a collision almost inevitable, until a second shadow split from the dim walls of the building's frame. The figure—a woman, perhaps—floated several feet out into the field, extending an arm into the evening, and just as Jon expected the eagle to land there—as he'd seen in films—it seemed somehow to mold itself into the darkness, one shadow absorbing the other until the bird had vanished completely, and its owner had followed.

The field was empty, the night still.

Jon glanced in disbelief, his heart racing—not with fear, but exhilaration.

Quietly, he latched the window, deciding even before he turned that this was a mystery that demanded some investigation. So determined, he tiptoed across his mother's bedroom, moving quietly so as not to wake her. In the time that he'd been at the window, she'd drifted back to sleep. She breathed quietly, peacefully, every breath like some traded currency, but for the moment, at least, her protests against the dream-demon had stopped.

She would still be alive tomorrow, he decided. And he would have a story to tell her when she woke.

3

In the basement, by lamplight, the Nightbreed argued.

"What do you mean *no shelter*?" Xxyzx insisted angrily. He hobbled across the dirt floor, trailing minuscule droplets of blood in a line toward Allyaphasia.

"You're *dripping*," said the guide, her voice at once both soft and hollow. Like a satin glove with no hand inside.

"Remind me again and it'll be your blood on the floor," the creature growled. "Love you though I do."

To human eyes, Xxyzx might easily have been the most *sapiens* among them—tall and slender, commonly built. He could have walked for an evening in the cities or towns—unnoticed were it not for his black eyes and ruby-red fangs. But his appearance had made him feel eternally *different*, and over a decade, he withdrew further from the race into which he'd been born. He'd chosen to live in books, scavenging human pages wherever he might find them—classics and porn magazines, pamphlets and maps (from which he'd renamed himself). His hatred for a species to which he felt somehow connected made for a bitter temperament, and seldom could he hold his tongue when given the opportunity to unleash it. He ranted frequently—fancied himself a self-tortured intellect—and blasphemed often on the subject of Baphomet.

He was an open book.

So Lylesburg had cursed him—a punishment given without trial, which was uncommon among the Breed, though in this instance nobody objected, nobody cared. The curse was thus—that every negative emotion, every terrible thought, would write itself across the creature's skin, in all tongues and languages. Every ember of anger would scribble itself in razor-thin lines across his flesh—the scripting eloquent, the bloodletting slight. Lylesburg had hoped that the pain might force Xxyzx to reconsider himself, to negotiate some pleasure from his own existence, and for a while it had worked. He had calmed.

But the humans had come with their torches and guns and Lylesburg was dead, having never lifted the curse. And Xxyzx, like all the Breed, bore his anger openly. Cast out and homeless with neither direction nor hope of salvation . . .

He bled frequently these days.

"Again," he insisted. "What do you mean *no shelter?*"

Allyaphasia contorted her neck and shoulders to facilitate the knitting of form and flesh. The eagle had nearly retaken its place across her back.

"In all directions," she said. "Only wilderness. We cannot make shelter by daybreak. We can only go back."

The crowd murmured in protest.

"Certainly, there must be—"

"Nothing," the mother insisted. "Roads. Fields. But no place to hide."

"We can't return," said Neptune. "Can't go back."

"Then what of here?" asked Jonas, picking cobwebs from between his horns. When he spoke, his lips failed to move, his mouth hung open in a dark, empty oval to allow the thing that lived in his throat—the puppeteer, the *real* Jonas—to speak in its shrill hiss.

Xxyzx scoffed loudly. "What of it?"

"We can all smell it," he said. "The death. From the house across the way."

Xxyzx winced as another few lines carved across his cheek. The German word for "idiot," the Arabic for "fool."

"Others will come," he responded. "For them, death is just an empty space. They can't stand the silence, the stillness. It's what they do, the humans—they find the empty and fill it."

"Well, we can't wait forever," grumbled another. "Or drift forever, too."

"And you'd have us do what?" demanded Xxyzx. "Dig? Rebuild?"

"Perhaps," said a voice. Not one, but many.

"On the backs of us broken few? Here, in this place, dare to do what Baphomet did, for all his power? To create a new home?"

The room fell silent at the prospect. Allyaphasia put a hand on his bloody shoulder, feigning her smile from memory.

"I'll try again tomorrow," she comforted. "One last time. And then we'll go."

Xxyzx turned, his brow an architecture of lines. "To where?" he asked, his voice trembling as the word "despair" cut slowly across his chest. *"To where?"*

Jonas pushed suddenly to the front of the crowd, his nose held high in the air. "Xxyzx, Allyaphasia . . ." he began. "I smell something."

The old monster rolled its eyes. "Yes, yes, death. We all smell it, Jonas, we all—"

"Not death," interrupted the creature. "Something worse, I think. *Life.*"

Even as he uttered the phrase, the woodwork creaked loudly overhead, the double-hatched doorway to the cellar pulled open and—

4

—there were monsters in the basement.

Standing atop the stairway, Jonathan tried to scream, but the terror caught dryly in his throat. He'd made his way across the field, ducking between a section of half-broken boards and quietly into the darkened barn. The smell of hay and damp cedar wafted into the night, masking another scent—musty and strange—which he'd never before encountered among the farm's earthy perfume. And beneath that odor, a noise—the chatter of whispered voices, half raised in argument.

He should have turned then—turned and run back to the house, rousing Albert toward the shotgun that his father had left behind. But he pressed forward, silently across the floorboards, between which small slivers of lamplight projected themselves like stars against the ceiling. With all the foolishness of youth, he cast open the cellar door—

And there were monsters in the basement . . . a group of them, looking slack-jawed and surprised, meeting his frightened glance with a fear of their own. Together, they seemed like some crudely sewn patchwork—a half-human quilt of magnificent colors and forms. Purple skin and mossy scales; wet, gelatinous masses and fully-fleshed forms. Some had horns, others tentacles. A few had neither. A few were . . . *worse*.

Finally, Jonathan gasped, a gesture that broke the frozen moment between them. He turned, terrified, rushing back up the stairway in small ten-year-old steps. Below him, his feet went *thunk-thunk-thunk* against the dusty plywood, masking a sound that he failed to hear until it was too late. Behind every *thunk*, a *click*, a spark—the claws of a creature against the damp cellar walls. It entered his periphery, demanding a glance, and he turned to find it not beside him, but crawling across the surface to his left, spider-walking in spite of gravity. A second, smaller set of arms had somehow torn themselves free from the hollow structure of the first, and the monster—all six hands clutching the walls—scurried along the concrete and in front of him, slamming the door with a thundering echo.

He was trapped, surely dead. He dropped his head in anticipation of the bite, or the blow, but none came. Instead, only—

"*Stop!*"

It was a voice of complete command, strong yet distinctly feminine, though not without a slight, shaking vibrato.

"I forbid this!" it called. "Not another child dead before my eyes!"

"Allyaphasia," hissed one of the creatures. Its mouth dangled open, teeth glinting, but despite the high-pitched voice, its lips didn't move.

"Neptune, bring him here," said another, this one far more like a human than any of the rest. He turned to the others, some of whom snarled, some of whom whimpered. "It was bound to happen. Hiding in basements and barns. Be thankful it was only a boy."

The creature behind him—Neptune, they'd called her—whispered quietly into his ear—"Don't scream, darling"—and before he could even consider doing so, she'd wrapped four of her arms around his chest, lifted him off the upmost step, and carried him down into the midst of the monsters.

"He's trembling," she said, half laughing into the room. "Fancy that. First time in my life I've ever been found *imposing*."

It was at that moment that Jonathan decided that he was dreaming. Whether it was the casual, lightly spoken manner of whatever thing had just moved him across the room, or the way in which the freakish assembly failed to meet a young boy's definition of "monster," Jon felt little immediate threat of being devoured or torn to pieces. And since such creatures did not, of course, exist—monstrous or otherwise—he felt, as one occasionally does in dreams, that however terrifying this might become, he would wake eventually. And so he spoke bravely in an attempt to hide his lie.

"I'm trembling because I'm cold, thank you," he said politely, a quip to which a few of the group laughed.

"And not out of fear?" said the half-human one, and from this distance, Jon could discern the strange pattern of cuts across his body. "We're monsters, after all."

"Xxyzx, please," said the woman who'd halted Neptune's attack. It took Jonathan a moment to realize that the creature before him was naked, clothed rather in an odd assortment of drawings across her skin. Her breasts were full; her body was slender. The dark lines of her tattoos curved across her frame, drawing his eye and allowing it to linger perhaps a moment longer than was proper. The shapes traced down along her midsection, folding into the crevice just above her thighs, and continued to her feet. It was the first time that Jonathan had ever seen a woman in a state of such nakedness, at least in the flesh.

"He's staring," chuckled Neptune.

"I am not," insisted Jon, using the exchange as an excuse to turn his attention away. "Or if I am, it's because I've never dreamt about monsters before."

"Dreamt?" asked Xxyzx. "You think this is a dream?"

"I may be ten," said Jon, "but even I know that monsters aren't real."

Jonas threw up his hands in a mockery of worship. "Praise Baphomet! Our suffering is diminished! If only because we don't exist!"

The tattooed woman turned. "Jonas, please. A month ago, there were things that even *we* might not have believed."

"Bite him, then," said Neptune. "Turn him into one of us. Make him immortal, make him strong—unsick and forever. Let a few centuries pass and see if he wonders when he'll wake."

"That's enough," said the woman. She kneeled slowly to Jon's level, putting her hands softly onto his shoulders. "What's your name, child?"

"Jonathan," he replied.

She smiled sweetly. "My name is Allyaphasia, Jonathan. I had a son your age, and another slightly older."

"Monsters have children?" he asked, suddenly aware of his own naïveté. "Can I see them, please?"

An emotion flickered across the woman's face, one he'd seen a number of times before, on the face of his mother, which was not so dissimilar. It was the expression she wore in her most somber of moments, when she allowed herself to be weak and honest and weep in his presence. It was the face that followed the words "I'll never see you marry, or your children be born."

"They died," said Allyaphasia.

"If this is a dream," began Jonathan, "then maybe I can dream them back. You can do that in dreams."

"Would you trust me if I asked you to close your eyes?" she inquired, and to his own surprise, he did. She put a hand to his forehead, delicate and soft, and he felt the creature's nails trail their way lightly across his skin, down over his eyelids and above his warm, rosy cheeks. It was a sensation at once both *calming* and *real*, as honest a touch as any he'd ever received in waking life, and when he opened his eyes a moment later he said, as if to himself—

"This isn't a dream."

5

An hour passed in the company of the one they called Allyaphasia. It was an hour filled with a child's questions, and with the patience of one who used to be a mother, she answered them as best she could. In the space behind them, where they sat gingerly on a damp bale of hay, the others paced nervously in the shadows.

She told him of Midian, the underground city—of its immense, cavernous walls and magnificent chambers. She told him of its birth, of Baphomet and their history, of their tragedy and their wanderings. She spoke of Boone and his becoming with neither judgment nor scorn. She told him the story of the Nightbreed as one might tell it to a man, and when he pointed this out to her, she said only, "Having seen what you've seen, you cannot help but become one, as I, seeing you, am a child once again."

He told her of his mother and of Albert. He spoke of his plans to run away after her passing—for which he said he'd prepared himself, though Allyaphasia didn't have the heart to say just how impossible that truly was. He stopped at one point in the evening and said excitedly, "You could stay here, or I could go with you," to which Allyaphasia simply laughed and turned the topic to some story of Midian.

And after an hour of conversation, the pacing Xxyzx finally broke free from the crowd and pulled her away to a quiet corner, saying, "Quit this, damn you. Quit this now!"

"I know what you're thinking," she began.

"And I you. Playing mother to incur our sympathies, as if the sight of you and the boy were some rite of protection." He paused, sighing, and leaned in closer. "They want to kill him, you know. Here in the barn. Then across the field for the sleeping mother and uncle. And then move on . . ."

"I won't allow that."

"You can't stop it!" He pressed his fist into the rafters behind her head. "If he proves too convincing, or brings them here, we're through. If we let them live, they'll invite more. The humans bring death, Allyaphasia—intended or otherwise."

"I can't let you kill him, Xxyzx," she said plainly. "Because if we do—if we slaughter a boy and his family—then we are, indeed, just as he claims. We're monsters."

Xxyzx growled heavily, an element of his nature of which he'd never quite disposed. "What then do you suggest?"

"Not me," she said, and in that moment, Jonathan appeared at her side, his face alight with words unspoken, calling her ears to the question she'd been waiting for him to ask.

6

"Will you turn my mother?"

The room erupted in whispered argument, for he'd addressed the question to them all, but Jonathan wavered not a bit. His mind had been turning in the time that Allyaphasia and Xxyzx had spoken, poring over the story of Boone, but mostly over the words that Neptune had uttered earlier.

"Make him immortal—unsick and forever."

"You can do this," he shouted into the deafening crowd. "You can help her. Why won't you help her?"

Allyaphasia moved to stand before him, putting herself between the child and the rabble. "Calm yourselves!" she cried.

"That last human we turned," began Jonas, motioning to the darkness of the room around them. "This is the result of that."

"Kill him!" cried some. "Kill them all!"

Jonathan, frightened but stalwart, clung to the woman's wrist. "Make them understand," he whispered, uncertain if she'd heard him.

"No killing," cried Xxyzx into the room. "There's been enough of that."

"What other option is there?" shouted Neptune.

Allyaphasia stepped forward, leading the boy with every step.

"Ours is a history of running," she insisted. "And too often of fighting—but never of helping. Never a gesture of kindness for fear of being vulnerable. Never a moment of forgiveness. We cannot expect from them what we are unable to give ourselves."

"We're broken, Allyaphasia!" cried Jonas.

"Then this is how we *mend*," she insisted. "By fixing ourselves."

She would have said more had Jonathan not stepped out from behind her, dropping a hand that reached back out for his own, and moved cautiously into the center of the room. Never before had he felt so small, so afraid, but if courage was the price, he would find it to pay.

"My mom is dying," he said, tears spilling from his eyes. "You can help her; you can do that. Whatever you are, you all were *born*. I'm just a kid with a sick mom and a dumb uncle and no *hope* except for you. And whatever you think we'll do, we won't, I swear, because she'll be *one* of you. And that doesn't matter to me as long as she's okay." He paused, weeping and embarrassed. "Your god left you, and I'm pretty sure that mine left me, too. So if all we have left is each other, then whatever we are, that's better than being alone, right?"

The room was silent. The world had fallen into a deep and lulling hush.

"She's dying," he concluded. *"Please."*

The silence lingered for a long, lasting moment until Neptune finally spoke.

"That's a smart fucking kid," she said. "I call for council."

"Council's dead," grumbled Jonas. "Council was a relic of Midian."

"We *are* Midian," replied Xxyzx. "And I second the call."

Reluctantly, the creatures began to assemble in the center of the room as Allyaphasia turned to Jon.

"You must go now," she said. "This will be a *long* process."

"Will they help?" he asked, but she didn't answer.

"Go now, back to your mother. Give her your love and return here tomorrow. We'll be waiting."

7

In the darkness before dawn, Allyaphasia stood in the cool, rustling grass of the field, gazing upward at the stars. She knew of their patterns and portents, understood the workings of far-off worlds on her own. She was an old mystic, last in a long line of sky-gazing fortune-tellers, but tonight, for all their power to be more so, she wished them only to be what they were— pinpricks in the darkness.

She heard Xxyzx before she saw him, and when the shadows parted to reveal his face, he looked exhausted.

"We've been at this for hours," he said. "With hours more to go."

"Jonas can smell it," she said. "We all can. There aren't many hours left."

A cricket sang its one-note song from somewhere in the darkness, and it took Xxyzx a moment to realize that it was doing so from the palm of Allyaphasia's hand. The creature was her own, molded from a slice of flesh across her forearm, and it chirped quietly into the night. The two friends stood there, together in the tallgrass, listening to its music.

"We're only ever saved by the mercy we show to others," said Allyaphasia after a time. "Lylesburg told me as much."

Xxyzx groaned at the name of the man who'd set him to bleed, but his skin remained unmarked. Nothing new had scrawled itself there. Rather, he only laughed—guttural and deep. "Lylesburg and his lessons," he muttered. "When did he spin you *that* fiction?"

"The day before the taking of Midian." She paused. "The day before he'd decided to remove your curse." She let the revelation hang delicately in the moonlight, and for a moment, there was only silence, save for the chirping of insects.

If Xxyzx reacted, Allyaphasia couldn't tell. "He said it to me after Boone arrived," she continued, "before the fire followed. He confessed that he'd been wrong to curse you. Admitted that peace isn't something to be forced, but discovered; that we have to come to it in our own way, in our own time. He would have healed you, Xxyzx. He was a good man."

She'd given him an opportunity to lament, she understood—to despair at the loss of a truth refused him. Instead, he simply said, "One day, love, you'll find your peace," words which led her to suspect that somehow, by chance, he'd begun to find his own.

"I believe now that I will," she replied after a while. "It's why I've decided to help the boy. Whatever the verdict."

Before she could speak, Xxyzx sighed mournfully into the evening chill. "Ally, please—"

"Oh, be still," she chided. "Do what you must, I'll understand. But if we are, the lot of us, more than just a tribe, greater than a simple pack of bickering drifters—if we are, by fate or family, *bound*—you'll allow me this, Xxyzx. All of you."

"It won't bring them back," the creature said plainly. "The dead stay dead. . . . But you already know that."

Allyaphasia turned and touched his cheek. For the first time in a long time, her hand came away bloodless.

"I'm a mother denied her children. I haven't the right to deny a child his mother."

She smiled, thin-lipped but honest, and the expression she wore was one of resolution. She had finished wandering, it was clear—finished mourning, finished apologizing for her tears. She had *decided*, and there were no requests left in her. Seemingly unchanged, the world had somehow remade itself, and in that moment, he knew that she was no longer Nightbreed. She was singular; she was her own.

"When?" he asked. "I'll be there with you."

"Tomorrow," replied Allyaphasia. "After nightfall."

Elizabeth Adler died the following morning.

8

Died, but not died. Half died.

Jonathan awoke to the sound of the dream-demon—not in his mother's head, however, but in his own. "It's time," said the shadow, vague against the light, a vision that Jonathan might have forgotten had it not carried him back into wakefulness.

Finally, my mother . . . he began to think, but stopped himself. He'd found the way to help, so long as they would agree.

He moved quickly from the bed, threw open his door, and saw Albert standing in the entrance to his mother's room, face sullen. He feared for a moment that he was too late, but the voice of the demon—or was it an angel—persisted inside his skull. "It's time" suggested somehow that there was time to be had, little though it might be, and it allowed precious few seconds for grief.

"She's alive?" he asked, the space between them immense.

"I woke her for breakfast," he stammered. "Oatmeal, the usual. But she won't open her eyes. I think you should say your—"

"I've gotta get to the barn," he said, bare feet rushing toward the stairwell.

"I don't think you understand," said his uncle.

"I can help," cried Jon. "*They* can help!"

"Who, Jon? Who can help?"

"The Nightbreed," he said, almost casually. "The monsters in the basement."

Albert stopped at the top of the stairs as Jon looked back up. It was the first time that his uncle had ever worn a human face, he thought, and it was one of sorrow. Jon knew it well and pitied him for the fashion.

"She's dying," said Albert. "Jon, son, *it's time*."

"No," said the boy by his place at the door. "Not quite yet."

9

He ran across the field, ignoring his uncle's calls, scrambled through the break in the barn wall and into the darkened cellar.

"She's dying!" he called loudly into the room. "Please, help! Please!"

From the shadows, a lamplight began to glow—then another, and another. The monsters stirred from their sleep, rousing into the shadows of the midafternoon. A few lay on improvised beds of dirt and hay; others slept in crossed-legged meditation, while others still hung from the rafters overhead. As the lamplight brightened the vague shape of the cellar, they slowly began to assemble, eyes squinted against the darkness. Xxyzx was the first to speak.

"We said to come at night, boy!"

"She's dying!" he cried. "Allyaphasia, she's *dying!*"

There was some commotion among the crowd as Allyaphasia appeared, exchanging nervous glances with Xxyzx across the room. From the space above, the distant shouts of Albert crossing the field could be faintly discerned, but Jonas had already sensed the threat from its smell alone. He looked frantically up the stairs, then back toward Xxyzx at the center of the Breed.

"Fool!" cried the puppet. "Who have you brought?"

"It's my uncle," said Jon, crossing the room toward the tattooed woman. "I didn't have time to wait. He's harmless, I promise, but we have to go now."

He took her hand, attempting to drag her forward, but she resisted, digging her feet into the earth below. "I can't—" she began.

"Can't what?" asked Jon. "Can't *why?*"

Before she could answer, Albert's voice sounded from the top of the stairs. His footsteps echoed off the creaking boards—one step, another—as he shouted down below.

"Dammit, Jon, this is serious. Your mother's ill and you're talking about monsters? It's not time to be a *child* now!"

He might have said more had he not breached the lamplight, nearly collapsing to the bottom at the sight of their assembly. His footing faltered as he yelped a nervous, half-formed scream, caught in his throat by Jonas's six-fingered hand. The creature rushed toward its victim, pinning him violently against the wall, yellow eyes against Albert's dull, muddy brown.

From his mouth, a set of pincers revealed themselves—spit-covered and sharp—extending past the creature's lips and hefting themselves against the meat of Jonas's cheeks. Thick, viscous choking sounds gurgled from the back of his throat, contracting painfully as if something were making its way *out*. From between his teeth, the glistening curvature of the puppeteer's head emerged into the light, soft and dark like so much mud, or shit. It was larger than it should have been, and oddly shaped, contorting itself impossibly into the open air. It had a mouth of its own—eyes and hands—like some cancerous newborn tearing bloody into the world, but rather than cry—or roar, as Albert might have expected—it trained its narrow slits on the terrified man and said simply—

"*Boo.*"

Albert fainted, an unintended gesture which Jon would later assume had saved his life. He was, for the moment, a threat averted. No need for a murder so late in the day.

Jonas's face fell back like a hood, absent of muscle or bone, as the puppet adjusted itself upright. "Tell him," it hissed to Xxyzx. "Tell him why his mother's going to die."

Jonathan looked back toward Allyaphasia. "What does he mean? I thought you would help. I *needed* you to help."

Before she could speak, Xxyzx interrupted. "We would have," he admitted. "We'd agreed. . . . But we can't go just now. Later, perhaps—"

"There is no later," he protested. "She'll be dead later!"

"It's why we're here," said Neptune from behind him. "Hiding in the dark. The sun can burn us. *Kill* us."

Jonathan moaned—half in mourning, half in anguish. The world seemed determined that a life would be taken this afternoon, and who was he to fight against the world? Just a boy, after all. Certainly nothing more.

"We can't cross until nightfall," said Xxyzx, leaning in toward the child, touching his face for the very first time. It was as real a connection as he'd made in centuries, so much that he barely felt the word "sorrow" script itself across his chest.

"I'm sorry," he said. "Truly, I am. If she lives—"

"She won't." Jon sniffed, weeping openly now.

"If she lives," assured Xxyzx. "We'll go. We'll invite her to be one of us. . . ."

He held open his arms to the boy, who sobbed into the comfort of the monster's awkward embrace. The child's body shook with its tears, pattering against his scarred flesh, trickling over words of sadness and scorn, melancholy and anger, and mixed with the blood there to trace soft, pink trails across the creature's skin. And in no small way, they hurt him more than Lylesburg's curse ever had.

"I could have helped," Jon cried, his voice muffled. "I could have saved her."

Xxyzx looked past the boy's head—took in the clean, soapy smell of his hair—and met Allyaphasia's eyes across the room. He was uncertain whether the glance had been one of permission, or whether she'd simply come to the decision on her own, but when she stepped forward and placed her hand on the boy's cheek, he was hardly surprised at her response.

"And we will," she said. "We'll save her together."

10

None of them tried to stop her; they knew it would be fruitless. None of them tried to argue that she was their guide and that without her they were lost. None of them made proclamations of love, or offered eulogies in her honor.

Rather, they followed her up the steps to the place where the sun split through the broken boards, pushing through the shadows that fell across the floor. They watched her turn for what they knew would be her final look, hoping against hope that it might be otherwise. They witnessed Xxyzx as he edged the shadows and embraced her tenderly.

"This is your peace?" he asked. She nodded without speaking, and he touched her face like a lover might. "And *this* has been mine." He kissed her—neither brief, nor lingering—and delicately pushed her away toward the boy.

"Move quickly," he said in lieu of "Good-bye." "It takes but a moment."

Jonathan offered his hand, looking back across the monsters in the barn, who seemed as certain as he that the world would take its death today.

"Ready?" he said.

Allyaphasia closed her eyes—conjured the faces of her children, whom she hoped to see again—and stepped into the sunlight.

11

When the Nightbreed would later speak of their history, storytellers would spin the crossing of Allyaphasia in the most romantic of ways. It was a tale designed for tears, after all, told and retold, made and remade. But it wasn't the truth, of course—history never is—and those who'd been there to see it would have told you that the reality was much, much worse.

She burned from the very beginning, from her first moment out among the light. It was a terrible pain, and for all her mother's bravery—for all her intended nobility—she screamed with every step. Her skin smoked and charred. Her hands; her feet. Her arms turned red in five simple paces—a deep, sunburn tan; brown in ten; and gray in twenty. She made the walk with her eyes closed, knowing that they would burn first, hoping that her lids would protect them long enough to cross the field. She relied on Jonathan to guide her, and despite her cries and frequent stumbles, he pulled her firmly, bravely, murmuring platitudes to keep her going.

By the halfway point, her hair had stiffened and cracked, falling to the ground like straw. Her exposed head sprouted red, pus-filled sores; her back gristled and hissed, and by the time they reached the dirt path toward the porch, her spine had become discernible beneath the half-cooked flesh.

"A few more feet," pleaded Jonathan. "Just a few."

They made it together, stumbling up the steps. Jonathan reached to pull open the screen door and turned to the creature beside him. Her right eye had blistered and burst, its juices leaking down her cheek.

He pulled her into the living room only half alive, but her strength was evident even in her weakened state.

"Which way?" she asked, and when he pointed to the stairs, she sighed.

Allyaphasia crawled to the top, step by step—half pulled, half dragged by Jon beside her—and down the hall into Elizabeth's bedroom. Jonathan pulled the curtain closed to block the afternoon sun.

"We made it," said Jonathan, following her to the side of his mother, and for the first time since stepping from the barn, he allowed himself to notice the tragedy that the sun had played upon Allyaphasia. Elizabeth lay there—eyes sunken, skin pale—and yet for all the damage wrought beneath her skin, she still, at least, looked human. There was nothing vaguely resembling Allyaphasia left of the creature across from him, and in that moment, Jonathan realized that he'd traded one loss for another.

He'd come to love this woman, this monster, and he wept for *her* now as much as his mother. He felt somehow as if they were the same.

As if to dispel the notion, Elizabeth muttered quietly.

"You," she said softly to the dream-demon. "Your face . . ."

Allyaphasia looked up at those words, taking Elizabeth's hand. "We're not alone," she said after a moment. "There are others here."

"It's just us," said Jonathan, thinking perhaps that she'd lost her sight completely. "The room is empty."

"One room is every room," she said. "And all rooms are one room."

Jonathan didn't pretend to understand, nor did Allyaphasia attempt to teach him. She simply reached for the soft flesh of Elizabeth's arm—of which there was little, for she'd wasted much—and asked of the boy, "Are you certain?"

He nodded, and Allyaphasia lowered her head, placing her lips over Elizabeth's skin, and bit down as if her bite were a kiss. Two small rivulets of blood flowed down her pale, alabaster hands onto the quilted blanket that his grandmother had knitted before her passing. He wondered for the first time by how long his mother might now outlive him, or his children, or his children's children—the missing of which had been her greatest dying regret.

"How long?" asked Jonathan, leaning over his mother's frail façade, when suddenly her eyes opened, meeting his own with a fire he'd not seen in months.

"Not long at all," laughed Allyaphasia as Elizabeth looked intently at her son.

"Jon?" she said, the gauze of her sleep still shedding from her eyes. She touched his face, his neck, his hair—smiling, half giggling. "He sent me back," she said. "The angel, he sent me back."

He kissed her, surprised at the warmth that had already returned to her body. He wrapped his arms around her neck as she winced. "Slow there, tiger. One step, then another," she said, but she only hugged him harder.

It wasn't until they'd parted that her eyes fell to Allyaphasia, and before Jonathan could think to tell her not to scream—to say that there was an explanation, and then explain it—Elizabeth smiled. "He said you'd be here," she whispered, tears welling, but not yet fallen. "That I'd know you by your eyes."

They were kind eyes, indeed, thought Jonathan, who asked only, "What did you see?"

"I saw him," said Elizabeth. "Clearly and for the very first time. The man in my dreams; the one who calls to me." She paused, raising her hand to the marred, blackened flesh of Allyaphasia's cheek. "He had a face like yours."

"Like *ours*," muttered the monster, her breathing labored, her dim eyes growing heavy. "Do you understand?"

Elizabeth nodded. "It was explained to me. And I accept."

Even Allyaphasia, who knew more of the world-behind-the-world than Jonathan could ever hope to learn, seemed confused by her words, but if she desired to know more, she said nothing. Instead, she turned to Jonathan, who'd made no pretense to hide his tears, and smiled.

"Kindly, dear, would you open the window?" she asked, her tired glance full of knowing. "So that I might see my son."

Jonathan hesitated, aware of the consequence, but Elizabeth simply nodded—a gentle, melancholy gesture—as if to give permission to them both. It was a moment between mothers, he understood, and not for him to share.

Elizabeth's eyes met those of the tattooed woman—as if parting at the start of a long journey—and she pulled herself back into the room's shade and shadows. In his corner, Jonathan reached for the curtains. A slice of light penetrated the narrow slit and fell across Allyaphasia's face. She closed her eyes against the sting and gestured him forward.

He drew the curtains wider, enough to allow the sun to pour down onto the creature in the center of the room, and as it did so, she began slowly to unravel. The tattoos that marked her skin pulled away, peeling toward the sunlight and rising into the shape of animals. Jonathan spied a titmouse emerge from the woman's skin, followed by a cat, followed by a snake.

The offspring weren't immune to the soft diffusion of sun, and as they separated and formed, one by one, they came back together in an embrace of species. They nestled into one another—taking suckle, taking safety—as the light dissolved their newborn forms, floating like ash into the air.

Allyaphasia was almost gone now, as well, a hollow framework from which countless lives had come and gone, but she was not wholly unrecognizable. Her smile persisted to the end. Elizabeth stepped forward from the shadows, unafraid of what effect the light might have on her fading humanity, and cradled the soft, wet tissue of the disappearing woman.

"I saw him," she repeated. "The man from my dreams. And he spoke to me of you."

The Breed no longer had voice, but her mouth moved breathlessly in the pantomime of a question: *What did he say?*

And with her first breath as a member of the tribes, Elizabeth told her.

12

When it was safe—when the sun had set—Jonathan led his mother across the field to the barn where the remaining Nightbreed paced nervously in the shadows. He helped her across the threshold and down into the crudely dug cellar where the creatures waited impatiently. They looked up curiously, their eyes passing beyond the stranger in their midst in search of Allyaphasia behind them, which she was not.

"Our woman?" asked Xxyzx. "Did she not make it?"

Elizabeth scanned the room with greater confidence than she had ever possessed in her human life, and with the strange audience before her, simply shook her head.

"Such a fucking waste!" cried Jonas. "Trading her for you! We're lost now!"

"Not entirely," said Elizabeth to the room, a timbre in her voice which Jonathan had never before heard. "My son and his uncle will be our eyes in the daylight; find us places to rest beneath the moon. We'll explain it to him when he wakes," she said of Albert's body slumped unconsciously in the corner.

Laughter spread among the crowd—tenuous and discordant. There were holes in their disbelief. She had put them there with only a scant few words.

"And what of it?" asked Xxyzx. "What of you?"

"Of me?" she asked, removing the veil from her head, revealing the shapes and mutations that Allyaphasia's bite had conjured there. Her features had changed considerably. The bones beneath her skin had reworked themselves, re-formed, but not without regard to her femininity. In truth, strange as it may have seemed, Jonathan considered his mother to be more beautiful in that moment than ever.

"Of me," she began, "I died. And in death I had a vision. A man, but not a man. Like me now, a half-breed. And in that vision he spoke, and in speaking asked me to address you thus. . . ."

The Nightbreed stilled, their attention rapt, and had Elizabeth known the long, suffering history of Xxyzx—upon whose skin the worst had been written—she might have been surprised to see the word "hope" appear there now.

On the stairs beside her, Jonathan took her hand.

"Tell them, Mom," he whispered quietly. "Tell them what the man told you."

Elizabeth smiled proudly at her son, running a hand through his delicate auburn hair, and turned to the roomful of unbelievers, prepared to make them less so. *"My name is Boone,"* she quoted. *"And these are my children. You are chosen among them. You are Cabal. And you will lead them to me."*

And so it was that Elizabeth Adler—newest of the Nightbreed—having spoken the words, began to make them true.

ABOUT THE AUTHORS

Karl Alexander is an award-winning novelist and screenwriter. He has published seven novels. Two have been made into films, including the classic *Time After Time*. His most recent book, *Time-Crossed Lovers*, was an Award Winning Finalist in the 2013 International Book Awards. He lives near his hometown, Los Angeles.

Timothy Baker is a retired firefighter and martial-arts instructor embarking on a new career in writing fiction. Having published a handful of short stories, Timothy is working to get his novel, *Hungry Ghosts*, into the light of day. An Oklahoma native, Timothy now lives on the stark high plains of southeastern Colorado and lives with his three cats: Gary, Spidey, and Mel. You can find his blog, *Bones Along the Road*, at skeletonroad.word press.com.

Amber Benson is a writer, director, actor, and maker of things. She wrote the five-book Calliope Reaper-Jones urban-fantasy series and the middle-grade book *Among the Ghosts*. She codirected the Slamdance feature *Drones* and (cowrote) and directed the BBC animated series *The Ghosts of Albion*. She also spent three years as Tara Maclay on the television series *Buffy the Vampire Slayer*. She doesn't own a television. You can find her online at www.facebook.com/amberbensonwrotethis.

Edward Brauer is an unsettling taste in the back of your throat; a broken promise of clear skies, still oceans, and birdsong. By day he speaks the forbidden tongue of computers, nurturing the many-tentacled network of a cosmetics company. By night he cloaks himself in formless shadow and writes weird fiction. He lives with his partner, Lindsey, and cat, Savvy, in a creaky, old house on the edge of Melbourne. You might catch his silhouette vanishing around the corner of a cobblestone laneway should you visit sometime, but if you're wise, you'll curb your curiosity and not follow. You can find him online at www.facebook.com/edward.brauer.75.

Longtime film critic turned novelist and screenwriter **C. Robert Cargill** has written for *Ain't It Cool News, Spill.com,* and numerous other sites as well as penning the film *Sinister* and the novels *Dreams and Shadows* and *Queen of the Dark Things.* He lives and works in Austin, Texas.

Brian Craddock is a storyteller and visual artist in Australia. He has toured the Outback of Australia and as far afield as Pakistan as a professional puppeteer, and currently works as a special-effects makeup artist for independent film. You can find him online at www.facebook.com/craddockfx.

Ernie W. Cooper lives in Concord, North Carolina, with his fiancée and their evil, breath-sucking cat. When he's not playing in other people's literary sandboxes, he makes movie magic happen at the local megaplex. Find him online at www.facebook.com/ernie.cooper.33.

Born somewhere during the latter part of the twentieth century, **Nerine Dorman** remembers what life was like before cell phones and the Internet. Yes, she is that old. By day she slaves away as a newspaper subeditor; after dark she makes authors weep and scribes her own tales of darkness and misery. Her book reviews and lifestyle editorial often appear in assorted South African newspapers and online. She worships at the altar of coffee, plays classical guitar, and is growing a forest around her house. One day she'll visit Egypt. For now, she'll dream. You can find her online at www.nerinedorman.wordpress.com and www.facebook.com/nerine.

Kelly Dunn's fiction first appeared in e-zines such as *Necrotic Tissue* and *Aberrant Dreams.* Her short stories have since been featured in the anthologies *The Dead That Walk, Midnight Walk, The Undead That Saved Christmas, Vol. 2,* and *After Death.* Kelly is the editor of the horror fiction anthology *Mutation Nation,* published by Rainstorm Press. Her alter ego, Savannah

Kline, has written an urban-fantasy novel, *Beloved of the Fallen*, published by Ulysses Press. Visit Kelly at kellysdunn.com.

Residing in the land of swamps and simulacra known more commonly as Florida, **Kurt Fawver** is a fine purveyor of literature both wondrous and horrific. He has published short fiction in numerous magazines and anthologies and has also released a collection of short stories—*Forever, in Pieces*—through Villipede Publications. You can find Kurt online at www .facebook.com/kfawver.

Nancy Holder is a *New York Times* bestselling author of approximately eighty novels and over a hundred short stories. She has received five Bram Stoker Awards for her supernatural fiction and a Scribe Award for *Saving Grace: Tough Love*, based on the TV show by the same name. This is her second tribute story to the master, having also appeared in *Hellbound Hearts*. Recent publications include *Buffy: The Making of a Slayer* and *On Fire: Teen Wolf*. She is the coeditor of the young-adult science-fiction anthology *FutureDaze2: Reprise*, from Underwords Press. She lives in San Diego. Tweet her @nancyholder.

Lisa Majewski is a screenwriter and animal activist who graduated with honors from the USC School of Cinematic Arts. Frequently asked when her love for the macabre began, she replies, "At birth."

Seanan McGuire is a professional author and amateur watcher of as many horror movies as she can get her hands on. She began pursuing both professions at approximately the age of six, which explains a lot. (She had more early success with horror movies and began publishing her fiction in 2009.) She also writes as Mira Grant, because one name was not enough. Seanan enjoys haunted houses, haunted corn mazes, haunted hotels, and the occasional cemetery. She also enjoys Disney Parks, creepy dolls, and spending time with her cats. You can find her at www.seananmcguire.com or on Twitter as @seananmcguire.

Shaun Meeks lives in Toronto, Ontario, with his partner, Mina LaFleur. Shaun is a member of the HWA and has published more than fifty short stories. His most recent work has appeared in *Shadow Masters*, an anthology from *The Horror Zine*, *Zippered Flesh 2*, *Fresh Fear*, *Someone Wicked*, *Van Gogh's Ear, Vol. 8*, and *Of Devils and Deviants*. His short stories have been collected in *At the Gates of Madness*, *Brother's Ilk*, and *Dark Reaches*. His new novel, *Shutdown*, is due out this year. To find out more or to contact Shaun, visit www.shaunmeeks.com.

Christopher Monfette grew up in Massachusetts as a lifelong lover of genre fiction. He began his career as an entertainment journalist for mainstay geek institutions IGN and G4 and transitioned to comic writing with IDW's *Seduth*, his debut collaboration with horror maestro Clive Barker. He later reimagined the Hellraiser franchise for Boom! Publishing, penning the first eight issues of the critically celebrated series. As a screenwriter, he's worked on feature adaptations from idols such as Barker and Stephen King and continues to develop original work in the realms of horror, science fiction, and action/adventure.

Weston Ochse is the author of twenty books, most recently two SEAL Team 666 books, which the *New York Post* called "required reading" and *USA Today* placed on their New and Notable lists. His first novel, *Scarecrow Gods*, won the Bram Stoker Award for Superior Achievement in First Novel, and his short fiction has been nominated for the Pushcart Prize. He lives in the Arizona desert within rock-throwing distance of Mexico. He is a veteran with twenty-nine years of military service and recently returned from a tour in Afghanistan. Visit him online at *Living Dangerously*—www.westonochse.com.

Ian Rogers is an award-winning Canadian writer. His debut collection, *Every House Is Haunted*, was the winner of the 2013 ReLit Award in the Short Fiction category, while his novelette "The House on Ashley Avenue" was a finalist for the Shirley Jackson Award. His short fiction has been published in *Cemetery Dance*, *Broken Pencil*, and *Shadows & Tall Trees*, and has been reprinted in several best-of-the-year anthologies. Ian is also the author of *SuperNOIRtural Tales*, a collection of stories featuring occult detective Felix Renn. Ian lives with his wife in Peterborough, Ontario. For more information, visit ianrogers.ca.

Lilith Saintcrow has been writing stories since second grade and does not ever plan to stop. She lives in Vancouver, Washington, with her family and

a small menagerie. You can visit her on the Web at www.lilithsaintcrow
.com.

Paul J. Salamoff has been working for over twenty-four years in film, TV,
video games, and commercials as a writer, producer, executive, comic creator, and makeup FX artist. He is the author of *On the Set: The Hidden
Rules of Movie Making Etiquette, The Complete DVD Book*; the graphic
novels *Discord, Tales of Discord, Logan's Run: Last Day, Logan's Run: Aftermath*, and *Logan's Run: Rebirth*; and issues of *Vincent Price Presents*. Salamoff owns the TARDIS console from the 1996 *Doctor Who* TV movie. His
website www.thetoptenmoviesofalltime.com reviews and recommends
movies in every genre.

Rob Salem is a writer, poet, artist, and musician currently living in the
Midwest. He also hosts an Internet radio show featuring underground rock
and metal, and when not pursuing any of those passions, he spends his time
indulging himself in early medieval history, good wine and beer, decent
cigars, and catching local rock concerts. He is somewhat of a modern no-
mad, easily prone to wanderlust, and enjoys traveling when he can, finding inspiration for most of his work in the people he meets and the places
he goes—the best stories, he feels, are rooted in the real world. You can
find him online at www.facebook.com/robsalem156.

David J. Schow has indulged this activity called "writing" for over thirty-
five years, yielding movies (*The Crow, Leatherface: Texas Chainsaw
Massacre III, The Hills Run Red*), television (*Mob City, Masters of Horror*),
eight novels (*Upgunned* is the latest), seven short-story collections, and an
award-winning compendium of his infamous *Fangoria* columns, *Wild
Hairs*. His other nonfiction ventures include *The Art of Drew Struzan, The
Outer Limits Companion*, and its celebratory follow-up, *The Outer Limits
at 50*. As expert witness you can see or hear him on over a dozen DVD
supplements and commentaries. Look him up.

Durand Sheng Welsh is a police officer in Sydney, Australia. He is a graduate of the Clarion Writers' Workshop 2008. His work has appeared in *Apex*
magazine, *Crossed Genres, Canterbury 2100*, and elsewhere. He is currently
working on a crime/horror novel.

Kevin J. Wetmore is an actor, director, and writer. His books include *Post-9/11 Horror in American Cinema* and *Back from the Dead: Remakes of the Romero Zombie Films as Markers of Their Times*. His work has also appeared in *Rue Morgue* magazine and *Horror Studies*. He teaches horror theater and horror cinema at Loyola Marymount University.

Stephen Woodworth is the author of the *New York Times* bestselling Violet series of paranormal thrillers, including *Through Violet Eyes*, *With Red Hands*, *In Golden Blood*, and *From Black Rooms*. His short fiction has appeared in such publications as *Weird Tales*, *Realms of Fantasy*, *Fantasy & Science Fiction*, *Year's Best Fantasy 9*, and *The Dead That Walk*, and he has other tales forthcoming in *Nameless Magazine* and *Black Wings IV*. He is currently at work on a new novel. You can find Steve online at www.facebook.com/stephen.woodworth2.

ABOUT THE EDITORS

Joseph Nassise has been writing urban fantasy and supernatural thrillers for over a decade, with more than twenty novels to his credit. His work includes the international bestselling Templar Chronicles series, the Jeremiah Hunt series, and the Great Undead War series. Nassise has been a finalist for both the Bram Stoker Award and the International Horror Guild Award. You can find him online at his official website, *Shades of Reality* (www.josephnassise.com), and at his Facebook page (www.facebook.com/joseph.nassise).

Del Howison is a journalist, writer, and the Bram Stoker Award–winning editor of *Dark Delicacies: Original Tales of Terror and the Macabre by the World's Greatest Horror Writers*. He is the cofounder and owner of Dark Delicacies, a bookstore known as "The Home of Horror," located in Burbank, California. He can be reached at Del@darkdel.com.